There was still a part of her in love with Paul, in spite of the new man in her life, in spite of her glittering career.

Her visit back to Bampton Hall was, ostensibly, to hear Paul's new opera, but in reality she needed to think about how she felt about Larry . . . and Paul.

But Paul had changed in the four years she'd been away. No one knew why he had been behaving so strangely, so out of character, but something, somewhere, was terribly, badly wrong.

Love Beyond All Telling

Jean Gregory

CORGI BOOKS

LOVE BEYOND ALL TELLING

A CORGI BOOK 0 552 12506 7

First publication in Great Britain

PRINTING HISTORY
Corgi edition published 1986

Copyright © Jean Gregory 1986

This book is set in 10/11 pt Mallard
by Colset Private Ltd., Singapore.

Corgi Books are published by Transworld Publishers
Ltd., Century House, 61–63 Uxbridge Road, Ealing,
London W5 5SA, in Australia by Transworld
Publishers (Aust.) Pty. Ltd., 26 Harley Crescent,
Condell Park, NSW 2200, and in New Zealand by
Transworld Publishers (N.Z.) Ltd., Cnr. Moselle and
Waipareira Avenues, Henderson, Auckland.

Made and printed in Great Britain by
Hunt Barnard Printing Ltd., Aylesbury, Bucks.

In the Stately Homes Handbook, *Historical Houses, Castles and Gardens*, the entry for Bampton Hall reads as follows:

'Bampton Hall, Moreton-in-Marsh, Glos. Bampton, dated 1765, is a fine example of Georgian baroque noted for the outstanding quality of its brickwork and set in spacious parkland. Originally the home of the Squires family, the house is now in use as an independent educational establishment for children unusually gifted in music and the arts. The Bampton Festival is held annually for one week every May in the school's own theatre, and evening recitals are given during the months of June to October.

'Further particulars from The Bursar, Bampton Hall, Moreton-in-Marsh, Glos. For times of opening, see opposite page.'

And, on the opposite page:

'Bampton Hall, Moreton-in-Marsh	3m. west of Moreton-in-Marsh on A44 to Evesham	April 2–7 daily then July 30–September 4, Weds, Fris & Suns.
Bampton Educational Trust		Admission Ho. & Gdns 50p. Chd & OAPS 25p.
House contains a remarkable collection of harpsichords & early pianos		Hotels & Restts in Moreton-in-Marsh.

No reasonable public transport.'

In the booklet on sale to the public at Bampton itself, the following information is given:

'The Hall lies three miles to the west of Moreton-in-Marsh in the heart of the Cotswolds. For almost two centuries the private residence of the Squires family, the house was left to the National Trust at the end of the last war and since 1959 has been run by the opera singer, Joseph Terrazzas, and his wife Ludmila Huhalova, former ballerina with the New York City Ballet, as a school for artistically gifted children.

'During the twenty-five years of its existence, the school has produced several musicians and dancers of note, including the composer Paul Salinger and the conductor Hugo McDonald, both of whom are now on the teaching staff of the school.

'The Bampton Music Festival, when pupils and ex-pupils combine to produce a week-long series of concerts and dance evenings, has achieved international recognition and ranks as one of the leading events in the British musical calendar.'

1

Paul was roused by the sound of the telephone: shrill and imperative, it came screaming up at him from the hallway below, disturbing him on the outermost edges of post-coital slumber. He lay for a second or so, counting the rings and waiting to see whether Hugo or Rose would make any effort to crawl out of bed and answer it. Needless to say, neither of them did. Hugo wouldn't budge as a matter of principle, and Rose, though a dear, good, sweet-natured soul, was indubitably the laziest woman on earth. The telephone went on ringing.

'What's the time, for heaven's sake?'

He groped on the bedside table for his glasses and peered through them at the travelling clock in its blue leather case. It looked as if it said twenty minutes past seven — unless it said five and twenty to four. He couldn't remember what time it had been when they had come to bed.

By his side, Virginia stirred, in protest.

'What are you doing?'

'Trying to see what time it is —' By dint of holding the clock about two inches away from his face he could just make out which hand was which: twenty past seven. Pm. It had to be pm. Virginia hadn't been here all night; she never stayed overnight. He dropped the clock back on the table. 'I suppose I'd better go and see what it wants.'

'Why? It won't be anything important.' Coaxingly,

she slid a hand up his thigh; let it linger a moment, suggestively, in his crutch. 'Ignore it.'

For a moment he was tempted, but then he thought: it could be Caroline. The cable had said simply DEPARTING SAN DIEGO 13.30 ARRIVING HEATHROW 9.30 AM SUNDAY TWA FLIGHT CHICAGO STOP WILL CALL SUNDAY PM TRAVEL MONDAY STOP LOVE AND KISSES CAROLINE.

Not without a certain reluctance, he threw back the bedclothes. Virginia, disgruntled, heaved them up again.

'They'll probably have rung off by the time you get there.'

'Probably.'

'So why bother?'

Because it wasn't every week that Caroline came over from the States, that was why bother. Not every week, not every month, not even every year.

'I won't be two seconds . . . back before you know it.'

He groped for his dressing-gown, trod barefoot across the carpet, out onto the darkened landing and along the passage to the stairs. There was a line of light just dimly discernible beneath the door of Hugo's room. For good measure he banged on the wall as he passed: a muffled cry of 'Go away!' was the only response.

Down in the hall, the calor gas heater had run out and already there was a distinct pall of frost in the air. (The Lodge, which had scarcely been altered since its Georgian beginnings, was primitive to say the least where its domestic and heating arrangements were concerned. American tourists thought it quaint until they discovered that someone actually lived there. He didn't know how Caroline was going to cope, after five years of the soft life.)

He reached the telephone, stubbing his bare toes as he did so on some unseen obstacle propped against the table, and clawed up the receiver.

'Hello?'

'Pauly? Is that you? This is Papa Jo here.'

'Hi, Papa Jo.' He stood on one leg, massaging his bruised toes with the hand that was not holding the telephone.

'I get you out of bed?'

'What, me?' He feigned innocence. 'On a Sunday evening I should be in bed?'

'I only wondered. Listen, I've just been going through Act I — I got some great ideas for a new ending. You want to come round discuss them? Or —' elephantine pause — 'you want we should leave it till tomorrow?'

Paul grinned.

'It's all right, Papa Jo . . . you're not interrupting any unfinished business. If it's important, I'll be round.'

'I think it's important. I think you need a new aria. Right at the end, where she leaves Thornfield . . . I think it needs something. Like maybe you could take the same theme you have in the duet, and you could —'

'I'll be round,' said Paul.

Virginia, predictably, was not pleased. He hadn't imagined that she would be, but time was of the essence, and daily growing more so.

'Just stay put and keep the bed warm. I'll be back as quick as I can, I promise.'

'I'll give you forty minutes,' said Virginia, 'and no longer.'

'Forty minutes it is. You hang on here and have salacious thoughts. . . .'

'Was that Paul you were just talking to?'

Papa Jo looked up, guiltily, from the telephone.

'He just called me.'

'*He* just called *you*?'

'Well —'

'Well?'

Ludmila stood, militant, in the doorway. Poised and upright, she showed few of those signs of physical deterioration normally to be remarked in one of her years (she was sixty-seven). A tall woman — unusually so, for a dancer — with the high cheekbones and slanting eyes of the East European, blonde hair pulled straight back off her forehead in the severe style of the classical ballerina, the inexorable passage of time was manifested less by any obvious ageing process than by the marked angularity of feature — the sharp line of the jaw, the lean, taut sinews of well-used muscle, stomach flat as a board even now, hard as iron to the touch, calves like ropes of tempered steel. In youth, Ludmila Huhalova had possessed a kind of beauty, cold and remote even as the Russia whence she came: age had taken that beauty and pared it to the bone.

She waited, now, as if upon some explanation. Papa Jo shifted his great bulk uneasily in his wheelchair.

'He's coming over . . . he wants to talk with me about the ending to Act I. He has this new idea —'

'You mean, you have this new idea!'

'I have this new idea . . . all right! *I* have this new idea. So we need to talk about it.'

'So it couldn't have waited till tomorrow?'

Papa Jo hunched a shoulder.

'You know Pauly.'

'I know Paul? I know you! The one of you's a young fool, the other's an old one. You think he doesn't have better things to do on a Sunday evening?'

'What he was doing was not wholesome. He was with that woman.'

'Which woman?'

'That fornicator with the red hair that works in the office.'

'Virginia Truscott?'

'If that is what her name is. I don't care to remember it; she offends me.'

'Well, she obviously doesn't offend Paul!' Ludmila spoke sharply. 'Why you can't just let him alone —'

'Because I grow anxious for him is why!' Papa Jo

pounded with his fist on the arm of his chair. 'He troubles me in my mind . . . he is not himself. I don't know what's happening, and I don't like it. He worries me, that boy. I know that there is something wrong.'

'We all know that there's something wrong, but until he chooses to confide in us it's no business of ours — not mine, not yours. It's certainly not your business who he chooses to spend his leisure hours with. God knows, he takes few enough of them. If he wanted to spend them jumping in and out of bed with the whore of Babylon, it still wouldn't be any of your business. As for dragging him round here on a Sunday evening —'

Papa Jo looked mutinous.

'He didn't have to come.'

'Of course he had to come! He's as crazy as you are — he doesn't need any encouragement. What are you trying to do? Give him a breakdown? You know he's been up till almost midnight every day this past week working on that opera? Did you know that?'

'So it's going to be a great opus! You think Verdi kept regular hours when he was making *Otello*?'

'Verdi wasn't suffering the after-effects of a car smash and a broken marriage . . . I'm telling you, if that boy doesn't ease up he's heading for trouble. You want that on your conscience?'

For a moment Papa Jo seemed crestfallen; then he brightened.

'Don't worry . . . after tomorrow, no problem! Caroline will be here.'

Ludmila shot a look at him.

'I hope you're not thinking to start on any of your meddling?'

'But now that he no longer has Diana. . . .' There was a note of entreaty in Papa Jo's voice. 'Paul was always very fond of Caroline. Don't you remember? How he wrote the music for her that year, for her to dance? How they used to walk together, hand in hand?'

'How that sentimental old fool Jo Terrazzas had them already paired off and marching up the aisle smothered in orange blossom ... for heaven's sakes, Papa! That was when they were kids. They haven't even seen each other in four years. For all you know, Caroline could have someone back home in San Diego.'

'Then if she has someone, why is she not married to him?'

'Because whether you like it or not this happens to be the second half of the twentieth century and not everyone subscribes to your outmoded views on the sanctity of holy matrimony. In any case, Caroline has her career to consider, and I will thank you —' Papa Jo, who had opened his mouth, somewhat sheepishly closed it again — 'not to give me the benefit of your male chauvinist views on *that* particular subject. Now —' Ludmila glanced at her watch, which she wore on a gold chain about her neck — 'I shall give you until nine o'clock. Not a minute more. If you're not through by then, that's just too bad.'

From the Lodge to the Hall was a distance of approximately half a mile — a pleasant enough stroll in the gentler months of the year, though none too agreeable on a freezing February night. There had been heavy snowfalls the previous week and the road was still rutted, the drifts piled man-high on either side.

Paul walked fast, coat collar turned up against the wind. As he rounded the bend approaching the gates of the Hall, from somewhere to his left he heard the sound of smothered infantile giggles: the next second and he found himself trapped in a crossfire of snow bullets, coming at him thick and fast from what seemed all directions. Yells of triumph rent the air. Little sods, he thought. He thought it without rancour, though he did rather wonder if they would have dared take the liberty of pelting Hugo as they were pelting him. Hugo wouldn't stand for any of their nonsense. Paul had had the uncomfortable feeling, these last few weeks, that he was losing control. They sensed that they could run circles round him.

He bent, to scoop up a handful of snow (some kind of gesture clearly had to be made) but before he could form it into the requisite shape an unluckily well-aimed shot had caught him a stinging blow on the cheek and sent his glasses flying.

'Truce!' He held up a hand. 'I surrender . . . only cowards fire on unarmed men.'

The hail of bullets ceased; the yells of triumph died away. There was a somewhat abashed silence as Paul squatted down in the snow and felt around, gingerly, for his lost property.

'Hey, I'm sorry —'

One of the kids had come and squatted with him.

'Who's that?' said Paul. 'Chris Kaufman? You ought to be ashamed of yourself ... chucking snowballs around like some delinquent.'

'We didn't meanta knock your glasses off.'

'I daresay not, but since you have, just watch where you're putting your big feet and concentrate on trying to find them for me.'

'They're right here —'

'In one piece?' He settled them back on his nose and studied the kid through them. He was wearing what looked like a goldfish bowl on his head: closer inspection showed it to be a plastic space helmet. 'Stupid American brat,' he said.

The kid grinned, unrepentant.

'You OK?'

'Physically, yes; psychologically, I very much doubt it.'

'You want me to come up the house with ya?'

'Why? Does it guarantee protection?'

'Sure; they won't attack while I'm there.'

'In that case, it seems the least you can do.'

They walked on together, through the gates. The kid barely came up to Paul's shoulder.

'Now that you've protected me,' said Paul, 'you don't think it might be a good idea if you took yourself back indoors and got those hands warmed up? Messing around in the snow in woollen gloves is hardly an occupation I would recommend for someone who is supposed to be making a career of playing the violin.'

'No; I guess not.'

'I guess not, too . . . go on, get on with you!'

The kid hesitated.

'You gonna call on Papa Jo?'

'Yes, why?'

'I'd better come see you up there.'

Paul frowned.

'Whence all this sudden solicitude for my welfare? You think I can't find my own way?'

'No, it's just that we've made this slide right outside in the drive and old Meat Loaf's been going on about it . . . saying how it's dangerous, an' all.'

'Mr Mitloff is undoubtedly quite correct. However, now that you've been good enough to warn me I shall pay due care and attention.'

'Yeah, well, just don't go stepping on it, will ya? Meat Loaf says anyone breaks their neck he's gonna hold me personally responsible.'

'Maladroit as I am,' said Paul, 'I shall not break my neck. Now, get back indoors and get those hands warmed up . . . and next time, try picking on someone your own size, will you?'

He made his way carefully round the side of the house (he had no trouble locating the slide: it gleamed its glassy warning plain enough for even him to see) and up the snow-covered path to what had once been a back entrance leading to the kitchen regions and which served now as front door to the Terrazzas' private apartment. It was Ludmila who came to let him in.

'Paul,' she said. 'Step inside.'

14

Obediently, he did so.

'Is it all right for me to come round?' One never felt quite certain, with Ludmila; she was not a person whom it was at all easy to get close to. Despite having been seven years at Bampton as a student, and having taught there for the past six, he had no sure idea even now what lay behind the mask. A heart of gold? or a black hole? He sometimes wondered if even Papa Jo really knew. 'I wouldn't have disturbed him,' he said, 'only he did ring me.'

'I know he rang you. Don't bang your head on that lintel. Everybody is always banging their head on that lintel.' She took his arm. 'Before you go in, I want you to know that I have set a deadline . . . I want you out by nine o'clock. Not a minute later. Is that understood?'

'Surely.'

'Just so long as it is. Papa's an old man, and he's a sick man. He's also a remarkably foolish man. Someone has to restrain him. In here.' She threw open the door to Papa Jo's sitting-room and firmly, still maintaining a tight grip on Paul's elbow, as if he were back again at the age of eleven and being summoned for an interview, propelled him inside. 'Nine o'clock,' she said. 'Remember?'

The injunction was addressed more to Papa Jo than to Paul. As the door closed, Papa Jo pulled an elaborately henpecked face.

'*Nine o'clock, remember* . . . how this woman runs my life for me!'

'Maybe I shouldn't have come?'

'Shouldn't have come? Shouldn't have come? If Madame had her way no one should come! I should be bundled into my bed every night like a baby and fed on hot milk and rusks . . . I tell you, Pauly, there's nothing like the love of a good woman. Come! Take a seat.'

He gestured towards the piano, heaving his chair round to face it. In the prime of life, celebrated and fêted throughout the civilised world for his

15

Caravadossi, his Rodolfo, his Radames, Papa Jo had been what is commonly described as 'a fine figure of a man'. Two cerebral haemorrhages, one immediately following the other, had put paid to his operatic career and confined him, in all his broken glory, to the indignity of a wheelchair, where he had been ever since: a crippled colossus condemned to immobility, his vast frame run to fat, only his spirit unquenchable.

'Tell me —' he eased the chair up closer — 'talking of good women . . . what time does Caroline come?'

'Some time tomorrow evening. We're waiting for her to ring.'

'And how long does she stay? Does she stay for the Festival?'

'I don't honestly know.' He didn't want to talk about Caroline; not with Papa Jo. The old man was too obvious. 'She hasn't said, but I don't imagine so.'

'You don't imagine so? Why you don't imagine so?'

'Well, the Festival's still three months away . . . I imagine she'll be wanting to get back to the States before then.'

In some ways, he couldn't help thinking, it might be better if she did. Whatever prospect there might once have been of any kind of a future for the two of them, that prospect was well and truly gone, even assuming she had not found someone else, which was by no means an assumption that could safely be made. He could not be the only person who had found her desirable. He had a sudden vision of her, as she had been on the last occasion on which he had seen her, four long years ago. She had come over to Europe, on tour with the company. He had gone down to London, with Diana, to watch her in a performance of *Firebird*. Afterwards they had had supper together, in some rather sleazy Soho night club chosen by the company choreographer, Larry something-or-other (Lundquist? Sundquist?) who for some reason he couldn't now remember had accompanied them. What he did remember, very clearly, was gazing at Caroline across the table, grave and beautiful, with her deep, dark eyes and Spanish-black hair, and wondering how in hell he had ever been capable of the folly of marrying Diana. . . .

'So she can't stay just for three months?' Papa Jo was still worrying at it. 'When she has been away for all these years? Rubbish and nonsense!' He looked at Paul, challengingly; daring him to deny it. 'I shall tell her she stays . . . in any case, she must do so, to hear the opus.'

Paul ran his fingers over the keyboard, picking out the theme from the love duet in Act I.

'I thought you had this great new idea you were anxious to discuss? If you want me to start tinkering and adding bits, you'd better get on and tell me what you had in mind, or I very much doubt whether there'll be any opus. . . .'

When he arrived back at the Lodge, Virginia had gone; at any rate, she was no longer where he had left her. He picked up the travelling clock and peered at it: twenty past nine. That wasn't too bad. She might at least have given him till then.

He went downstairs just to check (barking his shin, this time, against whatever it was that was propped against the telephone table) but she was nowhere to be found. From Hugo's room there seemed to be coming sounds of movement. He went back up and stuck his head round the door.

'So, the krakens wake . . . what a way to spend a Sunday evening!'

Hugo, crawling out from beneath the duvet like some emergent troglodyte, cast a jaundiced eye in his direction.

'And where have you been?'

'Round with Papa Jo, discussing Act I. What happened to Virginia?'

'The Creeper? Search me.'

'We only just woke up,' said Rose. 'By the way, I left a portfolio downstairs for you. It's got my sketches for Act I. Did you see it?'

He didn't tell her he had barked his shin on it — not to mention nearly broken his toes. It was already a standing joke in the household: if you've mislaid anything, just ask Paul what he's tripped over recently .... He was going to have to take more care, in front of Caroline.

'Is that the thing by the telephone table? Yes, I saw it. Thanks, Rosie. I'll take a look some time.'

'How about now?'

'I can't right now, sweetheart. Just leave it with me, hm?' He smiled at her, hopefully. He knew she would be disappointed, but he needed to be by himself, to study them first in the privacy of his own room. 'I promised Papa Jo I'd try and get something down for a new aria for Act I.'

'Tonight?' Rose removed a strand of hair which was lying across her cheek. She had a strange, almost pre-Raphaelite aura about her that made her seem not quite of this century. Her hair, waist-length, and of flaxen paleness, hung limp and straight from a centre parting on either side of a face that was a perfect oval, with broad, flat cheekbones and curious almond-shaped eyes the colour of topaz. She attired herself almost permanently, during the winter months, in blue jeans and baggy sweaters, hand-knitted for a person twice her size: in summer, ankle-length skirts of some soft, swirling material, pattered in vivid oranges and bright pinks of her own design, teamed with Hugo's cast-off shirts worn smocklike over the top. Paul had thought, originally, when he and Hugo had first seen her, throwing pottery in the arts and crafts centre which she ran, in somewhat desultory fashion, in Bampton Village, mainly for the tourist trade, that she was affected; when he had come to know her better, he had realised that she was not. There was no artifice about Rose. She was as she was, without seeking to impress. She knelt, now, on the bed, unselfconscious in her nakedness, anxiously scanning his face. 'You're not really going to sit down and start working again? Not *tonight*?'

'I have to, Rosie.' It was becoming a race against time: he needed to snatch at every spare minute. 'Just a couple of hours,' he pleaded, 'that's all.'

'That's what you said last night —'

'Oh, let him be!' That was Hugo, growing impatient. 'We've had all this out before. If he wants to kill himself, that's his problem. I've had it with performing rescue operations. Get your clothes on and let's go down to the boozer.' He looked at Paul. 'Are you coming?'

'I might join you down there later.'

'Don't force yourself.'

'It's just that I really do have to put in a bit of extra work on Act I. Papa Jo —'

'I don't wish to hear. You know what they say, don't you?' Hugo thrust his face close up to Paul's. 'All work and no play makes Jack a very boring little boy.'

'And honestly,' said Rose, 'it doesn't solve anything.'

He wondered what she meant by that. He wasn't trying to solve anything — just trying to finish his opera.

'You're wasting your breath,' said Hugo. 'He's a lost cause. Incidentally, Caroline rang while you were out. She's travelling up tomorrow evening — gets into Cheltenham six-fifteen. I said I'd drive in and pick her up.' He paused. 'Unless you'd care to?'

Paul shook his head. It was almost a year, now, since he had driven. Hugo still occasionally tried tempting him — 'You want to take over? You want to use the car?' He had said to him, just a short while back: 'You've only got to do it once and you'll find you're quite OK again. You know that, don't you?' Paul didn't know anything of the kind. He hadn't disillusioned him, however.

Hugo obviously thought he had lost his nerve. Well, so be it; he could live with that.

'I'd better go and give Virginia a bell . . . check whether she's mad at me.'

Virginia, when finally she deigned to answer her telephone, left him under no illusions.

'And where the hell did you get to? I've been sitting in that damned pub all on my Jack Tod for the last bleeding hour!'

'In the pub?'

'Yes, sweeticle . . . *in the pub.* Exactly where I said I'd be.'

He hesitated. There were, he knew, a number of people who were under the impression that he was fast losing his marbles, but as far as he was aware his memory had not yet started to give up on him.

'I don't recall you telling me you'd be in the pub.'

'For Chrissakes! What time did you get back?'

'About . . . ten minutes ago. You weren't here, so I —'

'So you didn't bother reading the note I left you?'

'Note? What note?

'I didn't see any note —'

'Oh, get knotted!'

The receiver was slammed down. He had the feeling that that was how it was going to stay — for this week, next week, and all subsequent weeks. He tried ringing her back, as a matter of form, but sure enough she wasn't answering. It rather looked as though he and Lady Virginia had reached a parting of the ways. Ah, well! It was probably about time. He pulled a rueful face at the telephone, picked up Rose's portfolio and went through to his study to get to grips with the new aria.

It wasn't until much later, when finally he gave up for the night and retired to bed, that he discovered the missing note: it had been strategically placed on his pillow, where it might reasonably have been assumed that not even he could fail to see it. In capital letters, in what looked like eyebrow pencil, she had scrawled, GOING DOWN TO SARACENS. WILL WAIT TILL 9.30. *BE THERE!!!*

He could understand that she was not best pleased with him.

2

White, upon white, upon white . . . pressing her cheek, like a child, to the window, Caroline watched as the fleeting fields sped past. Over forty hours since she had left San Diego: over three days since she had set eyes upon Larry. He hadn't been able to make it to the airport to see her off. One of the kids was having a birthday and his presence was required. He claimed not to be able to stand kids but he always went running whenever one of them got ill, or had a party, or there was a function on at school. Up until recently she had been easily able to suppress any slight unworthy twinge of resentment or neglect, arguing that such assiduous attention to parental duty could only be a good trait — one for which, in the future, she would hopefully have cause to be thankful. Now she knew differently. Parental duties, it seemed, had their limits, and as far as Larry was concerned he was already stretched to his. Bettina had been allowed the indulgence of mothering four of his offspring: Caroline was not to be allowed the indulgence of mothering even one.

'Enough is enough . . . I've been through that scene. Now all I want is a beautiful woman all to myself . . . is that too much to ask? I want you, not a parcel of goddamn squalling brats!'

And in any case, there was her career to consider. Caroline Ramirez, star of the Santa Rosalia Ballet Company, couldn't afford to waste nine precious months of her working life fulfilling a function which any Mexican peasant woman out of the fields could fulfil equally well (if not, indeed, a great deal better).

'What's the point of my bothering to write a new ballet for you if you're not going to be in a fit state to perform in it? Sorry, pumpkin, but it's just not on. We're grown people, not star-struck kids. Having a dear little baby isn't the fun thing you seem to think it is — it doesn't produce instant sweetness and light. You take it from me, it's nothing but a millstone hung around your neck ... I should know: I've had some. Four little millstones, all hanging on like grim death — and I tell you, frankly, I don't fancy the idea of having any more. What you do is up to you; it's your choice. I can't dictate. All I'm saying —'

All he was saying was, you go ahead and have it and that's it: finito. It's up to you. The choice is yours. . . .

In the circumstances, it hadn't been much of a choice. He'd swept her off to Vegas, afterwards, for a week of rest and recuperation. To give her, as he put it, a good time; make up for all she'd been through (but had he really the least inkling of what she'd been through?) She had never cared for Las Vegas and had no interest whatsoever in gambling: it had been Larry's idea of a good time, not hers. They hadn't exactly quarrelled, even though he had accused her of being too snooty and English to let her hair down and enjoy herself. It was always a sign of displeasure, with Larry, when he emphasised the English half of her parentage. When he was feeling affectionate, it was 'dumb chica'.

'Dumb chica,' he'd say, ruffling her hair.

'Sex-mad Swede!'

'Hold it! Hold it! You'd just better watch your language, chica.'

'You don't like being called sex-mad?'

'Who said it was that I objected to?'

He hadn't been too keen on the idea of her trip to England, but he hadn't suggested accompanying her:

Bettina had chosen this moment to move house and he had promised to help her get settled. She couldn't be expected to manage by herself; not with four little millstones all under the age of twelve. Last year when Caroline had proposed a trip back to England, Bettina had organised to go into hospital and have her womb removed, which had meant Larry staying behind to look after the brood. On that occasion Caroline had cancelled: on this occasion, she had not. Not out of any fit of pique, which was what Larry accused her of; simply the feeling that she needed a breathing space. She needed time to think — to evaluate. She could do neither so long as he was around. All she could do when he was around was play moth to his candle flame: a poor, weak, fluttering creature, too feeble-minded to resist the lure of his attraction.

He could have made it to the airport, had he chosen to exert himself. The drive over to Bettina's didn't take more than a couple of hours, two and a half at the very most; he could still have been there in time for the birthday. Instead, he had chosen to go off the night before: it was his way of punishing her. He had obviously felt bad about it, because he had telephoned her in London, that same afternoon, at her hotel. He had caught her just as she was on the point of leaving.

'How's the time your end?'

'Three o'clock — pm.'

'It's seven in the morning over here. How'd you like that? Seven in the morning and I didn't hit the sack till almost three. Is that devotion or is it not?'

She had resisted the temptation to ask him what he had been doing, and who he had been doing it with, until three o'clock in the morning. She had agreed that it was indeed devotion (which in a sense it was: Larry rarely if ever ungummed his eyes before 9 am).

'So how was the flight? Was the flight OK?'

'Well, I got here.'

'And how about the weather? Is it raining?'

'No, but it's been snowing.'

'Good; I hope it snows some more. I hope it snows so damn much you get sick of it and catch the first flight back... I want you back. You know that, don't you, you dumb chic? I don't want you doing a sneaky one on me and taking up residence. I need you back here, with me. In fact, I've been doing some hard thinking these past twenty-four hours ... I reckon it's about time I got things moving on the divorce front. Really; I mean it. Bettina's dragged her heels quite long enough. Next week when I go back up there I'm really going to start pushing. I guarantee — I give you my word. Time you get back those lawyers are going to have received their instructions and the ball's going to be rolling. How about that? Make you happy?'

I don't know ... restlessly, Caroline rubbed her cheek along the glass, clearing a space where her breath had made mist patches. Six months ago, it would have made her happy; now ... she didn't know. How was it you could love someone and not trust them? not even believe them? He had said it so often. *Bettina's dragged her heels quite long enough* ... she wasn't even sure, any more, that it really was Bettina who was doing the dragging.

They were coming into a station. Cheltenham? She hadn't been paying attention. She had chosen the train in preference to renting a car mainly for reasons of nostalgia, and had done nothing the entire journey save wallow in a prolonged orgy of self-pity. She sat herself up and smiled reassuringly at the couple of middle-aged American tourists sitting opposite.

'This is Cheltenham.'

They nodded, eagerly; grateful for her deigning to acknowledge them. Seeing the TWA labels still attached to her bags they had more than once attempted to engage her conversation. They were from Cedar Rapids, Iowa; where was she from? Was she American or was she British? Was she by any chance acquainted with this part of the world? They couldn't help remarking that she had c/o Bampton Hall on her address tags. Bampton Hall was in their Stately Homes Guide Book but it didn't seem to be open during the winter months. Of course it wasn't the best time to tour, they realised that, but they had come over for the birth of their first grandchild. You couldn't always regulate the arrival of grandchildren to coincide with the tourist season, could you? Anyway, they'd been told the Cotswolds was one of the places to come, so they'd come, in spite of the weather. Not that they minded a bit of snow, they saw plenty of that back home in Iowa. They probably didn't get too much of it where she came from ... San Diego, had she said? They'd never been to San Diego. Never been to California at all. Never been further than Denver, Colorado, which was where their son was resident. Their daughter lived in Hertfordshire; that was just outside of London. Her husband was in computers. Their son in Denver was a heating engineer. What did Caroline do, if it wasn't impertinent of them to inquire?

Caroline had been friendly, but remote; supplying the information requested — yes, she was American, but her mother had been British: yes, she did know this part of the world, she had been educated here: no, they didn't have much snow in San Diego: no, it wouldn't be impertinent to ask what she did, she was a dancer — in tones which, without exactly repelling, had scarcely invited further probing. It was a technique she had of which Larry did not approve. An unAmerican activity, he called it: freezing people out. Doing her 'English lady' act. Well, it didn't matter whether Larry approved or not, since he wasn't here to witness it.

The gentleman from Iowa — putting her to shame, not waiting to be asked — was already busy humping her suitcases down on to the platform for her, wanting to know if she could manage, whether she would like him to call a porter.

'No, that'll do fine, thank you. I'm being met.' She looked up the platform, expecting to see the compact and slender figure of Paul, but seeing instead the rangy six-foot frame and sandy hair of Hugo. She waved: he saw her, and waved back. 'He's coming right now.' She smiled again at the couple from Iowa. 'Have a good stay.'

'Who was that, then?' Hugo had advanced upon her in rapid strides up the platform. 'More wooden planks?'

'Don't be so disrespectful ... I'll have you know they've come all the way over from Iowa, just to fill the coffers of your English tourist trade.'

'Not *my* English tourist trade. Don't you Yanks ever learn?' Hugo bent his head, to kiss her. 'There is a subtle difference between the Scots and the English, you know. Anyway, how are you?'

'Fine,' she said. *I just got rid of a child that I desperately wanted by a man I have the misfortune to be in love with ... but other than that, I'm fine.* 'How about you?'

'Likewise, likewise ... here, let me.' He took possession of both suitcases. 'The car's just outside — Paul sends his apologies, by the way. He stayed on to see Papa Jo about some new aria they've cooked up between them for Act I.'

'Of course! His opera.' He'd written her about it; in rather more detail than she'd been capable, just recently, of taking in. '*Wuthering Heights*?'

'*Jane Eyre!*'

Jane Eyre. She knew perfectly well it was *Jane Eyre*. This was ridiculous, she must pull herself together. Her troubles were her own: no need to foist them on to other people.

'So how is Rose?' she said, 'Have you made an honest woman of her yet?'

'Rose doesn't want to be made an honest woman of! She'd belt me one if I even suggested it to her ...

marriage has become a very dirty word amongst a certain section of the female population, thanks to you and your mob of screaming banshee libbers. Marriage, babies, domesticity ... they'd be less insulted if you gave them a pickaxe and suggested they went down the coal mines.'

'The women's liberation movement has never been against the idea of women having babies,' murmured Caroline. 'Not, at least, as far as I'm aware.'

'You try telling that to Rose ... I mean, can you really imagine her? Changing nappies?'

'Yes,' said Caroline, 'since you ask. Although there's no reason on earth, of course, why *you* shouldn't be the one to change them.'

'Thank you,' said Hugo. 'That will be quite enough of that.' He dumped her suitcases and felt in his pocket for the car keys. 'I'm afraid we're going to have to stick to the main drag. I would have taken you back via the lanes, but they're well nigh impassable just at the moment. I trust you've come well prepared for the weather?'

'I've come prepared for snow and ice ... so long as the temperature doesn't rise above zero, I should be OK.'

'In that case, you'll be OK.'

('It rains all the time in England, doesn't it?' Larry had said. 'Doesn't it rain all the time? You know you don't like rain: you're a sun person, not a rain person ... you'll be back.')

They talked, safely and cosily, as they drove, of Papa Jo and Madame — of Bampton — of the old days.

'Remember Meat Loaf?' said Hugo. 'The rages he used to get into? *Ach, Ghrist! Vot are you beeble blayink at?*'

'It was Paul that used to really get him mad.'

'Paul used to really get a lot of people mad.'

'But Meat Loaf had it in for him ... *Chust because your farder was makink his own strink kvartet, iss no reason you should be thinkink to get away vid murder!'*

'*Vot in ze name of Gott is ze verld comink to?* — He's still with us, incidentally . . . old Meat Loaf.'

'He never is!'

'You'd better believe it . . . still trying to hammer home the rudiments of harmony and counterpoint.'

'For God's sake! He must be ninety if he's a day.'

'Seventy-eight at the last count.'

'Does he still have it in for Paul?'

'He did have, up until just recently. He seems to have mellowed a bit these last few months.'

'Could be Paul's mellowed a bit, too?'

'Could be . . . feel like stopping off at the Saracan's for a quick dram?'

'All right. Why not?'

She was not averse to the idea, although since they were now within a mere hundred yards of the Lodge gates she was mildly surprised at his suggesting it, the more so as she and Hugo had never really enjoyed any great degree of intimacy. It had always been Paul who was the link.

The Saracen's Head was as she remembered it: picture-book Elizabethan. Oak-beamed, sagging-ceilinged, diamond-lattice windows and plentifully horse-brassed. She wondered if the couple from Iowa would ever make their way there. It wouldn't have been any use bringing Larry; he didn't care for old buildings. The one time he and she had been in England together they had taken a quick trip up to Stratford-upon-Avon (she hadn't brought him to Bampton: they had steered well clear of that). They had stayed the night in a Tudor manor house converted to a hotel. Larry had done nothing but complain about the lack of central heating and the gurgling of the water tank, which had kept him awake. At breakfast next morning there had been no plastic pots of marmalade or pre-wrapped butter, and the table had been of wood instead of formica, which was unhygienic, because wood harboured germs. She had thought at the time that his lack of appreciation must in some way have been her fault — she had obviously laid it on a bit too thick, the beauty of the English countryside, the charm of the past. His refusal to be impressed was a perfectly natural reaction. After seeing him in Las Vegas, happy as a child surrounded by goodies, she had begun to realise that his distaste for anything older than the here and now was quite genuine: Larry was essentially a product of the disposable society.

'Cheers —' Hugo had raised his glass, waiting for her to do likewise. 'Here's to success.'

She responded mechanically: 'Success.' Whatever success might be. She was no longer sure that she knew.

'Well! That sounded enthusiastic.'

'Sorry.' She shook herself. 'I was miles away.'

'Not back in Lotus Land already?'

She laughed; trusting it didn't sound as forced to his ears as it did to hers.

'Give me a chance . . . I only just got here!'

'Hm.' He studied her a moment, frowningly, over the rim of his glass. He seemed to be making up his mind whether or not to say something. 'If I were to ask how long you intended staying, I suppose you'd instantly jump to the conclusion that I was anxious to get rid of you? Than which nothing, I hasten to add, could be further from the truth. Quite the contrary. The longer you stick around the better, as far as I'm concerned.'

'Oh? I shouldn't be in too much of a hurry to say something you may regret . . . I have a three-month leave of absence.' A three-month leeway, in which to make up her mind. Whether to rejoin the company, or whether to move on. (Whether to go back to Larry or make the break now, while she still could. *If* she still could.)

'Three months,' said Hugo, 'would be fine.'

It would?

'Ah!' she said. 'The Festival!'

'I wasn't actually thinking of the Festival, though

certainly you ought to stick around for it if you can.'

'I'd like to. It's been a long time since I came to one. Not since —' she thought back — 'not since the first year you and Paul took up teaching here. Do you remember? Paul wrote a piece for orchestra —'

'I remember.'

He cut across her, his voice clipped and curt with its brusque Scots overtones. She wondered again why he had brought her in here. Evidently not for the nostalgia trip.

'So how is this year's contribution coming along?'

'Pretty well. Mind you, it should: he's working at it like one possessed.'

'I guess it must be about the biggest thing he's ever done?'

'It's also going to be the best, but that's no reason to break himself up over it.'

'Oh, you know Paul ... he's a workaholic. Always has been. Who's going to conduct it? You, or him?'

'He's supposed to be.'

There was a pause. She waited for him to expatiate; and then, when he didn't: 'Supposed to be?' she said.

'If he hasn't killed himself with overwork by then.'

'Oh, now, come on! It can't be as bad as all that.'

'You think not?'

Quite suddenly, she got the message: he had brought her here to talk about Paul.

'I remember,' she said, 'when he was working on his string quartet ... he used to shut himself away half the night.'

'That was different. He hadn't been through then what he's been through this year.'

She looked at him, quickly.

'You mean, Diana?'

'Diana ... smashing the car up — I suppose he told you about that?'

'He mentioned something; he didn't say too much. Just that he'd had a bit of an accident.'

'It wasn't a bit of an accident, the car was a write-off. He was lucky to get out of it alive.'

She set down her drink.

'He never told me that . . . what happened, exactly?'

'He was driving back to Bampton one night after seeing Diana off. Some fool came at him out of a side road, he swerved to avoid him, wrapped himself round a tree . . . he was in hospital for nearly two months, having bits of glass picked out of him. It was during that time the Lady Diana finally decided on decamping — you know she'd already moved down to London? Said she couldn't stand being shut up at Bampton any longer. It was only supposed to be a temporary measure, until they got things sorted out. Then what with Paul being out of commission, and one thing and another . . . I don't think anyone was really very surprised. She'd always been on at him to quit teaching. She had this romantic daydream of a composer being someone who leads a life of gay social frenzy seven days a week and turns out the odd symphony or so in his spare time . . . God only knows how she ever got tied up with him.'

'She was pretty,' said Caroline.

'She was a bitch,' said Hugo.

Caroline shook her head; there wasn't really any comment she could make on that. She had never actually known Diana. She had been away on tour when Paul had met her; appearing as guest artist with the Santa Rosalia when quite unexpectedly (she could still remember the shock of receiving his letter even now) he had married her. The only occasion on which Caroline had been, briefly, in her company, was when the Santa Rosalia had come to London for a short season. Diana had struck her then as being beautiful — undeniably so — but lacking in either sympathy or depth of understanding; a reaction which she had attributed, at the time, to her own simple hurt and jealousy. Her affair with Larry, begun in a spirit of defiance, had been barely into its sixth month of life: you could not be off with the old love and on with the new all in a matter of six short months.

'He never lets on that much in his letters,' she said. (But then, how much did she let on in hers? She had never once mentioned Larry, other than in passing. Paul knew no more about the state of her emotional life than she did about his.) 'Did he take it very hard?' she said. 'Diana walking out on him?'

Hugo shrugged.

'Impossible to tell — he's been like a clam ever since it happened. All I know is that he's not the same as he used to be.'

'In what way?'

'Difficult to define. He just doesn't seem . . . with it, any more. Not clued up. Rose thinks it's overwork; I'm not so certain.'

'So what do you think it is?'

There was a silence. Hugo looked down into his whisky glass.

'God knows.'

'Have you tried asking him?'

'How do you ask someone if they're having a breakdown?'

She frowned.

'You really think he is?'

'I don't know.' Hugo tossed the remains of his whisky down his throat and stood up. 'I'm hoping, now you're here, you'll be able to tell me . . . shall we get back?'

On their way out they bumped into a girl wearing a green velvet pants suit and frilly blouse. She looked curiously at Caroline as they passed. Hugo nodded, briefly, but did not perform any introductions.

'Who was that?' said Caroline.

'Local bicycle.'

'The what?'

'Our friendly neighbourhood nymphomaniac. While hubby's away, the lady doth play . . . her name's

Virginia Truscott, and she works in the office, up at the Hall.'

'She reminded me a bit of Diana.'

'Really?' He shot her a quick glance.

'The hair,' said Caroline. 'That particular shade of red — and green eyes. Didn't Diana have green eyes?'

'You're right: she did.' The observation seemed to strike him as being of some significance. 'I'd never noticed before . . . that would maybe account for it.'

'Account for what?'

'The fact that Paul — if you'll pardon the expression — has recently been knocking the arse off it.'

The expression didn't bother her one way or another (Larry was not exactly noted for the purity of his language); she needed to pause for just a second, though, to test her reactions to the thought of Paul, in bed with the red-haired girl. She found that even after all this time, she didn't like it. The discovery rather shook her: she had considered herself immune.

'Ah, well!' She made a determined effort to speak lightly. 'I guess he needs to have some sort of an outlet. And if the lady's willing —'

'Oh, she's willing! Can't get enough of it, that's her only problem.'

'You don't think your Scots Presbyterian petticoats are showing just a wee tiny bit, do you?'

'I don't like the woman; I don't mind admitting it. Furthermore, what happens when her husband gets back? We just beam and nod and pretend it never happened?'

Larry, thank heavens, had already been separated from Bettina before he and Caroline had started living together. A broken marriage was one burden she did not have to carry.

'All that can be said in mitigation —'they had reached the car: Hugo slid into the driver's seat and leaned across to open the passenger door — 'is that a) she threw herself at him and b) he's somewhat restricted for choice these days.'

'*Paul?*' She was about to laugh, when a sudden thought clammed the sound in her throat. *He spent nearly two months in hospital having bits of glass picked out of him....* 'He's not —'

'Not what?'

'I mean ... the accident. It didn't —'

'Oh, he hasn't ended up like some kind of Frankenstein's monster, if that's what you're scared of. He does have the odd scar or two, but they're neither here nor there. He got off relatively lightly, all things considered. No, it's just that he has this phobia about driving — that's another thing you can do for him while you're here: get him behind the wheel of a car. Get him mobile again.'

'You mean he doesn't drive at all?'

'He hasn't, ever since it happened. That's why I say, he's restricted for choice ... a place the size of Bampton, there's not that much going. Mind you —' Hugo swung the car out of the pub forecourt and up the hill to the Lodge — 'having said that, he always did have lousy taste in women. Diana was a prime example. You're the only good one he ever picked; all the rest were rotten apples.'

It was not a reflection which brought much solace. Sooner, at the time, have been a rotten apple, so long as it had been the one of Paul's choice.

'I never knew why it was,' said Hugo, 'that you two didn't get it together.'

There had been a time when they might have done. She had often thought, if she hadn't been away on tour when Paul had first met Diana ... but maybe it wouldn't have made any difference. Maybe he would still have preferred Diana. He and Caroline had known each other too long. From eleven to eighteen they had lived in each other's pockets. Even during vacation time, more often than not, they had been together. Whenever it wasn't convenient for Linda to come over to England, or for Linda to have Caroline come over to the States (which had been the case more and more frequently as the years progressed) there had been a standing invitation to go back with Paul, to Marden.

The old house, on the edge of the Romney Marsh, had come to seem almost more like home to her than her real home — possibly because she had never actually had a real home, in any meaningful sense of the word. Linda, after her divorce from Raul, had led a butterfly existence, continually on the move; whilst Raul, in his capacity as foreign news reporter, had spent more time abroad than he had in the States. Caroline had once stayed overnight with him in a Paris hotel, before he took off for the Middle East, and had once spent a month with him and Julie-Dawn in their apartment in San Francisco — or, to be more accurate, with Julie-Dawn, who had resented her. Raul had disappeared for entire days at a time on secret missions to places where people were slaughtering each other.

On the whole, she had much preferred being at Marden, with Paul and the old ladies — Auntie Marion, who was crusty; Auntie Vi; soft as sugar; and Auntie Lily, who was the one who had got away. Auntie Lily had married and been deserted, but not before managing to have two children of her own. Sometimes they had come to Marden as well, but mostly it had been just her and Paul. It was nice for Paul, Auntie Vi had said, to have a companion his own age; and nice for Caroline, Auntie Marion had tartly added, to have somewhere to come when her own parents could not be bothered.

It had been nice, at the time. It was only latterly that she had wondered whether it might not have put paid to any future relationship.

Changing tack, as they drew up outside the Lodge, she said: 'Just so I know what the situation is . . . do I take it that Paul and this Virginia person are still in the thick of things?'

'They were, up until last evening; I'm not quite sure

what the current state of play is. The Creeper was looking daggers at him in Assembly this morning . . . with any luck he'll have suspended operations in honour of your visit.'

'He doesn't have to do that,' she said.

'Why not? Period of abstinence . . . do him good.'

Paul had not yet arrived back from the Hall: she said that she would walk up and meet him.

'If he's not through,' said Hugo, 'you can tell him from me that it's about time he was.'

'When he's talking about his *opera*? To Papa Jo? I wouldn't dare!'

As it happened, she didn't have to. She had just turned in through the Hall gate when she saw Paul coming around the corner. He was accompanied by a small child carrying a violin case and wearing a plastic space helmet on its head. The child was talking, earnestly: Paul was listening. She stood, watching, as they approached. She could see even from this distance that Paul had aged. His face was noticeably thinner, and more lined; his hair, thick and slightly curly, once as dark as hers, had begun perceptibly to grey at the edges. He was still a very good-looking man — she could understood all too well why the Virginia Truscotts of this world should make a set at him — but he was not the same as he had been, four years ago. Whatever he had been through since then had left its mark. (And might not the same, she reflected, be said of her? The Caroline Ramirez of thirty-two was certainly not the Caroline Ramirez of twenty-eight. Four short years . . . but a lifetime of emotional experience.)

She waited, by the great cedar of Lebanon, which once, for a dare, Paul had climbed to the very top and there appended, flaglike, someone's tutu. (And been soundly castigated for it by Madame; not for any damage he might have done either himself or the tree, but for wilful misuse of a ballet skirt.) Impossible to imagine this Paul, head gravely inclined towards his young companion, being incited by schoolboy jibes to perform an act of such purposeless folly. He had been, in those days, irrepressibly high-spirited. She found herself wondering if he still was.

She heard the child's voice piping, as they drew near. It was high and shrill, and spoke in tones of indignant self-righteousness.

'... how was I to know he was gonna go walkin' round there? At ten o'clock at *night*? I mean, ya'd have thought an old guy like that oughta to be in his *bed* that time o' night. Wouldncha? Wouldncha think he'd be in his *bed*? And why go walkin' round there anyways? When he'd already *seen* the thing? Why'd he wanna see it again? He'd already told me someone was gonna break their neck. Then he has to go an' *step* on it —' the child spared Caroline a mere cursory glance, without breaking the flow of its outpouring — 'he has to go an' *step* on it an' twist his stupid *ankle* already, an' then he tries to say it's *my* fault?'

'You can't say you weren't warned.' Paul walked on without even sparing her so much as a cursory glance. She might almost not have been there. 'You should have gone back and done something about it . . . put some salt on it, or something.'

'Well!' Caroline stepped out, on to the path. 'There's a fine greeting to give a person!'

Paul turned, sharply.

'Carly? Where did you spring from?'

'I didn't spring from anywhere . . . I've been here all the time. You were just so busy talking —'

He pulled a face.

'Sorry about that. Poor old Meat Loaf's gone and come a cropper on this young vandal's slide . . . OK, Chris, you can scarper! And take your troubles with you — you've only got yourself to blame.' The child looked at Caroline, pulled a ferocious face beneath its space helmet and stalked away, shoulders righteously hunched, to air its grievances elsewhere. 'So —' Paul took a step forward, and stopped. With the tip of a finger, he pushed his glasses further up his nose: a familiar gesture, remembered of old. 'Aren't you going to come and say hallo to me?'

3

'Are you quite sure,' said Caroline, 'that you wouldn't rather be the one to drive?'

'Quite sure, thank you.'

'It would make a lot more sense . . . seeing as you know the roads.'

On the contrary. Far from making a lot more sense, it would make no sense at all. Had she but known it, it would be highly dangerous, not to say downright suicidal — and he was not ready for that just yet a while. Certainly not so long as *Jane* remained unfinished. After that . . . he gazed through the passenger window at the vague blur of the fields, snow-white to the grey horizon. After that . . . who knew? In his more depressed moods, just recently, he had toyed with the idea, tossing it about in his mind as a final possibility, should the situation prove intolerable. In braver moments he resisted it, defiant in the face of the gods and their thunderbolts; but even in his braver moments he never quite dismissed it entirely. It was there, even now, spread like a safety net across the yawning chasm of blackness that lay beneath conscious thought. If the worst came to the worst. . . .

'So where shall we go?'

'Up to you. You're the visitor.' He knew all the local routes well enough to be able to direct her without difficulty. Provided she didn't want to venture too far afield, there should be no problems. 'Turn right out of the gates and we'll go to Burford . . . that do you?'

'Fine — though I'd still be happier if you were behind the wheel.'

He smiled, grimly. I doubt it, he thought. Aloud, he said: 'Why so shy of driving all of a sudden? I thought all you Yanks were born and reared in motor vehicles?'

'I wish you and Hugo would kindly stop referring to me as "all you Yanks" . . . when I'm over in England, I like to be English. In any case, there are *some* of us who still have the use of our feet.'

'I heard that in Los Angeles you could get done for walking.'

'That,' said Caroline, 'is Los Angeles. Los Angeles is not the whole of America, despite what the television may lead you to believe. OK! Which way do I go from here?'

'Take the first left, then left again at the roundabout; that'll bring you on to the A424. From there it's straight through to Burford.'

'Right.' She drove a while in silence, then: 'To be perfectly honest, the reason I don't care to drive is that I got lazy . . . too used to automatic gears. Humping this old bus feels like doing tank manoeuvres.'

'Never let Hugo hear you call his beloved Mk 2 Jag an old bus! It's his pride and joy.'

'Well, there you are . . . that's another reason.'

And equally as spurious as the first. There was only one reason why Caroline didn't care to drive, and that was that Hugo had been having a go at her.

Get him behind that wheel . . . get him mobile. He's only got to do it once —

'Paul?'

'Mm?'

'There's something I've been meaning to ask you.'

He stiffened; automatically on his guard.

'What's that?'

'Before I ask it, will you promise to give me an honest answer?'

'That depends,' he said, cautious.

41

'On what?'

'On what you're going to ask!' If she was going to ask what he thought she was going to ask —

'In other words, I don't know till I've tried? OK, so let me put it to you . . . am I cramping your style?'

'Cramping my style?' That was something he had not expected. 'What on earth do you mean by that?'

'I mean, me being here at Bampton . . . is it making things difficult for you? Because if it is, I can easily rent a car and go off and do some touring, as a good American should.'

'I thought you said that when you were in England you liked to be English?'

'No, I mean it . . . seriously. Three months is a hell of a time to park yourself on someone.'

He was silent, not knowing what to say. He wished he could tell her that as far as he was concerned she was welcome to stay for three years — to stay for ever. He had never cursed his own stupidity in failing to see what was there in front of him so much as he did now, when he could scarcely see it at all.

'What I can't quite understand,' he said, 'is why you should think that your being here is making things difficult for me?'

It was — but not in any way she could be thinking of. Before she came, he had taken certain basic safeguards to lessen, so far as he could, the possibility of embarrassing mistakes. For a start he had gone through their entire collection of records with a magnifying glass, arranging every single one of four hundred and odd discs in strictest alphabetical order, appending a large sign for Rose's benefit — PLEASE REPLACE RECORDS IN CORRECT SLOT AFTER USE. He had done the same in the kitchen, with all the staple commodities such as sugar, salt, coffee, etc., again with a notice for Rose's benefit. It was a necessary precaution, because without the notice Rose tended to pick things up in one place and put them down in quite another, depending solely and simply on where she happened to be standing at the time. Fortunately she was too indolent to have a similar penchant for moving the furniture about. He couldn't very well have stuck notices on that — they already thought he was suffering from some kind of phobia. Only the other day Hugo had inquired of him, with heavy sarcasm, whether he wouldn't care to stipulate how many inches from the sugar the salt should be kept, and at what angle the kitchen table should be placed.

'When you say difficulties,' he said, 'what sort, exactly, did you have in mind?'

'Well . . . shall we say, practical ones?'

He looked at her, sharply.

'The Lodge being so small,' she said. 'I just wondered if I mightn't . . . get in your way?'

His first thought was that Hugo had been regaling her with the standing joke — *if you lose anything, just ask Paul what he's tripped over recently*. And then he bethought him of something else Mr McDonald was likely to have gone shooting his mouth off about.

'If Hugo's been railing on at you about Virginia —' he knew they had crossed paths in the Saracen's, for Hugo had taken good care to apprise him of the fact — 'you needn't concern yourself on that account: she's a thing of the past.'

He would have given her up in any case, even if she hadn't got in first. He had bumped into her (literally) coming out of the office one day last week.

'I suppose it's too much to expect,' she had said, acidly, as they ricocheted off each other, 'that people who don't bother looking at messages that are left for them should go to the elementary trouble of looking where they're going.'

He hadn't attempted any explanation. Whatever he had said would have sounded phoney, and the relationship, such as it had been, had run its natural course. He and Virginia owed each other nothing.

'Actually,' said Caroline, 'she reminded me a bit of Diana.' There was a pause. 'Did you say make a left?'

'Left. Yes.'

'Even though it says Swindon?'

'Even though it says Swindon.' He had picked a route he could have driven blindfold. In the old days, before it had all gone sour, he and Diana had driven down every Sunday to have lunch at the Manor House. 'You'll find there's a turning off about a couple of miles further on.'

'I told you you should be in charge.'

'I am in charge — you're just the operator. Get on with the job.'

'Yes, sir! Whatever you say ... Swindon here we come.'

They drove in silence for a while. Paul sat, trying to make out the familiar landmarks as they passed.

'Does it trouble you,' said Caroline, at last, 'to talk about Diana?'

'Not in the slightest.'

It was true; it didn't. Most people steered well clear of the subject because they thought it would upset him. He himself didn't so much avoid it as see no cause for mentioning it. What had occurred between him and Diana had occurred, and was over. He felt neither bitterness, nor any inclination to apportion blame. They had both of them made the fundamental error of confusing temporary infatuation with the genuine article; the fact that as one of the direct consequences he should now be paying more dearly for that error than she, could scarcely be laid at her door.

'It's difficult to know,' said Caroline, 'whether to talk about things or whether to preserve a discreet silence ... you never told me too much in your letters.'

'That's because there wasn't too much to tell. It wasn't any great trauma, we just discovered we were incompatible.'

Which was something, no doubt, that anyone else

could have seen at the beginning. He hadn't seen it — hadn't let himself see it — until that night with Caroline, when they had all gone out to supper. It had come upon him then with a force which had rocked the very foundations of his being. The tragedy of his life was not that Diana had finally walked out of it but that she had ever walked into it in the first place. Too late now to repair the damage that had been done. Even were Caroline prepared to forgive his betrayal — for betrayal he knew that it had been — he was in no position to ask it of her. Caroline, besides, had some sort of involvement of her own, back home in the States. He was almost certain of it. She had received no less than three transatlantic calls in the short time that she had been here, the latest one coming that same morning, just before they had set out. As Hugo, in his clever way, had calculated, 'It's 5 am over there . . . must be either an emergency or a case of extreme devotion.' It obviously had not been an emergency; he could only assume it was extreme devotion. He had known that there must be someone — had known that even were there not he was still in no position to make any attempt at winning her back — but still he had experienced an unpleasant surge of what could only be described as common-or-garden jealousy.

'Is there absolutely no chance,' said Caroline, 'of you and Diana getting together again?'

She would obviously like it if there were. She would like him to be cosy and settled, so that she could concentrate on being cosy and settled with whoever it was.

'No way,' he said. He was very firm about it. There was no reason on earth, any more, for Diana to want him back and while some might say there was every reason for him wanting her, he believed he knew himself well enough to state quite categorically that pride would never allow it. He would not go crawling to anyone, least of all to Diana.

'You sound like you've slammed all doors,' said Caroline.

He shrugged.

'They were never really open . . . we just about managed to slide through the first as it was in the act of closing; and the rest, we found, were well and truly locked.'

She glanced at him, curiously. Or was it sympathetically? Perhaps a mixture of the two.

'I guess you didn't have a great deal in common.'

'That is certainly one way of putting it.'

'So where did you meet? You've never told me. Do you know that? You've never told me where you met her.'

Feeling too guilty, no doubt. (*Had* he felt guilty? Had he realised, subconsciously, even in the vortex of his first infatuation, that he was performing an act of treachery?)

'It's no secret,' he said. 'We met here at Bampton, during a Festival.'

Diana had been in the audience, and had attended the reception afterwards. She had made a beeline straight for him. He could still remember the brilliant, brittle beauty of her as she came across the room.

'I just had to tell you how much I *adored* your string quartet . . . that slow movement! Absolute heaven.'

Her elaborate praise, backed up as it was by no evidence of any musical depth or knowledge of technique, must surely have rung false even at the time. (Surely it must have done? He could not have been so deluded as actually to be flattered by her gushing superlatives?) Subsequently, during the course of one of their many rows, she had referred to that selfsame string quartet as 'the most monumentally boring piece of music it's ever been my misfortune to sit through'. On that day of their first meeting, however, they had both of them been carried away on a tidal wave of instant gratification. Emotions had run shallow: physical attraction was all.

Over the passion-ridden weeks that had followed

they had wooed each other in their chosen rôles, she the devout music lover and patron of the arts, he the trendy young composer: Rudolph Valentino of the concert platform. They had caught themselves in a mesh of their own making. With the honeymoon over, the need to keep up the pretence no longer quite so pressing, they had all too speedily discovered the truth of each other. Diana's artistic soul rose no higher than the level of the *Sunday Times* colour supplement: it was as much as she could do to distinguish Bach from Tchaikovsky, or retain even the simplest of melodies for more than five minutes after hearing it. As for the Rudolph Valentino of the concert platform, he had revealed himself as a sad stick-in-the-mud, more intent on getting to grips with the writing of his first symphony than doing the social round. In a moment of petulance, Diana had once screamed at him that 'I always knew I shouldn't marry a man who wore glasses!'

For a while, in an idiotic attempt at appeasement, he had tortured himself wearing contact lenses, which were for ever falling out and getting trodden on, and going to endless parties, which had tortured him even more, because he was too shy to talk to people and too bored to listen properly when they tried talking to him, so that Diana grew angry and told him he was an introvert and an isolationist, which was very possibly true. The final parting of the ways had certainly not been all her fault. Sympathy at Bampton lay with him, because at Bampton Diana had not been popular, but he did not doubt that in her own circles, up in town, she was much commiserated with on having chosen such a dull dog to get herself shackled to.

'False images,' he said. 'That was the trouble. She got led astray by the fact that I was sitting on a concert platform, scraping a violin and wearing a penguin suit ... also, as I recall, I hadn't had my hair cut for several decades. It gave me a rakish aspect which is totally misleading.'

'Oh, I wouldn't say that,' murmured Caroline.

Diana had. Diana had complained most bitterly. She had thought she was marrying someone she could show off, someone who would amuse her smart friends with a flow of nimble wit and repartee, not some diffident hermit crab which could be coaxed out of its shell only with extreme difficulty and on the rarest of occasions.

'Mind you, I blame Ludmila,' he said. 'She's the one who insists we get all dolled up.'

'The glamour of the occasion,' said Caroline.

Maintaining standards, was what Ludmila called it. She was of the old school, was Ludmila, when performers were *artistes* and the audience sat in splendour in their diamonds and their mink.

'Talking of the occasion,' said Caroline — 'hang on! Is this the turn off?'

He sat up, making a show of looking ahead through the window. It presumably had to be the turn off — the distance felt about right.

'Burford.' She swung the wheel over. 'You're a lot of help!'

'Sorry, I wasn't paying attention. You were saying, about the occasion?'

'I was merely going to ask how the opus was coming along?'

The opus, thank God, was approaching its last lap. There had once been a time when he had almost despaired of ever being able to finish it. Now he knew that come what may, by one means or another, he was going to get there.

The subject kept them safely occupied until they reached Burford. Caroline, unlike Diana, who had never given a fig for what he was writing, it could have been an opera or a concerto for Jew's harp for all the interest she had ever shown, seemed genuinely eager to hear details of the production.

'Who did the libretto?' she wanted to know.

He told her, Hugo and himself, with the occasional suggestion thrown in by Rose.

'We decided to start straight in on the meat of the book — Jane going to Thornfield and meeting Rochester. We've got a splendid Jane. One of Papa Jo's protégées. A seventeen-year-old — Deirdre Martineau. Lyric soprano, beautiful voice, clear as a bell . . . dead right for the part. We're borrowing Peter Hargreaves, by the way, from the Garden to come and do Rochester for us — oh, and Martina Lansmann's agreed to do Blanche. We just heard last week.'

'Big names! Hasn't Lansmann just been appearing at the Met?'

'That's right . . . Papa Jo twisted her arm. She's flying over specially — guest appearance.'

'And you're conducting?'

He hesitated just a fraction of a second.

'Yes,' he said. 'I'm conducting.' Nothing was going to stop him doing that. Not that he wouldn't trust Hugo to make a good job of it, but Hugo would have his chance later on. The first performance, at least, must be his. If he had to flunk out of subsequent ones, so be it; but at least let him have the first. 'Rose, by the way,' he said, 'has designed the costumes. Did she tell you?'

'Yes, she did. Are they any good?'

'Fine.'

'She seems to think you're not too impressed.'

'I am impressed! As a matter of fact, I'm more than impressed. What makes her think I'm not?'

'She didn't say. She just said, I don't think Paul's too happy with them.'

Damn! He knew why it was: it was because he hadn't had a private session, going through them with her. He had meant to, but then at the last minute he had chickened out, simply handing them back with a 'Thanks, Rosie. They're great.' She would have wanted to go into detail, pressing him to give an opinion on every least little item, pointing out this, asking about that . . .

he could never have survived it.

'Rose underestimates herself,' he said. 'She has real talent, that girl. If she weren't so —' he was about to say lethargic, but it sounded uncharitable — 'if she weren't so totally lacking in ambition, she could do well for herself.'

'There are more ways of doing well for oneself,' said Caroline, 'than knocking oneself senseless trying to get to the top of the pile.'

'Oh!' Was that supposed to be a reference to himself, or was he growing paranoid? He decided that he was growing paranoid. He had already reached the stage where he knew for a fact that everyone was watching him, waiting for him to slip up.

'Is this Burford?' said Caroline.

He sat forward.

'Yes.' It had to be; it couldn't be anything else.

'So where do we go? You have some place in mind?'

'The Manor House,' he said. 'About five hundred yards on your right.'

The Manor house had been Diana's favourite rather than his, but on that very count he knew it better than anywhere else. He couldn't go wrong at the Manor House. The only trouble he foresaw was with the deciphering of the bill, but he would doubtless find a way round that when the time came. He was getting quite adept at finding ways round things. On Caroline's first night home they had gone out with Rose and Hugo to the Bull, at Moreton-in-Marsh. He was not acquainted with the Bull, it was a haunt of Rose and Hugo's, and just at the start he had panicked, wondering how he was going to cope, but as it had turned out it had been surprisingly easy. When it came to ordering, he had simply waited till last, then ordered what one of the others had done: when it came to paying the bill, on which he and Hugo had agreed to go halves, he had cavalierly tossed it at Hugo with a request to 'Tell me the damage.' In spite of his paranoia, he found it amazing what you could get away with if you really put your mind to it — amazing, thank heavens, how much escaped people's attention when they weren't actively looking for it.

The Manor House, blessedly, had not changed: it was its same fossilised, fuddy-duddy self, just as it had always been. They were even ushered (by one of the statutory young ladies from Roedean, employed to impress visiting Americans) to the very table where he and Diana had last been ushered. He remembered how they had sat there and had one of their rows (as statutory as the young ladies from Roedean) about him giving up teaching and leaving Bampton. Diana had been wearing a green dress to match her eyes. He remembered the dress very well: she had been wearing it the following evening when he had driven her back to the station. It was one of the last things on earth he had been destined to look upon with any degree of clarity.

He smiled at Caroline across the table. She was wearing some sort of flame-coloured garment, or garments: he rather fancied it was a blouse and skirt.

'What are you having?'

She chose prawn avocado and venison ragout, a speciality of the house. With some misgivings as to his ability to handle the former without making a vile mess of both himself and the table, he followed suit. His main concern was to avoid the fiasco of sending something flying, which was what he was becoming increasingly prone to do. Last night, on the order of Ludmila (Ludmila being one who tended to issue orders rather than invitations) they had presented themselves for dinner with her and Papa Jo, during the course of which he had suffered the humiliation of upsetting a full glass of wine across the polished table. He was only glad that Hugo had not been there to remark it.

Today, by dint of exercising extreme caution, he actually managed to get through the meal without disgracing himself. The sticky moment came, as he had predicted, with the bill. He sat there for a while, toying with it, thinking over various ploys — 'What do you make this out to be?' or, alternatively, 'What the hell is this supposed to say?' (Except that he had tried that on once with Virginia, and she had obviously thought he was niggling about the amount. She had been quite aggressive: 'For heaven's sake! They couldn't write it any clearer if they tried.' On the whole, it was not a ploy he favoured.) He had just decided to risk a quick trip to the gents, taking the bill with him, when Caroline solved the problem by announcing that she was going to the ladies. He wasn't too bothered by a room full of total strangers witnessing his comic antics: by the time she returned he had succeeded not only in deciphering the amount but in writing out a cheque to cover it. All in all, he felt he had acquitted himself rather well.

'So what shall we do now, then?'

'What would you like to do?' He ought to have had something planned. He was going to be sunk if she opted for the full tourist bit, wanting to jump back into the wagon and drag him off for miles to stare at heaps of old masonry or clamber about over rocks. Apart from anything else, once they left the immediate vicinity he could no longer direct her. She wouldn't swallow a plea of 'Sorry, I wasn't paying attention' after more than the first couple of road signs. 'It's the wrong time of year,' he said, hopefully, 'for looking at things.'

'It is,' said Caroline. 'But you can't always plan the arrival of a grandchild to coincide with the tourist season.'

'You what?'

She laughed.

'Don't worry . . . not mine! Let's go for a walk. Isn't there a footpath somewhere round here, as I recall?'

There was: it was one he had walked many times with Diana. Some of their most bitter rows had been conducted along that footpath — in the fine weather. She wouldn't venture forth in snow or ice, nor in rain, nor mud, nor even a simple drizzle. Conditions had to be just right before Diana could be induced to leave the beaten track.

As they set off, down the main street, he said: 'So what's with the reference to grandchildren?'

'Oh, just a line I stole. No significance.'

He wondered whether to acccept it or not.

'Do you ever want any?' he said.

'Grandchildren?'

'Children.'

'Oh!' She tossed her hair back, over her shoulders. It was as thick and as glossy as he remembered it. People kept telling him how little she had changed. He had to take their word for it. All he could make out was the deep, velvety sheen of her hair, and the burning darkness of her eyes. All the rest was but a memory. 'I'm getting a bit long in the tooth,' she said, 'to think of that kind of thing.'

'Bit long in the tooth? I'll thank you, my girl, to watch your language! You happen to be speaking to an exact contemporary.'

'Sure, but my exact contemporary doesn't have to do the hard work ... besides, extra poundage put on at my time of life isn't so easy to get rid of. No one wants a fat flabby dancer.'

'I can't imagine you ever being fat or flabby,' he said. When she had kissed him, that first evening, and for a moment he had held her in his arms, he had been struck by the extreme slimness of her. She had felt more like a girl of eighteen than a woman of thirty-two. He wondered again about whoever it was, back in San Diego. 'You know something that strikes me?' he said. 'We have a one-way communications system in operation here.' He had noticed, even through the increasing haze which surrounded him, and the appalling cocoon of self-preoccupation which it engendered, that Caroline, thus far, had shown a determined tendency to keep very well away from personal matters. 'We've done a whole lot of talking about me and my career,' he said, 'but we hardly seem to have touched on yours.'

'There isn't that much to touch on.'

'No new rôles? No new ballets?'

She hesitated.

'Yes; as a matter of fact. Larry's working on a new ballet for me right now.'

'Larry?'

'Sundquist. You met him.'

'Of course.' Larry Sundquist; that was the name. He remembered it now. He was the one who had dragged them off to that God-awful night club in Soho. Strangely, he couldn't recall what the man had looked like. Smallish, undistinguished — but with the sort of tapwater charm that worked wonders on susceptible females such as Diana. And Caroline?

The main road swung round to the left: they branched off it, on to the footpath.

'Larry must be the one,' he said, 'who keeps calling you?'

'He needs to consult with me. About the ballet.'

'At five o'clock in the morning?'

'So what's it about, this ballet? Tell me about it.'

'Oh . . . it's based on a Mexican folk tale we dug up. Very ethnic.'

And that was all? It appeared that it was.

'All right,' he said, 'if you don't want to tell me about the ballet, tell me about something else . . . your fond mama and papa, for instance. Do you see anything of them?'

'Not so's you'd notice. Raul occasionally drops by for the odd day or two on his way some place else, Linda's gone and got herself tied up with a new boyfriend . . . half her age and very beautiful.'

'How many does that bring it to?'

'Don't ask! I started to lose count way back. I should say a round couple of dozen wouldn't be too much of an exaggeration. How about your folks? — Watch out for that branch.' He found himself suddenly seized by the arm and pulled sideways. 'Have you been down to Marden just recently?'

'I was there before Christmas.' He had waited till the worst of the scars had healed, after the accident. He hadn't told the Aunties about the accident, it would only have panicked them. Him and Diana splitting up had been enough for them to cope with, without his adding to it; though truth to tell they had never really liked Diana. She hadn't fitted in, as Caroline had. 'It's Auntie Vi's birthday next week; she's going to be seventy. I'm supposed to be going down there.'

'Why only supposed?'

Because he didn't know whether he could face it, that was why.

'Oh . . . I don't know.' He hunched a shoulder. 'I'm really too busy to spare the time just at the moment.'

'Too busy to spare the time for Auntie Vi? When she's going to be seventy?' Caroline's voice was reproachful. She thought he was being ungrateful and insensitive. 'Did you go when Auntie Marion was seventy?'

'Yes.' Auntie Marion had been seventy two years ago. There hadn't been any problem two years ago.

'Well, then! There you are! How can you possibly not?'

How could he possibly, was more to the point. Had it been only Auntie Marion and Auntie Vi, he might perhaps have braved it, but Vicky and Toby were going to be there as well. Auntie Vi had told him, happily, on the telephone last week: 'The children are coming over. Susan can't, because she's on duty, so the young ones are coming instead.'

He just didn't see how he could go through with it; not without giving himself away. Young Vicky, in particular, had eyes like a hawk. Only let him trip over the carpet a few times — blunder into the odd armchair, smash the odd glass, fail to respond when he ought — and she would know at once there was something up. Even apart from spoiling the occasion for Auntie Vi, it would subject him to what he was not yet prepared to face: the well-meant concern of those who cared about him. That, of it all, was perhaps the hardest part to bear.

'It's no good,' he said. 'I can't. I have to work.'

'You don't have to work: you have to take a break. Everyone needs to take a break from time to time. Not only that, it would break Vi's heart. You know you're her favourite.'

'I'll make some excuse.' He wouldn't hurt the old lady; not for the world. 'I'll have Hugo call and say I've gone down with the flu, or —'

'You won't have Hugo call, because Hugo will refuse to do it! So will Rose, and so will I.' She slid her hand through his arm, linking herself close to him. 'I suppose it hasn't occurred to you,' she said, 'that *I* should like to go? If you think I'd be welcome, that is.'

'You'd be more than welcome.' He couldn't tell her otherwise. 'Every time I go there they want to know how you're getting on.'

'I write,' she said.

'I know — they keep your letters to show me. They'd be over the moon if you went down.'

'Well, I'm not going by myself,' she said.

Perhaps, after all, he could find a way round it. If they just stayed the one night — he had proved this afternoon that it could be done. It was a question of acting circumspectly. Thinking before he did things.

'Let's say we'll go,' said Caroline. 'Please?'

'Oh, all right.' To tell the truth, he hadn't been too happy at the thought of letting the old girl down. 'If you really insist.'

They could go down to London on the Friday. It would give him a chance to do what he ought to have done weeks ago, except he'd kept telling himself that it

56

was all in the mind: things weren't really getting worse, it was simply a case of auto-suggestion. He'd been warned what the possibilities were — what might happen *if*. By some perverse subconscious action, he was obviously willing those possibilities into existence. Alternatively, if he wasn't subconsciously willing them, then it was a mere transitory phase due to strain, or stress, or overwork. Once he'd finished *Jane*, everything would be back to normal — or at least, as normal as it was ever likely to be. Normal enough to get by.

It was what he tried telling himself, though he knew perfectly well it wasn't true. He had known now for some time. He supposed it wouldn't actually hurt to make an appointment with old Bradbeer and get himself looked at. It might just conceivably set his mind at rest, and if it didn't — well, if it didn't, he couldn't be told anything he hadn't already guessed. The hell with it. They'd go down on the Friday and stay the night in a hotel, maybe take in a show and have a bite of supper afterwards. Just the two of them, by themselves. No Diana, no Sundquist. It would be almost like old times. He took Caroline's hand in his and squeezed it.

'I daresay,' he said, 'that you think you're being very clever, my girl, but I've sussed out what your little game is.'

'Oh?' She turned, to look at him. She sounded genuinely puzzled.

'You're just trying to get into Hugo's good books. Confess it! He's been telling you how poor old Paul's going bonkers, losing his marbles, heading for a freak-out . . . he's been on at you to try and get me to take some time off, hasn't he?'

'He did say he thought you were overdoing it.'

'Overdoing it! That's putting it mildly. Told you I was heading for the loony bin, more like.'

'Well . . . not in so many words, but he is pretty worried about you.'

'So you're trying to curry favour, huh? Trying to get yourself a gold star?'

'I know what *would* get me a gold star ... if you would be very brave and drive us home.'

She didn't know what she was asking. If he could have done it, he would, just to make her happy; just to convince her there was no need for concern.

'Won't you?' she said. 'To get me a gold star?'

'Carly, I'm sorry.' He stopped, where he was, in the lane, and turned her slowly by the shoulders to face him. He tipped her chin up with one finger. 'I can't,' he said. 'Not even to get you a gold star. . . .'

4

'I mean,' said Rose. '*Look.*'

She threw open the door of the kitchen cupboard: Caroline looked. On the top shelf, ranged in a neat row in descending order of height, were salt, coffee, sugar, tea, right on down the line to peppercorns, chili powder and minced garlic. A large notice, in printed caps, was stuck to the inside of the door with Scotch tape: PLEASE KEEP CONTENTS OF CUPBOARD IN ORDER.

'He goes raving berserk,' said Rose, 'if one dares misplace anything by so much as a centimetre . . . he put salt on his cornflakes the other week and then blamed me.' She settled herself back again at the kitchen table; cosy, if not elegant, in a brown wool dressing-gown of mottled check which belonged to Hugo. 'He's done exactly the same with the records. Not just Bach-Beethoven-Brahms, but quartets before quintets, and piano sonatas before violin sonatas . . . he says it makes for ease of reference.'

'Which I suppose it does,' said Caroline.

'But it's not like Paul. He used to be so easy.' Rose stirred at the biscuit tin with lethargic finger, in search of something titillating. 'I don't ever remember him being short-tempered in the old days; not even with Diana. Anyone else would have wrung her neck, but not Paul. Truly, you wouldn't believe the amount of stick he took from that woman. Because he loved her, I suppose.' She brooded glumly for a moment. 'I don't know. Now he gets mad over every least little thing — over *nothing*. Nothing at all. Absolutely *stupid* things. Really trivial. I used to leave my bicycle just outside the front gate, you know? Now if I leave it there he accuses me of trying to break people's necks. I mean, where else am I supposed to put it?'

In the garage? wondered Caroline; but didn't say so. Rose was good-hearted: she meant well. Her concern was quite genuine.

'*And* he never looked at my sketches.' She picked out a Garibaldi and nibbled at it half-heartedly. 'I know he doesn't care for them, I don't care what he says.'

'Rose, that's not true! He does care for them. He told me so.'

'He's just saying it,' said Rose.

'He's not just saying it. If he were saying it, he wouldn't be going ahead and using them, would he? Can you imagine Paul putting his precious opera at risk by agreeing to costumes he didn't think were up to standard?'

This was obviously a view which had not previously struck Rose. For a moment she seemed willing to be comforted, but then: 'If that was the case, why didn't he want to go through them with me?'

'I guess because he thought they were OK as they were.'

'I don't think he's even bothered to look at them,' said Rose. 'I made some alterations on Jane's first act costume the other day and when I showed it to him, do you know what he said? He said, which one's that?'

Caroline sat, cradling her coffee between both hands. She bent her head slightly, so that her hair fell forward, covering her face.

'He was probably thinking about something else. You know what he's like.'

'He wasn't thinking about something else . . . we'd been *discussing* the costumes. We'd actually been sitting here, at this table, *discussing* them. Sometimes,' said Rose, 'I think he looks at things and simply doesn't see them.'

Caroline kept her head bent over her coffee cup. Rose didn't know what she was saying. If she did, she wouldn't have said it, any more than Caroline herself could summon up the courage to do so; for to say it out loud, to say it even in the silence of one's mind, actually to formulate the words, was tantamount to admitting it as a possibility. It could not be a possibility. She refused to accept it — and yet it would not be dismissed. It all fitted in just a little too neatly for comfort; all made rather too much (albeit disturbing) sense of her own observations over the past couple of weeks.

On Saturday evening, she and Paul had been summoned by Ludmila to dine with her and Papa Jo. Paul had been reluctant, which at the time had struck her as odd. He had pleaded by way of excuse that Ludmila put the fear of God into him: Caroline had laughed, and told him to think up something better. Later, as the evening progressed, it had come to her that possibly it was Papa Jo who had been the real reason for his unwillingness. Papa Jo had behaved as only he could. Loud, jovial, and tactless, like an overgrown child that has burst the bonds of parental control, he had carved a collision course through the conversation with all the diplomacy of a steamroller.

'So!' (To Caroline) 'You are not married? Neither is Paul any more, you know. That woman has left him. We are all glad of it. Why pretend otherwise? She had no heart, that Diana. I don't know why he ever married her in the first place. Do you remember, when you were here at Bampton as a little girl, how you and Paul used to walk together hand in hand? The love birds, we used to call you. Did you know that? You had your names for us, but we had ours for you. The little love birds ... wasn't that so, Madame? Isn't that what we used to call them? And now here they are, all grown up, and Caroline not married, and Paul once again on his own —'

For herself, she had not minded so much; it was Paul

she had felt for. Ludmila had done her best to stem the flood — 'That's quite enough of that. They don't want to hear you carrying on about when they were children. You get on and eat your food before it starts congealing. We've had more than enough of your voice for one night' — but even Ludmila was as no more than a pebble in the unleashed dam of Papa Jo's benevolence.

'How I deplore all your -isms!' he had once declared with fervour, at a mock general election organised by Paul in his student days. 'Let us do away with all -isms and have human kindness instead!'

Such a simple, if well-meaning, philosophy, could not but come to grief in practical application: Papa Jo's human kindness ran away with him. In his earnest desire to see those about him neatly paired off and made happy, he caused untold agonies of hurt and embarrassment. It was Paul, finally, who had brought it to an end, by the timely expedient of upsetting his wine glass. She had thought it was timely: she had thought it was expedient. After yesterday, she was no longer so sure. Sometimes, Rose had said, I think he looks at things and simply doesn't see them. . . .

His adamant refusal to drive had puzzled her even before yesterday. It was true he had never been a particularly enthusiastic driver, she could perfectly understand that for the first month or so after the accident he might have had qualms, but to be without transport in this part of the world, dependent for one's mobility on the goodwill of others, was to render oneself virtually a cripple. Knowing Paul as she did, she would have thought the loss of his precious independence would be sufficiently abhorrent to overcome any fears as to his ability to handle a vehicle.

On the drive to Burford she had kept a close watch for any signs of nervousness in him as a passenger, but there had been none: he had appeared perfectly relaxed and at his ease. On the way back, however, they had come by a different and more roundabout route, one of her choosing rather than his. It was one he was not so familiar with, and twice, coming up to junctions, he had perceptibly hesitated, waiting for her to read the signs before directing her. The third time he had been busy cleaning his glasses; and thereafter, to spare his feelings, she had not asked.

She had sensed, over lunch, that there was something amiss. He had made a show of studying the menu, yet she had had the distinct feeling he was not actually reading it. She could not have said why, could not have pinpointed the reason for her feeling, but instinctively, when he was pouring the wine, she had edged her glass towards him, making certain it was positioned correctly, just as outside, in the lane, the same instinct had made her pull him to one side to avoid an overhanging branch. Again, she could not have said what it was that prompted her; only that at the time it had seemed the natural thing to do. Another second and she was convinced he would have walked straight into it — he had shown no awareness of its proximity either before or after she had removed him from its path. When he had confessed to her, a few minutes later, that he was in two minds whether to go down to Marden for the old lady's birthday, she had known for sure there was something wrong.

Auntie Vi and Auntie Marion had been both mother and father to Paul ever since the premature death of Richard Salinger, from leukaemia, at the age of thirty-five, followed by the tragic suicide of his wife three months later. Richard had been their adored younger brother, handsome and talented, with all the world at his feet, and they had loved and worshipped him as only two devoted spinsters could. That love and worship, on his death, had been transferred to Paul. Paul, henceforth, was to be the light of their life: their pride and their joy and son by all but birth. But if the old ladies — Auntie Vi in innocent openness, Auntie

Marion with somewhat more reserve — had poured out their orisons upon the altar of their love, the passage of emotion had not been all one way. Paul in his youth may have been thoughtless, but in his adult years he had more than made up for it. She remembered once, in pre-Diana days (life had become pretty well divided into pre- and post-Diana) when Auntie Vi had had a bad dose of pneumonia which had landed her in hospital, he had even foregone attendance at a first performance of one of his own works in order to be there at her side. A man who would do that, she argued, would not back out of an old lady's seventieth birthday celebrations unless he had some very good reason.

'Compulsive tidiness —' Rose picked up the biscuit tin and peered vaguely into its depths — 'is one of the symptoms of inner disturbance . . . it betokens a state of considerable anxiety.'

It could also, thought Caroline, betoken the need to be able to locate things when you could no longer see where they were. She cast her mind back, over the two weeks since she had been here. Had she ever, in that time, seen Paul pick up a newspaper? read a book? She surely must have done. Others, beside her would have noticed if he were having difficulty. There was a limit to the amount you could hide from people.

'Rose,' she said. 'What happened to Paul when he had his accident?'

'He was driving back,' said Rose, 'after seeing Diana off.'

'Yes, but I mean . . . injury wise?'

'Oh! I don't really know; not for certain. He never really talks about it. I don't think he likes to. All I know for certain is they had to dig about nine million bits of glass out of him. We weren't actually here at the time. It was school holidays, you see; we were abroad. At some music festival or other. . . .' Her voice tailed off. 'We always seem to spend our holidays at music festivals. Hugo was conducting, of course. Paul was supposed to be coming over, and then suddenly we heard he'd been in this accident. By the time we got back he was more or less recovered.'

'I noticed he had a few scars, still, on his forehead.'

'Yes, they've almost faded,' said Rose. 'They were quite bad at first. It's where they had to dig the glass out of.'

'I guess —' Caroline hesitated, choosing her words. 'I guess it's pretty lucky he wears spectacles? Saved it going into his eyes.'

'You can lose your sight that way,' said Rose.

Caroline looked at her, across the table, but Rose's pale, madonna face remained as bland as ever. She plainly did not share Caroline's particular apprehensions. Perhaps, after all, it was only imagination.

'Oh, well!' She pushed away her coffee cup. 'This is no good, I must get moving. I have a class at ten.' She was taking classes every day, with the advanced students. In return, she herself was giving a daily class to a select band of pupils handpicked by Ludmila.

'Thank God I'm not a dancer.' Rose replaced the lid on the biscuit tin and stood up, yawning. 'I suppose I'd better look in at the shop, just in case the odd intrepid tourist shows up ... life is all go, isn't it? Have you noticed? I fly about like the Red Queen, getting nowhere.'

'Don't you mean the White Queen?' said Caroline. She had vague memories of the Red Queen being a fast, frenetic, busy sort of lady.

'No,' said Rose. 'The White Queen had it easy. I simply never seem to stop ... I suppose that's one of the curses of being a career women.'

'Oh, we're all career women now,' said Caroline.

'I know. Isn't it hell? It certainly wasn't like this in my mother's day.'

'Why? What did she do?' Caroline was intrigued: she knew nothing whatsoever about Rose's mother.

'She didn't do anything,' said Rose. 'She lived in Tunbridge Wells and had me. That was enough, in those days. Now we all have to prove we can do everything that men can do ... but who, I ask you, in their right minds, would *want* to do what men do? I wouldn't. Not if it means inventing horrific bombs to kill people with. It's all their fault, you know. Women would never have invented such things.'

'They probably mightn't have invented airplanes or motor-cars, either', ventured Caroline. Not that she felt particularly strongly about the subject; not just at this moment.

'So who cares about aeroplanes and motor-cars? Nasty smelly things. *And* dangerous. I tell you,' said Rose, 'if men had been kept for breeding purposes only, which is what they pretty well soon will be, what with sperm banks and all the rest, if they don't manage to blow us all up beforehand with this accursed bomb of theirs, this world would be a far better and healthier place to live in. Granted we'd be about a thousand years behind as far as technology is concerned, but we'd till the soil and hoe the land, or whatever it is you do with land, and we'd all be a damn sight happier.'

'I wonder?' said Caroline.

'Well, I certainly would be,' said Rose. 'I'd sooner squat by an unpolluted river bank and wash my clothes by hand any day of the week than have the benefit of a washing machine and Blue Daz and the threat of radiation poisoning for ever hanging over one ... I meant to go on a Peace March last month. Unfortunately, I was overcome by a fit of lethargy at the last minute and never made it.'

Caroline was amused: the thought of Rose being attacked by anything so energetic as a fit of lethargy....

'You can laugh,' said Rose. 'But I'm warning you, it's no laughing matter. Unless, of course, you find it funny, the prospect of the world being atomised.' She looked at Caroline, rather hard. '*Do* you find it funny?'

Hastily, Caroline, straightened out her features.

'I'm not smiling. Believe me.'

'So why don't you do something about it?'

'Do what? Go shoot all the eggheads?'

'Come on a rally with me ... come next weekend. Trafalgar Square. Make a stand, declare your principles.'

'Rosie, I can't next weekend. I promised I'd go down to Marden with Paul.'

The excuse sounded feeble, but her life at the moment embraced a narrower compass than Rose's evidently did. To have an abortion, or not to have an abortion? To stay with Larry, or not to stay with Larry? It was difficult to take the cosmic view when such was the nature of one's preoccupations. Now, it seemed, there was Paul who must be added to the list.

'I would've come —' she would; just to show solidarity — 'but I can't leave him high and dry.' He wouldn't go if she weren't there to keep him to it. He would invent some excuse and back out.

'Make him come with us,' said Rose. 'It's about time he started getting into things again — he gave it all up, you know. Because of Diana. She used to nag him so. I seem to remember that before he met her he was quite committed.'

'He did his share of flag waving.'

'Which is more than Hugo ever did. Hugo,' said Rose, 'is really so intolerably *narrow-minded*. Not to mention being an arch chauvinist. I mean, honestly.' She brooded a while. 'It's just as well you're taking Paul away.' (Taking? wondered Caroline. Did Rose think him not capable of getting anywhere under his own steam?) 'Marden, Trafalgar Square ... it doesn't really matter. Just so long as he has a break. Ever since Diana left him, he's been driving himself like there was no tomorrow — which, of course, there may very well not be. However, that's no reason to kill oneself prematurely. Would you believe we woke up at three o'clock one morning and found him still at it?'

'Yes, Hugo was telling me. He seems to be scared Paul's heading for some kind of a breakdown.'

'He might be *pushing* himself into some kind of breakdown. What's important,' said Rose, 'is to discover why he's doing it. I have a theory about that.'

'You do?'

'Yes. Would you like to hear it?'

'Why not?'

'Well, it's really very simple . . . he's sublimating.'

There was a pause.

'Sublimating?' said Caroline.

'Yes.'

'Sublimating what?'

'His need for someone. Someone to love.'

Caroline laughed.

'Why, Rosie, I never knew you were such a romantic!'

'There's nothing romantic about it. Love is need. Need isn't romantic, it's a basic fact of life. Most people's life. Not everybody suffers from it. Hugo, for example. Hugo doesn't really need anyone. So long as he's got his music, that's all that matters. He doesn't *need* anyone to love. He thinks he does, but actually he doesn't. Paul on the other hand thinks he doesn't — or tries to *make* himself think that he doesn't — whereas in point of fact he quite desperately does. Therein,' said Rose, 'lies the root cause of his problem, resulting in overwork, compulsive tidiness, and not having the elementary good manners to look at my sketches.'

Would that it were that simple, thought Caroline. Rose could, of course, be right — but she very much feared that she was not.

'The day will come,' said Rose, 'when the male of the species will be kept frozen and bottled, to be used solely for purposes of procreation. I'm only surprised that in America you haven't got there already.'

'Don't worry,' said Caroline. 'We're working on it.' It

was the very thing that Larry had so venomously complained of, when she had first broken it to him that she was pregnant: *That's all you goddamn women ever want us for ... profuckingcreation.* She turned, abruptly, and headed for the stairs. She didn't want to think about Larry; not just now. She had enough on her plate, thinking about Paul. 'I must go and get my gear together. I'll be late.'

On her way along the landing she passed Paul's bedroom. She had not been into Paul's room since arriving at Bampton; there was no reason for her to have done so. Now, on impulse, she pushed open the door and looked in. Her eyes went at once to the bedside table: a travelling alarm clock was all that stood on it. Not a book or a magazine in sight. She remembered, in the old days (pre-Diana) that his bedside table had always been piled high. She had been well acquainted, then, with the contents of his bedroom — not that he and she had ever shared an apartment, but there had been a time, nonetheless, when she had spent more of her nights in his bed than her own. Paul was the first lover she had ever had: the only one apart from Larry. She had been attracted often enough to other men, had had offers in plenty had she cared to take them up. Somehow, for her, the need to consummate every fleeting passion with a night in bed had just not been that great. She claimed no special virtue thereby, nor had she ever felt inclined to jealousy of Paul's many and varied conquests. They came, they went; they were not important. Or so she had always believed. It was Diana who had changed all that: Diana, too late, who had awoken her to the true nature of her feelings where Paul was concerned.

Guiltily, now, she shut the door on his invaded privacy. She had not told him of Larry; what right had she to pry into what he quite obviously did not wish her to know?

Downstairs she found Rose, still in her dressing-gown, perched on top of the calor gas heater varnishing her finger nails with silver varnish.

'Incidentally,' said Rose, 'I almost forgot ... your boyfriend rang again yesterday, when you and Paul were out. He said he'd try again this afternoon. Round about four — our time, that is.'

'Right,' said Caroline. 'Thanks.' As an afterthought, she added: 'He's not my boyfriend, by the way. He just happens to be writing a new ballet for me.'

'Oh, I see,' said Rose.

She didn't sound very convinced. Caroline could hardly blame her: that was the fourth call Larry had made since she had been over here. He had called yesterday morning to inform her that he had 'had things out' with Bettina, and that Bettina, finally, had agreed to go along with a divorce.

'I'm seeing the lawyers first thing Monday.'

Even now she didn't know whether to believe him. It had all happened so often before.

No; that was not strictly true: he had never actually before gone so far as to say that Bettina had agreed. Before, she had always been made a convenient scapegoat. Perhaps this time he really could be serious?

For the moment, perhaps, he really was serious. So long as she was in England he was serious. Come the middle of May, when she went back to the States (*if* she went back to the States) it would doubtless be the same old story: Bettina had changed her mind, Bettina was making waves, it wasn't so simple, what about the children?

One of these days, thought Caroline, I will wake up to the fact that Larry Sundquist is a bastard.

She already had woken up to the fact. Just didn't care to face it, that was all.

Going into school, she met the Kaufman kid. He had abandoned his customary space helmet and instead of a violin was carrying a vast pile of text books, clamped somewhat precariously into place by his chin. He grinned at her familiarly over the top of them.

'Hi.'

'Hi,' said Caroline. 'You need a hand?'

'That's OK, I can manage. Hey! I just remembered.' She turned.

'What's that?'

'Paul says you're driving down to London Friday. Is it OK if I ride with you?'

'Sure.' She had no objections to the child accompanying them.

'He said I was to check with you first.'

'OK, so you've checked. It's all right with me, if it's all right with Paul. You have something special to do down there?'

'My old man's coming over.'

'You mean your father,' said Caroline.

'That's what I said . . . my old man.'

Caroline looked at him.

'Why is it American kids are so obnoxious?'

'That's what Paul's always saying. Between you and me, I think he's a xenophobe.'

'Some people,' said Caroline, crushingly, 'are enough to make one.'

At the end of class, Ludmila crooked an imperious finger, beckoning her to one side. Back in San Diego, Ms Caroline Ramirez would haughtily have ignored such a summons: here at Bampton, old habits died hard. Meekly she went across.

'Madame?'

'I hear you've finally gotten Paul to take a break.'

'Yes, we're going down to visit his aunts, in Kent. Only a long weekend, but —'

'A long weekend,' said Ludmila, 'is a long weekend longer than anything else he's had just recently. How do you find him?'

The question was put so abruptly it almost had her off balance.

'How do I find him?'

71

'You find him changed?'

'Well —' She was guarded. 'Four years is quite a time. I guess we've all done a bit of changing in four years.'

'You haven't noticed anything . . . untowards about him?'

She fenced.

'In what way, untowards?'

'You saw how he sent that glass flying at dinner the other night.'

'Yes, I'm sorry about that. I hope the wine didn't stain?'

'I'm not worried about stain!' Ludmila dismissed the notion, impatiently. 'I'm more worried about Paul. He strikes me as being very tense.'

'I think perhaps he was a bit on edge . . . all that talk of Diana.'

'Nonsense!' said Ludmila. 'It wasn't that at all.'

Caroline waited for her, in that case, to offer some other explanation. Instead, with sudden change of tack, taking her by the arm in proprietorial fashion, Ludmila said: 'Tell me about this ballet Sundquist's writing for you.' She had already asked her about the ballet on several previous occasions: Caroline had already told her all there was to tell. Anything, however, was preferable to being subjected to an inquisition about Paul. She didn't know what, or how much, Ludmila suspected, but if Paul had wished the world to be made aware of his problems he would presumably have come out into the open and declared them; the fact that he had not would seem to indicate very clearly that he preferred to do battle by himself.

With forbearance, therefore, she told yet again the story of the ballet. Ludmila listened, and nodded; seemingly well pleased.

'It sounds good. A good vehicle. You'll do it, of course?'

The question, she had to assume, was rhetorical; at

any rate, she was spared the necessity of answering by Ludmila pausing scarcely long enough to give her the chance.

'Three months is a considerable time to be away. I wouldn't like to think you were throwing everything up. Not at your age. You still have any years to go.'

She smiled at that.

'Many? Six if I'm lucky!'

'So six years is six years... not to be sneezed at. You sacrifice those six years now, and by the time you're sixty you'll be wondering why in hell you didn't cling on to them with both hands while you still had the opportunity. In any case, who says you have only six years?'

'I do! I don't intend to be aching and groaning my way through daily class in the company of seventeen-year-olds when I'm fast approaching forty.'

'Forty,' said Ludmila, 'is nothing. Nothing! I wish you girls would get it into your heads that I don't train you up just to drop everything and go plummeting into armchairs at the first creak of a joint. I had to, but my case was different. I had Papa Jo to consider. You're free: take advantage of it. Good morning, Lydia! Why are you running? The rules of the establishment are quite clear: students shall walk the corridors in decorous fashion at all times save in case of fire. Is there a fire? No? Then kindly moderate your pace.'

'Yes, Mme.'

The unfortunate Lydia, red-faced, bobbed a curtsey; Caroline took the opportunity to espace. Ludmila's homilies were beginning to be rather pointed, though it was difficult to see exactly what she feared. From which direction did she sense danger? From here at Bampton, or from across the Atlantic? Whichever, she could do without being lectured at.

She had an hour's break before she was due to take her own class. She wiped herself down, pulled on sweater and leg warmers and went off to the staff-room for a coffee. She felt almost back in her student days, walking the corridors (in duly decorous fashion) in practice costume. She could not but look back on those days with affection — and perhaps just a hint of wry amusement? It was quite true, what Papa Jo had said. There had been a period, in their late teens, when she and Paul had gone everywhere together locked hand in hand. The Siamese-flaming-twins, Hugo had called them, with all the disparagement of a contemporary as yet untouched by the pangs of love. She smiled; indulgent, at such distance, for the lost euphoria of youth. Anyone might have been forgiven, in those far-off days, for expecting a happy-ever-after of her and Paul.

She saw Paul as she passed by one of the music rooms. He was there with Papa Jo, and a girl who could only be his Jane Eyre — small, slim, dark, demure. She paused a moment, unobserved, to watch through the glass panel of the door. Papa Jo, in his wheelchair, seemed from his outstretched arms to be exhorting. She still remembered with pleasure the day he had implored Paul, in a school production, to 'Sing! Sing like Isolde!' She and Hugo had had a lot of fun with that. She looked at Paul, now. He was at the piano. He had no music on the stand, but then she supposed he quite likely would not; not if he were playing his own work. He presumably had every note of it safety locked away inside his head.

She went on her way to the staff-room, which she found uninhabited save for Meat Loaf, drinking coffee from the coffee machine and eating digestive biscuits out of his own personal tin, his injured ankle, still ostentatiously bandaged, propped on a footstool before him. She never quite knew how to address Meat Loaf. Paul and Hugo had reached the stage of casually addressing him as Victor, which was something Caroline had not yet been able to bring herself to do. In student days the old man had been both a figure of fun, with his perpetual, throttled cries ('Ach, Ghrist! Vot are you beeble blayink at?') and, at the same time, a figure to be feared, for Meat Loaf, if crossed, could be malicious. Paul especially he had held in aversion, as now it seemed he held the Kaufman boy. In many ways the little Kaufman reminded her of the young Paul: cocksure, impatient of restraint, taking his own gifts very much for granted. A pain, certainly; but far from unlikable.

'Ah,' said Meat Loaf. 'Caroline. Have a beeskit.'

He held out the tin. Surprised, she helped herself to a digestive. Since when had Meat Loaf started doling out his private rations?

'So.'

He positioned his injured ankle more comfortably on its stool and settled back, as if for a cosy chat, into the depths of his chair. Caroline looked at him warily. What did he mean, so?

'So how are you findink our young friend?'

It was Ludmila all over again. Suddenly, everyone wanted to know about Paul — at least, she assumed he was referring to Paul. Maybe not.

'Young friend?' She went across to the coffee machine. 'You mean Christopher?'

'Do not talk to me of that child! If he were not superb on violin, I demand he be booted. I am meanink Baul.'

'Oh! Paul.'

'How are you findink him?'

'Pretty good,' she said, 'considering what he's been through.'

He pounced.

'You vould say that vat he hass been though hass had bad effect?'

'Would you?' countered Caroline.

Meat Loaf regarded her reproachfully.

'Is this a debate? Do ve try to sgore boints? I ask begause I veel concern: I vish to know if you, too, feel concern. If you do not, then maybe I am made a little bit more happy.'

75

She felt chastened. Perhaps she had misjudged the old man. Hugo had said, had he not, that time had mellowed him?

'What is it,' she said, 'that makes you not happy?'

'I vatch.' With grave deliberation, Meat Loaf dunked his digestive in his coffee. 'I ask qvestions.' The digestive was removed; flabby and coffee-sodden. In the nick of time, he transferred it to his mouth. 'I find that these qvestions haff no answers. Or answers —' he pulled out a handkerchief — 'that can only disturb. Therefore I say to you, I am not happy.'

There was a pause. Caroline sat in silence, not knowing how to reply. She, too, had asked questions: she, too, found answers that disturbed. Whether they were the same questions and the same answers was something which could not be put. Loyalty to Paul forbade it.

She was still searching for words that did not come when the door opened and Paul himself appeared. He made no acknowledgement of the other occupants of the room, but went straight across to the coffee machine. That was fair enough, thought Caroline. He was preoccupied; his thoughts still running on his opera. You couldn't expect him to switch off all in a matter of seconds.

Meat Loaf lowered his injured leg to the floor and went over to join him at the table.

'Goot mornink, Baul.'

'Morning, Victor. How's the ankle?'

'Better than it has been: vorse than it ought to be. That child is a moral delinkvent. Ve haff gompany, by the vay.'

'Oh?'

Paul turned.

'Only me,' said Caroline. She spoke quickly, lest there be any embarrassment. 'I came in for class.'

'Of course, I was forgetting . . . want a coffee?'

She hesitated; then: 'Yes, why not?' Guiltily, trying not to look in Meat Loaf's direction, she set down her cup, still more than half full, and took the one that Paul was holding out.

Meat Loaf, as he left the room, paused and looked at her. Slowly, he shook his head.

He knows, thought Caroline.

She wondered how many other people also did.

5

They drove down to London the following Friday morning. The snow had cleared, but a wintry hail of rain now gusted across the fields in its place, turning the landscape bleak and sodden. Larry would have been pleased, had he known. He asked her every time they spoke whether it had started raining yet. It was a game that he played: if all else failed, the weather would defeat her in the end. He had asked her again on Monday, when he had called to tell her that he had seen the lawyers and that 'everything was in hand'.

'Has it started to rain yet?'

'No,' she had said, 'it's too cold for rain.'

Larry had chuckled; obviously contented.

'Is that so? Me, I'm just off to the pool. Lie in the sun, think about the new ballet. . . . '

They were coming up to a roundabout. At her side, Christopher's voice piped authoritatively, giving her directions: by Paul's suggestion, he was sitting in the front.

'We don't want the brat getting car sick.'

'Car sick? Who gets car sick?' Chris had been indignant. 'I don't get car sick!'

'Well, you can still sit in the front . . . do a bit of map reading. Make yourself useful.'

It had to be said, he was better at it than Paul.

They stopped off, on the motorway, for a coffee. It was the first time she had had a chance to observe Paul in an environment with which he was not intimately acquainted. As they left the car he took her hand, tucking it through his arm in familiar fashion. It was not necessarily anything to go by: simply because they had ceased to be lovers did not mean they had ceased to feel affection.

At the entrance to the restaurant was a step. She resisted the impulse to warn him of it. It was Chris who did so.

'Just watch ya don't trip over, now . . . I don't wanna get the blame same as I did the other day.'

'The other day,' said Paul, 'you deliberately, and with malice aforethought, obstructed my path.'

'There ya go again! Always puttin' it off on someone else!'

'Yes, well, you have to make allowances for the onset of senility . . . by the time one reaches thirty, one has very little going for one.'

'Listen, if you're as senile as all that,' said Caroline, 'why don't you take a seat and let me and Chris go get the coffee?'

'Yeah, that way we might just get to drink the stuff without losin' half of it.'

'You just park yourself there and rest your ancient old bones.'

There had once been a time when he would most strenuously have resisted such a suggestion, albeit one made partly in jest: now he accepted it without even so much as a token show of protest. She reminded herself that the climate had changed since she and Paul had been young together. In the days of their teens gentlemen had still studiously walked on the outside, raised their hats, footed the bills — and Paul, brought up by the two old ladies, had been nothing if not a gentleman. Larry would have thought it all very quaint.

'Say, could I ask you somethin'?' said Chris.

'Go ahead. What is it you want to know?'

'I was just wondering . . . why doesn't Paul drive any more?'

'Oh —' she hunched a shoulder. 'I guess he doesn't feel too happy about it, since the accident.'

'My old man was in an accident once. He said the best thing to do was just get straight back in.'

'He did? What do you want to drink? Tea or coffee?'

'Coconut milk shake.'

'They don't have coconut milk shakes.'

'I know a place that does.'

'So go there!'

'I can't, it's back home.'

'In that case, don't complain. All the world is not MacDonald's . . . have a hot chocolate.'

'Oh, OK, if I have to.' Chris was silent a while, swinging on the hand rail like any other eleven-year-old; then: 'You know this accident?' he said.

'Mm hm?'

'It didn't do somethin' funny to his eyes, did it?'

She looked at him frowning.

'What makes you ask that?'

'Well, I dunno . . . he's been acting really weird just lately.'

'How do you mean? what kind of weird?'

'Like —' Chris screwed up his face, trying to think of examples. 'Like the other day, I held the door for him and he went an' knocked straight into me?'

She did her best to make light of it.

'The show of politeness was probably too much!'

He stared at her, reproachfully, even as Meat Loaf had done.

'It wasn't that. It was more like he just didn't see me.'

'He was probably preoccupied. He'd probably just been working on his opera.'

'He'd just come from assembly,' said Chris.

'Well, there you are! Papa Jo —'

'It wasn't Papa Jo, it was Meat Loaf, an' he's borin' as shit. Ya know what he did yesterday? Paul, I mean?'

'No. What did he do yesterday?'

'Sat down on a piano stool that wasn't there.'

80

Cold fingers clenched at her stomach. She looked across at Paul, sitting patiently where they had left him, at a table by the door. He seemed to be looking in their direction. She found herself wondering if he could actually see them. . . .

'I suppose,' she said, lightly, 'you all laughed like cretins?'

'We tried to, but just about nobody could. I mean, he really wanted us to. He said, OK, you guys, I'm givin' you one minute to have a good laugh, and then he stood there an' he timed us, and boy, that was a real turn off!'

'Why so? Too embarrassed?'

'I guess. Plus feelin' kinda sorry for him. I mean really,' said Chris, 'that kinda thing is not funny.'

You can say that again, thought Caroline. She picked up the tray. Chris, ducking under the rail, waited until she had passed through the check-out.

'You don't think he's goin' blind or somethin', do ya?'

Out of the mouths of babes, she thought. . . . She forced herself to speak calmly, choosing her words with care.

'I think,' she said, 'that perhaps he doesn't see quite as well as he used to, but I also think it's something he'd rather people didn't talk about, so if you want to help him, the kindest thing you can do is pretend not to have noticed. Unless of course he says anything. I don't know —' she hesitated, not certain just how much understanding could be expected of an eleven-year-old — 'I don't know whether that makes any sense, or —'

'Yeah.' He nodded, thoughtfully. 'I guess it does . . . I guess it was like when I had my appendix and didn't want my sister to know. I nearly died on account of not wanting my sister to know.'

She was intrigued, in spite of herself.

'Why in the world was that?'

'Why in the world did I nearly die or why in the world didn't I want my sister to know?'

'Well . . . both, if you like!'

'I nearly died because my appendix ruptured and they only just got me to the hospital in time, and I didn't want my sister to know because by sister is a fink. If she'd known I was having these pains she'd have really taken advantage. It would have made her feel really superior. I guess that's why Paul doesn't want people to know . . . in case they take advantage. Wouldn't you say?'

'Maybe something on those lines,' murmured Caroline. She obviously had a lot to learn about the minds of eleven-year-olds. . . .

Kaufman senior was staying in Park Lane, at the Dorchester. He was of that breed of men whom Larry despised above all others: an artist by proxy. (A financier by profession.) Caroline, not sharing Larry's prejudices, found him affable if a trifle over-engaging. His knowledge of music was all too palpably nil, his respect for its practitioners exaggeratedly earnest. (Christopher, firmly included amongst the ranks of those practitioners, took respect as his infant due, treating his worshipful parent with the benevolent contempt of one too young as yet to have learnt proper reverence for the power of the almighty money-bag, which alone, in a mis-ordered world, made possible the flowering of his precious talent. Some day, thought Caroline, he would learn; and then what? Gratitude? Humble recognition? Or simply an augmentation of contempt?)

They were pressed to stay and have lunch. For her part she would not have objected; it was Paul who declined, making the excuse, which was true enough, that he had an appointment to keep. In fact the appointment was not until late in the afternoon. He had given her no details, and she had prudently not asked, but something, she would hazard a guess, to do with Diana. For all his show of indifference, his flat denials that there was any chance of a reconciliation, she could not believe he would let go that easily. Diana, whatever harsh things people might say about her, had undeniably been beautiful; and he had loved her once — well enough to marry her. There had never been any talk of marriage where Caroline was concerned.

They ate quietly, by themselves, at their own hotel; a genteel establishment in the hinterland of South Kensington.

'Is it all right?' Paul wanted to know.

'The lunch? It's fine.'

'The hotel. We could have gone somewhere grander, but I thought you'd prefer this. I thought it might bring back memories . . . 24 Redwood Gardens?'

Twenty-four Redwood Gardens . . . she had almost forgotten it. Not the place, but the actual address. The place itself was for ever engraved on her memory.

'Your apartment,' she said.

His little, spartan, two-room box of an apartment, where one bright summer's day, a lifetime ago, she had ceased to be a virgin and become instead his lover.

'How long is it now,' she said, 'since you were there?'

'Six years this September. When I started at Bampton.'

And just before he had met Diana. At least she had the solace of knowing that Diana had never slept with him at Redwood Gardens.

'Should we go take a look at it?'

'Why not?' he said. 'If you're in the mood for nostalgia —'

She had not been, until he mentioned it; but since he had, she supposed it could do no harm. Whatever pain there had been, had long faded. If she could not now look back in tranquillity, she never would.

'Do we have time to go after lunch?'

'Loads.'

'OK, you're on.'

'How about this evening? What would you like to do this evening?'

'Mm . . . just sit over dinner and talk?'

For a moment he seemed tempted, but then, almost reluctantly, shook his head.

'We ought to do something — go somewhere.'

'A concert?'

'You're sure you wouldn't rather the ballet?'

'No way! I'm on vacation, remember? Besides, I can't stand to have you complain all the time.'

'*Me?*'

'Yes, you! Or had you forgotten? Your immortal remark? *Music —*' she mimicked his accent, impeccably English — *is either too good to be desecrated by having people jump around to it, or too bad to be glorified by the name of music.*'

'I said that?'

'You said that.'

He pulled a face.

'Pompous young ass!'

'I think,' she said, kindly, 'that you were going through your Oscar Wilde period.'

'Epigrammatically only, I trust!'

'Well, whatever . . . you were certainly unbearable to sit through a ballet with.'

'I wouldn't be now; I promise you.' He reached for his wine glass — just fractionally off course. Unobtrusively, she shunted it towards him. 'I've mellowed since then.'

'Like Meat Loaf,' she said.

'Meat Loaf?' He sounded surprised, as if the thought had not previously struck him. 'Yes . . . now you come to mention it, I had noticed a certain sentimental sogginess setting in. He's been almost humanoid just recently.'

Even Meat Loaf, thought Caroline, was not without compassion.

Shortly before the end of lunch she was called to the telephone.

'Friend Larry?' said Paul.

She imagined that it had to be. He must presumably have called her at Bampton and been given the number of the hotel. Such determined pursuit was beginning to assume almost the dimensions of assault and battery. She picked up the receiver.

'Hallo?'

'Ms Ramirez?'

'Speaking.'

'This is Rod Kaufman here.'

'Oh, Mr Kaufman!' She didn't know whether to feel disappointed or relieved. 'I'm sorry, I didn't recognise you.'

'No reason why you should. Listen, I was wondering, I'm having a little dinner party tonight in my suite here at the Dorchester, would you and Mr Salinger be insulted if I were to invite you to come along? There's one or two people I'd really like to have you meet . . . Layton Berry, for example, of ICP. Do you happen to be acquainted with him by any chance?'

She did not happen to be so; and neither, as far as she was aware, did Paul. Her brain, which split seconds ago had been rapidly sifting through excuses for yet a second time declining an invitation, now abruptly shifted gear and went into overdrive. Layton Berry was head of one of the most powerful organisations in show business: International Concert Promotions had half the top-ranking artists in the western hemisphere on its books. For herself she had no particular burning desire, any more, to be promoted. She had secured her own personal niche, and while it might not perhaps be at the very topmost branch of the tree it was as far as she had any ambition to climb. Certainly she had no hankering after the glitter and glamour of international stardom; she left that for Larry, who had hankering enough for both of them. Larry would give his right arm to make acquaintance with the top mogul of ICP. Strange, then, that it was not of Larry whom she thought; not at the time. At the time it was Paul who sprang immediately to mind. Paul and his opera, his precious *Jane*.

Unblushingly abandoning all pretence of prior engagements, she accepted the invitation for seven-thirty that evening and went back to the dining-room to break the news to him. Predictably, he was not happy about it. She had known he would not be: even in the old days he had been a most reluctant socialiser.

'Do we really have to?'

'We do now I've accepted the invitation.'

'Can't you ring back and unaccept it?'

'Paul, you don't seem to understand.' She paused, as they emerged from the hotel, to put up her umbrella. (How Larry would laugh....) 'Layton Berry could do great things. I mean really. If we could coax him down to Bampton —'

'I'm not good at coaxing! I'm only good at writing music.'

'Yes, but you need to have your music played, don't you? You need to have people hear it?'

'Caroline,' he said, 'don't bully me! I don't want to go and have dinner with all these boring people.'

'It's not *all these people*, it's only half a dozen — and who says they're going to be boring? They could be just as bright and scintillating as you are.'

'I still don't want to go and have dinner with them.'

'Well, you're going to.' She was very firm on the point. 'There are times we all of us have to do things we don't want.' Such as having abortions. It had been necessary, if she were to keep Larry, but she had not enjoyed it. Paul, no doubt, would not enjoy the Kaufman dinner party. She felt for him, but if he would not confide in her, there was little she could say by way of comfort. 'It's just one of those things that has to be done. I know it's difficult for you — watch the kerb. I know you don't like to meet people —'

He stopped.

'What made you say that?'

'In case you weren't looking where you were going.'

'No, I mean . . . that bit about it being difficult for me.'

'Oh! I was just being charitable. Assuming that you were shy rather than deliberately antisocial.'

He was silent a while.

'Has Ludmila said anything to you?'

'About what?'

'The other night — when we went round to dinner.'

'Why on earth should Ludmila have said anything?'

'I don't know . . . I just thought she might have done.'

'Well, of course she hasn't!' She lied, determinedly. She hadn't realised that it worried him so much. 'How egotistical can you get? Thinking everyone's talking about you!'

He smiled at that, but only faintly.

'Don't go getting all freaked out.' She squeezed his hand, beneath the umbrella. 'Tonight won't be anywhere near as bad as you seem to think.'

I am becoming a bore, thought Paul. An introverted, paranoiac bore . . . of course Ludmila had not said anything! If she suspected, even for a moment, the state that he was in, she would not rest at merely saying things. Ludmila was one for action — swift, decisive, and if necessary, brutal. She would be swayed neither by sentiment nor by any misplaced sense of loyalty. Ludmila owed allegiance to no one and nothing, saving only Bampton itself: she would not carry passengers.

Strange, though, about Meat Loaf. Caroline was quite right, there had definitely, of late, been a softening of attitude. Looking back, he could even date it, quite clearly, to a morning a couple of months ago when like the clumsy fool that he was becoming he had walked slap bang into the sharp edge of a filing cabinet in the office and cut his forehead. Meat Loaf and

Virginia had both been there to witness it. Virginia had been unsympathetic — hardly surprisingly: she had suffered just a little too much, over recent weeks, from Paul's growing capacity for making a court jester of himself. It had been Meat Loaf who had expressed concern. It had struck him at the time as being out of character. It was not like Meat Loaf to be solicitous, especially where ancient enemies were concerned. Could it be —

'Watch it,' said Caroline. He felt himself jerked suddenly sideways. 'That was a lamp standard you nearly wrapped yourself around.'

'What?' This was no good. He was going to have to take a grip on himself, or he would have Caroline joining the ranks of those who plainly thought him ripe for the nut house. She probably already did. He was finding it increasingly difficult, even when he could make out the rough general shape of things, to judge distances, which meant he had either to fumble and grope or chance his arm and pray. Sometimes luck was with him: sometimes it was not. She must by now have noticed and be wondering, and he hardly helped his cause by walking round in a paranoiac haze, bumping into lamp posts — or by making all that absurd amount of fuss over one small dinner party. So what if he did make a spectacle of himself? What if he were to throw glasses of wine here, there and everywhere, including over Layton Berry? Just laugh it off, that was the thing to do. Only let Bradbeer give him the reassurance that he needed and he would do more than just laugh it off, he would turn it into the biggest joke of all time. He would surprise the lot of them, and especially Caroline. The hermit crab emerging from his shell. . . .

'Down here?' said Caroline. 'Wrexham Gardens?'

'Yes.' He stepped out, confident: this was a part of the world which he knew. 'Down here and turn right . . . the third house along.'

*   *   *

She had been wrong about the pain. It had dulled, but it had not gone. Seeing the house, unchanged, familiar as it had ever been, brought it all back with an intensity she had no longer thought possible: the first acute shock of receiving his letter, the long, bitter months of hurt which had followed. She had learnt, at least, not to be bitter. Had there been even the slightest trace it must surely have been routed by Paul as he was now, for the Paul she had come back to was not the Paul who had half broken her heart, all those years ago. The Paul of former days had had about him an air of almost arrogant conviction, an unshakable certainty in his own powers, both mental and physical: no woman he could not have conquered, no mountain he could not climb. His reserve then had seemed an aloofness, It seemed now to stem more from reticence and self-doubt.

'So there you are,' he said. 'Twenty-four Redwood Gardens.'

Did she detect just the faintest note of query in his voice? *Tell me, for God's sake! Is it, or isn't it? Put me out of my misery....* She did so.

'As ever was,' she said.

'As ever was.'

They stood for a moment in silent contemplation. Paul did not suggest they ring at the door and ask to go up. She was glad of it. Dwelling on the past was a too masochistic pleasure for her present mood.

'So what would you like to do now?' he said. 'Call in at Frank's for a nostalgic coffee?'

'If you like.'

Memories of Frank's were not as bittersweet as memories of the flat, though Frank's, too, was full of ghosts. They had sat there by the hour together, back in the old days. It was in Frank's Paul had outlined to her the plan of his first symphony — sung to her the melody from the sublime slow movement of his string quartet — discussed with her his plans for the writing of an opera (on the fall of the Roman Empire . . . a far cry indeed from *Jane*). It was in Frank's, too, that she had told him of the invitation to dance with the Santa Rosalia. A year in California — a year away from Paul. Ought she, for the sake of her career, to accept it? They had both solemnly agreed that she ought. Frank's, she had sometimes thought, had a lot to answer for. . . .

It was not the same as it had been. It was still called Frank's, but it had obviously changed hands. The front was new and glossy, the service high-powered.

'This place has altered,' said Paul.

'It has,' she replied.

'Ah, well . . . I suppose one can't expect everything just to stand still. At least the house was the same.'

She wondered why it should matter to him. Was it merely the common desire of approaching middle age that the things of youth should stay for ever as they had been? Or did he have regrets for the path that he had chosen? Regrets, alas, as she had learnt, were sterile. What had been done, had been done. Time could not now be turned back upon itself.

'What were you and Chris talking about when you got the coffee this morning?'

'Oh . . . this and that. Nothing very spectacular.'

'I suppose he told you what an abject idiot I made of myself yesterday?'

'No.' That made the second time she had lied. 'Why? What did you do?'

'Only sat down on a piano stool that wasn't there.'

'That must have amused their infantile minds.'

'Oh, it did; enormously. Loud titters all round.' She raised an eyebrow: it was not the tale as she had heard it from Chris. She was prepared, on the whole, to give credence to the child's version. 'I'm suprised he didn't regale you with it,' Paul told her.

'There you go . . . being egotistical again! I asked you before — why should you think everyone's talking about you the whole time?'

'So what did he talk about?'

'I really can't remember. The usual kid stuff. It's nearly four o'clock by the way. What time do you —'

'Four-thirty. I'll walk you back to the hotel then get a cab.'

'If you're going into town, could you drop me off some place? Would that be convenient?'

'Surely.'

'Anywhere will do, so long as there are shops. I need to buy something for Auntie Vi, I don't have any present for her yet. What sort of thing does she like? Does she still like to dress up and titivate?'

'Vain as a young girl! Buy her something pretty and you can't go wrong.'

'I'll do that.'

He dropped her off in Regent Street.

'I'll see you back at the hotel. I shouldn't be too long . . . expect me round about five-thirty. OK?'

'OK.'

She waved as the cab bore him off. He still had not told her where he was going: she still had not asked. There had once been a time when they had shared every least thought, but that time had long gone. Now they guarded their secrets; wrestled alone with private anguish, each enclosed from the other.

She took her time choosing a present for Vi, finally settling (as she remembered the draughts in the old house at Marden, and the creeping damp which came off the Marsh) for a wool and mohair stole patterned in swirling loops of vivid mauve and scarlet. Auntie Vi had always been one for bright colours — 'Like a jackdaw,' as Auntie Marion, scathing, had been used to say.

After making her purchase she took tea, in silent dignity, like a dowager, in the Ritz; for no better reason than she knew it would annoy Larry. Larry was no anglophile. 'You fuckin' British,' he had once yelled at her, during the course of an argument, 'you're all the fuckin' same ... keep your thumbs up your fuckin' assholes!' She wrote to him, now, demurely, on a sheet of headed notepaper, as she sat sipping tea and eating muffins.

> 'Dear Larry, Here I am in London, at the Ritz Hotel, eating muffins ... outside it is raining (you will be delighted to hear). I am dressed sensibly for the weather in long boots and mackintosh. I even — wait for it!! — have an umbrella ... can't get more English than that! After years of ceaseless sunshine, I actually find that a bit of rain makes quite a welcome change —'

Even as she wrote the words, she wondered why she was doing it. Why should she want to upset and annoy him? It was, she could only suppose, a gesture of bravado. Look at me — see how well I am doing! See how independent of you I am.... But was she? All very well to play games. So long as he was still there — still bombarding her by letter and by telephone — she could afford a bit of a display. But if the calls were to stop, the letters cease to come —

She looked down again at what she had written. For a second she was tempted to destroy it, but then, at the last, she let it stand. One could go on being a doormat for just so long.

It was gone five-thirty by the time she arrived back at the hotel. She had fully expected Paul to be there and waiting; instead, she was handed a message by the desk clerk:

> 'Mr Salinger rang, he will not be able to keep the dinner engagement, he asks you to make his apologies.'

He might at least, she thought, have had the goodness to call back and tell her in person.

6

The rain had degenerated into a sullen, drizzling downpour. The large spattering drops that had shot like hailstones out of the winter sky had given way to a thick mist of all-enveloping dampness, cold and grey and bleak, clinging to the body like a limp wet glove.

Bradbeer had told him nothing that he did not know. Nothing.

He pushed his wet hair down inside his coat collar. It had grown too long again, he should have had it cut weeks ago, but what did it matter? What did anything matter? *Now?*

Nothing mattered now save getting his opera finished. After that —

He stepped off the kerb into the rain-sodden murk. From somewhere in the vicinity of his right ear came the loud snarling of brakes. A voice bawled at him out of the gloom: 'What's the matter with you? You blind or something?'

Not yet, sir: not quite. Give it time. A couple of weeks — couple of months? Bradbeer would not be drawn into committing himself. And yet the verdict had been quite uncompromising:

'I'm sorry,' he had said. 'I am so sorry. I only wish I could hold out some kind of hope.'

The only faint ray that he had been prepared to offer was the last-ditch sop that maybe, just maybe, if he were exceedingly blessed, he might yet retain sufficient of his cloud-besmeared vision to be able to inform himself when night was at hand.

'It's not much, I know —'

But there you are. Take it or leave it. It's all I have to offer.

Bradbeer had done his best. There was no way in which he could cushion the blow, but still he had done his best. He had sat Paul down, in a soft armchair, and plied him with brandy and spoken to him kindly, and gently, as if he were a child. You must try to be brave — it has happened to others. You are not the only one. And you will learn how to cope. You would be surprised how people do. Think of Beethoven —

Who was deaf.

Deaf! So how much worse! For a composer, that is. At least you will be able to *hear* the music that you write.

And how, dear God, was he supposed to write it? Must he end up like Delius, with some scribe doing it for him?

And Ludmila? What of Ludmila?

Of course you must stay on, my dear Paul! You surely don't think I'd ask you to leave, just because you can't see?

Like hell.

Had he really, at this point, disgraced himself by putting his head in his hands? Surely he could not have done? Not in front of Bradbeer?

He would like to think that he had not; but all he could remember was Bradbeer placing an arm about his shoulders.

'I'm sorry . . . I am so sorry. I only wish I could be more optimistic. But that's the way it is, I'm afraid. The eye is a delicate organ. It will take just so much and no more. If an operation would help —'

But an operation, it seemed, would not. All he could do now was sit back and wait. Pray for a miracle, if you believe in such phenomena — but of course you don't, do you? You gave up all that sort of nonsense, years ago. You matured: you grew out of it. Well, young man, that is your hard luck. All I can suggest is you go and talk to the social workers. See what they can do. If you're very good and ask nicely, they might give you a white stick so you won't be run over in the dark. They might even give you a special watch to tell the time by, and teach you how to pour a cup of tea without spilling it over the side of the cup. You mustn't be depressed, there are all sorts of clever things you can be taught to do. Lace work, crochet work, answering the telephone ... You could even take up piano tuning. With your background, that's something you ought to be able to manage. But whatever you do, you mustn't let it get you down. Remember (as the Aunties would say) suffering is sent to try us. There is a purpose in all things. God rules: God is OK. What a pity you don't believe in him! I always find him such a comfort. One can talk to him, you know, and tell him one's problems.

Dear God, if you're listening — which of course He always is — *Dear God, I have to say that I don't altogether understand why you've inflicted this load of misery on me, but I'm sure it's for my own good and in my own interests and that God DOES know best, so I will bear with it patiently, God, and go on loving you, and not kick against the pricks or rebel against the teachings of my childhood* ... that way, you see, these terrible things don't happen. It's only because you left the shelter of the fold. If you'd stayed inside with the rest of us like a good boy you wouldn't now be tramping the streets of London in the pissing poxy rain unable to see where the hell you're going.

He stopped, took off his glasses, wiped them with the end of his tie, which was fast becoming as sodden and useless as his handkerchief, and stuck them back on his nose. He might just as well not have bothered. He still couldn't see where the hell he was going. Not that he cared. He only knew that he had to go somewhere;

had to keep walking. Until he got things sorted out. He couldn't go back to Caroline in this state.

She had not yet arrived in from her shopping trip when he rang. He had been relieved about that. Leaving a message might be the coward's way out but it was the best way, at the moment, that he could think of. He wouldn't have trusted himself to speak: she would have guessed at once there was something wrong. The last thing he wanted was to have her worried on his behalf. Let her go to her dinner party and have a good time, which was more than she would be able to do if he were there, staggering round like some drunken half-wit, unable to communicate. By the time she got back he would have taken a grip on himself; come to terms, at last, with the reality of the thing. It was what he should have done weeks ago. Months ago. Bradbeer had told him nothing he had not already known. Nothing.

So how come it had knocked the guts out of him? Was Bradbeer God, that he should have to wait for His Word to confirm?

He didn't believe in God. But he did believe in Bradbeer. He could hardly do otherwise, confronted as he was by the evidence (or fast-growing lack of it) of his own eyes.

Someone was shouting at him again — at least, he supposed it was at him. There were not very likely to be two rain-blinded moles stumbling across the road at the same time. He was going to have to take more care, if he didn't want to end up under the wheels of a car. Which he didn't. Not just yet. Not until he had finished that opera.

Bradbeer had said the rate of likely deterioration was impossible to calculate. He had said that it could be a matter of months — or it could be a matter of weeks. He had been definite about only one thing: now that the process had begun there was no known way of halting it. He had hoped that it would not begin. It was not inevitable — sometimes one was lucky. He had thought that Paul was going to be so, but Paul had not been. (Paul had turned away from the true faith and brought the wrath of God upon himself.)

When he was younger, he had been amongst the devoutest of the devout. He had gone to Mass every week, made regular confession of his youthful sins, genuflected, crossed himself, lighted candles, sprinkled holy water, generally done everything a good Catholic should. God and the Aunties had been pleased with him. Now they were not; and only see what had befallen him.

It had nearly killed Auntie Vi, when he had renounced the Church. She trembled even to this day, in fear of his immortal soul. Auntie Marion, being made of sterner stuff, did not tremble, but he knew, all the same, that she yearned every bit as passionately as Auntie Vi for his return to the fold. The pressure was there every time he paid a visit. It was a loving pressure; loving and gentle, as befitted the beliefs they so earnestly espoused. His own beliefs were neither quite so loving nor quite so gentle, being concerned rather with the travails of this world than the delights to come in the next, but he espoused them nonetheless firmly. He was not yet ready to abandon them, only because of personal misfortune.

Misfortune? He laughed out loud, like a lunatic. It seemed to him at this moment a weak enough way in which to describe his plight. He would hesitate, perhaps, at tragedy; but . . . misfortune?

All right. Misfortune. Others had learned to cope, so would he.

He reached the kerb. Resolutely, he stopped; took off his glasses, wiped them dry yet again, put them back on. He was at some kind of major crossing. He could tell from the noise of the traffic, the constant hissing of tyres on the wet road surface. Headlamps zoomed up at him, disembodied rings of brightness, zipping past one after another like so many flying objects coming at him out of the night. He waited what seemed an age, until the traffic came to a halt, the flying objects ceased to fly. He saw them, standing stationary, away to his left, neatly ranged in three parallel rows, stretching back into the dim distance of his vision. Since they were to his left, and since there were three rows of them, he worked out logically that he was not only at a major crossing but that it was also a one-way street; and since the traffic had now stopped, it was safe for him to go over. Boldly, pleased at his own cool assessment of the situation, he stepped into the road. One did not have to succumb to helplessness and dependence. It was all a question of using one's head. Keeping one's wits about one. One listened, one waited — and one crossed.

He had taken about half a dozen steps when with a rush and a roar the flying objects were upon him again. Not the same flying objects as before, but new ones, coming from a new direction; still from his left, but from a different angle. Too late, he perceived his error. He stood, frozen, trapped like a rabbit in the firing line of a thousand oncoming guns. Traffic surged crazily, parting either side of him. A cacophony of angry horn blasts joined with the frenzied screeching of tyres. Paul stood where he was and did not move.

His one coherent thought was for his opera....

'Got a light?' said the girl. It was the third time she had asked him. She wondered if he were deaf and dumb. She had watched him, out there on the street, playing chicken with the traffic. How he had survived, God alone knew. Now he sat opposite her, in Big Sam's, dripping wet, cradling a mug of hot tea, not appearing to hear a word that she said.

She reached out and touched him on the back of his hand. He started, and looked up.

'A light?' she said. 'For a fag?'

'I'm sorry.' He shook his head, apologetically. 'I don't smoke.'

The girl shrugged her shoulders. She called across to Sam behind the bar.

'Chuck us a book of matches, Sam, will ya? — Ta.'

She had a thick East End accent, glottal stops that screamed aloud and all the vowels tied up in knots, but the tone of the voice was interesting in its contradictions. It was rich and deep, like brown velvet: it was harsh and grating like a sieve full of pebbles. Momentarily, he was arrested; sufficiently moved to exert himself and discover what the owner of such a voice could look like. He took off his glasses and for the umpteenth time wiped them, as best he could, on a damp patch of tie. His hair was as wet as if he had just washed it, the water dripping into his eyes, and down his neck, and generally everywhere. He brushed it away, impatiently. The girl chuckled.

'That'll teach you to go swimming without a bathing cap . . . takes all the curl out, doesn't it?'

Paul put his glasses back on and her image became slightly clearer. Not very much so, because the tie had been too wet to do more than smear, and even if it had not been he had long passed the stage of being able to make out detail. She seemed to be little more than a child; a tiny, fragile creature with big bush baby eyes and flapping elephant's ears that stuck out on either side of a little spider monkey face. He wondered if she were pretty. She might well be, but he had no way of telling. He would never have a way of telling from now on. He would talk to people and have not the least idea whether they were beautiful, or ugly as hell. Perhaps, he thought, it didn't really matter.

He pushed his wet hair off his forehead and she grinned and held up one of her own inch-long locks between finger and thumb.

'Just can't do a damn thing with it when it's wet, can you?' she said.

Paul smiled, in spite of himself.

'Here —' She grabbed a handful of paper napkins, leaned towards him and began briskly to rub at his hair with them. 'That's better.' She sat back and studied him anew. 'Don't look quite such a drowned rat now.'

'Thank you,' he said. He said it with genuine gratitude. He felt suddenly quite powerless to do anything for himself. The incident out there just now, in the traffic, had shaken him more than he had realised. He closed his hands round his mug of hot teabags and felt the warmth bringing back some of the life into his benumbed fingers. 'What time is it?' he said.

He was wearing a wrist watch: she wondered why he didn't look at it. She turned, and glanced at the clock on the wall.

'Eight o'clock, just gone.'

Eight o'clock; just gone. It had been five-thirty when Bradbeer had sent him out into the world, naked and defenceless, to find his own way home. (To be fair to Bradbeer, he had been anxious to know whether he could manage. He had wanted to call him a cab: it had been Paul who had refused.) Now it was eight o'clock; just gone. That meant he had been walking the streets for two and a half hours — had no more idea than the man in the moon where he had landed up. He supposed, if he were to ask, the girl would instantly conclude that he was some kind of mental defective. Well, that could not be helped. There was no other way.

Yes, there was: there had to be. He must learn cunning.

'Tell me,' he said, 'what would the nearest underground be?'

'Isn't one; not within easy distance. Where'd you want to go?'

'South Ken.'

She might have known it would be somewhere like that. He had that sort of an accent.

'You'd do better getting the bus,' she said.

He stuck to his guns.

'I'd rather go by tube.'

'You'll have to walk a bit. It's nearly fifteen minutes away.'

Nearly fifteen minutes away; and he still didn't know where he was. He had not sufficient energy to pursue it. He raised his mug of hot teabags to his lips. It tasted like dishwater full of saccharine, but it was at least hot. His clothes were beginning to stick to him like a damp skin graft, cold and clammy. He felt quite inadequate to the task of getting himself back to the hotel, by bus, cab, tube or any other means. Suddenly, desperately, he wanted Caroline. He wanted to sink down, like a child, into her arms and weep. Abandon himself to an orgy of woe.

Mary, pray for me! Jesu —

'Are you all right?' said the girl.

'What?' Slowly, he raised his head. His glasses had steamed up and reduced her once more to a blur. Mechanically, he took them off and began yet again to wipe them.

'I said, are you all right?'

'Yes . . . yes, I'm all right.'

'They haven't just dragged you out the canal, or anything?' She leaned across the table and unceremoniously twitched open his raincoat. 'God almighty,' she said. 'You'll get pneumonia, walking round like that. It's asking for trouble.' She considered him a moment, her head to one side. He must have been on the tramp for hours, to get as wet as that. Problems with his girl, maybe? Walked out on him? Had a row? Or his wife, could be, he wasn't as young as that. About the same age as herself, she'd reckon. Certainly not a boy any more. 'You'd better come back to my place,' she said. 'Come and get yourself dried off. You can't go all the way to South Ken in that state . . . come on!'

She stubbed out her cigarette and clattered her chair back from the table. He stared up at her, unseeing, still mechanically wiping his glasses with the damp end of his tie.

'That's not doing much good, is it?' she said. 'Give 'em here!' He felt the glasses snatched away from him. Seconds later they were restored, newly wiped and clean. He settled them back on his nose.

'OK?' said the girl. He nodded. 'Coming, then?'

Obediently, he stood up.

'Well, come on!' she said. 'Don't just stand there, catch your death of cold . . . what's the matter? Think I'm going to rape you, or something?'

He ran a distracted hand through his hair.

'I don't —'

'Don't what?' She waited, impatient.

'I don't . . . know where we are —'

'What d'you mean, you don't know where we are?'

He didn't know where they were. He didn't know how he had got there. He didn't know how to get back. Numbly, he shook his head.

'Come on,' said the girl. 'You'll be all right with me.'

Outside, in the street, car tyres were still hissing on the wet road. Instinctively, as they approached the kerb, he drew back.

'Now what's the matter?' said the girl.

Nothing; nothing was the matter. He had just been told that by the end of the year, if not a great deal sooner, he would be as blind as a bat, but apart from that, there was nothing the matter. Why make such a fuss? There were far worse things that could befall a person. Ingrowing toenails, bunions, beriberi —

'So what you dithering for?'

'I was just — trying to work out — which part of London we were in —'

She looked at him, curiously.

'Caledonian Road.'

Caledonian Road? How in God's name had he come to be in the Caledonian Road? He'd never been there in his life before. He didn't even know where it was.

Somewhere north. That was all he knew.

'So are you coming, or not?'

He nerved himself to step off the kerb. This was how it was going to be from now on: having to trust people — having to rely on them. He had better start growing used to it.

'You haven't been on the booze, have you?' said the girl.

'No,' he said. 'I haven't been on the booze.'

'I didn't think you had.'

She was plainly puzzled. He wondered why she was bothering with him. For all she knew, he could be dangerous. (For all he knew, she could have a tame gorilla waiting indoors to clobber him.)

'This way.' Firmly she guided him. Despite being so tiny, her grip on his arm was like that of a steel vice. She need not have troubled: he lacked the strength of mind to shrug her off, even had he wished to do so, which in fact he did not. He had reached that stage of mental, and consequent physical, exhaustion where on his own he would be helpless. She could take him where she chose, do with him as she would. He would put up no resistance.

She lived in a dilapidated terrace, just off the main road. Even he could tell that it was dilapidated. Some of the houses had been demolished, some seemed to be derelict, the windows boarded up and planks nailed across the doors. Hers was the last house in the row. He squinted at it, through the drizzling damp and the tarnished yellow glow of the street lamps, but could distinguish very little. From the fact of the front door standing open and the floorboards being bare, he deduced that it was possibly a squat.

'Up here,' said the girl.

She led him up a narrow, uncarpeted staircase, through to what seemed to be a bedroom. Or maybe it was a bed-sit. There was some sort of covering on the floor — linoleum, he fancied, from the feel of it — but the windows appeared to be curtainless and the furniture sparse.

'Got any change?' said the girl. 'For the meter?' He handed over a couple of fifty p pieces and a ten, which was all he had. 'Ta. Should keep us going for a bit. Here!' He found a towel thrust at him. 'You get out of those wet clothes and start drying off.'

Zombie-like, obedient to her least command, he removed his dripping raincoat; and having removed it, could not think what to do with it. He stared round, blankly, towel in one hand, raincoat in the other, making puddles on the floor. 'What shall I —'

'Give it me!' Efficiently, she whisked it away from him. He saw her toss it up into the air, where, as if by some divine intervention, it remained suspended. He wondered how such a miracle could occur. He didn't believe in miracles: there must be some logical, physical explanation. He racked his brains to try and think of it.

A line! That was what it was. A nylon line, which he could not see.

His own powers of deduction pleased him greatly. Had he been Cro-Magnon man with dodgy eyesight he would instantly have leapt to the conclusion that superior and unearthly forces were at work. But he was not Cro-Magnon man. He was twentieth-century man. Walked upright on two legs, shaved his face, did not let himself be taken in by all the gibberish about unearthly forces. Big Daddy God Father, God Mother, Son —

'I thought I told you,' said the girl, 'to get those clothes off?' She yanked at his tie, wrenching it undone. 'Come on! Let's have that jacket. Give us your arm.' Obediently, he held out his right arm. 'That's the way,' she said. 'Off with it.'

She was humouring him. She had obviously decided that he was a lunatic; harmless, but a lunatic.

'Now the rest,' she said.

With practised hand, she started to undo the buttons on his shirt. At any other time it might have been quite a pleasurable experience. Now he only stood, like a mindless robot, doing as he was told.

'Want a blanket?' said the girl. 'Or shall we get into bed?'

The decision was beyond him: he left it to her.

'Might as well get in,' she said. 'Place takes a bit of time to warm up.'

He had never felt less like making an effort. In ordinary circumstances he would have found his unexpected rescuer, with her shorn locks and elfin figure, appealing enough. Whatever her motive she had certainly been good to him, bringing him in out of the rain, taking charge when he was in no fit state, mentally, to take charge of himself. One would have thought the least he could do in return was show his appreciation in the way she obviously wanted. God knows, it was little enough to ask — or would have been, in the normal course of events. Today, try as he might, he found himself incapable. It was a novel situation, and one that he was very far from relishing, but for the moment, it seemed, there was little he could do to remedy matters.

'Boy, have you got problems!'

She sat up in bed and looked down at him. He was unable to make out the expression on her face, it was only a vague white blur, but she sounded sympathetic rather than derisive. He propped himself on one elbow.

'I'm sorry,' he said. 'I'm not as a rule so useless.'

Far from it; Virginia would testify to that. Not even Diana had ever had any complaints to make on the score of sexual incompetence. A social inadequate he might be, but he had never failed in his duties as a lover.

'Honestly,' he said, 'I'm not usually like this.'

'I'll believe you,' she said. 'Thousands wouldn't, but I'll take your word for it.'

He grimaced.

'I'm afraid it rather looks as though you'll have to.'

The girl reached across and clawed up her cigarettes and book of matches from the linoleum-covered floor.

'You want to tell us about it'

Tell her about it? Tell her about what? Tell her why a piece of equipment he had hitherto been accustomed to rely on for instant response should of a sudden decide to pack up?

'I guess I'm just not on form,' he said.

'So talk!'

'About — what, exactly?'

The girl hunched a frail shoulder. She lit her cigarette and tossed the match away, then groped under the bed for the old tin saucer that served as an ashtray.

'About whatever it is that's screwing you up.'

Paul sat by her side in the narrow divan, hugging one knee to his chest. Without the benefit of even the rudimentary degree of clarity conferred by his glasses, the shabby room seemed almost cosy. He could dimly perceive the glow of the gas fire and the red pinpoint of her cigarette, but for the rest it was nothing more than vague shapes in the shadows. He was quite unable to make out any of the details, unable even to see her face with any exactitude, but for once he preferred this world of semi-darkness which over the last few months had been gradually enclosing him. He felt no particularly urgency, at this moment, to be able to take stock of his surroundings or of other people's reactions. His very helplessness seemed in its own way to be a form of protection: a convenient mask behind which to hide. If he could not see her, he could almost manage to persuade himself that she in turn could not see him. It made him feel comparatively safe from her probing questions, her evident determination to look down deep into his troubles and sift her way through them until finally she dug out the truth.

'I don't just mean about you not being able to do anything,' she said.

'Though God knows that is bad enough.'

'Balls.' She crushed out her cigarette. 'I don't give a damn about that. That wasn't the reason I brought you back. Nor that.' She jerked her head towards his clothes, strung out on the unseen line to dry. 'That wasn't the reason, either.'

So what was?

'Reason I made you come back,' she said, 'is that I was scared you might be going to do something silly,'

Like throw himself under a passing bus. She had seriously thought, back there in Big Sam's, watching as he walked out into the traffic, that he was trying to get himself killed. Even now she wasn't so sure that he hadn't been; if not consciously, then subconsciously. It had crossed her mind at one point that he might be a bit daft in the head (it had crossed her mind that she must be pretty daft herself, taking the chance that she had). She really hadn't been that much attracted to him; not to begin with. He looked better now that he was warm and dry, with his hair only slightly damp and the tangles combed out. He looked less desperate. Less ... haunted. Vulnerable, without his glasses — he obviously couldn't see as far as the back of his hand without them, but then she wasn't at all sure how much he could see with them, if it came to that. The way he kept stumbling and fumbling, there'd got to be something wrong.

'Tell us,' she said. 'Tell us what it is that's eating you ... talk about it. Get it out of your system. Don't keep things bottled up, it's not good for you.'

He made a vague gesture.

'What's the point?' There was nothing that anyone could do. They were his problems, not hers. He said as much: 'I should only be unburdening myself at your expense.'

'Oh, crap!' She banged a fist, impatiently, into the pillow. 'Don't give me that load of crap! Your problems aren't your exclusive property, for God's sake! No man is an island, brother, and don't you forget it. Stop being so bleeding stoical and stiff-upper-lip. Who d'you think you're kidding? Anyone can see you're in dead trouble, they've only got to look at you.'

Was it really as bad as all that? He supposed it probably was. But he would pull himself together: he would learn how to cope. And without crying on any shoulders. That kind of self-indulgence he could do without.

'Listen, you —' The girl jabbed a finger into the centre of his chest, pushing him back against the wall. 'We've all got to live in this lousy rotten stinking world until we die; right? Right. And the only way we're going to make it bearable is by spreading a bit of the old brotherly love. You agree with me? Yes? So, OK, then! Out with it — get it off your chest! You're never going to see me again, so what the hell?'

Paul stood by the uncurtained sash window, leaning against it with his forehead resting on his folded arms. The rain had dried up and the night sky was high and wild, with white clouds racing and a shrouded moon. He could just make out its shape, pale and faintly luminous through the ragged gaps of cloud. He shifted his position slightly, pressing his cheek to the cool pane.

'*There's night and day, brother; both sweet things —*' He ran a finger up the glass, tracing lines in the condensation. '*Sun, moon and stars, brother; all sweet things. . . .*'

'*There's likewise a wind on the heath*', said the girl. She left the bed and walked over to join him at the window. '*Life is very sweet, brother; who would wish to die?*'

There was a long silence. Paul turned, very slowly, towards her.

'You read?' he said.

She tilted her chin.

'That surprises you? That I should read?'

'It surprises me that you should read George Borrow . . . not many people do.'

'I read everything,' she said. 'Everything from the *Holy Bible* to *Forever Amber*. It takes your mind off things.'

She stood for a while by his side, at the window, staring out as he had done across the darkened rooftops.

'I just wish,' she said at last, 'that I could be of some help.'

Paul straightened up. He took her small face between his hands, exploring her features with fingertips already become more sensitive than the organs of sight. She was not as young as he had originally thought. He could feel the roughened texture of her skin, the lines in the corners of her eyes. He wondered again why she had bothered with him: why she lived all by herself in this shabby room and read George Borrow and *Forever Amber* to take her mind off things. She had problems of her own, no doubt of that. And who knew but they might not be far worse than any of his?

'You have helped,' he said, gently. 'Believe me

'But there's nothing I can actually do, is there?'

No; there was nothing she could actually do. There was nothing that anyone could actually do. Bradbeer had been very clear about that. This was a battle he was going to have to fight by himself. Sooner or later the rest of the world would have to know, and then, doubtless, there would be a multitude of willing hands all too eager to assist him: a myriad eyes to see for him, ears to hear and mouths to speak, as if by losing one sense he had lost all three and become worse than useless; but not yet, please God. He was not yet ready for that. When the time came he would submit gracefully, but for the moment he had not reached the stage of surrender.

'You've done as much as anyone could,' he said. He might have added, *and far more than I had any right to expect.* 'I'm only sorry I was such a wash-out.'

'I told you, forget it. It's not that important.'

He pulled a rueful face. To her it might not be; to him it represented yet another nail in the coffin containing the tattered shreds of self-respect. For a moment he was almost tempted to have another try, see if this time he could do any better. He peered at his watch, without avail: the smallness of the hands defeated him. He really didn't know why he bothered to go on wearing the thing, except that if he didn't he supposed some busybody would notice and start wondering.

'What time is it?' he said. 'Is it late?'

She took his wrist. 'Nearly midnight.'

'Christ almighty.' He had been there four hours. Self-respect would have to go hang: Caroline would be back from her dinner party and starting to worry if he didn't get a move on. 'It's time I was off. I've imposed on you quite long enough.'

'You won't go doing anything bleeding stupid?'

'I won't go doing anything bleeding stupid.'

She fetched his raincoat and jacket off the line.

'I'd better come down and help you find a cab.'

'There's no need,' he said, 'really. I'll manage.'

'Don't be flaming daft.' Roughly, she pushed his jacket at him. 'How d'you think you're going to tell a cab from any other vehicle?'

7

'And then, you see —' Auntie Vi, in excitement, rummaged amongst the collection of greetings cards ranged along the mantelshelf — 'I had this.'

She handed Paul a folded square of paper. He took it, and unfolded it. There was a pause.

'May I see?' Caroline craned forward, over his shoulder. 'TO DEAR AUNTIE VI WITH ALL OUR BEST LOVE ON HER BIRTHDAY FROM MICHAEL SHEILA NICOLA AND LOUISE ... a greetings telegram! All the way from Australia. Isn't that nice?'

No one, except perhaps Vicky, appeared to notice the fatuousness of the remark. At eighteen, Vicky had emerged from the coltish tomboy that Caroline remembered into a highly personable young adult of as yet indeterminate gender. Long-legged and lean-hipped, with tiny breasts and broad, boyish shoulders, she exuded the sort of ambivalent sexuality that few men of mature years appear able to resist. Almost certainly, she was aware of it. She subjected Paul to a titillating mixture of coquetry and reverence, calculated — if not deliberately, at any rate with full consciousness — to provoke and inflame. Paul, so far, had responded with avuncular caution. Flattered, no doubt, at being the object of youthful attention; possibly amused; almost certainly aroused.

'Well, well!' He refolded the cable and handed it back again to Auntie Vi. 'Michael and Sheila.'

'All the way from Australia.' Vicky shot Caroline a

malicious glance. 'Isn't that nice?'

'Isn't it?' said Paul.

'I think so,' said Auntie Vi. She nodded, beaming, at Caroline. 'Michael is Bunny's boy, you know. Bunny Lavington, my cousin.'

'Our cousin,' said Auntie Marion.

'Well, yes of course, dear. Our cousin. That goes without saying.'

'Then why did you not say it?'

'I suppose one didn't think.' Flustered, Auntie Vi restored the cable to its position on the mantelshelf. 'This one with the roses is from Polly Knott, who used to be our best friend when we were at school.'

'No, she didn't,' said Auntie Marion. 'She might have been your best friend, she certainly wasn't mine. Don't go saddling me with her, I couldn't stand the woman.'

'I never knew that,' said Auntie Vi. She turned, in distress, to look at her sister. 'You never told me that before.'

'You never tried to make out she was my best friend before.'

Vicky giggled. Auntie Marion shot her a glance of malevolent triumph: she enjoyed scoring points off Auntie Vi.

'Well, anyway,' said Auntie Vi, 'she sent me a card, which I think was most thoughtful, considering I haven't seen her for almost twenty years.'

'Some best friend,' said Vicky.

Auntie Vi looked hurt.

'Who's that one from?' Caroline pointed, at random. 'That one at the end?'

'Oh!' Auntie Vi snatched at it, gratefully. 'This is from Nicky — Paul will remember Nicky, won't you, Paul? Show it to Paul, Caroline. He'll like to see a card from Nicky.'

Obediently, Caroline handed it over.

'From Nicky,' she said.

'Old Nick the Greek? Used to run the Copper Kettle?

112

I thought he'd gone back to Athens?'

'He did,' said Auntie Marion. 'I presume that is why he writes in Greek.' Vicky giggled again. 'Read it out. See if you can make sense of it. *I* certainly can't.'

'Not much use me looking at it,' said Paul. 'I'm not a Greek scholar. You want to try old Toby over there. He's supposed to be some kind of linguistic whizz kid, isn't he?'

Toby, who at a year older than his sister possessed none of her self-assurance and little, as yet, of her sexual allure, sat forward with long-limbed eagerness on his chair.

'I'll have a bash, if you like. Mind, I don't guarantee to be able to understand it, I only did Greek for a couple of years.'

'But —' Auntie Vi was looking bewildered. No wonder, thought Caroline. She took the card away from Paul.

'*Remember the salad sandwiches* — or is it salami? It looks like salami to me.' She passed it across to Toby. 'What do you make of it?'

Toby stared at it, blankly.

'It's in English —'

'If that's what you call it.' Auntie Marion snorted. 'Salami sandwiches! What, pray, is the man talking about?'

'I can't imagine,' said Paul. He held out a hand. 'Let's have another look.'

Toby held out the card: Caroline took it: gave it back to Paul. How much longer, she thought, did he mean to keep up this pretence? After only a couple of hours she was finding the need for constant vigilance beginning to take its toll; and if of her, how much more of him?

She watched, with pity gnawing at her heart, and an irritable counterforce of exasperation, born of her own frustrated concern, as he feigned reading.

'Salami.' He shrugged his shoulders. 'Search me. He must obviously have fed you some salami sandwiches at one time.'

'Not to my knowledge,' said Auntie Marion.

'Well, that's definitely what it says.' He stood up, carefully negotiated a path through the maze of furniture to the mantelshelf, and settled the card in front of the clock. On his way back, not quite so careful, he knocked into the coffee table. Had Caroline not prudently been keeping her foot against it, there would have been a small disaster with the coffee.

'Clumsy,' said Vicky, teasing.

Paul reached the security of the sofa and sank down again, beside Caroline.

'It's this place,' he said. 'It grows more like a museum every time I come here.'

Auntie Marion's head rose up, beaky and wattled, like a chicken's, on the end of her neck.

'Do you accuse us of hoarding?'

'Cluttering,' said Paul, 'is the word I would use. Isn't it about time you got rid of some of this junk?' He waved a hand, impatiently. 'It's all worthless. There isn't a single piece that isn't chipped or fucked up.'

There was a silence, into which Vicky giggled again; whether as a nervous reaction or because she found it amusing, Caroline could not decide.

'I mean, let's face it,' said Paul, 'it's all come off rubbish tips.'

This is too much, thought Caroline. She stood up.

'Let me at least remove the tray, before you decide to send it flying.'

He shot her an injured glance: she ignored it. That he was under considerable stress she did not doubt, but that was no reason for taking it out on the two old ladies. She went through to the tiny kitchen, accompanied by Auntie Vi bearing the coffee pot, followed seconds later by Auntie Marion. They were obviously anxious to talk to her, to sound her out, in privacy, about Paul.

'He seems a bit tense —'

'A bit on edge.'

'Not quite himself —'

'Not at *ease*.'

She made the time-honoured excuse, pressure of work. They were soothed. The magic words 'his opera' were enough. All was instantly understood: all instantly forgiven.

'We have not seen as much of him these last few months,' said Auntie Marion, 'as we should have liked; but of course, if he has been working on His Opera —'

'It was good of him,' said Auntie Vi, 'to spare the time to come down at all. And to have dear Caroline as well —'

'That,' said Auntie Marion, 'is an added bonus. I cannot tell you,' she said, 'what we suffered from The Other One. Hoity toity little madam. Nobody at all, and thought herself the Queen of Sheba.'

'Whereas Caroline,' said Auntie Vi, 'who is Someone — we have all your photographs, you know. Right from when you were little, and used to come here from Bampton. Remind me to get them out later on and show you.'

'Never mind the photographs,' said Auntie Marion, 'where is The Sherry?'

They ran the sherry to earth, eventually, beneath the kitchen sink, nestling amongst the scouring powders and detergents.

'Harvey's Bristol Cream,' said Auntie Marion.

'Bought specially,' said Auntie Vi, 'for The Occasion.'

Caroline remembered, with a smile, that it always was. She hoped Paul would be gracious enough to drink a thimbleful. If there was one thing he couldn't stand, it was sweet sherry. In the past, prompted by good manners and a nice nature, he had always downed it with every show of enjoyment. In his present mood, she placed no reliance on either his manners or his nature.

They returned, in procession, Indian file along the

narrow passage, to the front room, Auntie Vi bearing the sherry proudly before her on a silver tray complete with six genuine eighteenth-century sherry glasses. The decanter, also, was genuine eighteenth-century.

'Auntie Vi,' said Vicky, 'you shouldn't have bothered.'

Auntie Vi beamed.

'Oh, my dear, it's no trouble. I like to get the old things out occasionally.'

'As a matter of fact,' said Paul, 'we were just thinking of popping down to the Woodman's for a quick nip before lunch, if that's all right?'

Caroline was nettled: he knew perfectly well about the Bristol Cream.

'No, it is not all right! What's the matter with staying here and drinking sherry?'

Paul at least had the grace to hesitate; Vicky had not even that much. She screwed up her face, cheeky and freckled.

'You can't *drink* sherry . . . you can only sip at it.'

'Drink!' Auntie Marion, like Caroline, was obviously put out. 'That's all you young people ever seem to think about. There's a great deal too much of it goes on, if you ask me.'

'Paul drinks,' said Vicky, 'and he's not a young person.'

'He is to me,' said Auntie Marion.

'But he's going grey!' said Vicky. She tweaked, flirtatiously, at a lock of his hair. 'You need a touch of the old Grecian 2,000, my man.'

'Thank you,' said Paul, 'I prefer to do my growing old gracefully, if you don't mind. Sweetheart —' he bent and kissed Auntie Vi; missing the eighteenth-century decanter, as he did so, by merest fractions of an inch. 'We'll have the sherry later. Before dinner. How's that?'

Auntie Vi was easily bought: one kiss and she was his.

'Oh, get off with you!' She gave him a little push. 'Go and enjoy yourself.'

'Only a quick one,' said Paul. 'I promise. Be away no more than half an hour. Carly?' He held out his hand, plainly expecting her to take it. She was displeased, however, and would not. If he were so keen to go, then let him go by himself. Let him see how well he could manage, without her at his side to keep an eye on him. Little Vicky might not be quite so keen to play the flirt after he'd made himself look ridiculous, bumping into the odd lamp post and falling up a few kerbs. Paul frowned. 'Aren't you coming?'

'I'd just as soon stay here,' she said, 'if it's all the same to you.'

She could see that he was in a quandary. It was his own fault. She didn't mind covering up for him in front of the old ladies — why he should be so desperate to keep his problem hidden she could only speculate, but since he evidently was, and since she was the one who had pushed him into coming here, she felt duty bound in some measure to stand by him. She saw no reason, however, why that protection should be extended to include trips to the local hostelry in order that he might pursue a middle-aged dalliance with a child almost fifteen years his junior.

'You go,' she said.

He let fall his hand.

'Not without you.'

She was conscious of having scored a victory. A minor one, perhaps; but a victory nonetheless. Tacitly he had admitted that he could not do without her. She ought to have felt gratified; instead, she looked at him and felt ashamed. What kind of victory was it that must be won at his expense?

'Oh, for goodness' sake!' She slipped her hand through his arm. 'If you're going to sulk. . . .'

'The Aunties are so funny,' said Vicky. 'Do you

remember, Tobe, that song we used to sing? When we were little? *Dear, dear, what can the matter be?*' Her clear soprano rang out, mischievously, across the saloon bar of the Woodman's. '*Two old ladies locked in the lavatory? They were there from Monday till Saturday, Nobody knew they were there....*'

The words fell into a silence. Toby, embarrassed, buried his nose in his beer mug.

'What a very silly song,' said Paul.

'We were very silly people,' said Vicky, 'One is, you know, at ten years old.'

'One is not supposed still to be so, however, at eighteen.'

'Well, but really, you must admit . . . they are a couple of goons.'

'The Aunties,' said Paul, 'are all right.' He took out his wallet and extracted a five-pound note. 'Who wants to go and get another round?'

It was the third one he had bought. Caroline, no lunch-time imbiber, stuck to fruit juice, Toby to his beer. Both Paul and Vicky were on shorts. Vicky, she suspected, from bravado; Paul, normally the most moderate of drinkers, in search of Dutch courage. What had occurred the previous night she could only conjecture, but whatever it was it had plainly done nothing for his morale. She had been there, shortly after midnight, when he had returned to the hotel: he had walked straight past her, in the lobby, without even seeing. Numbly she had watched as he made his way towards the lifts — as he ran his hand across the surface in search of the call button. Only when she saw him depress the button marked DOWN had she galvanised herself into action: it had suddenly seemed too much like spying, to go on sitting and watching and him unaware.

'Paul?' She had hastened after him, across the lobby; unobtrusively pressed the UP button. 'Are you all right?'

'Of course I'm all right.' He had turned on her, made irritable by her solicitude and the discovery that he was not, as he had thought, alone. 'Why shouldn't I be all right? What are you doing here, anyway? Why aren't you in bed?'

'I just this minute got back.'

It was a lie. She had been back for over half an hour, sitting brooding in the lobby with a gin and tonic, trying to convince herself that if he were round with Diana, getting it together again, it would be the best thing by far that could happen. She had known at once, seeing him as he stood there by the lifts, that wherever he had been, and whatever he had been doing, it was not an occasion for rejoicing. He had looked to her like one defeated. She had tried a little gentle probing, a demonstration of concern, but he would have none of it. Roughly, he had rejected all overtures. He was perfectly OK, there was nothing to worry about, he would thank her (not actually spelt out in words, but clear enough for all that) to leave him alone and stop fussing. She had had no option but to do so.

In the morning, over breakfast, he had made a very conscious attempt to atone for any incidental churlishness that may have manifested itself, asking her how the dinner party had gone, apologising for having to back out ('I just couldn't make it': no explanation), wanting to know what she had bought for Auntie Vi. On the journey down to Marden he had lapsed into a silence from which, apart from the odd brief comment as to the scenery or the state of the roads, she had not roused him. He had excused himself from navigating on the plea of having a headache, and to prove the point had removed his glasses and sat for the most part of the journey with his eyes firmly closed. He need not have gone to such lengths; she had no wish to embarrass him. She had in fact taken good care to check out the route beforehand.

Vicky, coming back from the bar with a double

Scotch for Paul and a Bloody Mary for herself (leaving Toby, typically, to follow with the beer and fruit juice) wanted to play darts. Or, to be more precise, wanted Paul to play darts.

'With three double Scotches inside me? Have a heart!'

'Well, I've had three Bloody Marys . . . come on!' She tugged at his sleeve, trying to coax him to his feet. 'Don't be such an old fuddy duddy! I've been practising all winter.'

'In that case, you'd beat me hands down.'

'That's what I want to d ... get my revenge for past defeats.'

'You mean you want to humiliate me?'

'Yes! Why not?'

'Because it wouldn't be kind. I'm growing old and must be treated gently . . . why don't you play with Toby?'

'I can play with him any day of the week. Anyhow —' she sat down, pouting — 'he's useless.'

'So am I,' said Paul.

'You never used to be!'

'No, well, I'm losing my faculties. As you so generously pointed out, my hair is starting to turn grey.'

'I like men with grey hair; it's distinguished. Don't you think so?' Vicky applied, archly, to Caroline. 'Don't you think he looks distinguished?'

'It's no use asking Caroline,' said Paul. 'She knew me in the flower of my youth.'

'Likewise in your snotty-nosed brathood.'

'I deprecate that remark! Brathood I may have passed through, but I was never snotty-nosed.'

'You were still pretty gruesome. How about that time you climbed the cedar of Lebanon and came back down with your ass hanging out your pants?'

'All right, all right! How about that time little Ms Ramirez fell in the lake and got her frilly knickers wet and had to take mine off me to get back home in?'

'Frilly ones?' said Vicky.

'Oh, sure,' said Caroline. 'He used to wear them with forgetmenots round the edges.'

'You,' said Paul, 'are asking for it.'

You, thought Caroline, might be said to be doing the same. She smiled.

'Don't be shy! Why not confess it? Frilly knickers and nail polish, and curlers in your hair . . . well, you can see for yourself. He still resorts to the hair curlers.'

Vicky giggled, happy to be back again in the conversation.

'I thought it was a home perm!' She draped herself, still giggling, across Paul's chest. 'Is it? Or is it natural?'

'Wouldn't you like to know?' said Paul.

'Shall I pull it and see?'

'Why? What good would that do?'

'It might be a wig —'

Toby had his nose back in his beer mug again. She didn't blame him. That sister of his needed a good sharp kick up her sexy little butt. Unfortunately, Paul was not the person who was very likely to do it for her. She wouldn't exactly accuse him of playing up to the child, but he plainly was not disliking Vicky's attentions. She supposed, to be fair, there wasn't one man in a million who would. The girl was attractive, no doubt about that. She remembered, in latter years, when she had accompanied Paul down to Marden and Clive and Susan had been there, with the two kids, how it had always been Vicky who had claimed all the limelight, clambering about Paul, hugging him, kissing him, putting on a display even at that tender age. It had been left to Caroline to coax Toby out of his infant and adolescent shyness. Paul, too reserved himself to help others in similar plight, had never made more than half-hearted attempts to form a rapport.

Vicky, now, had taken a comb from the back pocket of her jeans and was happily combing his hair into different styles, giggling as she did so.

'If you grew it a bit longer I could plait it . . . can I take your glasses off? You look loads better without them. Do you really need to wear them all the time?'

'Not really,' said Paul, 'no.'

'Then why do you?'

'Because if I didn't I should probably fall over and break my neck.'

'Then you do need to. You must be extremely short-sighted. Why don't you try contact lenses? You'd look much better with contact lenses, wouldn't he? Don't you think so?' She appealed again, roguishly, to Caroline. 'Don't you think he'd look better with contact lenses?'

'What I think,' said Caroline, 'is that it's high time we were heading back for lunch.' She had had enough of the floor show even if Paul hadn't. 'Anyone coming?'

Paul stood up; reluctantly, it seemed to her.

'We'll take some wine back with us.'

'You don't think you've had enough already?'

'Not nearly enough. I've hardly begun.' Firmly, he possessed himself of Vicky's hand. 'Come and help me choose something.'

All right, thought Caroline. If that's the way you want it.

Outside the Woodman's, clutching his two bottles of wine, he hesitated. She left him to get on with it. If he could suffer the child combing his hair and draping herself over his chest and generally making a spectacle of the pair of them, then he could suffer her holding his hand on the way home. If she let him walk into a lamp post or trip over his own feet, then that was just too bad. *Tough shit*, in Larry's inimitable vernacular. He'd asked for it.

Determinedly, she walked on ahead with Toby. The boy seemed pathetically grateful for any attention that was paid to him. They talked, amicably, and with growing ease, about the United States — about California — about Los Angeles. Los Angeles, it transpired, was his Mecca.

'I really mean to go there some day. Next year, if I can. I'm hoping to get an exchange.'

Automatically, she said that in that case, of course, he must be sure and come down to San Diego. To herself, silently, she added the rider: always provided that I am still there. She had as yet come to no firm decision on the point. Last time Larry had called it had been to reassure her that all was going ahead 'according to schedule'. She presumed he had been talking about the divorce rather than the ballet, but for some reason she had chosen not to ask.

From behind, came a yell. She turned, to see Vicky and Paul, still some distance off. Vicky was flapping a hand, and pointing.

'That's the marsh road,' said Toby. 'It'll be boggy as hell.'

'In that case —' deliberately, she spun on her heel — 'you and I will just keep straight on.'

She and Toby arrived back just as Auntie Vi was beginning to panic.

'I wondered where you had got to. Luncheon is all ready. The table is all laid —'

'Where are Paul and Victoria?' said Auntie Marion.

'Oh, they chose to go tramping off across country. They should be back any second.'

'They took the marsh road,' said Toby.

'Then that was exceedingly foolish of them. At this time of year? Paul at least ought to know better.'

'I expect she made him' said Toby.

Paul and Vicky turned up ten minutes later. Both were liberally plastered in mud; Paul, in addition, had a graze on his forehead and a cut hand.

'He fell over,' said Vicky. 'In the mud.' She giggled. 'At least we managed to save the wine. . . .'

The day, from that point on, became fraught. Almost immediately there was conflict between Auntie Vi, who wanted to play mother — wanted to bring out the lint, the bandages, the cotton wool, the sticking plaster — and Paul, who wanted nothing so much as to be left alone.

'It's only a graze,' said Vicky.

'Grazes can go septic. Let me at least get some warm water and bathe it. A bit of TCP —'

She had her wish, but at the expense of Paul's already battered image. Caroline could readily understand that for him the easiest way — perhaps, indeed, the only way — of coping, because the way least damaging to his pride, was to make light of the incident. Auntie Vi's tender determination to build it up could not but wreak psychological havoc. He drank defiantly throughout lunch, joined glass for glass by Vicky.

'If your mother were here, my girl,' said Auntie Marion, 'she would soon put a stop to all this guzzling.'

Vicky pulled an impudent face.

'Well, she's not, so she can't!'

More was the pity, thought Caroline. Susan might at least have had some measure of control over the girl. She remembered, when she and Paul had been young, how Susan had browbeaten them, bossing and bullying with all the ruthlessness of seven years' seniority. The Aunties, even Auntie Marion, were quite unequal to the task. Paul alone might have wielded some influence, but Paul was too busy redeeming his shattered image, keeping up a light flirtation and a string of jokey comments which Caroline found irritating in the extreme but which Vicky, from her constant giggling, appeared to consider the very acme of wit.

After lunch, they had to play games: Vicky, it seemed, could not sit still for more than five minutes at a stretch without doing something. First of all they played a game called Botticelli, the rules of which, as relayed by Vicky —

'Someone thinks of a person, then we all take it in turns to ask questions, and if you get the answer "yes" then you can challenge them, like saying "A breed of dog beginning with A", because you have to go through the alphabet, and then perhaps the person might say Afghan, and then you might say Airedale, and then if the person can't think of any more —'

'Alsatian,' said Auntie Marion.

'Yes, but if he can't think of any —'

'That's ridiculous! I'm sure there must be plenty.'

'Yes, but that's not the point. If he gives up —'

The rules were so exceedingly complex that Auntie Vi quite failed to grasp even the basic fundamentals, with the result that Vicky grew impatient, and Auntie Vi grew tearful, and Auntie Marion, exulting in her own mental superiority and finding herself thwarted, became rather cross and rude and accused her sister of having a brain like a parrot.

'What do you mean, is it a man? We've already established that it is! What's the point of keeping on asking the same question over and over? For goodness' sake, woman! You have a brain like a parrot!'

'Let's play something else,' said Paul.

'Thank you, I do not wish to play something else! I happen to find this particular game both stimulating and amusing. If *she* would only apply herself —'

'We could always play Monopoly,' said Toby.

No one save Auntie Vi, who said that she liked Monopoly, especially when she could build houses on Park Lane, took the least notice of his suggestion. It seemed to be generally agreed, however, that Botticelli was not going down too well. They argued for the next half-hour over what they should play instead. Auntie Vi wanted to play something called Dumb Crambo, which she said she had played as a girl.

'You get up and you mime things —'

'Oh, that!' said Vicky. 'They do that on the television.'

'Cards,' said Toby.

Auntie Marion said that cards were an insult to the intelligence; what was wrong with pencil and paper games?

'Too much like hard work,' said Paul.

'Anyway,' said Vicky, 'Paul couldn't play anything that needs thought processes, he's far too squiffy . . . let's do that thing we used to do at Christmas.'

'Murder,' said Toby.

'Not Murder, you idiot!'

'I know a game,' said Caroline. 'It's called Lords and Ladies. What you do —'

'I've already decided,' said Vicky, crushingly. 'We're going to do the thing we used to do at Christmas. How Does it Resemble Me . . . someone goes out of the room — Paul! You go out of the room —'

'Not me,' said Paul. 'I'm too squiffy.'

'Not for this, you're not.'

'Yes, I am. I'll fall over.'

'Oh, all right! Toby, you go out of the room.' Toby, obediently, left the room. 'Now, what we have to do, we have to think of an object, like —'

'Santa Claus,' said Auntie Vi.

'*No!* It's got to be something that's in the *room*.'

'Flower pot,' said Paul.

'Flower pot?'

He shrugged.

'Isn't there one?'

'Oh, all right, we'll make it flower pot. Then when Toby comes back he has to ask each one of us, How does it resemble me? and we have to say, and he has to guess —'

On the whole, it was not a success. Auntie Vi embarrassed both herself and Toby by replying to his inquiry with the serene observation that 'It has a hole in its bottom'; a situation which was not helped by both Paul and Vicky instantly falling over each other with laughter and Auntie Marion tartly informing her sister that 'If you intend to lower the standard to one of smut and obscenity I shall absent myself. Simply because you do not have the elementary brain power to cope with the more intelligent type of game —' When it was Paul's turn to leave the room he flatly refused to go until taken in hand by Vicky (a task she patently enjoyed) and being forcibly led out there. On his way back, attempting to chart a course between tables and chairs, he tripped over the edge of a rug.

'That,' said Auntie Marion, 'is the Drink Talking.'

Vicky gave a merry peal of laughter.

'I told you he was squiffy!'

At six o'clock — much, Caroline suspected, to the relief of everyone, including Paul — she and Toby took their leave. They had to be at a party, Vicky explained, at Canterbury.

'Lucky old Canterbury,' said Paul.

'You want to come? You can, if you like.'

'Good God, no! I loathe parties.'

'They'd probably be a bit young for you, anyway,' said Vicky, kindly.

'That's right, I told you . . . I'm getting ancient.'

'Certainly getting *clumsy*.' She kissed her fingers, pertly pressing them to the strip of sticking plaster on his forehead. 'Hope you don't go septic. . . .'

With the departure of what Auntie Vi called 'the young folk', a sense of peace descended — of peace, yet also, it seemed, of anti-climax. It was as if, without the sexual challenge of Vicky's presence, Paul lost all incentive. Opting out, with the bottle of Bristol Cream to keep him company, he left it to Caroline to bear the main burden of the conversation. Auntie Vi had brought out the promised photographs: Caroline it was who duly examined and exclaimed, passing each across to Paul with suitable identifying comment. He accepted them phlegmatically, appearing to take for granted her constant flow of pictorial chit chat. Did it never occur to him, she wondered, how consciously she was going out of her way to make life easier for him? Did he think, when he was with her, it was merely by providential twists of fate that he managed to avoid accidents, managed to keep out of embarrassing

127

situations? She could only suppose that he did. One believed, by and large, what one wanted to believe.

At eight o'clock, she went out with Auntie Vi to prepare supper.

'You don't think, do you,' said Auntie Vi, 'that Paul is drinking just the tiniest bit more than is good for him?'

She was very sure that he was, but did not personally relish the prospect of being the one to bring it to his attention. Where angels feared to tread, Auntie Marion, intrepid, stepped in.

'Paul,' she said, 'give me that sherry.' She held out a hand. 'Come along, now! You have had more than enough.'

If he is vile to Auntie Marion, thought Caroline, he can go hang.

There was a pause.

'I'm not a child, you know,' said Paul.

'Then do not behave like one!' Deftly, Auntie Marion repossessed herself of what remained of the sherry. 'Get up to the table,' she said, 'and eat your supper.'

Paul rose, a trifle insteadily, to his feet. Caroline tucked her hand into his. I'm only doing it, she thought, because he wasn't vile to Auntie Marion. If he had been vile, she wouldn't have lifted so much as her little finger. As it was, she steered him safely to the table, charted him safely through the meal. She thought she noticed Auntie Marion looking at her rather oddly once or twice, but nothing was said and any slight uncertainty on Paul's part was presumably put down to an excess of sherry. Shortly after supper, he announced that he had a headache and should like, if no one objected, to go to bed.

'By all means go to bed. Bed is sometimes,' said Auntie Marion, 'the Best Place.'

'Especially if one has a headache,' said Auntie Vi.

'Eespecially if one has been drinking too much,' said Auntie Marion.

A flicker of irritation passed across Paul's face.

'I have not been drinking too much. I simply happen to be rather tired and have rather a headache and should like to be in bed.'

'That's right,' said Auntie Marion. 'You go there.'

'Let me get you some hot milk.' Auntie Vi was already up on her feet. 'Hot milk and aspirin. That's the best thing.'

'Alka Seltzer, more like.'

'For crying out loud!'

With sudden violence, Paul scraped back his chair. Caroline closed her eyes. Any minute now....

The expected explosion did not materialise. She heard the door open, heard it slam shut. When she opened her eyes, both Paul and Auntie Vi had disappeared.

'That young man,' said Auntie Marion, 'has not been the same since marrying Diana.' She considered a moment. 'It is a great pity,' she said, 'that you ever went back to America.'

Caroline sat up for another hour. She was weary herself, but the old ladies were eager, once again, to talk about Paul: after all that had occurred, she could not but feel they were owed that indulgence.

'I suppose,' said Auntie Vi, wistfully, 'there is no chance of his coming back to the Church?'

She was very certain there was not, but to crush all hope seemed unnecessarily brutal. She could still recall the anguish it had caused, that summer long ago, when the young Paul had brashly announced his departure from the paths of organised religion. To Caroline had fallen the rôle of emotional buffer. Then as now the old couple had poured out upon her all their doubts and their anxieties. To this day they mistakenly credited her with having some influence over him. If she were to urge —

'He listens to you,' said Auntie Vi.

She was wrong: Paul had never listened to her. It had

always, in the past, been she who had listened to Paul. She promised, however, that she would talk to him.

'He is plainly troubled,' said Auntie Marion. 'And he is more likely to confide in you than he is in us.'

I doubt that, thought Caroline.

It was almost eleven-thirty when she went up to bed. Paul's room, as she passed it, was in darkness. She paused a moment outside the door, but hearing nothing continued along the twisting passage to her own room. Marden, originally, had been two small cottages belonging to 'employees of the Harbour Board' back in the days (over three centuries ago) when the sea had come up almost to the very doorstep. The marshes since then had been drained, and had receded, the cottages knocked into one, with a double staircase up which it had been the delight of the young Paul and Caroline to run screaming in school holidays. Visitors, now, slept in what was grandiloquently known as 'The Guest Wing', comprising two tiny bedrooms and a miniature bathroom with cast-iron Victorian bath and flowered wash-stand and lavatory.

When she had first come to England, at the age of eleven, Caroline had thought all English houses were like Marden — either like Marden, or like Buckingham Palace. It had come as a severe disappointment when she had gone home for the weekend with a girl from Bampton and discovered that many, if not indeed most, people lived in ordinary modern dwellings complete with plastic frontage and underfloor heating. It was not what the guide books had led her to believe.

Marden had at least gone some way toward restoring her faith: she was fond of the old place still. How many nights had she undressed and slept in that same doll house room? Every detail of it — the old-fashioned, black-leaded grate, diamond-paned windows and uneven floorboards, covered in rugs hand-made by the Aunties — was as familiar to her now as in the far-off days of her adolescence.

She had undressed, and was about to climb into bed, when there was a tap at the door.

'Carly?' The door opened a crack and Paul's head appeared round it. 'All right if I come in?'

There had once been a time when such a question need never have been asked.

'I thought you were asleep?' she said.

'I can't sleep. My head's like a wasps' nest, everything buzzing.'

She did not make the obvious retort: people who drink too much ... it would not have helped, and was very probably not the reason.

'What's it buzzing with?'

'Oh ... this and that.' He perched himself on the edge of the small oak chest which served as a dressing-table. 'What have you been up to down there?'

'What have I been up to down there? I haven't been up to anything down there.'

'So what have you been talking about?'

'Oh!' She sank down, on to the bed. 'This and that.'

He frowned, and was silent a while, swinging one pyjama-clad leg. He was wearing a blue silk dressing-gown which looked as though it had come from one of the more exclusive London stores. That would be Diana's doing, no doubt. Paul had always been a neat dresser, but never a showy one. (Unlike Larry, who loved nothing so much as to peacock. She must remember to buy him a dressing-gown like Paul's: he would be in his element.)

'I suppose,' said Paul, 'the old ladies took the opportunity to do a bit of pumping?'

'About what?'

'What do you think?'

'They're certainly concerned for you,' she said, 'if that's what you mean.'

'They're always concerned for me.'

'So what's new?'

He went on frowning, and swinging a foot.

'Do they have any reason?' she said.

'Do they ever?'

'I don't know, I'm asking you.' He said nothing. 'Paul? Do they?'

'Of course they don't! Just because I choose to have a drink or two — *what's wrong with Paul? what's the matter with Paul?*' Cruelly, he mimicked their voices; the thin, high, stridulating voices of old age. 'I suppose they think I'm turning into an alcoholic?'

'No; I don't think so.'

'So what do they think?'

'I don't know what *they* think, but I'll tell you what *I* think . . . I think that for someone who came down here to celebrate an old lady's seventieth birthday your behaviour was enough to make a skunk sick! Of all the thoroughly mean and selfish ways to carry on —' She was mad at him, now, and justifiably so. If after all these years he still did not trust her sufficiently to take her into his confidence, to say out loud that he needed her help, then it made a complete farce of everything that had ever been between them. She had given him ample opportunity: he had chosen to ignore it. Very well, then. Let him lick his wounds in private and not come running to her in search of sympathy. 'You ought to be ashamed of yourself! You spend half the morning down at the pub, half the afternoon encouraging that child, half the evening drinking yourself silly —'

'Carly! Don't be cross with me.'

'That's right: now we're off on the old self-pity jag! First you behave like a rat —'

'I know! I know I did!' Suddenly he was on his knees beside her, down on the hand-made rug, his head muffled in her lap. 'I know I behaved abominably, but don't be cross with me . . . please, Carly . . . not now!'

'Why not now?' (And if not now, when?)

'Because I want you,' he said. He raised his head: she realised for the first time that he was not wearing his glasses. His eyes, without them, were just as bright, just as blue, as they had ever been; but she was aware, even as he looked up at her, that a light had gone out of them.

'Paul,' she said. She took his head between her hands 'Won't you tell me what it is that's wrong?'

'I am telling you! I'm telling you as plainly as I can. . . .'

He was; without knowing it. If she had had the least vestiges of doubt, they disappeared now as she gazed down into his eyes.

'Carly?'

Caroline Ramirez, she thought, you are a fool. . . .

8

'You're quite sure,' said Hugo, 'that you don't want to change your mind and come?'

'No way; not feeling like this.'

Hugo looked at him, sympathetically.

'The head's really bad?'

'Like the inside of an old boiler.' It was partially true. He had spent the day locked in his study, poring over pupils' composition exercises with the aid of a magnifying glass, and his eyes were aching if not his head. Even if they hadn't been, he had no intention of allowing himself a second time to be inveigled into eating dinner under Ludmila's eagle-eyed gaze. He knew that she was watching him, waiting for him to make mistakes. It was something that he sensed. She had not said anything, and possibly it was only the old paranoia raising its ugly head yet again, but he preferred to take no unnecessary risks. Life was quite hazardous enough as it was, without going out of his way to court disaster.

'You realise,' said Hugo, 'that you're deserting a comrade in his hour of need?'

'Go on, you'll have a whale of a time ... Ludmila all to yourself? What more could a man ask?'

'If I come back a nervous wreck, I shall lay it directly at your door.'

'Not mine' said Paul. 'It's your woman who's responsible. If it hadn't been for her, dragging Caroline off to go and make an affray —'

They'd set out together, yesterday afternoon, all done up in their duffle coats and jeans, to join the peace marchers in Hyde Park. They had wanted Paul to go with them, but he had a load of work to catch up on. Everything, these days, took him at least three times as long as it used to do. He was very conscious of the fact that over these past few weeks his sight had deteriorated to a degree which would have alarmed him, had he not already been to Bradbeer and heard the worst. Now that he knew, he could cope with it. That first night, when Bradbeer had broken it to him, had been rough; the news, just for a while, had knocked the stuffing out of him. But now that he had had a bit of time to accustom himself to the idea, he found he was beginning to acquire an almost philosophical acceptance. Blindness was an affliction he could have done without, but it was no great tragedy. Not the end of the world. Other people managed to lead full and productive lives: so would he.

That, at least, was the theory. In weaker moments he still had to battle against depression, but the original burst of panic, thank God, seemed to have abated. He could contemplate the ultimate closing of the door, if not with eager anticipation, at any rate with a certain fatalistic calm. That did not mean, however, that he was prepared to go and make a clown of himself in front of Ludmila. Plenty of time for that later on.

'You'll miss all the goodies,' he said to Hugo, 'if you don't get a move on.'

'You're a rat,' said Hugo.

'I have a headache,' said Paul.

'You're still a rat.' Hugo opened the sitting-room door, walked out into the passage, poked his head back in again. 'If you have a headache, *don't work.*'

He had, in fact, fully intended doing so, but for once found himself forced to concede defeat: his eyes were not only aching, they felt hot and inflamed. Bradbeer had said he could do no more damage than had already been done, he could read twenty-four hours a day and it would make no difference to the rate of deterioration; for all that, he was prepared to swear that he could see appreciably less now than he had been able to earlier in the day. He would rather preserve what little he had left to him for as long as he could, eking it out bit by bit, than dissipate it all in a few mad binges of visual activity. For all his brave philosophical acceptance, he was not exactly looking forward to the day when he opened his eyes on total blackness — although he supposed it would not actually happen like that. Bradbeer had seemed to think it would be more in the nature of a gradual sliding. Not that Bradbeer really knew. He had admitted as much. No two cases, he had said, were ever quite alike. One could only wait and see. (The pun Paul charitably assumed to have been unintentional.)

The front door slammed. He heard Hugo's feet scrunching on the gravel, heard the front gate open and close, and knew that he was alone. He went across to the record collection and selected a Beethoven quartet — op. 127, always provided it had been put away in the correct place — and stretched himself out full length on the sofa to enjoy a couple of hours' uninterrupted solitude. He could not remember the last occasion on which he had been alone in the Lodge; not completely alone. It brought an immediate sense of relief — relief mainly from the constant pressure of having to act out a part which he was no longer equipped to play, but relief, also, from the paranoiac fear of being watched: of being caught out in some piece of buffoonery, squeezing shaving cream on to his toothbrush, crawling on his hands and knees across the carpet in search of some glaringly obvious piece of lost property. And yet, even as it brought relief, it brought a sense of isolation. To be alone was to be a prey to one's thoughts; and his thoughts, try as he might to turn them elsewhere, led always, and inevitably, to the self-pity of fear.

Self-pity it was that tempted one into acts of which subsequently one was ashamed. Acts one most bitterly regretted. He should never have made love to Caroline, that night down at Marden. She had cried, afterwards, lying there in his arms. She wouldn't tell him why, but he had known, instinctively, that it was because of him. Because once he had betrayed her, and now had done so again, taking advantage of her, playing on the love she had borne him, and which he had flung back in her face. He ought never to have done it. He had known it even at the time, but the demands of self-pity had ruled supreme: he had needed comfort, and at her expense he had found it. Hardly a very noble achievement. Now — to punish him? — she had gone off with Rose to demonstrate solidarity, leaving him all alone with Hugo to fend for himself.

It terrified him to reflect how little by little, insensibly, over these last weeks, he had come to rely upon her. He had not realised, until that weekend with the old ladies, just how helpless he had become when taken out of his natural environment. Life even at Bampton was growing increasingly fraught. In his composition classes he was having to depend almost entirely upon the goodwill of his pupils. He was still able, in privacy, with the aid of his magnifying glass, to decipher their efforts for himself, but it was a long and laborious task and one that he was by no means certain he would be capable of performing in another week, two weeks' time.

Individual rehearsals for *Jane* he could still cope with reasonably well, but full orchestral sessions were becoming something of a nightmare. He had always been less of a martinet than Hugo, more inclined to give the kids free rein, trusting to their basic integrity and sense of fair play. It had worked well enough in the past; in general it still did. But once or twice just recently he had had the uncomfortable feeling that it was they who were controlling him rather than the other way round.

Some of the older ones seemed puzzled by what (he could not but recognise it himself) was a change in his demeanour. Outwardly he strove to appear the same as he had ever been: he joked with them, allowed them to be familiar with him, raised no objection to the occasional swear-word or odd bit of impertinence. The difference lay in the fact that his basic confidence had been undermined, and the kids plainly sensed it.

Some, such as the little Kaufman boy, had begun to treat him with an air of almost patronising tolerance — poor old dopey Paul, who might be able to write music but couldn't even be trusted not to trip over his own shoelaces. Others — the shyer ones amongst them — tended to withdraw, embarrassed no doubt by his strange antics and growing incompetence.

A few, though only the odd one or two, took advantage. Unfortunately, even the odd one or two could create havoc if they so wished. No one had yet tried putting tintacks on his chair, but it could be only a question of time. They had already discovered he was vulnerable to practical jokes. Funny cushions which farted as you sat on them he didn't mind, he could laugh at that as well as anyone, but he had to confess to being rather shaken the day a trombone had suddenly appeared in the midst of the first violins. It hadn't been so much the sound which had emitted as the awful moment of revelation: they could do these things and get away with it. The entire orchestra could re-shuffle itself and him none the wiser until the minute he raised his baton and cacophony broke forth. Small wonder the kids were beginning to think he was ripe for the nut house.

As the weeks went by, he was finding himself increasingly having to resort to trickery and cunning in order to survive. He had, for example, counted exactly how many paces there were from the door of the staff-room to the coffee machine; from the coffee machine to the window, where stood a chair of such unparalleled discomfort that he could be reasonably certain of its never being occupied. This chair he had appropriated for his own use. It might leave ridges in his backside but at least it removed one of his worst fears, that of lowering his carcase on to somebody's unsuspecting lap, for in artificial light it was not always possible, now, for him to distinguish shadow from substance.

It was for that same reason that he avoided the canteen, save at the least populous hours of the day, when the majority of the tables were empty and he might select his place with confidence. Likewise, he had taken the precaution of fixing a small strip of sticking plaster beneath the handle on the door of the men's lavatory, for although the door was the fifth one down from Virginia's office (still just about identifiable by its glass partitions) pressure of traffic along the corridor made the counting of doors not always a feasible proposition, which meant he had to rely on his judgement as to what sort of distance he had covered.

He had measured it once and found it to be approximately thirty paces, but that had been on a clear day when there were no foreign bodies to impede him. It could be awkward if he misjudged — the next door along was the one to the women's lavatory. The one before was the broom cupboard, which wasn't quite so awkward but nevertheless looked foolish. He had in fact gone sailing into it on one over-confident occasion and had had to back out, laughing rather too heartily and loudly chiding himself for absent-mindedness, just in case anyone had happened to observe him. It had been after that that he had had recourse to the sticking plaster.

Lately, also, he had developed what he had thought was a foolproof technique for coping with the perils of morning assembly, loitering in the staff-room, on some pretext or other, until all the rest of them had gone, then turning up at the nth minute, when the doors had been closed and everyone was safely inside. That way, since members of staff took up their places down the side of the hall in whichever order they happened to arrive, he could slip unremarked into the last, unoccupied seat, right at the back and just inside the door. It also had the advantage of making for a quick exit afterwards, before the mob was set loose to go on the rampage.

The system had worked as smooth as clockwork up until a few days ago, but like every system ever devised it had turned out to have its weak spot. Last Tuesday, he had discovered what that weak spot was. Blithely, grown a bit cocksure, he had gone marching up to the double doors, stuck out a hand to push them open — and found himself punching into empty space. For a second, such was the shock of it, his brain had ceased to function. All he could think was, what had happened to the door? And then, from the place where the door ought to have been but wasn't, he had heard Ludmila's voice: 'Don't you intend coming in, Paul?' Rather too coincidentally, it had been that selfsame day, after Caroline had announced her intention of going off for the weekend with Rose, that Ludmila had sent forth her summons: he and Hugo were to attend for dinner with her and Papa Jo on Saturday night.

'Why?' he had said to Hugo, when the command had been relayed.

Hugo had shrugged.

'Search me. Feels sorry for us, I guess.'

Rubbish. Cant and froth and ludicrous nonsense. Ludmila never felt sorry for anyone — and what was more, she never did anything without a motive. He had made up his mind, there and then, to have a headache.

The record which he had so carefully selected came to an end. Someone had obviously put it away in the wrong place, because it hadn't been Opus 127, it had been Opus 132. Rose might not be able to tell one from the other, but there was in fact a quite considerable difference: they happened to be two quite distinct and separate pieces of music. It would be a great help, therefore, if they could be kept in their quite distinct and separate places in the record collection; ie, before and after Opus 131. It surely wasn't too much to ask?

Grumbling to himself, he removed the disc from the turntable. He had left what he had thought was Opus 131 slightly pulled out of the cabinet as a marker, but how did he know now whether it was 131 or 127? How did he know what anything was, without actually taking it out and playing it? Either that, or trailing all the way upstairs to fetch his magnifying glass, and he didn't see why he should have to. People ought to be capable of putting things away after them. God knows, he had asked them often enough.

He wondered, as crossly he took a chance and rammed home Opus 132 on the far side of what he could only hope to be 131, whether they would learn to be a little more considerate when they discovered the truth.

'So Paul has a headache.' Ludmila pushed a dish of marshmallows toward Hugo. 'That's too bad.'

'He did ask me to apologise,' said Hugo. Ludmila seemed to have doubts as to the genuineness of the excuse. It was the third time during the course of the evening that she had come back to it. He found even himself wondering, now, whether there really had been a headache or whether it had been a put-up job, though he could hardly imagine an evening with Ludmila inspired that much dread. Gorgon she might be, but a free meal, when all was said and done, was a free meal, and whatever her shortcomings Ludmila always provided an excellent spread: she had everything sent in from a restaurant in Broadway. 'He was stretched out on the sofa when I left him. He did look pretty rough.'

'Poor Paul. I wonder what brought that on?'

'Not the Opus,' said Papa Jo. He waved an

admonitory finger. 'Don't you go blaming the Opus.'

'As a matter of fact,' said Hugo, 'the Opus, as far as I know, has ceased to cause problems. At any rate, he seems to have stopped knocking himself out over it.'

'That is because Caroline is here. Caroline is a good influence. She always has been. Do you remember, when they were young —'

'For heaven's sakes!' said Ludmila. 'Don't go starting on that again.'

'We used to call them the love birds,' said Papa Jo. 'The little love birds, because they would walk everywhere hand in hand.'

'Yes ... they were rather nauseating, weren't they?' Hugo, blandly, helped himself from the dish of marshmallows. He had already consumed a good half of them, but since Paul wasn't here to eat his share he might just as well eat it for him.

'I wonder,' said Ludmila, 'if it could possibly be psychological?'

There was a silence.

'What are you talking about?' said Papa Jo. 'They walked hand in hand! They were in love.'

'That was their glands, you fool! What I'm talking about is Paul's headache.'

'Oh! That. So who does not have a headache from time to time? What *I* am talking of —'

'What you are talking of is neither here nor there. You know,' said Ludmila, addressing herself to Hugo, 'that last time, when he came round with Caroline, he had a little accident?'

Hugo choked, into his napkin.

'You mean, he couldn't wait to get to the bathroom?'

'I mean,' said Ludmila, 'he upset a glass of wine.'

'Really?' said Hugo. He racked his brain for something else to say, since something, plainly, was expected. 'That was clumsy.'

'Very.'

'What's all this? What's all this?' Papa Jo was

growing impatient. 'So a man upsets a glass of wine! So what is a glass of wine that such a fuss should be made?'

'No one's making a fuss,' said Ludmila. She looked again at Hugo. 'I merely mentioned it. As a possibility.'

'I see,' said Hugo; not seeing anything. It was one of Ludmila's characteristics to be cryptic, but this time she had lost him.

'A man doesn't care to make a fool of himself, after all.'

'No,' said Hugo. He wondered what subtle message she was trying to convey. The gist of it would seem to be that Paul's headache had been manufactured psychologically because last time he had come round to dinner he had upset a glass of wine and didn't like making a fool of himself. It was perfectly true, of course, that Paul *was* a bit of a clumsy sod. Only the other day he had sent Hugo's shaving mug shattering into the bath, and last week had gone and wrecked some special pot that Rose had brought up with her from the shop to show Caroline. As for the number of breakages in the kitchen, they had become legendary.

Had Paul always been so clumsy? He was damned if he could remember. Like he couldn't remember if he'd always worn glasses. Had there been a time, back in their boyhood, when he hadn't? Rose had snapped at him the other day that it was about time he went and had his eyes tested and got himself something a bit stronger — pebble lenses, if necessary. It was unlike Rose to be sharp, but she'd been pretty cut up about that pot. Presumably Ludmila felt the same about the glass of wine. 'Paul's trouble,' he said, 'is that he goes around with his head in the clouds. Half the time, he just isn't here.'

Papa Jo exploded.

'And should we expect him to be? Is the man not an artist? Do we not make allowances for the creative genius?'

Not to the extent of excusing sheer cussed, wanton, bumbling inadequacy, thought Hugo. Not if it meant smashing other people's property and throwing glasses of wine all over the place. It had to be said, in certain respects, just recently, Paul had become somewhat of a liability. It wasn't until now that he had really stopped to consider it.

'One asks oneself,' said Ludmila, 'whether there might not be something on his mind?'

'Well, of course there is something on his mind! Dio mio! Will you listen to this woman? You think people write music the way other people make pasta? Writing music is a great gift, and great gifts make great demands. So maybe at times he is a little forgetful — a little crazy. So we have to understand. He needs looking after, not that people should grow angry and shout.'

'No one to my knowledge,' said Ludmila, 'has so far done either.'

'No, and no one, to my knowledge, is being there to look after him! What are these two foolish young women doing, going off to make a nuisance of themselves?'

'Who says they're foolish?' snapped Ludmila. 'One of those bombs ever gets to go off, it'll be more than just a nuisance, you cretinous old fool!'

Across the table, Papa Jo closed one eye at Hugo in a conspiratorial wink. Hugo smiled, but with the side of his mouth that was hidden from Ludmila. She was already of the opinion that he was an arch chauvinist — a view wholeheartedly shared by Rose. It was that, as a matter of fact, which had been the indirect cause of the weekend jaunt. He only hoped Papa Jo would not pursue the subject, because frankly it was not one he felt any inclination to discuss. He was not overproud of the part he had played. Rose had been railing on, astride her usual hobby horse, the general vileness and futility of the male of the species, and he, like a prize lout, had allowed himself to be goaded into losing his temper. Not only into losing his temper, but into actually yelling at her.

'You and your women's lib crap . . . you're all mouth! Nothing but mouth! What do you ever actually do? Sweet FA! Just sit around the place stuffing yourself on cream buns and chocolate, trying to make out it's my fault the world's going bananas and threatening to blow itself up. It always is my fault, isn't it? I suppose it's my fault you sit there stuffing yourself day after day and getting fat? I suppose in some way I'm to blame for that, as well as for the Bomb and pollution and women getting raped? It sometimes seems to me I'm to blame for just about everything round here. If you ask me it's about time you got off your great fat fanny and started putting some of the action where your mouth is!'

The very next day, she had announced that she and Caroline were going off together on some peace march, to show solidarity and do their bit. They had not asked him to accompany them. Not that he would have done, even if they had. He left that sort of quixotic gesture to people like Paul, a born supporter of futile causes if ever there was. He was surprised he hadn't gone with them. He knew they'd invited him, for Rose had made a special point of telling him so. Paul, she had intimated, was one of the few, one of the very few, who might just possibly be spared when the great Day of Female Reckoning came. Hugo needn't think that he stood any chance: he would be one of the first for the chop. She had then had the infernal nerve to suggest they took the car, so they could get down there in style. He had drawn the line at that: they either got there under their own steam or not at all. Rose had tossed her head and said 'You needn't think a bit of male piggery is going to put us off.' Great daft cow. He only hoped she didn't go and do something stupid and get herself arrested. She was maddening as hell, but on the whole he'd rather she were here than not. On the whole.

Papa Jo was demanding to know why he and Rose did not get married. It was a question he put regularly at least three times a year: 'Why do you not get married and start a family?'

He was regularly given the same answer at least three times a year, but either he deliberately forgot or wilfully refused to believe that it could be true.

'We don't see any reason to get married. Rose doesn't want to start a family.'

On his other side, Ludmila, talking in counterpoint to Papa Jo, was launched into some story about Paul and a door. He couldn't quite make it out — it seemed to have something to do with morning assembly. Paul had been coming in late for morning assembly. Had Hugo not noticed? (He couldn't say that he had.) He had been coming in late and seating himself right at the back.

'Always at the back. Now, I don't see any reason a person would always choose to sit at the back unless it was to keep himself hidden. And I don't see any reason a person would want to keep himself hidden unless —'

Unless? He didn't hear the next bit: Papa Jo's voice was louder and more insistent than Ludmila's.

'Rose doesn't want to start a family? This I do not believe! This is only what she is saying, not what is true. Every woman wants to start a family! Is it not so, Madame?'

Bombarded on both sides, Hugo found himself picking up only fragments of the tale Ludmila was telling. The fragments were incomplete ('For a couple not to have a family is the greatest misfortune on earth! Madame will agree with me. Will you not agree with me, Madame? For a couple not to have a family —') yet even in their incompleteness they made a kind of sense.

This morning, when the post had arrived, it had been Paul who had collected it from the front door mat. Hugo, coming down the stairs, had said 'Anything for me?'

'Here —' Paul had thrust the whole lot at him. There

had been five letters in all: one for Caroline, from the States, one for Hugo, the rest for Paul himself. Hugo had opened his there and then; Paul had put his in his pocket, unopened and unread, not even bothering to look at the envelopes to see where they had come from. He hadn't really thought anything much about it at the time. It was only now that it struck him.

'Do not think,' said Papa Jo, earnestly, 'that because Madame and I have no family it is because we have never wished for one. Quite on the contrary! It was fate which said we should not be blessed. Was it not, Madame? Was it not fate which said that we should not be blessed?'

Ludmila ignored him.

'And then again —' she said.

And then again, thought Hugo.... Last night, after Rose and Caroline had departed, he and Paul had taken themselves down to the Saracen's for a plate of shepherd's pie and a couple of jars to soothe their wounded egos — well, soothe Hugo's wounded ego. He had honestly never thought Rose would find the strength of mind (let alone of body) to go off and desert him for a whole weekend simply to cavort about the streets of London with a load of other crackbrained loonies. Who the hell did they think was going to listen to them? He had been disappointed in Caroline, lending her support. Caroline was usually so sensible. Now it seemed even she had gone and got the bug.

'Hugo,' she had said, 'you are just so reactionary it's not true!'

He wasn't reactionary, he was simply being pragmatic. The whole thing was a farce: a complete waste of time. According to Paul, it was a demonstration of the will of the people, but since when, he would like to know, had the will of the people ever counted for anything? It was all claptrap. He'd heard it all before. Paul always had been part of the lunatic fringe where politics was concerned. What he had never been was lazy;

yet last night, in the Saracen's, when it had come to his turn to buy a round, he had coaxed Hugo into going and doing it for him. He had made the excuse that he had bruised his toe, which may or may not have been true — he had certainly stubbed his foot quite badly against the kerb on the way there.

Again, at the time, Hugo had thought nothing of it. Paul was always tripping over things, it had become almost a household joke. But had it been a household joke a year ago? Or was it something that had only happened recently? He couldn't decide; but looking back, to the days when Diana had been with them, he was inclined to believe that it was something that had only happened recently. In which case —

'It was not for want of trying,' said Papa Jo. 'I can assure you of that. We tried, did we not, Madame? Did we not try? Dio mio, how we tried!'

'I don't think Hugo really wants to hear all about that,' said Ludmila. 'Why don't you just leave people alone? He and Rose are quite happy as they are.'

'How do you know?' said Papa Jo. 'Hugo might be. But what of Rose? What of —'

'*Will* you be quiet?' Ludmila turned on him, angrily. 'Always trying to run people's lives for them!'

'*I? I* run people's lives? How can you say such a thing?'

'Quite easily! And I'll say it again if there's any more of it! I never knew such a man for meddling.'

The double act continued. It might have been amusing, had worrying notions about Paul not begun to filter through to his consciousness. Incidents he had long forgotten, or had not even been aware of noticing, now came back to niggle at him. Paul, in the garden, failing to catch a tennis ball casually tossed at him across the space of a few yards — Paul, pouring hot tea all over himself — Paul, not even acknowledging him as they passed within hailing distance on either side of the village street. . . .

Ludmila was no fool; he had never thought her one. Was it possible she had picked up on something which the rest of them had signally failed to register?

It seemed that she had. As he left, at ten pm, she pressed his arm and said: 'See if you can find out about Paul . . . it's important we should know.'

He said he would find out what he could; but how in hell, he thought, was one supposed to set about it?

9

If her public could see her now ... weary, but on the whole content, Caroline kicked her feet out of her shoes and stretched her legs across the carriage to the seat opposite. Beside her sat Rose, slumped in a heap with her cheek pressed against the glass. Rose, to say the least, looked a trifle the worse for wear: she was sure that she herself looked no less so. She ran her fingers through her hair, sorting out the tangles. Her tights, she suddenly noticed, had holes in both big-toe areas. Never mind her public seeing her now, it would be enough if Larry were to do so.

'What in the name of Richard Millhouse Nixon have you been *doing* to yourself?'

There was nothing more distasteful, in Larry's eyes, than a badly groomed female. He didn't even like her wearing jeans just to slop around the house in. Jeans and duffle coat and big baggy sweater (stolen from Paul) would really freak him out. Likewise, if he'd called while she was away and been told that she had gone on a peace march — it would, quite definitely, rattle him. Going on peace marches was not the sort of activity he expected from his leading dancers, and especially not from one hitherto as undemonstrative as Caroline. Once, watching a Jane Fonda movie on the television, he had ruffled her hair and said, 'Thank Christ you're not one of the banshee breed ... when you see women like that it really makes you wonder if they should ever have been given the vote.' She had felt ashamed, sitting there, saying nothing; but still she had gone on sitting there — and still she had said nothing. How often had it happened like that? Caroline biting her tongue, subjugating her true self, all in exchange for a rare moment of affection. . . .

If Larry had called and Hugo had answered the telephone, he would have found himself talking to a soul mate. They could have had a good transatlantic bull session on the horrors of political women. She hoped it would be Hugo who had answered rather than Paul. Larry was suspicious of Paul. 'This guy you went to school with. This composer guy . . . what's his name?' He was always pretending to have forgotten Paul's name. It was his way of dismissing him: a man without a name could scarcely be counted as competition.

And a man without sight?

She had wept, after Paul had made love to her. It had distressed him; he had wanted to know why. He had thought that it was his fault — that he had upset her, making demands he ought not to have made. He had been wrong: it was not for herself alone that she had wept, but for them both. For opportunities lost, and the golden glory of youth that had gone. For her, and the child she had not had: for him, and his stubborn pride, which kept him locked into silence. It was a silence which was as difficult for her to break as for him. More than once, that night, as they lay in each other's arms, she had been on the point of making the attempt; each time, her courage had failed her. Was it because, deep down, she had no wish to know? No wish for the *responsibility* of knowing? Let her fears remain unconfirmed, and she might allow herself the luxury, even now, of believing them to be exaggerated. No one else seemed to have noticed anything amiss. She had thought for a while that Meat Loaf might have done so, but that, she had since decided, had been but a figment of her too active imagination. Certainly Rose and Hugo appeared to have no inkling. So how was it she should see what others did not? She turned, to look at her silent companion.

'Rose,' she said, 'have you ever noticed —'

She stopped.

'Noticed what?' said Rose. Her voice was muffled, the tears coursing unchecked down her cheeks.

'Why, Rosie!' Caroline, concerned, swung her legs to the floor, groping with stockinged feet for her shoes. 'Whatever is wrong?'

Rose withdrew a hand from deep inside the recesses of her duffle pocket. It was clutching a damp handkerchief, screwed into a ball. She blotted despondently at her face with it.

'I'm such a slob,' she said.

Sternly, Caroline repressed the desire to smile.

'What in the world do you mean by that?'

Rose hiccuped.

'I never seem to *do* anything . . . I never seem to make any *effort*.'

'Now, how can you possibly say that? When you've just done more in three days than some people stir themselves to do in a lifetime!'

'Yes, but it took *him* to make me — I only did it to prove him wrong.'

'So there you are, then! You've proved him wrong!'

'No, I haven't.' Rose dissolved again into tears. 'I've proved him right . . . I'll never find the willpower to do it again. I know I won't! I'll just go back to sitting around doing nothing . . . stuffing myself with chocolates and getting fat.' She dabbed with the damp ball of handkerchief at her eyes. 'I am getting fat,' she said, 'aren't I?'

'I wouldn't say you were getting *fat*,' said Caroline. A little plump, maybe, but then most people got a little plump. Most people could afford to do so. There were times when she wished she could herself.

'I am getting fat,' said Rose. She pulled open her duffle coat, almost defiantly. 'Look at that.'

Caroline looked.

'Yes. Well —' It wouldn't do for a dancer, but Rose wasn't a dancer. Rose had more sense. 'Just a bit of exercise,' she said, 'that's all it needs.'

'You think it would get rid of it?'

'Of course it would!'

'You guarantee?'

'Sure — if you're prepared to keep it up.'

'I'd really get to be as slim as you are?'

You might, thought Caroline, if you don't mind half starving yourself and going through God knows how many hours of sheer hell every day.

'Actually,' said Rose, 'I'm nearly five months pregnant.'

'You're *what*?'

'Nearly five months pregnant ... it doesn't seem quite so bad, does it, when one knows that? One's entitled to get just a little bit fat, when one's pregnant.'

'So they tell me,' said Caroline. She would have been in her eighth month by now, if she hadn't given way to emotional blackmail. Not that it was Larry's fault. She had only herself to blame: the choice, ultimately, had been hers. It was she who had opted for abortion, which some called murder. She had often wondered about it, whether it had been a boy embryo or a girl that she had caused to be torn out of her. She had never asked. She didn't expect they would have told her, anyway; they probably didn't even look. Just chucked the whole bloody mess into the incinerator. Another few weeks and it might have been a live pink baby, kicking in its cot. She swallowed.

'Are you shocked?' asked Rose.

'Shocked?' Why should she be shocked?

'Shocked at me going ahead and having it.' That, she thought, would be a strange thing to be shocked about. 'I've signed hundreds of petitions, you know ... defending a woman's right to do what she likes with her own body. Abortions on demand, and all the rest of it. It's what I believe in. Firmly. I do! It's just that when it actually came to the point —'

'You couldn't face it.'

'Don't,' said Rose. 'It's too awful.'

'I don't see what's so awful about it. You didn't sign any petitions saying women *had* to have abortions.'

'No, but I've said over and over that it's better than bringing an unwanted child into the world . . . oh, God!' Rose removed some strands of damp hair that were sticking to her cheek. 'Why does one talk so glibly? It always rebounds.'

'Do I take it,' said Caroline, 'that you don't actually want the baby?'

'Who knows?' Rose, dispirited, humped a shoulder. 'Who knows what I want any more? I don't.'

'So what does Hugo say?'

'Doesn't say anything . . . haven't told him.'

'You mean he hasn't *noticed*?'

'Hugo wouldn't notice,' said Rose, bitterly, 'if I grew two heads and turned sky blue pink. All he knows is I'm stuffing myself with chocolates and getting fat.'

'Then surely it's about time,' said Caroline, 'that you put him right?'

Rose waved her handkerchief, lethargically.

'I suppose so.'

'Oh, come on, now, Rosie! You can't keep a thing like this from him. I mean, unless —' She hesitated, struck by sudden doubts.

'Oh, it's his,' said Rose. 'I haven't consorted with other men.'

'So why haven't you told him?'

'Because he'll crow,' said Rose. 'He'll exult over what he calls feminine frailty.'

'But won't he be pleased?'

'Maybe. Maybe not. I don't know. He might even get all sentimental and want us to get married.'

What wouldn't one give, thought Caroline, for the odd bit of sentimentality. . . .

'I imagine you wouldn't exactly object to the idea?'

'Grant me *some* principles!' said Rose. 'If I gave way on that, I wouldn't have anything left.'

Caroline looked at her, curiously.

'You really feel as strongly as all that?'

'Don't you?'

'Well —'

'The institution of marriage,' said Rose, 'was entirely man-made to protect the interests of the propertied classes.'

'Quite.' Paul had sternly informed her of the fact on more occasions than she cared to remember. Why, then, had he gone ahead and married Diana?

'It reduces women to the status of chattels. Besides which, it's utterly futile and ridiculous for two people to pledge lifelong union. It's naïve to the point of imbecility.'

'Of course, you're quite right.' Diana, presumably, had insisted. Perhaps it had been the only way he could get her into bed with him.

'Legalised prostitution,' said Rose. 'A licence to screw. That's all it is.'

Was that all it had been in Paul's case? Certainly he hadn't been accustomed to have women hold out against him. If Diana had indeed done so, it must have come as a rude jolt to his ego. But maybe it had not been that at all. Maybe he had quite genuinely and sincerely believed himself to be in love with her.

'Tell me,' said Rose. Her clear, topaz eyes rested solemnly upon Caroline. 'Would *you* get married? To Paul, for instance?'

'Paul?' The question took her of guard.

'I mean, obviously,' said Rose, 'if he were to ask you?'

She hedged.

'Since the question is purely hypothetical —'

'You can give a purely hypothetical answer.'

That's just the trouble, she thought: I can't.

Rose shook her head.

'I suppose you'd rather have this Larry person.'

155

She was spared the necessity of replying by their arrival in Cheltenham. She remembered, just a few weeks back, how Hugo had come to meet her, and how she had been surprised (and perhaps a little disappointed?) that it had been Hugo rather than Paul. This morning, there was no one: they were reliant upon the bus, which ran once in every hour.

'It really is the most tremendous bore,' said Rose, 'Hugo being so piglike. If Paul still had his car, he'd have let us take it like a shot. Have you managed to get him driving again yet, by the way?'

'Not yet,' said Caroline.

'He'll have to pluck up his courage soon; either that, or take to a bicycle. Life without wheels of some sort is just about impossible. I mean, what's he going to do when you've gone back home? Get taxis everywhere?'

'I guess he'll have to. And talking of taxis, why don't we grab one?'

'Do you think we ought?' Rose looked doubtful. 'It doesn't strike one as being quite fitting. In the circumstances.'

'If Hugo knew the condition you were in, he'd probably have said it wasn't quite fitting that you should have gone off in the first place.'

'He said that anyhow. He thinks we're mad and hysterical and ought to leave it to men whether we get blown up or not . . . that's why he wouldn't let us have the car. To teach us a lesson. If he sees us come back in a cab he'll jeer himself silly.'

'Let him.' Determinedly, Caroline led the way across the station forecourt to the cab rank. She had done her share of demonstrating. She had a class to take at two o'clock, she wasn't going to hang around Cheltenham for another forty minutes only to impress Hugo. 'When are you going to tell him,' she said, 'about the baby?'

'Oh, I don't know.' Rose trailed listlessly behind her across the forecourt. 'Today, tomorrow . . . some time.'

'I really think you ought to do it straight away. After

all, whatever one thinks of them —' and let's face it, they weren't all like Larry: some men might actually welcome such a piece of news. (Paul, for example? Would Paul?) — 'they do have *some* rights in the matter. Not a great many, I grant you; but some.'

Rose sighed.

'I suppose so,' she said.

The Lodge, when they arrived back, was empty. Caroline went upstairs to have first soak in the bath, Rose sat down in the kitchen, amongst the clutter of breakfast dishes which no one had bothered to wash up. Idly she examined the remains of what they had eaten for breakfast. From the scatter of crumbs it looked like nothing more substantial than toast and marmalade. She hoped Hugo wouldn't expect her to settle down and become a model housewife, doing cooked meals three times a day and vacuuming beneath the furniture. It wasn't her scene. Maternity was one thing: domesticity quite another.

She pushed the dirty dishes to one side. She knew that Caroline was right, she had to tell him. She ought to have done so weeks ago. Months ago. While there had still been time. If she had told him right at the beginning, when she had first suspected, she wouldn't now be sitting here with her gut sticking out and an insatiable desire to cram herself with chocolates and grow fat. Hugo would have said: 'I presume you want to get rid of it?' Taking it for granted. What else could she want? His very tone of voice would have been a challenge. How, in the face of that, could she have gone back on her stated principles?

'You mean you're actually going to *keep* it? After all your mouth? All your big talk?'

Oh, Hugo would have had a field day. Probably still would. But nonetheless, he had to be told.

Caroline called to her from the hallway: 'Rosie? I'm off.'

"Kay.'

Firmly, she put the biscuit tin away from her and went upstairs to have a bath. She wondered what it must be like to be Caroline, always so calm, so sensible — so *organised*. Caroline would never go getting herself pregnant. She knew exactly where she was going in life; had it all mapped out, both personally and professionally. If ever she had been in love with Paul (which was what Hugo maintained, except that what did Hugo ever know about anything?) she had obviously long since got over it. Even this Larry, who kept calling her all the way from California, seemed to rouse no turmoil within her. There had been a message waiting for her on the hall table, in Hugo's handwriting: *Caroline, your boyfriend called. Told him you'd gone off to do a Jane Fonda. Said you MIGHT be back Monday (always provided you hadn't gone and got yourself arrested).* Caroline had simply read it, pulled a wry face, and dropped it without comment into the waste bin. Perhaps she was one of those rare beings who was so genuinely bound up with her career that she had no need of emotional entanglements. If that were so, thought Rose, she didn't know how lucky she was. Glumly, she contemplated the mound of her belly as it rose, hippo-like, above the level of the water. How she had ever come to get bound up with Hugo. . . .

The slamming of the front door announced that one of them was back. She listened; and could tell from the decisive tread that it was Hugo. With her big toe, she unhooked the plug and reached out for the bath towel. This was it: the moment of truth.

He was out in the kitchen, amidst the débris, making himself a coffee.

'Hallo,' said Rose.

'Hi.' He spoke without troubling himself to turn round. 'I heard you were home, I bumped into Caroline. Want a coffee?'

'Yes, all right. Why not? Since you're making one.'

There was a silence. She waited for him to ask her how it had gone, cavorting with the loonies, but he said nothing. She could only assume he was still displeased. Too bad. She pulled the biscuit tin towards her.

'So what brings you back here at this hour of the day?'

The compelling desire to see you, my dove. To tell you how happy I am to have you here again. To take you into my arms and kiss you and tell you much I missed you. . . .

'I had a free period,' said Hugo. 'I wanted to do a bit of thinking.'

'Oh? What about?'

About us, my dove. You and me.

'About this.' said Hugo.

From his back pocket he pulled a folded sheet of paper, which he tossed on to the table, scattering toast crumbs. Rose picked it up, and unfolded it. It was a sheet of headed notepaper, completely blank apart from the name and address of the school — Bampton Hall, Bampton, nr Moreton-in-Marsh, Glos — and a signature, written further down on the left-hand side. The signature was Paul's. She looked at it, uncomprehending.

'So what is it?'

'A petition,' said Hugo. 'Anti-vivisection.'

'Oh.' She looked at it again. 'Who's getting it up?'

'I am.'

'*You?*' She hadn't known he cared. She hadn't known he cared about anything save his precious career.

'It was all I could think of on the spur of the moment. It needed to be something that I knew he'd support.'

She frowned.

'What are you talking about?'

'Anti-vivisection.'

'So?'

'So he signed it!'

159

'I can see he signed it... I'm obviously not with you.'

'For Christ's sake, woman! A blank sheet of *paper*?'

'Well, why not? If he was the first.'

'Because I told him,' said Hugo, 'to make sure and read it. Check what he was putting his name to.'

There was a pause. The kettle boiled; Hugo made the coffee. Rose sat, staring down at Paul's unsuspecting signature on the blank page. He never had looked properly at her costume designs. She had thought at the time that it was unlike him, he was usually interested in every least detail. And then there were the records, all neatly ranged in the record cabinet. Not just Bach-Beethoven-Brahms, but quartets before quintets, piano sonatas before violin sonatas... she shook her head.

'It doesn't prove anything.'

'It proves he can't see what the hell he's doing!'

'He probably didn't even bother to look.'

'You don't have to bother to look... not when there's nothing to look at.' Hugo set the coffee mugs on the table. 'Don't you see what it means?'

Deliberately, she folded the paper.

'It means,' she said, 'that you played a pretty filthy trick on him.'

'You think I enjoyed it? You think I got some kind of a buzz out of it?'

'I should have thought there might have been a kinder way of going about it.'

'Oh! So what would you suggest? I ask him outright? *What's the matter, old chap? Can't see quite as well as you used to?* For crying out loud!' Hugo yanked angrily at a chair. 'It doesn't exactly give me any thrill that one of my oldest and closest friends appears to be going blind!'

A shiver ran up her spine.

'Don't say that!'

'So what the hell am I supposed to say? I tell you, he can't see what he's doing! I've been here with him all weekend. I've been watching him —'

'Spying on him!'

'Not spying on him!' Hugo banged his fist down on to the table. The coffee mugs bounced, spilling coffee into the scattered crumbs. 'Hoping against hope that I'd got it wrong — but I haven't! *I* know I haven't, *you* know I haven't. Why else do you think we've got all these poxy daft notices all over the place? Why else do you think he keeps breaking things and falling over things and generally behaving like a cretin? Why do you think he's given up *driving*? Because he can't flaming well see to do it!'

Rose said nothing for a moment; then: 'Supposing that you're right —'

'I know I'm right!'

'— what is he going to do?'

'What's more immediately to the point,' said Hugo, 'is what am I going to do?'

She looked up, quickly.

'How do you mean?'

'Well —' He pulled his coffee towards him. 'We've got the Festival coming up. He's supposed to be conducting.'

'Only his own work.'

'So what difference does that make? He still can't see what the hell he's doing!'

'Perhaps he doesn't need to. He probably knows it all by heart.'

'For God's sake!' said Hugo. 'It's a bloody *opera*.'

'I don't think he'd attempt it,' said Rose, slowly 'if he didn't think he could manage it.'

'And how in God's name does he think he's going to see what's going on on stage when he can't even see a blank sheet of paper when it's two inches in front of his eyes?'

'I don't know.' She could be stubborn, when she chose. 'All I know is that it's his opera, and if he wants to conduct it —'

'Everyone else can go hang. Yes, all right! All right!' Hugo held up a hand, forestalling any scathing comments. 'I know perfectly well what you think of me. I know you think my heart's made of concrete and I'm totally lacking in any of the finer feelings, but just reflect upon one thing: it's not going to help Paul any if he makes a cock-up of it.'

'Nonetheless,' said Rose, 'it has to be his decision.'

'He may not be given the choice . . . it may be taken out of his hands whether he likes it or not.'

'Oh?' She spoke sharply. 'Why's that?'

'Ludmila suspects. In fact, I think she's pretty certain. She's just waiting for confirmation.'

'Don't give it to her!'

'It's all very well saying don't give it to her, but what do I do if she comes up and asks me? Point blank?'

'Tell her you don't know. It's true! You don't. You're only guessing.'

'*Guessing?*' said Hugo. He jabbed a finger on to the sheet of paper. 'What more proof do you need than that?'

'He'd have told us,' said Rose.

'Not if he's hoping to get away with it until after the Festival.'

'Get away with it? You talk as if it's some guilty secret — as if it's something he has to be ashamed of! Hugo, if it's true, *what is he going to do?*'

'Well, it won't stop him writing music, that's for sure.'

'Yes, but apart from that?'

'What do you mean, apart from that?'

'Apart from writing music! All the other things . . . looking after himself —'

'Oh!' Hugo drained his coffee and stood up. 'We can discuss all that later. The important thing right now is the Festival.'

She stared at him, unbelieving. There are times, Hugo McDonald, she thought, when you are incredible.

'I don't suppose,' he said, 'that Caroline has ever mentioned anything?'

'No. At least —'

'What?'

'She did once ask me about the accident. About what happened. I remember she said something about it being lucky that he wore glasses.'

'What made her think it was lucky, for God's sake?'

'Well . . . I don't know. She seemed to think it might have saved him getting splinters in his eyes.'

'Just the opposite,' said Hugo, 'I should have thought.' He pulled open the door. 'I think I'd better have a word with her. She might know something we don't.'

'Hugo —'

'Yes?' He turned, impatiently, obviously anxious to be off. 'What is it?'

'Oh, nothing,' she said. 'It'll wait.'

It had waited nearly five months; another few hours weren't likely to make very much difference.

It was gone three o'clock before he ran Caroline to earth: she was sitting in the canteen with Paul, eating sausages and chips. He bought himself a coffee and went over to join them.

'Strange time of day to be eating lunch,' he said.

'I had a class at two. I didn't have time for anything before. You may remember,' said Caroline, sweetly, 'that we didn't get back from our little outing until almost one o'clock . . . thanks to a certain person being too damn mean to let us have the loan of his car.'

He grunted. That hardly explained why Paul, also, was consuming sausages and chips at three o'clock in the afternoon. He said as much: 'What's he doing, stuffing his mouth at this hour?'

'I happen not to like crowds,' said Paul. 'How's the petition coming along?'

'The —? Oh. Yes.' The petition. He felt pretty bad about that. Rose was quite right, it had been a shabby trick. He wished now he hadn't done it. It was just that at the time it had been the only thing he could think of. 'I — ah — I've given up on it.'

'What was that?' said Caroline.

'Anti-vivisection petition.' Paul chased a piece of sausage round his plate. 'He talked me into signing it.'

'*Hugo* did?'

'I'm not all bad, you know,' said Hugo. 'At least one per cent of me is really quite nice.'

'Oh, yes?'

'Just because you and Rose have got your knickers in a twist —' the piece of sausage that Paul had been chasing finally eluded him and fell on to the table: Paul, not realising, went on chasing it — 'on account of having to use public transport for once in your pampered lives —'

There was a pause.

'Yes?' said Caroline.

He pulled himself together.

'— that's no reason for slagging me off.'

'Slagging you off? As if I would!'

'As if you would!'

'I might on occasion call you a reactionary old bigot —'

'Too kind!'

'Or even a Neanderthal throwback —

'Why be polite? Why not say what you really mean?'

'Not in public, Hugo, please!'

Paul looked up.

'What's going on?' he said.

Across the intervening space Hugo's eyes met Caroline's. With guilty haste, they switched their gaze.

'Nothing,' said Hugo. Deftly, he replaced the piece of sausage on Paul's plate. 'You just get on and eat your lunch.'

Afterwards, on his way to take class, he was stopped by Ludmila.

'Ah,' she said, 'Hugo. . . I've been meaning to talk with you.' In an eagle-like grip she took his arm, piloting him off down the corridor. 'What we were discussing the other night —' She lowered her voice. 'About Paul.'

'Oh, yes?'

'Did you manage to find out anything?'

'Well — no,' he said. 'Not really.' He signs his name to blank sheets of paper, and he pushes bits of sausage off the edge of his plate, and how in the name of all that's wonderful he thinks he's going to get up on a rostrum and fight his way through a full-length opera, God alone knows; but apart from that —

'Nothing?'

He hunched a shoulder.

'Other than the fact that he's had a bit of a rough time of it just recently —'

'I see.' Ludmila looked at him, searchingly. 'So in your opinion, he's perfectly fit to conduct?'

'I'm sure if he weren't,' said Hugo, 'he'd be the first to say so.'

10

Monday evening, Larry called. She had been expecting it.

'What's all this garbage about peace marches? What in hell are you getting up to over there?'

She had expected that, too. What she had not expected was the suggestion that he should come over and join her.

'I could take a couple of weeks off ... why don't I come over and keep an eye on you? We could go across to Paris, maybe. Do a bit of touring.'

'That would have been really great,' she said. 'Unfortunately, I'm pretty tied up here at Bampton just now.'

'Tied up?' There was a sharp note of suspicion in his voice. 'How do you mean?'

'Well, with these classes and all ... I told you, I was taking class every day?'

'So chuck it.'

'I couldn't do that,' she said. 'I promised Ludmila I'd be here till the end of term.'

She had promised no such thing, but that afternoon, in the staff-room, Hugo had come up to her.

'A word in your ear? Somewhere private?'

They had gone out together, into the grounds, and there he had confided in her his worries about Paul. She had known, then, that the time for playing ostrich had passed. The problem existed: she could no longer pretend that it did not. She had more or less made up her mind that come what may she would stay on until the Festival. She would see Paul safely over that hurdle before she left him to fend for himself.

She waited, with mixed emotions, for Larry to suggest that if she could not make Paris, then maybe he should come over to Bampton, but he did not; merely told her she was a damn fool to go and get herself roped in.

'I thought you were meant to be taking a vacation, for Chrissakes?'

'I am! In between classes I'm lazing around doing sweet bugger all.'

'That's not the way I heard it. The way I heard it you were screaming around the streets of London with a mob of malcontents . . . what's gotten into you?'

'I guess it must be something to do with the climate. It's stopped raining at long last.'

He grunted. He didn't like the fact that it had stopped raining: the rain had become a symbol. She wondered why she had mentioned it. It was exactly the sort of remark calculated to bring him over post-haste.

'The sun came out yesterday,' she said. 'I didn't know what it was at first . . . some kind of queer light in the sky. It stayed out for almost half an hour.'

'Big deal,' said Larry. 'Just don't let it go to your head.'

He made no more mention of joining her: it was, she supposed, just as well. It would be manifestly impossible, with Larry on the scene, for her to give Paul the time and attention he was going to need were he to stand any chance of emerging unscathed from the ordeal of the Festival. In Hugo's opinion, she knew, for he had made no bones about telling her so, she was simply wasting her energies.

'No way, just *no way*, can he get up there and conduct. If he thinks he can, he's kidding himself.'

'But you'll be there.' She had pleaded with him, on Paul's behalf. 'If anything were to go wrong — I mean really, disastrously —'

'I could step into the breach. Sure. But what do you suppose that would do for him?'

Hugo had argued they would be acting in the best interests of Paul and the production — and, by extension, the school itself — by stopping all pretence and confronting him outright.

'Let him know that we know — give him the opportunity of discussing it. Find out, for God's sake, exactly what's going on! Ask him point blank, if necessary, just how much he can see and how much he can't.'

She could not but admit the force of his argument; only, emotionally, she still shied away from it.

'He's fought so damned hard to keep it from us —'

'Yes, but for how much longer?'

When he's ready, she thought; in his own time. Don't force him.

Hugo had eventually agreed, although with reluctance.

'I still say we could be of more help to him if we officially knew.'

It was possible that he was right; but equally possible that for the moment they could be of most help if officially they did not know. She could see that for one so basically reserved as Paul, the surrender of his independence would be a blow almost more crushing than the loss of sight which occasioned it. Let him, for as long as he could, enjoy the illusion of self-sufficiency.

On Tuesday, at a staff meeting, Ludmila announced that the following Friday evening, from six o'clock to nine, she would be holding a soirée. She trusted it would not be too short notice; but it went without saying, even if it was, that everyone would be expected to attend. Ludmila's soirées were an institution. According to Paul, they were unadulterated hell — 'a modern version of the Inquisition'. Hugo confirmed.

'It's when she gives you the once-over. Vets you out. Decides who's for the chop and who's been a good boy and can stay on. She usually leaves it till nearer the end of term.'

The fact that on this occasion she had chosen to bring the date forward seemed ominous. They discussed the implications of it, later that same day, while Paul was up at the Hall taking a rehearsal.

'We all know why she's doing it,' said Rose. 'It's a witch hunt. She's out to trap Paul into betraying himself.'

Caroline frowned. Even knowing Ludmila as she did, the theory sounded a trifle Machiavellian. Hugo obviously thought so, as well.

'She doesn't have to go to those lengths. If she really wanted to find out, there are plenty of far easier ways of doing it.'

'Yes, like getting up petitions,' said Rose. 'Except that it takes a real rat to sink that low.'

A shadow of irritation passed across Hugo's face.

'It's not a question of sinking low, it's a question of protecting the interests of the school.'

'Oh, crap!' said Rose. She turned back to Caroline, discounting Hugo. 'Even if it isn't deliberate, the effect's going to be the same. She's still going to find out. Have you ever been to one of her do's? She holds them in the Conservatory, amongst the potted palms, and she spends the entire evening juggling people about. It's like being in some mad Shakespearian production, everyone constantly on the trot to somewhere else . . . good Gloucester, come hither, and thou, bold Worcester, get thee hence to Hereford, and noble Percy, go thou yonder . . . she has this mad thing about making people circulate. It's all done for a purpose, of course. She's scared stiff of insurrection . . . terrified that people might start forming cliques and ganging up. The first thing she'll do when we arrive is forge through the middle of us, scattering us in all directions . . . Rose, dear, you go and talk to Virginia — Caroline, there's Victor, standing in a corner — Hugo, Papa Jo wants a word with you —'

'She only does it to keep things moving,' said Hugo. 'There's no ulterior motive.'

'You want to bet?'

'Oh, don't be so infantile!'

'Well, whatever she does it for, Paul's not going to survive a whole evening of it, is he?'

No, thought Caroline; he's not. She remembered the weekend down at Marden. He would never have survived that if it hadn't been for her, and that had been in surroundings where he had spent his childhood. Most assuredly he would not manage to get through an evening such as Rose had described.

'If he wants to keep up appearances,' said Hugo, 'he doesn't have any choice. Another headache and he'd blow the whole thing wide apart.'

Did his tone really imply, *and no bad thing, either*, or was that only her imagination? Hugo, as if sensing disapproval, shook his head.

'There's no way he can get out of going, Carly. He'll just have to take his chance.'

He didn't stand any chance; they all knew that.

'You mean we're just going to throw him to the wolves?' said Rose. 'Just stand by and watch and do nothing?'

There was a pause.

'It's got to come out some time,' said Hugo. 'Better now, at some in-house do, than in public, at the Festival.'

Rose looked across at Caroline.

'Is that what you think?'

'I don't know, Rosie. I guess —' she spoke apologetically, feeling herself almost a traitor — 'I guess in some ways Hugo's right. I'd hate the thought of him making a fool of himself in front of an audience.'

'So what you're saying is, let him make a fool of himself on Friday and then he won't be given the opportunity of making a fool of himself in front of an audience, because Ludmila won't let him?'

'Well — yes.' Reluctantly, she admitted it. 'I suppose.'

'All right,' said Rose. 'So you're thinking of Paul. He —' she nodded, contemptuously, at Hugo — 'is thinking of the school —'

'And of Paul! It's not going to do him much good if he fucks things up, is it?'

'All right, so you're both thinking of Paul . . . so what I'm saying is, why can't Paul be allowed to think for himself? What right do we have to assume that we know better than he does? He's the one it's happening to. If he'd wanted people to know, he'd have told them; the fact that he hasn't speaks for itself. At least, it does as far as I'm concerned.'

'So what exactly,' said Hugo, with heavy sarcasm, 'are you saying? Apart from Paul being allowed to think for himself?'

'That *is* what I'm saying — he *has* thought for himself. He's come to a decision: he's prepared to take a chance that he can keep things hidden until he's achieved what he wants to achieve, which is, quite obviously, to conduct his opera, and what I say is that we ought to respect that decision and stand by him and do what we can to support him, not just wash our hands and say well, that's his hard luck, and if he bumps into the potted palms ha ha too bad —'

'Nobody ever did say that,' said Hugo.

'It's what you implied . . . *he'll just have to take his chance.* You know damned well that if we don't rally round he'll be lost before he even starts.'

'But what can we do?' said Caroline. 'If Ludmila's going to scatter us all to the four winds —'

'Keep an eye on him; unobtrusively. Always try and have one of us near him. Get to him before she does.'

'It'll never work,' said Hugo.

'Oh, so you're not even going to try? You're just going to stand there and watch?'

'I didn't say that! Don't be so quick to jump down a

person's throat. Naturally I'll give him a hand if I see he's in trouble and I happen to be nearby —'

'And if you happen not to be, that's his problem?'

'Well, there's not much point galloping to the rescue like a herd of bull elephants, is there?'

'Precisely! Which is why we've got to be on the watch-out.'

It was Marden all over again, thought Caroline — except that this time they had Ludmila to contend with. Privately she could not help but agree with Hugo: not only would they never get away with it, but sooner or later people were going to have to know, and in the long run it could save a lot of heartache and embarrassment if they knew now rather than later. Loyalty to Rose, alone, forbade her saying so. If Rose were prepared to aid Paul in his endeavours, she could only do likewise, mistaken though those endeavours might be.

'Well?' Rose was regarding Hugo challengingly. She obviously took Caroline's support for granted. 'Are we agreed? Do we stick by him?'

'Oh, don't worry!' Hugo spoke tetchily. 'I won't let him go bumping into the flaming potted palms.'

Paul had known, the minute Ludmila made her announcement, that his time was up. This was it: Armageddon. He had no doubts as to the outcome of the battle. Ludmila would win hands down, because Ludmila held all the trump cards. She was not only on her home ground, but she it was who would determine the rules of combat and the weapons to be employed. Not that Paul had any weapons, other than his recently acquired cunning, and that was hardly likely to avail him very much in a room full of people all talking nineteen to the dozen, not to mention a liberal selection of potted plants and tubs of greenery scattered at random about the floor. They in themselves presented an obstacle course that would be his undoing, never mind the additional impedimenta of human bodies.

In his first panic-stricken frenzy he thought of falling down the stairs and twisting his ankle, but a moment's reflection told him that Ludmila would never buy it. She was already suspicious. Paul absent, or Paul limping with a stick and conveniently confined, like Papa Jo, to one spot, would only confirm what he was pretty sure she had already half guessed; likewise if he were to smash his glasses (his second panic-stricken thought) and claim immobility without them. Nobody who wasn't already as blind as a bat could be rendered so by the simple expedient of removing a pair of spectacles.

Having dismissed both accident and breakage, he toyed for a while with the idea of seeking a private interview and casting himself upon Ludmila's mercy.

'If I can just conduct *Jane* — just the first performance. That's all I ask. After that, I don't mind, I'll go away somewhere and learn how to do tatting and tell the time. But please ... just let me have the first performance!'

The only trouble was, he wasn't sure that Ludmila had any mercy. She had certainly never shown any signs of it, and would, he supposed, be well within her legal rights to demand his immediate resignation. An untrained blind man (consciously, now, he forced himself to think in such terms) roaming the premises, in charge of anything up to sixty youngsters at a time, could almost certainly be said to constitute a safety hazard. He had realised that the other day, during an orchestra rehearsal, when the fire bell had rung. The children, fortunately, had known what to do, and it was in any case a mere practice drill; but had it not been, and had there been panic — he had been shocked, perhaps for the first time, into full awareness of his own inability to cope. In any situation of real emergency he would be not only useless but a positive hindrance. If Ludmila should exercise her right —

some might even say her duty — to suspend him forthwith, who should blame her?

He decided, after much thought, that casting himself on Ludmila's mercy would be simply to sign his own death warrant. He would be signing it just as surely by attending at her soirée, but at least that way he would not go down without a fight, and one never knew but at the last moment something might even yet occur to save him. The heavens could open, there could be an earthquake — flood, fire, tempest — Ludmila herself could be turned into stone, catching sight of her own reflection in the glass. Alternatively, he could go along and sit with Papa Jo for the duration. She probably wouldn't let him, but it was worth a try. Just so long as he didn't make an utter and total abject fool of himself, holding converse with a potted palm, proffering apologies to a tub of greenery . . . for one in his position, it seemed about as much as he could reasonably ask.

He very nearly came to grief within the first few seconds. Entering the Conservatory with Caroline, he found himself instantly and roughly torn asunder by Ludmila. That he had been prepared for: what he had not been prepared for was a potted something-or-other lying right across his path, under his feet, at the very first step that he took. He was almost tempted to believe that she had placed it there on purpose. It was Meat Loaf, by some act of providence appearing at his elbow in the nick of time, who saved him.

'Ach, Ghrist! These wretch'd liddle blants. Alvays one must be looking vhere one dreads.'

One would, thought Paul, if only one could. Desperately, amidst the hubbub, he sought a route to some safe haven.

'Where's Papa Jo?' He cast about him: a futile gesture. The room was full of fog, with blurred shapes slowly lumbering in its midst. One had, however, to put up some kind of a show.

'I come vith you.' Companionably, Meat Loaf interlocked his arm with Paul's. 'Alvays is best avay from Ludmila.'

They reached Papa Jo without mishap and stood a while (Ludmila would not allow of any chairs: chairs led to little groups of people, heads together, doing their own thing) drinking some kind of fizzy French wine that passed for champagne and discussing production details for *Jane*. Next week the principals were coming down and Papa Jo was to start working with them. He wanted to ask Paul, what did he —

'Some other time!' Ludmila's voice cut imperiously across the conversation. He had known that it would, before very long. 'I will not have these private confabulations going on! This is a social gathering, not a workshop. Paul —' firmly she took him by the elbow — 'why don't you go over there and speak with Virginia? She's all by herself and looking lonely. Go along now ... off you go!'

She shushed at his backside as if he were a chicken. Reluctantly, he moved forward. He hadn't the faintest notion where Virginia was to be found, nor the least desire to speak with her even if he had. Directly in front of him there seemed to be a little knot of people; it was either people or potted palms. Taking no chances, he edged sideways — and cannoned rudely into a body coming at him from the opposite direction. Ludmila was almost certainly watching.

'Oops!' A hand clutched at his arm: the voice was Rose's. 'Sorry about that ... wasn't looking where I was going.'

'Me neither. I'm supposed to be on my way to talk to Virginia ... you haven't happened to see her, by any chance?'

'She's over there, by the windows. Actually, I —'

'Rose!' (He had been right: Ludmila was watching him like a hawk.) 'I want you to come over here and have a word with Miss Dillinger. She'd like to discuss the possibility of your giving pottery classes. I told her —'

Rose was borne off; he was left alone and stranded, on the edge of a babbling sea of humanity, interspersed with potted palms. By staring long and hard he could just manage to locate the windows: getting over there was another matter.

'Hi!'

He jumped.

'Carly?'

'Who else?' He had thought, for a moment, that it might be Virginia. 'Where are you off to?'

'Nowhere in particular. Just wandering, aimlessly.'

'That makes two of us. Want to wander together?'

Gratefully, he took her hand.

'Why not?'

They stood for a while, together, at the windows, but the idyll could not last for long. The first to break it was Wanda Sharling, one of the academic staff, on an exchange visit from California. Ludmila, she said, had sent her over to talk to Caroline: Ludmila had also sent Virginia over to talk to Paul. Little by little, by degrees, they became separated. Once more he found himself on his own — except that this time he was on his own with Virginia. After a bit of preliminary skirmishing:

'So glad you could make it,' she said. 'Madame was saying only this morning what a pity it would be if you were to have another of your headaches.'

Just as well he hadn't tried the sprained-ankle trick — or the broken glasses. He wondered if Ludmila had actually gone so far as to voice her suspicions to Virginia. That could be why she had detailed the woman to come and talk to him, to do a bit of probing and find out.

'I don't know why she refers to them as *my* headaches,' he said, 'seeing as I scarcely ever suffer from them.'

'Just when it's convenient?'

There was a mocking note in her voice. He couldn't decide whether she was deliberately carrying out Ludmila's instructions or whether it was a simple case of teasing. It was disconcerting how little one could tell from voices alone. They did say that if you lost one sense those that remained became more acute. He didn't know if that were true or not. It could just be that faute de mieux one learned how to cope. Doubtless, in the not too distant future, he would discover.

'How's the eyesight these days?'

'What?'

'Read any good notes just lately?'

Good notes? What was she talking about, good notes? What did she mean? Doh re mi, a b c —

'I mean, it was there,' said Virginia, 'large as life, lying on the pillow . . . you could hardly blame me for being a bit peeved.'

'Oh!' That sort of note. He knew, now, what she was talking about. She was obviously still nursing a grievance from the night she had gone down to the Saracen's and he had not turned up.

'Over half an hour I waited for you. I felt a right lemon.'

'Yes, I'm sorry about that, I —' He what? He couldn't remember what excuse he'd made, if any. She'd been in too much of a dudgeon at the time to listen to excuses.

'I just don't see how you could have missed it,' said Virginia.

'No; I don't. I suppose I — simply didn't look.'

'I should have thought the bed would be the first place you'd have looked . . . knowing you.'

'Yes —' He sought, desperately, for a way of escape, but there was none: blind men, he was discovering, could not just turn on their heels and walk off. Not unless they were willing to run the risk of crashing headlong into unseen obstacles and knocking themselves senseless, which he was not. Not, at any rate, in company. What he did to himself in private was another matter. He had already cut himself, scalded himself, bruised himself, very nearly decapitated himself.

'How about another little drinkie?' said Virginia.

For just a second he thought she was offering him some. He was about to hold out his glass, when he realised ... she was suggesting he might like to go across to the makeshift bar and replenish hers for her. It presented certain problems (to say the least). The bar was somewhere over by the door: he was somewhere over by the windows. If he cut a straight line across the centre —

The chances were he would knock himself senseless.

It wasn't even a choice between two evils; it wasn't any choice at all. He had no option.

'All right,' he said. 'Let's have your glass.'

The way he saw it — or, to be more accurate, did not see it — he could either strike out boldly and hope for the best, or shuffle with uncertain tread and pray they would take him for drunk. He opted for the former, and struck out, boldly.

It was Hugo, this time, who came to his rescue.

'Where the bloody hell do you think you're going?'

He played it cool: 'Going to get a refill.'

'Oh! I thought for a moment that you were trying to make a quick get-away.'

Why? Why had he thought that? Was he headed in the wrong direction? No, he couldn't be: the drinks table was over by the doors.

'Hellish, isn't it?' Hugo placed a hand on his shoulder, turning him very slightly. (His blood ran cold: he must have been off course.) 'The booze is the only thing that makes it bearable. What are you on? Sootch, or fizzy stuff?'

'Fizzy stuff.' He held out the glass: a hand removed it from him. Hugo's, he presumed. 'It's not for me, it's for Virginia.' Even if it hadn't been, tanking up on a twelve-year old malt (Papa Jo would have none other) would be a mug's game, for one in his situation. He had difficulties enough as it was, without rendering himself even more incapable. He wondered, uneasily, if Hugo had actually noticed that he was off course. 'Where's the She Dragon?' he said.

'The female Fuehrer?' There was a pause, while Hugo (as he must suppose) looked around. For good measure, Paul also made pretence of doing so. Vague blurs moved shadowlike through the mist. He suddenly realised his own folly: Ludmila could be standing within two paces of him and he none the wiser. He really must learn to be more circumspect.

'She's over there,' said Hugo. 'Closing in on Papa Jo.'

Greatly relieved, he turned his head in the direction he remembered Papa Jo to have been sitting.

'Ah, yes.'

'She's going to break it up between him and Meat Loaf . . . that's it. He's been given his marching orders. Too long in one place. Could be dangerous. Here. One glass of fizzy stuff.'

'Thanks.' He reached out a hand, by some happy fluke making contact first time. Now all that remained was to get back again to Virginia. That was not going to be so easy. Perhaps he ought just to stand here and —

'Watch out . . . she's heading this way.' With sudden urgency, Hugo grabbed his arm. 'Let's beat it!'

Somehow or other, by some miracle, the evening was got through. Minor mishaps there were (he had trodden rather hard on someone's foot, and still did not know whose) but no major catastrophe, none of the abject buffoonery which he had feared, though there was a bad minute or two towards the end when finding himself isolated, abandoned without warning in the midst of the hubbub, he came perilously close to panic. His concentration, after almost three hours, had gone, and with it all ability to judge either distance or direction. He could no longer make any sense of the shifting patterns of light and shade which swirled all about him; could no longer distinguish windows from wall (possibly because they had drawn the blinds?) nor tell from sound alone whether the doors lay to his left or to his right. Presence of mind, in that moment, deserted him. Had it not been for Caroline, materialising out of the darkness, he would have lost his head entirely and done something foolish and irrevocable. As it was, he clung to her with the desperate fervour of a drowning man.

'Hey, now!' she said. 'It surely can't be as bad as all that?'

The tone of her voice was rallying, yet seemed to hold a note of compassion. Almost as if she knew — but that was not possible. Nobody knew. Not even Ludmila for certain. He had gone to the greatest of pains to ensure that they should not.

With an effort he pulled himself together; forced himself to speak normally.

'What time is it?'

'Almost fifteen minutes to nine.'

Almost fifteen minutes to nine. Another quarter hour to go. He knew within himself that he couldn't make it; he had had enough, he was through. Ludmila had beaten him. All he wanted was to go home. Back to the Lodge with Caroline, there to lie in her arms, rest his head on her breast and pour out his woes. *No man is an island, brother* — and don't you forget it.

'Carly —'

Why couldn't he say it? Take me home, get me out of here . . . for God's sake, help me!

'Don't worry.' Gently, she prised open his fingers, freeing her arm from his frenzied grip. 'I'll stick around.'

As his panic subsided, he felt ashamed and idiotic.

'Sorry about that.' He attempted a laugh, not too successfully. 'I don't know what came over me . . . I just suddenly felt I was going mad.'

'It's OK,' said Caroline. 'No need to explain.' She

squeezed his hand. 'Just hang loose, it'll soon be over....'

'So there you are,' said Rose. 'It worked.'

'I suppose so.' Hugo acknowledged it, grudgingly. 'After a fashion.'

'What do you mean, after a fashion?'

'Well, it's glaringly obvious, isn't it?' He yanked his tie over his head, not bothering to unknot it, tossing it impatiently on to the chest of drawers. 'You only have to look at him to see that he doesn't know whether he's coming or going ... he'd have walked slap bang into the doorpost if I hadn't stopped him.'

'Yes, but the point is, you did stop him. Didn't you? That was the whole object of the exercise.'

'It won't have fooled Ludmila, don't kid yourself.'

Rose turned, aggressively, from her contemplation of her face in the dressing-table mirror.

'To hear you speak anyone would think you didn't want it to have fooled Ludmila.'

'Yes, well, you already know my views on that. I won't shop him, but I'm far from convinced we're doing him any service, covering up for him like this.'

It had rattled him tonight, seeing Paul amongst a crowd of people. Watching him these last few days — in the staff-room, in the corridors, at home in the Lodge, safe on familiar territory — it had sometimes been difficult to believe that there could be anything seriously amiss. Hugo had, in fact, almost succeeded in persuading himself that the trouble was confined solely to close work, to reading, writing, driving the car. This, obviously, was the reason Paul had not pulled out of conducting. He might not be able to decipher the score when it was directly under his nose, but that scarcely mattered, since he had every note of it inside his head. What mattered was that he could still see well enough over a distance to be able to distinguish what was going on on stage.

Ludmila's little soirée had finally and firmly put paid to that particular illusion. He knew now that Paul could no more distinguish what was going on on stage than he could decipher a score when it was directly beneath his nose: his sight, for all practical purposes, be it near work or far, was non-existent.

'It's not going to be very funny, either for him or anyone else, if he loses his way after the first few bars.'

'Why don't you just leave it to him?' said Rose. 'He knows what he's doing.'

Hugo looked at her, irritably. How did she know whether or not Paul knew what he was doing? It was all very well for her, making these bland, simplistic assumptions: she wasn't the one who was going to have to step in and pull the chestnuts from the fire if he got up there on the first night and went all to pieces.

'He's just as professional as you are, you know.' Rose reached across the dressing-table for her hairbrush. Her belly, as she did so, flopped forward against the pink flannelette of her nightdress. 'You're not the only one round here with standards.'

He was moved to sudden anger: her and her bloody self-righteous pronouncements.

'For Christ's sake, woman! Look at the state of you ... stuffing yourself with chocolates! You look as if you're five months pregnant.'

With a small, unamused smile, Rose began on her nightly ritual of beating her hair.

'Dear me,' she said. 'And there was I, thinking you'd never notice. . . .'

'Don't tell me,' said Ludmila, 'that you didn't notice? She stuck with him like a leech for the last half-hour.'

'Holding hands ... just like the old days.' Papa Jo smiled, benevolently, and made a little crooning noise to himself. 'The lovebirds all over again.'

'Lovebirds, poppycock! She was protecting him —

they were all protecting him. Covering up for the fact that he can't see.'

'*He* can't see?' Papa Jo raised both hands heavenwards. '*She* can't see! There it is, right beneath her very eyes —'

'I can see well enough, I thank you,' said Ludmila, crisply, 'what's beneath *my* eyes.'

What was beneath them right now was a Papa Jo made maudlin by an excess of alcohol. She was wasting her time trying to get through to him. Roughly, she shunted his wheelchair up to the bed.

'Get yourself in there, you drunken old fool.'

With Ludmila's help, Papa Jo heaved his bulk out of the chair.

'Just a useless heap of blubber. That's all I am ... blubber. Like a big white whale on the sea shore.'

'A big white walrus, more like.'

She rolled him into bed, adroitly pulling the covers back. Long years of practice had made her adept. At first when he had been struck down there had been a nurse — two nurses. One for day and one for night. But Papa Jo hadn't liked having nurses. It had affronted his dignity, that strangers should do things for him. Ludmila had been the only one he could tolerate — the only one with whom he felt comfortable. Ludmila, after all, was his wife. What she did, she did for love: what they did, they did for money.

Ludmila had not been a natural, but she had learnt. Over the years, she had accustomed herself. Sometimes, as now, when the whisky had got to him, he became remorseful. Why had he ever taken her out of her rightful setting? She had shone like a jewel — the brightest star in the crown. What a dancer she had been! Pavlova had had nothing on her. And beautiful — so beautiful! Still she was beautiful, even now. But him; what of him? Nothing but a great jellified mound of lard. Couldn't even get himself into bed without her help — couldn't even perform his marital

duties when he got there. How long was it since they
had made love? Half a century? More? He ought never
to have taken her away from the ballet. She ought to
have divorced him, blubbering heap that he was. She
would be better off if he were dead. Why did she not let
him drink, and carouse, and stay up late, and do all the
things that he liked to do? That way, he would soon be
gone and she could enjoy herself once again. Find herself a real man — one who would treat her as she
deserved to be treated.

'A man who can still behave as a man, and not a
eunuch . . . what use have I ever been to you? Couldn't
even give you bambini —'

'Just stop being so self-pitying, you stupid old drivel-
ler! As if I ever wanted any anyway.'

'Ah, you say this just to make me feel better — but *I
know*. I know what you went through.'

No, you don't, thought Ludmila. She climbed into the
bed beside him, reaching up as she did so for the light
switch. Papa Jo had not the least idea what she had
gone through, for the simple reason that she had taken
very good care to keep it from him. She had been
twenty-four at the time — so young, so beautiful! She
had been beautiful: photographs there were in plenty
to tell her so — at the peak of her career, the years of
perfection, leading dancer with the recently-formed
Carnival Ballet of New York, and Papa Jo away in
Europe, on a six-month tour. An abortion had been
easy enough to arrange. He had never even known that
she was pregnant.

She had felt no qualms about it, suffered no pangs of
conscience. Why should she? She had made it very
clear, right from the start, that her career was the
most important element in her life. Even her husband — her rich, handsome husband, with his mass of
thick black hair and Neapolitan charm, and only the
barest hint of the paunch that was to come — even he
must take second place to her career.

The gynaecologist had told her, after the abortion, that she had quite possibly thrown away her only real chance of ever having a child. She had, so he said, 'a bumpy womb': she was most unlikely ever to conceive again. Not, at least, without an operation. She had refused the operation, preferring to live with the bumpy womb. Far from distressing her, the news had brought only relief. She had never told Papa Jo, but she had stopped taking precautions and that had pleased him, good Catholic that he was. He had thought, in his innocence, that it proved him right: Ludmila, at heart, was the same as all other women. She wanted babies, the more the better. Rosy visions of a whole nurseryful of cherubic, bouncing infants had instantly filled his horizon.

For a year or two it had kept him happy, before the dream at last had started to fade as the bouncing infants failed to materialise. Papa Jo had gone to have himself checked out: irony of ironies, he had a low sperm count. Not low enough (as she well knew) to rule out all possibility of his fathering a child, but low enough nonetheless for him to heap all blame upon himself and castigate himself as a failure. Then, for the first time, she had known a few shreds of guilt. By way of reparation she had gone back to the gynaecologist for a progress report on the bumpy womb, but she had left it too late, the condition had deteriorated beyond all hope of amendment. The bumpy womb was removed, and with it Papa Jo's last chance of fatherhood. If three years later she had voluntarily sacrificed the remaining decade of glory which might still have been hers, in order to fulfil that dual rôle of wife-and-nurse which so ill became her, it was, perhaps, no more than she ought to have done — but still it had not been without a severe internal struggle, nor, during the intervening period, had she always been free from private feelings of resentment.

Those feelings had been with her this evening, as she

contrasted herself with Caroline. There was a girl who had the world at her feet. If for any reason she decided against returning to San Diego, not a ballet company between here and the Urals but would be glad of the opportunity to snatch her up. Just so long as she did not tread the same path as all those years ago Ludmila Huhalova had done. . . .

Watching her tonight, with Paul, Ludmila had had the uncanny sensation of stepping back in time, almost three decades ago. There had been a party, she remembered, which she had attended with Papa Jo, a few months after his first stroke: before he had been confined to immobility, but when they had known, already, that he would never sing again. She had been at the same stage of indecision then as she suspected Caroline of being at now, save that in her case there had been the clear call of duty, of loyalty towards a stricken spouse. Caroline need be influenced by neither. Paul had had his chance, many years ago: he had chosen not to take it. She owed him nothing, therefore, and it would be an act of the sheerest folly were she to negate herself and her own gifts out of some mistaken allegiance to whatever bond may once have been between them.

A pity beyond all telling Lies hid in the heart of love . . . but love, thought Ludmila, was a snare and a delusion. Personal fulfilment was all that mattered in this life.

By her side, Papa Jo grunted and gulped in his sleep. He had always slept heavily, even before his strokes. Ludmila, by contrast, had suffered all her life from long bouts of insomnia. His snoring, in the early days, had frequently driven her almost to screaming pitch. Once, long ago, she had suggested separate beds. He had asked her, what was she suggesting, a divorce?

She stretched out a leg across the bed and prodded him, none too gently, with her big toe. The grunting stopped.

'What was that you were trying to tell me,' said Papa Jo, 'about Paul?'

'Don't let it bother you.' She lay on her back, hands folded, madonna-like, over her breast. Thus had she lain on her cold tomb at the end of *Romeo and Juliet*. Miguel Casala had been her Romeo; they had made a good partnership. She wondered what had happened to Miguel. He had been heartbroken when she decided to leave the ballet. He had begged her, pleaded with her, not to desert them. When she had left the Company, so had he. He could not dance, he had said, without his beloved Ludmila. The last she had heard, he had been running his own company down in Buenos Aires. That had been ... how long? Twenty, thirty years? He could be dead by now. If not dead, an old, old man. He had been almost five years her senior. That would make him ... seventy-three. Seventy-three was not so very old. Not if a man were in good health.

'I wish to know!' Papa Jo spoke querulously. 'You said I should speak with him —'

'In the morning.' She turned over, embryo-like, knees curled into belly. (Ballet of the Unhatched Chicks. Miguel had done the choreography.) 'We'll talk about it in the morning.'

11

Paul was up early next morning. Over recent weeks he had taken to setting his travelling alarm for six-thirty and dragging himself out of bed within minutes of its waking him. He was finding, these days, that he needed the extra time. So many small tasks which once he had performed without even stopping to think now required a supreme effort of concentration out of all proportion to the final nature of the achievement. Dressing had become a particularly tedious affair. He tended, so far as circumstances permitted, to stick to the same few, safe, routine garments, and had had the foresight (when still possessed of sufficient vision to make use of such a commodity) to eject all but the soberest of colours from his wardrobe, on the grounds that a chameleon-like merging with the general background was vastly to be preferred to an inadvertent walking of the streets decked out like a maypole. No one, he reasoned, was likely to be startled out of his senses by the sight of a man wearing blue shirt, green sweater, black trousers and brown socks, whereas scarlet and yellow, innocently combined with sky blue and grass green, might conceivably give rise to a certain amount of comment.

His shirts, now, were of three colours only, and each colour cunningly distinguished by its own mark. If the label had been removed, he knew that the shirt was a white one: if the label had been cut in half, that meant it was blue: and if the label were intact, then it was pink.

Socks, likewise, now came only in black and navy, trousers were either charcoal grey or blue denim (easily identified by touch alone), sweaters and ties, like shirts, were distinguished by the state of their labels.

The system, on the whole, worked well — so far as he knew. No one had actually exclaimed out loud at the sight of him; not at least, in his hearing — but still it was time-consuming and fiddly, having to grope his way through labels, the more so when he had the occasional brainstorm and could not for the life of him remember what was supposed to represent what. Part of the problem was that sweaters and ties came in a different assortment of colours from shirts. He wondered how other blind people managed. Maybe their memories were better trained, and they didn't have sudden blank patches when they forgot the meaning of their own specially devised symbols. Or maybe their symbols were simply more obvious — they did not have to contend, as he did, with the need to maintain secrecy. Sometimes, when she had one of her rare bursts of domesticity, Rose would kindly offer to include his washing with hers and Hugo's, or press a few garments for him 'while I'm about it'. It wouldn't do to have distinguishing marks that were too glaringly in evidence. She had already commented on the growing sombreness of his attire, and speculated on the fact of so many of the labels being cut through. It was, she said, exactly what they did in sales.

He had made a mental note, for the future, to avoid sales like the plague. That would really screw his system, to have someone else slashing things in half.

Today being Saturday he didn't bother messing with labels but simply pulled on his dressing-gown (blue silk, purchased for him by Diana. Very fussy about clothes, Diana had been. She wouldn't be at all pleased with the current state of his wardrobe). The time was six-forty. Hopefully, at such an hour, he would be the only one up and about. He liked to get down to the kitchen before any of the others, it meant he could fix breakfast at his own tortoise like pace without being self-conscious. Most of his breakages only came about because he knew he was being watched, which made him nervous and therefore clumsy. He scarcely broke anything at all when left to his own devices.

This morning, when he arrived down there, he was disconcerted to find there was someone else already in occupation. He sensed it the minute he opened the kitchen door. (Perhaps they were right after all about one's remaining senses growing more acute: he found now, as a rule, that he was immediately aware of another's presence.)

'Hi.' It was Rose. She was somewhere over by the sink. 'You're up early.'

'I might say the same for you.'

'I know, I couldn't sleep. I've been lying awake half the night, thinking. Want a cup of tea? I'm just putting the kettle on.'

'Love one.' Carefully, he pulled a chair out from the table and sat down. 'What's kept you so busy, then?'

'Hugo,' said Rose. He heard the soft slip-slop of her slippers across the flagstoned floor; the clatter of the kettle being placed on the stove, the scrape of a match and the small sizzle as it ignited. 'He's suddenly gone all soppy and sentimental and wants us to get married.'

'Oh? What's brought that on?'

'This, basically.'

This? for a second, he panicked. What was this? Something he was supposed to be looking at?

'Feel,' said Rose. She had come over to him; was taking his hands and pressing them to her belly. It felt soft, and pleasantly rounded.

'My goodness!' he said. 'Who's been eating a lot of chocolates?'

'Aproximately five months' worth,' said Rose.

'Five months?' He was startled. Rose was five months pregnant and he had never noticed? How did one explain that away? Someone might at least have had the goodness to mention it to him.

'Oh, don't worry,' said Rose. 'You're not the only one . . . Hugo didn't know himself until last night.'

'You mean, *he* didn't notice?'

'Would you expect him to?'

'Well —' He laughed. He could afford to laugh, now. He obviously wasn't the only one with defective eyesight. 'I would have thought, being so intimate as you are —'

'That he could scarcely fail . . . wonderful, isn't it? I should say he's the one that could do with wearing glasses, not you.'

For all the good they did, Hugo was welcome to them. He only went on wearing them for show; in moments when he could be sure of being alone, he invariably removed them. He put up a finger to push them further up his nose, a reflex gesture governed entirely by habit, and realised at the last minute that he hadn't bothered to put them on. Feeling foolish, he changed course, digging his hand into his pocket and bringing out his handkerchief instead.

'So the discovery's brought on a fit of the old let's-settle-down-and-be-respectables, has it?'

'You'd better believe it,' said Rose. 'I honestly never knew he was so *bourgeois* . . . he'll be wanting a mortgage and life assurance next.'

'What's the problem? You don't fancy the idea?'

'Well, really,' said Rose. 'In this day and age . . . what on earth is the point?'

What, indeed? Not very much, as far as he and Diana had been concerned.

'How about keeping Hugo happy?'

'But it's such a negation of principle! Everything I most strongly don't believe in. It surely can't be right to do what one doesn't believe in simply in order to keep someone else happy . . . I mean, would *you*?'

Some might say that he had — and had received his just deserts.

'I don't know, Rosie.' He shook his head. 'I'm hardly the best person to come to if it's advice you want, the mess I've made of things. I'm not exactly a shining example, am I?'

She was silent a moment, doing things over by the sink.

'Why *did* you marry Diana?' she said. She came back to the table, clinking cups. 'Or would you rather I didn't ask?'

'I don't mind you asking; I'm just not sure that I know the answer. . . . Because I was infatuated, I suppose.'

'Yes; that's what Hugo says.'

Oh! It was, was it?

'He always says you should have married Caroline — if you were going to marry anyone, that is.'

'Hugo seems to do rather a lot of pontificating.'

'Well, naturally,' said Rose, 'we discuss you.'

'Oh! Naturally.'

'Well, it is natural! Don't be silly, you can't expect us not to take an interest in you.'

He wasn't too sure, just at this moment, that he wanted people to take an interest in him. Only let them overdo it and take a bit too much, and they would stumble upon truths he had no wish for them to stumble on.

'I thought,' he said, mildly, 'that we were talking about you and whether or not you were going to make Hugo happy?'

'And what about him making *me* happy?'

'Wouldn't he?'

'Oh! I don't know. I expect so.' Rose opened the refrigerator and clonked a bottle of milk on to the table. 'One can't look for perfection, after all. It's just that I do sometimes get rather worried.'

'What about?'

'Well —' She was standing by the table, rustling something. 'If he'd been alive in Hitler's Germany, you don't think he'd have been one of those people who put Art Above All Else and simply closed their eyes to what was going on, do you?'

'Probably — left to himself. But not if you'd been there.'

'Hm.' Opening a fresh packet of tea, that was what she must be doing. Now she was pouring the contents into the tea caddy — taking it over to the teapot. 'So you're saying it's my bounden duty to marry him? To act as his conscience, stop him turning fascist.'

'Well, I wouldn't put it quite as strongly as all that, but I do believe you have a certain humanising influence over him. Seriously, Rosie —' he wondered if he dared risk going over to her. Better not. She might be holding kettles of boiling water — 'he's not so bad, old Hugo.'

'No, so he informs me. *He* says —' just as well he hadn't risked going over, she was busy pouring water into the teapot — 'he says I could do a damn sight worse.'

'So you could.'

'Yes, well, of course, I'd expect you to say that. Why is it, I wonder, that men are always so matey-matey?'

'The other day you were complaining they were war-like!'

'They're both,' said Rose. 'When they're matey-matey it's because they're ganging up together to make war on women.'

'I see.'

'No, you don't, you don't see anything.' How true. How very true. 'Men never do,' said Rose. 'They're idiots. Why don't you ask Caroline to stay on?'

Now what was she up to?

'To what purpose?' he said, casually.

'To live with you . . . *Come live with me and be my Love, And we will all the pleasures prove That hills and valleys, dale and field,* etc. etc.' Vigorously, Rose banged the lid down on the teapot. 'You know the sort of thing.'

'That was Christopher Marlowe,' he said. 'He was a homosexual.'

193

'So what? It's all the same. Why don't you ask her?'

'Because I don't think she'd particularly want to live with me and be my love.'

'She might. How do you know if you don't ask?'

How did you ask if you'd nothing to offer? Lightly, he said 'I see you're taking it for granted that *I* should like it.'

'Well . . . wouldn't you?'

It would have been safer by far to deny it — better for his pride, as well. *Oh, I'm through with all that sort of nonsense! I'm going to concentrate on being a fulltime misogynist from now on.* The words were there: he just couldn't find the wherewithal to articulate them.

'Wouldn't you?' said Rose.

'Whether I would or I wouldn't . . . it's too late, Rosie. Far too late.'

'Why?' She had come back to the table; was sitting down, next to him. 'Why is it too late?'

'Apart from anything else —' he strove for jocularity, which was something that didn't suit him even at the best of times: he had never been a jocular sort of person — 'apart from anything else, there's friend Larry, isn't there?'

'You don't want to let him put you off.'

No? When he had his full complement of senses? Probably had eyes like a hawk, didn't even need glasses for reading.

'After all,' said Rose, 'you're here on the spot, he's several thousand miles away.'

'Yes, and rings her without fail two or three times every week.'

'She doesn't seem to get too excited by it.'

'She wouldn't; she's not the type.' Just as he was not jocular, Caroline was not excitable. Caught between the volatility of Raul, and the neuroses of Linda, Caroline had educated a calm gravity, an almost remoteness, which alone, perhaps, had allowed her to survive the maelstrom of her earlier years. He had often wondered, if she had permitted herself a degree less control, screamed a bit louder for her share of the attention, whether he might have avoided the fatal mistake of Diana.

'It's always worth a try,' said Rose. 'I'm all for people trying.' She picked up the teapot: he heard her pouring tea. 'Are you coming?'

'Coming where?' he said.

'Back upstairs.'

'Oh. No, I think I'll stay down now I'm here. Get some breakfast.'

'At seven o'clock? On a *Saturday*? Don't be so daft!' Rose picked up her tray and walked to the door. He would have opened it for her, except that he was scared of hitting her in the face. 'Breakfast's on me this morning . . . bacon and eggs for four. Or would you prefer kedgeree? You'd better make the most of it while it's offered, it might be another eighteen months before I come over all domestic again.' Her voice, by now, had gone out into the hall. She called to him, impatiently. 'Aren't you coming? I've got your tea on the tray.'

It seemed he had no option. There was a growing number of things, these days, about which he had no option. Options, he had to conclude, contracted at roughly the same rate as vision. Soon there would come a time when he didn't have any at all. Then it would always be 'Do what you're told', 'Go where you're taken', 'Eat what you're given'.

Rose came to a sudden halt at the top of the stairs. He only just managed to avoid a head-on collision.

'I've got a cup here for Caroline,' she said. 'Why don't you take it in to her?'

'Well?' Ludmila looked militantly at Papa Jo. 'What do you intend to do about it?'

Papa Jo, uncomfortable, hunched a shoulder.

'I dunno . . . it's maybe not so bad as you think.'

'For heaven's sakes!' She turned, impatiently, and began slapping cream on to her cheeks. 'He can't even see to cross the room! If it hadn't been for Caroline and the others running to his rescue every five minutes he'd have fallen flat on his face ... I tell you, it was a conspiracy. Anything rather than let the old She Dragon know.'

Papa Jo, a large pink mound clothed in striped nightgown, sat silent and troubled against the pillows.

'There has to be some reason.'

'Of course there's some reason! He knows darn well that as soon as it comes out into the open his job is in jeopardy —'

'No!' The word was rapped out, unexpectedly firm. Ludmila, exasperated, laid down her pot of cold cream.

'What do you mean, no?'

'I mean no!' Papa Jo thumped a hand the size of a carpet bag on to the bedside table, setting glass and water jug in vibrant motion. 'No, and no, and no! Paul is a good teacher, he has done excellent service to this school. He stays. No matter. I don't argue.'

She tightened her lips.

'And the Festival? He still gets to conduct?'

'If he thinks he can do it, he will do it. If he thinks that he cannot, then he will come to me.'

'When?'

'When he feels good and ready is when! We have to trust him.'

Ludmila shook her head.

'Papa, you're a fool ... the Festival is only three short weeks away. This is one time when sentimentality has no place. We can't afford just to sit back and wait.'

'We can afford! What do you think Hugo does all this time? Twiddle with his thumb? He knows the score as well as Paul.'

'I still think you should talk with him.'

'And what do I say?'

'You ask him! You put it to him: is he having difficulties? If so, is there anything that can be done, or is it going to be permanent? Is there going to get *worse*? If it's going to get worse, then how does he propose to organise himself? He can't just go on as if it's not happening. He has certain loyalties to the school. We need to know ... is he going to be here with us next term? Is he going to be able to cope? We have to plan, and so does he.'

Papa Jo heaved a sigh. It travelled in ripples down his body.

'If this is true, it is a tragedy,' he said.

'Sure it's a tragedy! But it's no good closing your eyes to it. That doesn't help Paul, it doesn't help anyone.'

There was a silence.

'Well, if you're not going to speak to him,' said Ludmila, 'I guess I'll have to.'

'I'll speak with him, I'll speak with him! Just give me a day or two. I need time.'

'Time is exactly what you don't have.'

'Please,' said Papa Jo, 'be reasonable ... it's only yesterday you tell to me all this. It has come as a shock. I have to think out what I am to say.'

It was a pity, reflected Ludmila, that he did not more often adhere to such a principle. It would save a great deal of unnecessary embarrassment.

'Leave it with me,' said Papa Jo. 'I reflect on it.'

'Hi, there!' said Rose. 'We've brought you some tea.'

'Oh ... that's nice.'

Caroline, sitting up in bed, saw Paul and Rose framed together in the doorway. Rose had on a pink flannelette nightie, Paul was wearing his blue silk dressing-gown.

'There you go,' said Rose. She thrust the tray into Paul's hands, briskly removed a couple of cups and gave him a little nudge forward. 'See you for breakfast in about an hour. OK?'

'OK,' said Paul. He seemed a trifle dazed. He stood,

with the tray, as Rose hooked a foot round the bottom of the door, adroitly closing it behind her as she made her exit.

'Here,' said Caroline. She scrambled out of bed. 'Let me get it.' Meekly, he surrendered it to her. 'Rose is up a bit betimes, isn't she?'

'Yes. She's been awake half the night pondering the vexed question —' he moved towards the bed; seated himself, none too certainly, on the edge of it — 'of whether or not to make Hugo a happy man.'

'Don't tell me he actually wants them to get married?'

'On account of the baby. You knew about that, of course?'

'Rose told me, a few days back.'

'Would that someone had told *me*. Would you believe, I hadn't even noticed?'

Yes, she thought; I'd believe. She ought to have passed on the news, but there hadn't really been an opportunity.

Correction: there had been plenty of opportunity, she just hadn't cared to make use of it.

'I take it,' she said, 'that Hugo's pretty bucked?'

'I suppose he must be, wanting to make an honest woman of her ... poor old Rose! She thinks it's the beginning of the end.'

She handed him his tea.

'In some ways, I guess it is.'

'Oh?' He raised an eyebrow. She noticed that he wasn't wearing his glasses. He looked vulnerable, almost naked, without them: stripped of all form of defence.

'Well, nothing can ever be quite the same again,' she said, 'can it? Maybe for Hugo; certainly not for Rose.'

'It was her choice. She didn't have to have it.'

She looked at him.

'Meaning what, exactly?'

'Well —' He shrugged. 'She could have got rid of it.'

Caroline made a sudden, angry gesture.

'All this glib talk! Get rid of it . . . what do you think it is? A bad tooth?'

The gesture was lost on him: the tone of her voice was not. He seemed surprised.

'I thought you were one of the pro-abortion lobby?'

'Nobody's *pro* abortion, for Christ's sake! Abortion's a last resort, not a first option. Why does everyone always have to try and make it sound so goddamn *cosy*?'

He pulled a face.

'I'm only going by what Rose has always said.'

Crossly, because the point was valid, she snapped: 'Yes, so now she's discovered different!'

Simple envy, that was all it was, Simple envy of Rose, who had been braver than she and now had a five-month-old embryo inside her to prove it. She didn't have to take it out on Paul. It wasn't his fault.

'The chances are,' he said 'that once she's had this one she'll get bitten by the bug and start screaming for more. It would never surprise me. She's always struck me as being basically the maternal type.'

'Is that so?'

'Well, let's face it, she's not exactly what you'd call a hard-bitten career woman, is she? I can see that for someone like you the choice would obviously be far more fraught.'

Why? Because she *was* a hard-bitten career woman? My career, right or wrong? First, last, and all the time? Resentment welled up anew. All very well saying it wasn't his fault: if he hadn't gone and married Diana —

'What's the matter?' asked Paul.

She swallowed.

'Nothing's the matter.'

'Did I say something I shouldn't?'

Yes: five years ago, when you walked up the aisle and said 'I do'. She pushed her hair back over her shoulders.

'Drink your tea.'

He sipped it, thoughtfully. She could see he was still

trying to puzzle out what it was he had done to upset her.

'I'm sorry about last night, by the way,' he said.

'Last night?' He hadn't upset her last night.

'All the fuss I made. At the end.'

'Oh! That.'

He had stood there by himself, lost and forlorn, in the centre of the room, like a dog abandoned in a snowstorm. She hadn't been aware, at first. It had been Hugo, frantically signalling to her over Ludmila's head, who had drawn attention to his plight. When she had gone to him, and he had realised who it was, he had clung to her in a way which plainly betokened he had very nearly reached the end of his tether. If he could only bring himself to give up the unequal struggle and admit that he needed help, it would surely make life so much easier?

'I honestly don't know what came over me . . . I just suddenly felt that if I didn't get out I should start screaming. A sort of temporary claustrophobia, I suppose.'

Still he felt the need to justify: the need to explain.

'Paul, you don't have to,' she said. 'I do understand, I promise you.'

He looked at her, warily. His gaze — she couldn't help remarking it — was not quite focused. It was more noticeable without his glasses.

'I've always been an idiot at parties, haven't I?' he said. There was a note almost of pleading in his voice: confirm that I have always been an idiot! Confirm that it's not something new.

'Pretty well always,' she said.

'Was there ever a time when I wasn't?'

'Perhaps when you were a little boy —'

'No,' he said. 'I remember once grizzling in a corner because I wanted to go home.' He grinned, a trifle ruefully — but happy, all the same that he had averted danger. 'Seems as if I haven't changed much, doesn't it?'

'I guess it does, she said.

'I asked him,' said Rose. 'I said to him . . . why on earth did you ever go and marry her?'

'Really,' said Caroline. She didn't want to talk about Paul marrying Diana. She didn't want to hear about them. Not first thing on a Monday morning. She reached behind her, into the cupboard, for the cereal packet. 'Someone's gone and swiped the Rice Krispies!'

'Here,' said Rose. She brought them up off the floor.

'What in God's name are they doing down there?'

'I put them down there; just now. Out of the way. Anyhow, as I was saying —'

As she was saying, she had inquired of Paul why he had married Diana, and Paul had said that he supposed he must have been infatuated.

How very interesting. She slopped milk on to her Rice Krispies.

So what?

So that just went to prove, said Rose, that he had never really been in love with her. Only thought that he had.

So what difference was that supposed to make? It hadn't stopped him going ahead and marrying her, had it? Living with her, sleeping with her —

'Hugo always says,' said Rose, 'that he should have married you. If he'd had any sense.'

She spooned up a mouthful of Rice Krispies and concentrated on eating them.

'Of course —' Rose spoke wistfully — 'I suppose it's a bit late in the day now. From your point of view, I mean. You've already found someone else.' She paused, in hopeful fashion. Caroline remained mute. 'And anyway, one has to face it . . . it's not everyone would want to take on the responsibility of a man in Paul's situation. I mean, assuming there's nothing that can be done. Which, of course, there very well might be. I mean, you'd think there'd be something. Surgery, or something. Wouldn't you?'

'You would,' said Caroline. He must presumably have looked into it. He wouldn't go down without a fight. As Rose had said, you'd think there'd be something.

'If there isn't,' said Rose, 'it's going to make life pretty tough for him. Heaven only knows how he'll manage.'

'He'll manage.' Caroline swallowed the last of her Rice Krispies and took the empty dish across to the sink. She couldn't sit here discussing Paul, she had a class in twenty minutes. 'People always do, one way or another.'

She had managed — one way or another — when she had thought her heart was breaking. She had gone on that same night and danced the name part in *Giselle* as she had never danced it before. (And, please God, would never dance it again.) Hearts did not break and life did not stop. Paul would manage.

'Do I take it you're off?' said Rose. She sounded reproachful. She had obviously been looking forward to a nice, cosy, female chat about Paul and Caroline finally getting it together after all — but of course it wasn't everyone would want to take on the responsibility of a man in Paul's situation. Certainly not a hard-bitten careerist putting personal achievement above all else.

Deliberately, Caroline rinsed the Rice Krispie bowl and up-ended it in the rack.

'I'd like to stay and gossip,' she said. 'Unfortunately, I do have other commitments.' If hard-bitten careerist was how they thought of her, then she might just as well live up to her image. 'Have a good day.'

As if the heavy innuendo of Rose were not sufficient she found herself subjected, later in the morning, to the weighty tread of Papa Jo's elephantine trampling. He shot out of a door, conspiratorially, in his wheelchair, as she was passing on her way from class. He had, quite obviously, been lying in wait.

'Psst! Caroline!' He beckoned. 'A word with you.'

In her innocence, she wondered what he wanted: it was, inevitably, to talk about Paul. Suddenly, everybody wanted to talk about Paul.

'If what Madame says is correct, that he really and truly doesn't see so well any more, then what is he to do? Who is he to turn to? For my part, when disaster came, I had Madame. I thank the good Lord that I did! Without her, I should not have survived — I should not, to tell truth, have wished to do so. But Paul . . . who has he? No one! In the wide world . . . no one! This woman, this Diana —' he made a noise indicative of contempt. 'A painted butterfly! More useless than a butterfly. She doesn't even give him bambini. And not even ashamed of it! She talks of it, quite openly. I ask her one time, and you know what she says? Oh, Papa Jo, she says, you're so out of date! You're so behind the times! Everybody takes the pill these days, she says . . . this is a married woman that talks! And then she walks out on him. She leaves him, by himself, when most he has need of her . . . crippled in an accident, unable to see —'

'Papa Jo!' She was moved to protest. God knows, she had no love for Diana, but this was heaping blame where none existed. 'I never heard that he was *crippled* — and the chances are Diana never even got to be told about the problem with his eyes. It's presumably only got really bad these last couple of months. People would have noticed otherwise.'

'Well, anyway —' Papa Jo brushed aside her objections: they played no part in his argument — 'the fact remains . . . who is he to turn to? Who is to care for him? *She* will not; that is very obvious. Rose is to have her baby, you will go back to America —' he paused; looking at her, hopefully. She said nothing. Papa Jo sighed. 'You will go back to America, and then where will he be? Left to struggle all by himself.'

Just as I was, thought Caroline. Papa Jo was even less subtle in his approach than Rose. She found herself torn between an exasperated affection on the one hand and growing feelings of resentment on the other. She did not doubt but that Papa Jo's concern was equally as disinterested, equally as benevolent, as that of Rose; still she could do without being dragooned. Let Paul plead his own case — he did it quite eloquently enough without the need of their intervention. Impossible to look on him as he had been the other night, at Ludmila's soirée, without experiencing a pang: without knowing an impulse to yield to those emotions which still came most naturally to her where Paul was concerned.

'All men need a good woman.' It was one of Papa Jo's favourite hobby horses. 'No man can manage on his own — am I not here to testify? But Paul . . . how is he to find one? Now?'

'I shouldn't imagine he'd have too much difficulty,' said Caroline. He never had had, in the past. They had come flocking. Hurled themselves at his feet, like so many silly garden flowers, asking to be trampled on. She supposed, looking back, that she had hurled herself along with all the rest.

No; that was untrue. She had never hurled herself. She had lingered, a shrinking violet in the shadows, waiting for him to reach out a hand and graciously pluck her from obscurity when once he had tired of all the pushing, bright-coloured daffodils, the flaunting fuchsias and aristocratic orchids lying crushed and wilted beneath his feet. It had never happened. One of the aristocratic orchids had stolen a march: had gone waltzing in ahead of her and carried off the prize.

'Well, well,' said Papa Jo. 'There is nothing one can do, alas! Paul has chosen his bed and now he must sleep in it. Not all women are so ready to make sacrifice as Madame. She is something special; I have always known this. If Paul had only had the good sense — but that is enough talking of Paul! Let us talk of you, instead. When do you return to your ballet company?'

Oh, Papa Jo! thought Caroline. You are so transparent. . . .

'I haven't yet decided,' she said.

'Ah.' He digested this. 'So you haven't yet decided?

'Not yet.'

She still had another few weeks before she need take the final step of committing herself. She supposed, when the time came, she would probably do so — if Larry were still going ahead with the divorce. He had assured her, the last occasion on which they had spoken, that everything was in the pipeline.

'But you know these lawyers . . . take their goddamn time.'

She wasn't sure, even now, whether she really believed him.

'So,' said Papa Jo. 'You are in two minds, hm?'

'Two?' she said. 'Half a dozen! Papa Jo, I have to dash . . . I promised Madame I'd look in on her juniors.'

'Sure,' he said. 'You go.' He waved her away, happy at the discovery he had made: she hadn't yet decided. . . .

'Hasn't yet decided?' said Ludmila. She looked with narrowed green eyes at Papa Jo. What had the interfering old buzzard been up to this time? 'What do you mean, she hasn't yet decided?'

'She hasn't yet decided whether or not she goes back.'

'Of course she's going back! Larry Sundquist's writing a new ballet for her. She told me all about it. What were you doing, talking with her, anyway?'

'Oh —' Papa Jo wafted a hand. 'Just sounding her out.'

'You have no business to be just sounding her out!

You stick to your own side of things. Paul's your pigeon: Caroline is mine. Lord alone knows what harm you may have done.'

'No harm.' Papa Jo beamed. 'Maybe when she stays to marry him, you will say, for once, that I have done a good job. . . .'

12

On Thursday morning, just as class was finishing, Virginia appeared in the studio with a message that Ms Ramirez was wanted urgently on the telephone. Caroline glanced automatically towards Ludmila, seeking permission. One might be Ms Ramirez, but still one did not absent oneself from class without having officially been dismissed.

'Please!' Ludmila, all graciousness, inclined her head towards the door. 'It could be business.'

It seemed hardly likely, since almost nobody knew that she was here. She had purposely kept quiet about her visit to Bampton. She had wanted the time to herself, a period in which to reflect and be at peace, away both from Larry's sphere of influence and the public eye. She had impressed this on Paul before she came, and she knew that he had passed it on, for at their very first encounter Ludmila had assured her her desire for privacy would be respected.

'I know what it's like to be always under scrutiny . . . my God, don't I! Two and a half decades I had of it, right from when I was thirteen years old, when I danced *Les Présages* for de Basil. The baby ballerinas they used to call us . . . Danilova, Riabouchinska, Baronova, Huhalova . . . oh, I was glad to get out, I can tell you! One can have just a little too much of it, public adulation.'

In her own way, Caroline often thought, Ludmila was as easily readable as Papa Jo. More devious, perhaps, but every bit as transparent.

'I don't know who it is,' said Virginia, as she led the way to the office. 'He didn't say. But a man of some kind.'

The man of some kind turned out to be Larry. He had never called her at the school before — she was faintly surprised that he should even remember the name of it. He was always stubbornly resistant to memorising details of her life in England. Just as Paul was always 'this guy you went to school with', so Bampton tended to be 'this place you studied at'. She never knew whether it was pretence, or whether he had, quite genuinely, managed to expunge the names from his consciousness.

'Did I get you out of class?' he said.

Wonders would never cease: he had even registered the fact that she was taking class every morning. . . .

'No,' she said. 'We were just through.'

'I guessed you might be.' He sounded smug. 'I timed it specially . . . to the dot.'

She was suspicious.

'Why aren't you still nicely tucked up in your bed?'

'At this hour of the day?'

'Well —' She did some rapid finger calculations. 'Unless you've taken to exceptionally early rising —'

'Ten o'clock's not that early. I'm usually out by that time.'

She held the receiver from her ear, regarding it frowningly for a second.

'Where are you?'

'Paris.'

'*Paris?*'

'I suddenly got chica-sick . . . couldn't stand the thought of not seeing you for another three weeks. Listen, how long will it take you to get over? Couple of hours?'

'Larry, I told you!' She could have wished that Virginia were not here. Had she known it was going to be Larry, she would have had the call transferred some-

208

where more private. 'I can't get away, I'm committed.'

'So get uncommitted! I've made all the arrangements this end. Just give me a call when you know which flight you're on, and I'll come and pick you up. You have a pen handy? I'll give you my number. It's one-four —'

'Hang on.' She turned, and gesticulated at Virginia. 'Do you have a pen and paper? Thanks. OK, go ahead.' She took down the number, and the name and address of the hotel. He had already, it seemed, booked them both in; taking it for granted that she would meekly do his bidding.

'Larry, this is ridiculous,' she said. 'I really just can't walk out on people like this.'

'You'd rather walk out on me? After I've come all this way to see you?'

She might have retorted that if he had wanted to see her as badly as all that, he could just as easily have caught the plane to London as to Paris — could just as easily, even now, jump on the next flight and come over to Bampton. Thoughts of Larry and of Bampton, however, did not merge happily together: she left the words unsaid. Out of the corner of her eye, she saw Virginia sorting files in a filing cabinet.

'Look, why don't I call you back later?'

'When you've got your flight booked. Like I said. Do you go from London, or is there some place nearer?'

'London, I should think, but —'

'Whichever way, you have to be here by tonight. I'm not sleeping by myself again. You know the way I feel about hotel beds. It's been bad enough back home, these last few weeks. I've really missed you — you know that? Really one hell of a lot. I'll be honest, I wasn't too sure that I would. I mean, I knew I *would*; what I didn't know was just how much. Well, now I do. Now I've discovered. And I'm here to tell you, I really don't like it, not having you around. I need you, you dumb chica. I sometimes think you don't quite appreciate that. You think, oh, Larry, he doesn't give a damn.

He has his work, that's all he cares about. Well, maybe that's the impression I put over, but if so it certainly isn't the right one. I mean, what I'm trying to say, I just don't function without you. Not physically, not spiritually, not any damn way. Why else would I suddenly drop everything and come running? Larry Sundquist chasing half round the world after some dumb chica who stands there and says she's *otherwise committed*? Can you imagine the havoc that would wreak with my image? It's already wreaking havoc with my psyche. It just is not what I expect of myself. This is the first time in my life that I have ever *chased*. You know what I mean? I am not a chasing sort of guy. So don't give me any more of that committed bullshit. You want to see me still a whole man, you do like I did . . . you drop everything and you come. Right now. OK?'

'Larry! For heaven's sake!' She was torn, as so often with him, midway between laughter and exasperation. 'What you're asking me to do —'

'Is drop everything and come . . . *now*. For my sake. Because I need you . . . *please*?'

She hesitated.

'Look, I can't just — I mean — I'd have to consult with Ludmila.'

'So go and consult with her!' She noticed he didn't make any pretence of not knowing who Ludmila was. To forget the names of Huhalova and Terrazzas would be going a bit too far along the path of absurdity even for Larry. She was faintly amazed, all the same, at his being so readily amenable to the idea of consultation. A brief 'Fuck Ludmila!' would have been more in accord with the Larry she knew and loved. 'You run along' he said, 'and ask her, then call me back and tell me which flight you're arriving on — and when I say arriving, I mean today. Got it?'

Thoughtfully, she replaced the handset.

'Everything all right?' said Virginia, brightly.

'Yes . . . fine. Do you have any idea where I would

find Madame right now?'

Virginia turned her neat copper-gold head to look at the master timetable, pinned behind her on the wall.

'Right now, she's probably in her study.'

'Is it OK if I go along there?'

'Oh, I'm sure,' said Virginia. 'Seeing as it's *you*. . . .'

If she had been surprised by Larry's amenableness, she was even more so by Ludmila's. She would have expected at the very least a sharp reminder that 'success brings its own obligations . . . never forget, when you get to the top, what you owe to those still at the bottom.' It had been one of her favourite maxims, back in student days. Now she seemed cavalierly unconcerned for those still at the bottom: her interest lay solely in those at the top.

'Of course you must go over to Paris! If that's where your choreographer is, that's where you ought to be.'

'I'd just feel so bad,' said Caroline, 'suddenly abandoning all the kids.'

Just feel so bad, she might more truthfully have said, suddenly abandoning Paul. Not that he had any claims on her. He had long since forfeited his right to make emotional demands, and indeed was not doing so — or not in any conscious manner. Still she could not be quite easy, turning her back on him. She had thought Ludmila would put up more of a fight. She had given her every opportunity.

'That was Larry,' she had said, 'calling from Paris. He wants me to drop everything and go over there. I told him I couldn't possibly, I'm fully committed here at Bampton.'

Now here was Ludmila, actually urging her to go.

'If Sundquist wants you in Paris, then you get off there straight away. The children have already enjoyed an unexpected bonus. Nobody could expect you to stay on just for their sake. Go tell Virginia to arrange a flight for you.'

Virginia, at her most efficient, had her booked

within seconds on to a flight leaving from Gatwick at
16.00 hours. Dutifully, she called Larry to tell him, and
then was faced with the task of breaking it to Paul. It
was not one which she relished. When she discovered,
from Meat Loaf, that both he and Hugo were closeted
with Papa Jo and the principals up in one of the main
rehearsal rooms and were likely to be there for the rest
of the day, she could not in honesty have denied that
relief was the first emotion to flood over her. She hastened
back to the Lodge, packed a couple of bags,
called a cab, scribbled a quick note — *Paul, forgive
abrupt departure, have had to go off to Paris unexpectedly
re ballet. Will be back in time for Jane, never fear!
Love, C.* — propped it in a prominent position on the
kitchen table and was off.

It was only later, sitting on the British Airways jet
that was taking her to Larry, that she realised what
she had done: she had left him a note which she was
almost certain he could no longer see sufficiently to
read. The one consoling thought was that Rose would
be bound to reach home before he did. Rose would read
it. Rose would find some way of telling him. And tomorrow,
or in a day or so, she would call him from Paris.

Six-thirty am. Paul reached out a hand and punched
the alarm, somewhat irritably, into silence. He lay for
a while, trying to muster the necessary strength of
mind to peel back the covers and start on the tedious
business of gathering up the day's apparel. The inclination
to do so was even less than usual. A general
feeling of malaise hung about him, weighing him down,
turning his limbs to lead, his head a block of concrete
atop a body too feeble to move. It was like the early
days all over again — the days immediately after
Bradbeer had finally admitted that his luck had run out
and there was nothing that anyone could do. He had
woken every morning, then, feeling as he felt now.

But he was supposed to have beaten it, wasn't he?

He was supposed to have come to terms with it — to have accepted the fact that he was going blind (to all intents and purposes *had* gone blind). He had determined that it was not going to make any difference: he was going to be one of those who learnt how to cope. For crying out loud, he *was* coping! Hadn't he coped with Ludmila's soirée? More by good luck, perhaps, than good judgement, but still he had survived. Ludmila might suspect, but she didn't actually know. Nor did Rose and Hugo, they hadn't the least idea. Nor, most important of all, had Caroline. If she had, she would never have gone off to Paris without saying goodbye.

Angrily, he threw back the bedclothes. This was ridiculous! Ridiculous and pathetic! That a grown man — he snatched, at random, at the first shirt that came to hand — that a grown man should lapse into infantile self-pity all because he hadn't been said goodbye to. Common sense told him that it hadn't been feasible. He wouldn't have thanked her for bursting in on a rehearsal, and anyway she was far too professional even to dream of it. If she'd left him a note he couldn't have read it; not unless she'd printed it in caps two inches high, and even caps, these days, were starting to defeat him. She, on the other hand, was not to know that. So why hadn't she left one for him? He ignored, for the moment, the question of what he would have done if she had: the hurtful thing was that she had *not*. It had been Rose who had broken it to him.

'Apparently she was called over to Paris quite suddenly. Something to do with the new ballet. She's promised to be back in time for *Jane*.'

Back in time for *Jane* — and then what? He felt round for his jeans, which seemed mysteriously to have disappeared. Off to the States, with friend Larry?

Well, and why not? What else did he expect her to do? Sit around at Bampton ministering to his every least little need? It was no part of her mission in life to act as unpaid guide dog; nor would he want it to be. So drop the self-pity, all right? Just snap out of it. Pull yourself together.

The jeans were on the floor: he ran them to earth by the simple, if inadvertent, expedient of catching his foot in them and nearly sprawling headlong. He just managed to stifle the four-letter word which rose to his lips. (Not out of any regard for the purity of his language, merely to avoid waking Rose and Hugo. Yesterday evening, on his way to bed, he had tripped over a piece of torn linoleum in the bathroom and sent a glass tooth mug shattering to the floor. It had caused practically a full-scale panic. Hugo had arrived at the gallop, even Rose had put on a bit of a spurt. He didn't want to do anything else foolish; not just yet a while.)

From nine until ten that morning he had a composition class: from ten-thirty until twelve an orchestral rehearsal. The former he could cope with quite adequately. He had a modus operandi worked out which seemed to suit both himself and his pupils, causing the minimum of embarrassment to himself, the minimum of inconvenience to them. Were composition classes all he had to contend with, he could have contemplated at least the immediate future without too much foreboding. Alas, they were not: orchestral sessions had also to be got through.

Vaingloriously, for a while, he had kept up the pretence that such sessions held no fears. A bunch of kids was a bunch of kids — and Bampton Hall a select establishment in the heart of the Cotswolds. Had it been a tough comprehensive in the Liverpool Docks he might have had some cause to liken himself, as he mounted the rostrum, to Daniel entering the lions' den. It was not, however; and if he couldn't control sixty highly-motivated and well-intentioned eleven-to-sixteen-year-olds, then he wasn't fit to call himself a teacher. Blind or sighted, it should make no difference: sheer force of personality, together with the authority vested in him, should be sufficient to carry the day. Such, at least, had been the theory. Over the weeks, sixty highly-motivated and well-intentioned eleven-to-sixteen-year-olds had slowly but surely eroded it, until now there was nothing left to cling to and he was down to hard, rock-bottom, unpalatable truth: such sessions scared the shit out of him.

Today's, deceivingly, set off with a bang, on time and without a hitch. The kids were all settled and in their places, ready and eager; he himself managed to get from door to platform without fumbling, stumbling, tripping over unseen objects or in any other way behaving like a buffoon. He took them through the overture, the entr'acte, the journey from Thornfield: they played with a beauty that was almost heart-melting. He might have known it was too good to last.

'OK,' he said, 'that was fine. Great. Let's go back to bar —' he couldn't remember which bar it was. Sometimes, by some lucky fluke, he could, and would then make a show of consulting the score: today he simply flipped back a few random pages for the look of the thing. 'Let's return to where the first violins —'

He was interrupted by a shrill scream, proceeding from somewhere in the middle of the woodwinds. The scream was promptly echoed by another, and then another, the whole accompanied by a panic-stricken clatter of chairs and the sound as of music stands rapidly overturning.

'What the hell is going on?'

No reply; only more screams, this time with the addition of yells and shouts and stamping feet. Someone giggled: unmistakably hysterical. Standing on the rostrum, in isolating darkness, it seemed to Paul as if all pandemonium had broken loose. He rapped with his baton.

'Will somebody please enlighten me as to what the hell is going on?'

By way of response came only one shrill and terrified

screech above the general uproar. His blood ran cold. This was the very thing he had feared above all else: a situation beyond his control. Anything could have happened. Fire could have broken out, the floor caved in, someone dropped down dead —

Without thinking, he stepped down off the rostrum and plunged forward. The next second, and he was seeing stars. All about him, as if at the touch of a button, the noise subsided. He couldn't make up his mind, either then or later, whether it actually did subside or whether for a moment or two he lost consciousness.

'You OK? You OK?'

The voice repeated itself insistently, and with increasing urgency, in his ear. He put out a hand, connected somewhat groggily with what he took to be the edge of the rostrum, slowly pulled himself to his feet.

'What in hell —' he staggered slightly: someone took his arm — 'what in hell was all that about?'

'It wasn't anything ... honest! Just some fink let three filthy great spiders out. The girls didn't like 'em too much.'

'For crying out loud —'

'You wanna come an' sit down? Get him a chair, someone! Someone get him a chair!'

He heard the sound of a chair being scraped across the floor. At the same time the door was thrown open. A kind of hush fell upon the room.

'Paul?' Hugo spoke sharply. 'What's the trouble?'

He managed to straighten up: attempted a grin. Once he'd lost the ability to laugh, he was done for.

'No trouble ... I just tripped over a filthy great spider.'

'You did *what*?'

'He trod on a music stand. It kinda flew up and hit him.'

'Oh! So that was what it was. It felt like a tarantula wearing steel-tipped boots.'

For all its feebleness, the sally produced a few

laughs — almost instantly muffled. He guessed that Hugo had had something to do with it.

'Are you all right?'

'Just about.'

'Want me to take over?'

'Mm-hm.' He shook his head: to let Hugo take over would be fatal.

'At least go and get something put on that cut.'

'It can wait; it's only a scratch.' He turned, cautiously, and stepped back on to the rostrum. 'OK, you lot! Excitement over. Let's get back to business.' He reached out for his baton: it wasn't there. He must have been holding it when he went and trod on the music stand. *Damn*. 'Has anyone seen —'

'Here y'are.'

The baton was slid, unobtrusively, into his hand. He wondered how it was he had ever thought the Kaufman kid a pain in the arse. He could, when he wished, be positively helpful.

'My thanks.' He inclined his head. 'Now, if order is restored . . . shall we continue?'

Somehow or other, he got through it. It was almost worse than Ludmila's soirée, but he managed it. It was not until afterwards that the reaction set in. He sat in his chair, his hard lumpy chair which no one else used, over by the windows in the far corner of the staff-room, and felt for a moment that he was going to be sick. The sweat broke out, cold and clammy, on his brow: his skin enfolded him in a shroud of damp gooseflesh, wetly clinging, icy to the touch, as the room and its shadows slowly came and went. Suddenly, on the back of his neck, a hand was placed.

'Bent forvard! Put your head betveen your kneess.'

Meat Loaf?

'Do! Like I am tellink you!'

He had thought he was alone. He could have sworn —

'Bent! Bent!'

Obediently, he bent. Meat Loaf kept his hand where it was, on the back of his neck.

'You stay.'

You stay, you sit: lie down, come here ... was he never to have any say in the matter? Maybe they would teach him to do parlour tricks. *Beg for Mummy ... oh! What a clever boy!* Pat him on the head, chuck him a biscuit, want to go walkies?

Gingerly, he sat up. To his relief, the room was still.

'OK,' he said. 'I'm OK.'

'So what you do?' He felt Meat Loaf's fingers brush his hair to one side, where the music stand had struck him. 'Looks bad. You fall?'

'I — tripped over something.'

Meat Loaf grunted. There was silence; then the sound of the coffee machine being operated.

'Here.' A plastic beaker was thrust into his hand. 'Bleck goffee. You drink.'

You drink, you eat: sit up, lie down. Die for the Queen, sing for your supper ... there's a good boy! Such a clever dog!

He felt Meat Loaf watching him, and instinctively sat straighter.

'That's fine,' he said. 'I'm fine now.'

'What you drip over?'

'A music stand. Silly of me. Wasn't looking where I was going.' He took a sip of black coffee: it was repulsive. 'Keep my head in the clouds, that's my trouble.'

'Tell me,' said Meat Loaf. 'Why you not go to Papa Jo?'

'Papa Jo?' He looked up, frowning. There had been a note of what sounded suspiciously like compassion in Meat Loaf's voice. (*Compassion? Meat Loaf?*) 'Why should I want to go to Papa Jo? I'm not going to sue anyone. It was entirely my own fault.' He put up a hand and dabbed at his forehead: it felt tender to the touch and was covered in a hard crust of dry blood. 'You know what a clumsy sod I am.'

'If you vould get yourself a stick it vould be eassier, I think. And safer, too. Before you do yourself some real harm. But in any case, my young friend, you vould do vell to go to Papa Jo. I think you find,' said Meat Loaf, 'that when it comes to crunch, he is man behind vheel. You go to him, you talk to him. Like vhen you were little boy. You tell him your troubles, he listen. Alvays better —' his voice moved away, across the room — 'to get it off chest. Now, if you vill excuse, I haff glass.' The door was opened. He could hear the busy corridor noises drifting in from outside: footsteps clacking on the wood-block floor, the high-pitched chatter of kids' voices. 'You are alone, by the vay,' said Meat Loaf. 'There is no one else here.'

The door closed. For a long time Paul sat silent, cradling his plastic beaker of coffee. The thought uppermost in his mind was: he knows. Meat Loaf knows . . . how many days, weeks (*months?*) had he done so? And if he, then who else? It was not very likely that Meat Loaf would be alone. Ludmila, he knew, suspected. Did others, too, have an inkling of the truth? More than an inkling? Was everybody, perhaps just sitting back, watching with silent sympathy his pathetic blunderings, waiting for the day when he finally gave in and threw himself on their mercy?

Meat Loaf was right: in his heart, he knew it. The time had come when he must go to Papa Jo. It had probably come weeks ago, but he had been too stubborn to admit it. It had taken an incident such as today's to convince him. If he couldn't conduct even a simple rehearsal, how in God's name did he think he was going to get up there and fight his way through an entire performance? He supposed, deep down, he had known all along that it was a pipe dream. Had it not been for the comforting presence of Hugo, ever there in the background, ready to take over if things went wrong, he could not have afforded to indulge in it for even half as long as he had.

Determinedly, he drank his coffee and stood up. *If it were done when 'tis done, then 'twere well it were done quickly* ... it had taken him months to come to it, but now that he had, he wanted it to be over.

He walked briskly down the corridor to the office, running one hand along the wall as he went, checking the number of doors. (A necessary precaution, the office being no longer even faintly discernible by its glass partitions, save on rare days of brightest sunlight.) He tapped briefly on the door, opened it and stuck his head round.

'Virginia?'

'Virginia's at lunch.' The voice was Ludmila's. This time yesterday he would have cursed his ill luck: today he no longer cared. If he had given himself away, he had given himself away. It hardly seemed to matter any more. 'Did you want anything I could help you with?'

'Well ... not really. I was wondering whether it would be possible to speak with Papa Jo, or whether he was still rehearsing?'

'He's relaxing just at present. Was it something urgent?'

The temptation, even now, was to say no: to cut and run while the opportunity still offered.

'Not — urgent, exactly, but I would like to get it over with as soon as possible ... it's something I need to discuss with him.'

He was in no doubt that Ludmila knew exactly what it was. He could feel her, measuring him with her eyes.

'What have you done to your forehead?' she said.

'Nothing.' He ruffled his hair, in a belated attempt to cover it. 'Just a slight cut.'

'Have you had someone take a look at it?'

'Er — not yet,' he said. 'No. I was —'

He found his chin suddenly pushed up, as Ludmila, presumably, inspected the damage.

'That's nasty,' she said. 'You'd better get along to Matron and have her put something on it for you.'

'Yes, I will.'

'You just make sure that you do.'

'I will; I promise.'

'You're going to have to start taking a bit more care of yourself, young man. It's us who's responsible for your safety, you know. If you were to have a bad accident, here on these premises, we'd be the ones who were liable. You know that, Paul, don't you?'

'Yes,' he said. 'I know.'

'So you want to go see Papa Jo?'

'I — think I ought.'

'You'd better go across,' she said. 'I'll call and tell him you're on your way.'

He found Papa Jo in his study, a room fortunately almost as familiar to him as his own bedroom.

'Papa Jo?'

'Pauly! Come in, come in.'

He closed the door behind him, stepped carefully into the room.

'I'm sorry to disturb you at this time of day, but —'

'You don't disturb me! If Ludmila tells you I am asleep, then it is a lie: I never sleep in the middle of the day. Never! And even if I do, you know that I am always pleased to see you. Pour a couple of drinks and come and sit down.'

Paul hesitated. He knew roughly where the drinks cabinet was located: whether he could actually walk across to it without crashing into something else on the way, or, alternatively, missing it entirely, was another matter. Well, he could but try. He set off, treading a cautious path across the carpet.

'To your right!' sang Papa Jo. 'To your right!'

He stopped; as if a chasm, quite suddenly, had opened before him. So what had he expected? If Ludmila had had her suspicions, she would obviously have shared them with Papa Jo.

'Mind the chair, now,' said Papa Jo. 'You're going to fall over it.'

He swallowed; forced himself to put out a hand — felt the back of a chair; edged his way round it.

'That's it, keep going . . . a little more to your left . . . to your left! Now you're there. You can stop. The drinks are right before you. I'll have a Scotch.'

Gingerly, he felt amongst the bottles, trying to discern from the shape which was which.

'Not that one!' said Papa Jo. 'That's gin. You want gin?'

'No; not particularly.' He held up another. 'How about this?'

'That's better! Here, let me.'

He heard the creaking of Papa Jo's wheelchair across the floor, found the whisky bottle being taken from his grasp, heard the clinking of glassware.

'Come!' Papa Jo took his hand, placed it on the back of the chair. 'Come and sit down, we talk over here.'

Ensconced in the red leather wing chair in whose engulfing depths, as a small boy, summoned to the study for one of Papa Jo's periodic chats, he had squirmed and wriggled as his manifold crimes were brought home to him, he felt a sense almost of relief: the same relief he had felt when, as that same small boy, he had haltingly confessed to some piece of petty mischief only to discover that Papa Jo had known about it all along.

'Always come to me, Pauly; always tell me. Better I hear from you than from others.'

It was advice which perhaps he would have done well to heed in later life. To have confessed to Papa Jo right at the beginning might have spared him much embarrassment.

'So, then?' said Papa Jo.

'So —' He felt round with one hand for a side table. 'I obviously don't need to tell you why I'm here.'

'No.' Papa Jo spoke gently. 'You don't need to tell me. I knew that you would come . . . sooner or later. I have suspected for some time that all was not well.'

'For long?'

'Mm . . . . .' He could imagine the accompanying

gesture of the hand: so-so. 'For a while. I said to Madame
... he will come. When he is ready. In the meantime, we
must be patient. We must wait. It is of no use to push.
When he wish us to know, he will come and he will tell
us. Until then —' Until then, they would politely
pretend not to notice. If it looks like he's going to bump
into something, move it out of his way: if he doesn't see
you coming, step to one side. Let him go on with his little
game of make-believe for as long as it pleases him. One
day he will come to his senses. 'Well,' said Papa Jo.
'And so now you are here.'

He grimaced.

'Only because I don't have much choice.' Self-
delusion could go just so far, and no farther. This morning, for him, had marked a watershed: from this point
on, the dreaming had to stop. All right, then! Let it stop.
Say the words — put an end to it. *Hugo is going to have
to take my place at the first performance....*

'Hugo is going to have to take my place,' he said, 'at
the first performance.'

There was a silence.

'It is what I feared,' said Papa Jo. 'I hoped it would
not be true; but it is what I feared.' The wheelchair
creaked: Paul felt his hand taken and held. 'Pauly?'
The big carpet-bag hand was warm and firm over his.
'Things are really so bad with you?'

'Bad enough.'

'Too bad for you to conduct?'

'Papa Jo, you saw me just now ... if I can't even see
to find a bottle of Scotch, I certainly can't see to conduct an opera.'

'But you can see —' Papa Jo's voice held an element
of pleading — 'for ordinary things?'

He smiled at that, in spite of himself.

'If finding a bottle of Scotch isn't an ordinary thing,
I'd like to know what is!'

'But to read? To write? You see to do this? If I fetch
you a score —'

He was silent.

'But you can see me all right? Sitting here? You can see me?'

'Papa Jo —'

'Not even that? You can't even see me? So why you wear your glasses? If you can't see . . . why you wear them?'

'Force of habit. I can always take them off.' He did so. 'It makes not an atom of difference.'

Or perhaps it did make a difference: perhaps it made a difference that to him was not discernible. For the first time, he could sense that Papa Jo actually believed what he was telling him.

'The accident? In the motor-car?'

He inclined his head: the accident. In the motor-car.

'And there is nothing —'

'So they tell me.'

There was a pause.

'Pauly —'

'I'm sorry,' he said. 'I should have come to you far earlier. I don't know whether you'll want me to resign straight away, or —'

'Resign?' Papa Jo sat back with a thump in his chair. 'What you talk about, resign?'

'Well, I'm not exactly qualified as a —' the words stuck in his throat, even after all these weeks of forcing himself to think them: it was the first time, aloud, that he had ever said them — 'as a blind person, am I? I'm not exactly qualified to have charge of kids.'

'So what you have to do to get qualified?'

'I don't — really know.' He hadn't, in truth, given the matter much thought. He had been too bound up in the immediacy to spare any consideration for the future. 'I suppose — one has to — get rehabilitated, or something.'

Bradbeer had told him to contact the social services, but needless to say he had never done so. He had had visions of them giving him a white stick and telling him

224

to practise with it, up the garden path. He had thought, at the time, that he would not be seen dead with a white stick. Now, Meat Loaf's words rang in his ears: *If you would get yourself a stick, it would be easier, I think....* There had been occasions, just recently, when he had thought so, too.

'Listen,' said Papa Jo, 'I don't know about this rehabitation, whatever it is — what is it?'

'Some sort of training course, I imagine.' Bradbeer had told him, but he hadn't bothered to listen. 'They teach you things ... how to cook and — tell the time and — walk about without crashing into tables and suchlike.'

'You need to be taught? You can't find out for yourself?'

'Well —' It did seem rather foolish, now he came to think of it. Surely to God, with a bit of practice —

'If you want to go away on a course,' said Papa Jo, 'then you go away on a course — but you come back here! This is your home. Is where you belong. Don't I always say? Here at Bampton we are one happy family?'

It was true; Papa Jo always did say it. But no one, to Paul's knowledge, had ever heard Ludmila express such a sentiment. He voiced his doubts — Papa Jo brushed them aside. Paul had Ludmila all wrong. That was the great tragedy of Ludmila: everyone had her wrong. She did not show herself to her best advantage. Beneath the stern exterior there beat a heart of purest gold. Did it not speak for itself? Any woman who could do what she had done — and anyway, it was not up to Ludmila. Ludmila would go along with whatever Papa Jo decreed.

'If I say you stay, then you stay.'

'Even If I'm no longer capable of functioning properly?'

'How you should not be capable? You are a musician, yes? Not a football player.'

225

'I am also supposed, for my sins, to be a teacher.'

'So, teach! What is to stop you? Maybe is not so easy just at first, but you find ways round. You learn.'

'And while I'm doing so?'

'While you do so, we must be patient. Just as you must be. So, you make mistakes! You trip up, you fall over — what you do to your head? I only just noticed. Someone hit you?'

'I trod,' said Paul, 'on a music stand.'

'So you trod on a music stand! Next time you be more careful.'

Next time he would tread on a banana skin. Or an oil slick. Or a patch of ice. There were plenty of other things beside music stands. He had hardly started yet.

'Look,' said Papa Jo, 'where else you go? If you don't stay here, where you belong ... where you go instead?'

Where, indeed? The Aunties, he knew, would be only too eager to have him permanently resident at Marden. Auntie Vi would smother him with small attentions, wait upon him hand and foot; do his laundry, buy his clothes, cook his meals, run his errands. As a way of life, it would be intolerable. Sooner muddle along doing things for himself, slow and hamfisted though he might be, than relinquish all independence. But could he justifiably stay on at Bampton, working at only half strength? It was no use deceiving himself. It took him, these days, on average, twice as long to perform even the simplest and most basic of tasks as it took anyone else. There were certain tasks he couldn't perform at all, and never would be able to. Ingenuity had its place, and perseverance, too; but no amount of either could restore his lost ability to mark a piece of written work or read a score.

'Pauly —' Papa Jo was leaning forward: he could feel his breath warm on his cheek — 'how long now since you don't see so well? A couple of months, maybe? Bit more?'

He hadn't been able to see so well for the past two terms. It had only been this term, however, that it had really started to inconvenience him — only the past few weeks that he had existed in a world of almost total blackness. He hunched a shoulder.

'A month or so.'

'A month or so. So you tell me, truthfully . . . in that month or so, you been incapable? You let people down? Any of your students ever complain?'

'N-no, but —'

'So what's the problem? You manage so far; why you not go on managing?'

'Because —'

'Because —?'

He sat for a moment in silence; not trusting himself to speak.

'Because why?' urged Papa Jo. Paul felt his knee squeezed in a grip that was undoubtedly intended to be bracing. It was not Papa Jo's fault if it had precisely the opposite effect and succeeded in very nearly reducing him to a state of lachrymose imbecility. 'Pauly? Because why?'

He ran a hand through his hair.

'Because I've — lost confidence, I suppose. Plainly and simply, I — I can't control them any more. I know it, they know it.'

'So what they do? They play you up? Behave like little devils?'

'It's nothing malicious.' He was quick to defend them. 'They're OK in ones and twos, it's just when I'm faced with a whole horde of them together —'

'They make merry with you.'

'Any kids would. It's only natural.' Some fool floundering about, tripping over his own feet, knocking himself out on music stands, they were obviously going to take advantage. The temptation was irresistible. He didn't blame them. Unhappily it was a bit late in the day now to do very much about it: whatever authority he may once have possessed had been well and truly undermined. There could be no going back over lost ground.

'I tell you,' said Papa Jo; he gave Paul's knee another squeeze. 'What you got to do, you got to do what I did: you got to learn to accept help. You got to learn to *ask* for it. You go walking round pretending you don't need it, then sure, you land in trouble. People laugh at you, they get mad at you, they play jokes on you. They think you're just a clumsy fool. Just a clown. But you say to them, look, I need help . . . that's a different cup of tea. You tell those kids, you say to them, I don't see so good no more, I need you to do things for me, and Bob is your uncle! They are only too happy. They are not bad children; only they have to know what is wrong. They have to understand. Once they are told — no problem! I guarantee. They behave like angels.'

Paul grinned, rather ruefully.

'I beg leave to doubt that!'

'But you will try? Yes? You will go to them — you will tell them. You will say, please, children, I need you to look after me —'

Papa Jo, he thought, you don't know what you're doing to me. . . .

'If you would prefer,' said Papa Jo, 'I can always call the school together and I can tell them for you. But I think is far better they hear it from you. Believe me,' said Papa Jo, 'this is not what I would say to everyone. I would not, for example, say it to Hugo.'

No, thought Paul: Hugo was the sort who could maintain authority without having to crawl and beg. There were, without any doubt, great benefits to be derived from being a martinet. Blind, deaf and dumb, Hugo would never let a parcel of kids run rings round him.

'There are those,' said Papa Jo, 'who can ask, and there are those who cannot. Hugo is one who cannot. You are lucky: you are one who can. You maybe do not know it, because so far you have not had to do it; but you will see. You will find out.'

It seemed, once again, that he was to have no choice. If Papa Jo were willing to take a chance and keep him on, braving even the wrath of Ludmila, the least he could do by way of reparation was sink his pride and throw himself on the kids' mercy — always assuming, that is, that they had any. On balance, he was inclined to accept that they probably did. A modicum, at least. If he didn't altogether share Papa Jo's belief in their essential goodness, neither did he go along with Hugo's more jaundiced view. The kids were all right: it was the telling them that was likely to be the worst part.

'So, that is settled,' said Papa Jo. He patted Paul's knee, sat back again in his chair. 'For the moment you will carry on as you are. After the Festival, when we have more time, we will talk again. You will tell me what you can manage and what you cannot, and we will make arrangements. These things can be worked out. There are no difficulties so great they cannot be solved. Maybe you take fewer pupils, maybe we buy special equipment; we discuss it all later. In the meantime, you will not worry. The opus is finished, Hugo will conduct, there is no cause for concern. That is agreed; yes?'

'There is just one thing —'

'What is that?'

'You don't think it would be better if Hugo were to take over my orchestral sessions, do you? In view of the fact that he's going to be the one to conduct?'

'No.' Papa Jo sounded sympathetic, but firm. 'I think it is far better if you continue. Hugo will have enough on his hands as it is. Unless, of course —' He paused. 'Unless what you are saying is that this is one of the things you can no longer manage?'

Was he saying that? Perhaps he was. After all, it wasn't really reasonable, was it? That he should be expected to get up on a rostrum and conduct sixty-odd kids that he couldn't even see? No one could argue that that was reasonable.

'If this is the case,' said Papa Jo, 'then naturally we must make different arrangements. I wouldn't want to push you into doing something that is too much for you.'

Or perhaps what he was really saying was, I made an abject idiot of myself this morning and I don't want to have to go back again and face them. Perhaps that would be rather nearer the truth.

'You would be happier if we make new arrangement?'

The immediate relief would, without any doubt, be overwhelming. He stood up, orientated himself in the direction of the door.

'Don't worry. It's nothing I can't handle. Only a bit of cowardice . . . I'll get over it.'

'You go to them,' said Papa Jo. 'You tell them. They will be good children, I promise.'

I only wish, thought Paul, that I had your faith. . . .

Slowly, he made his way across to the door. He found, to his distaste, that without the need for pretence he was already and automatically starting to do those very things he had hitherto taken so much care to guard against — stretching out a hand before him as he walked, testing with each step for possible danger. Pride, before, had prevented him; given him a boldness which seemed in retrospect little short of insanity. He remembered with a shudder stepping out into the road, in the middle of the traffic, the night that Bradbeer had finally broken the news to him. It shook him now as it never had at the time. It was as if this morning's contretemps, minor (some might even say ludicrous) though it had been, had not only severely dented his ego but had also torn a gaping hole in whichever organ it was that housed his supply of courage. Never again, he thought, would he step out into a road without thinking: never again walk through a door without wondering what he was going to encounter on the other side of it. Caution doth make cowards of us all. . . .

For all that — or perhaps because of it — he reached the door without mishap, guided only by a couple of sharp directives to go 'more to your left . . . to your left!' (But this time yesterday he would have reached it with no directives at all.)

'Papa Jo —' He stood, awkwardly, one hand on the door knob. 'I'd like to say thank you, except I'm not very clever at this sort of thing . . . would it be ungracious if I asked you to take it as read? The fact that I am very grateful?'

'Grateful? Who wants grateful? Save your speechmaking for the bambini!'

He pulled a wry face.

'I'll do that.'

'By the way —' Papa Jo flung it at him, casually, as he went through the door. 'When does Caroline come back?'

'I'm — not certain.' The last thing he wanted to talk about was Caroline. 'In time for the Festival, I believe she said.'

'In time for the Festival . . . well, that is something. She has not yet made up her mind, you know, whether or not she goes back to America. Why do you not —'

'Papa Jo! Please!' Paul held up a hand. 'Don't spoil it.'

He thought, as he closed the door, that he heard a sigh.

13

'OK, you lot! Settle down, and pin back your lugholes ... before we get started, there's something I have to say to you.'

Slowly, and as it were reluctantly, the normal pre-rehearsal cacophony of sixty assorted instruments being simultaneously plucked, blown and scraped, faded into silence. It was a silence of expectancy, not altogether unmixed with apprehension. The message, quite obviously, had got across: what he had to say was something rather more than a cordial 'Good morning' — possibly something to do with yesterday's little episode?

'Right. Now —' He was only going through with it because he had promised Papa Jo. He had lain awake half the night, rehearsing what to say. *It may not have escaped your notice — you may possibly have had cause to wonder —*

The air of expectancy increased: so did the apprehension. He could feel it coming at him, in waves. He cleared his throat.

'You may possibly have had cause to wonder, these last few weeks, how it is that you have been able to get away with murder in front of me.' Confusion. Awkward shuffling of bottoms and crossing and uncrossing of legs. 'The reason, of course, is very simple — some of you may even have guessed it. If you haven't, then let me tell you ... the reason you have been able to get away with murder is that I have been unable to see you.' He paused. 'In this unhappy, or some may say happy state, depending on whether or not, as a bunch, you are deemed worth looking at, I still find myself; which means that, if you wish, you will still be able to get away with murder. It's entirely up to you. If you choose to run rings round me, then there's not very much that I can do about it. I'm the easiest person on earth to play blind man's buff with. I think, after yesterday, you probably realise that. All I can do is throw myself on your mercy — trust you not to take advantage. Papa Jo, he says to me, you tell those kids. You say to them . . . I don't see so good no more, and Bob is your uncle! They behave like angels . . . well, now, I'm not so naïve as to believe *that*. The day you lot start behaving like angels I shall know I'm really in trouble.'

Laughter. Relief, intermingled with embarrassment. Embarrassing having to listen to all this stuff about him not being able to see, but a relief, all the same, to know he wasn't going to slag them off.

'Having said that,' said Paul, 'I don't reckon you're quite such a load of barbarians as some people make you out to be. At any rate, I have to pray you're not, because from now till the Festival it looks like we're stuck with each other. That means that I'm going to have to rely on your sense of fair play — and you're going to have to be patient with me. Come next term, I'm hoping to have got things a bit more together. Just at this moment, I'm not finding it too easy, so if you could kindly avoid leaving music stands lying around where I'm liable to trip over them, I'd be very much obliged. Likewise, if you see me about to walk head-on into a brick wall, I'd certainly appreciate it if you'd take the trouble to stop me. What I'm trying to say' (because I promised Papa Jo) 'is that there are going to be occasions when I shall need a bit of help, and if you're not too shy to give it, then I promise you I won't be too proud to accept. In other words, I'm not going to bite anyone's head off for offering to take me across the road when I don't want to go. I assure you, I shall be only too grateful of any assistance anyone cares to offer. Incidentally, I won't actually be attempting to conduct any performances, you'll be relieved to hear. Mr McDonald will be taking my place for those, so you'll be in safe hands as far as that's concerned. Until then, if you could bear with me — perhaps even try pretending that I *am* Mr McDonald? So that if anyone has any bright ideas about letting loose an army of stag beetles or hooded cobras, maybe they'd just like to forget them ... I'm sure I don't need to remind you that Mr McDonald doesn't have quite the same robust sense of humour as I do — and unlike me, he can see only too well. Eyes both fore and aft, and all in good working order, so no more funny business. All right?'

Vigorous murmurings of assent, accompanied by much moving about and clattering of feet.

'So ... anyone got any questions they want to ask?'

It appeared not: he guessed they were too bashful.

'OK, then, now I've got that off my chest and we all understand each other, let's get under way. I want to take it right from the top and work straight through.'

The atmosphere, just at first, was strained. He had stopped being just-Paul, and had become Paul-who-couldn't-see, Paul-who-was-different-from-other-people. They weren't sure, any more, how to treat him. He could feel them on their best behaviour, stiff with the effort of demonstrating goodwill and the desire to please. It affected their playing: he said as much.

'You're sounding like a bunch of outraged spinsters forced to play Knees up Mother Brown in front of the high altar! There's no need to go all pious on me. Just because I can't see any more, that doesn't mean I've suddenly become a different person. You don't have to pussyfoot around as if I'm made of porcelain ... I won't crack in half if someone plays a bum note or mucks up their entrance. Let's take it again — and this time give it some stick. Blind I may be, deaf I am not: I should like to hear *my* music as *I* wrote it.'

By the end of the rehearsal, normal relations had been restored — almost restored. (Almost normal.) He was aware even now of a reserve on the part of the less outgoing: a tendency on the part of almost everyone to handle him with caution. He supposed it was inevitable. He could only hope that soon they would grow accustomed to his incapacity and cease to regard it as being in any way remarkable: to be subjected to special treatment was what he had all along most dreaded. As he was leaving the studio, a hand plucked at his sleeve.

'Hi! This is Chris. You going down the staff-room? Want me to come with you?'

He had been finding his own way from rehearsal studio to staff-room for the past month or more, in ever deepening darkness; he hardly required the assistance of an eleven-year-old to get him there. He couldn't very well reject the offer, however, after his brave words of earlier.

'That would be helpful,' he said.

'You want me to keep a hold of you?'

'No, I'm all right indoors.' He forced himself to speak amiably. 'It's only outside I get a bit lost.'

'Why doncha get yourself a stick? That's what most people do that can't see. They have these special ones that fold up almost to nothin' so's ya can hide 'em away when ya don't need 'em. Like umbrellas. That's the sort of thing you want. Either that or a dog. Some people have dogs. I guess on the whole I'd sooner have a dog. Which'd you?'

Just at this moment, he would sooner not have either. He knew, of course, that he would have to. He couldn't keep making excuses for not venturing further than the Lodge gates.

'You gonna learn Braille? All that stuff with the dots?'

'Er — no. No, I shouldn't imagine so.'

'Why not?' The child's voice was accusing: what's

the matter with you, you lazy slob? 'You don't learn Braille, how ya gonna read?'

'Well . . . maybe later on. When I have time.' When he'd learnt to cope with all the other, more pressing, day-to-day practicalities; maybe then. They presumably had a system of musical notation. He wondered if anyone had ever transcribed a full score — if anyone without sight had ever managed to read a full score. He didn't mind about books so much, they could be heard on tape, or on the radio, and newspapers were surely no great loss in a person's life; but to lose the ability to read a score — that was something that really scared him. Worse, even, than losing the ability to be freely mobile. One could always get around somehow, even if it did mean branding oneself for all to see with a white stick or a guide dog. Being unable to read a score made him feel almost bedridden.

'Mindja,' said Chris, 'it coulda bin worse . . . think of Beethoven.'

He was bored with thinking of Beethoven. Bradbeer had told him to think of Beethoven. And anyhow, he was far from convinced that it *had* been worse: Beethoven, after all, had still retained the ability to read a score.

In the staff-room, Hugo was waiting for him.

'Coming up to the canteen?'

Coming up to the canteen? Going down to the staff-room?

'Yes, I suppose so,' he said.

There was nothing to be gained, any more, from skulking about in corners until the coast should be clear. Everyone must be au fait by now with the state he was in — or if they weren't, they very soon would be. He was no longer troubling to disguise the fact (even if he wasn't exactly going out of his way to advertise it: the idea of toting a white stick, like some badge of crippledom, was one he still had not completely come to terms with).

He knew that some people knew by reason of their coming up to him and quite openly commiserating. With others he guessed, from their sudden and assiduous desire to be of service: doors were held open, chairs pushed forward, notices on notice boards loudly read out for his benefit. It was no use resenting it: and indeed, now that it was actually happening he found it less difficult to bear than he had imagined. If he were to be honest, it brought welcome relief from the pressure, the never ending, relentless pressure, of having to keep up the appearance of a normality he no longer possessed. He could feel for a door handle without being self-conscious, help himself to a coffee from the coffee machine without being scared that someone might be watching, noting his uncertain gropings for the right button, his clumsy movements as he positioned the cardboard cup. He didn't even have to martyr himself, sitting in the hard lumpy chair over by the window; not unless he wanted to. He could fumble his way round a whole selection of chairs, or simply ask someone to guide him to one. (In theory: it would be a while yet before he could actually bring himself to descend to it in practice. For the moment he preferred to stick with the old hard lumpy job and retain his independence.)

'So how did it go?' said Hugo.

'Not too bad.'

'Kids behave themselves?'

He smiled.

'Like angels....' It wouldn't last, of course; he wouldn't want it to. But just for the moment it made a pleasant change. 'Not a whiff of mayhem from start to finish.'

'So I should bloody well think! Little sods.'

'They weren't to know.'

Rose and Hugo hadn't known; not for certain. They had wondered, Rose said, over recent weeks, but they hadn't actually known. He had been relieved about that. He had almost managed to convince himself that the entire school had known, watching in silent concert, discreetly pretending not to notice as he ricocheted off the walls and blundered into music stands and tried to open doors that unaccountably weren't there.

'If *we* didn't guess,' Rose had said, 'I'm quite sure nobody else did. After all, we're the ones that live with you.'

He had wanted to ask her, how about Caroline? but he hadn't been able to bring himself to. Not at that point. It was only later, much later, when they had borne him off to the Saracen's and befuddled his brain with double brandies, that he had found the courage.

'Rosie,' he had said, 'did Caroline ever —'

'Ever what?'

'Ever give any sign that — she knew?'

Rose had hesitated; just long enough for him to notice.

'Would you rather she didn't?'

Her, more than anyone.

'But Paul, sweetheart, she'll have to know some time —'

'I know! I know!' Common sense told him as much. If she didn't know now, she would have to know some time — presumably when she came back over for the Festival. He could hardly expect the whole school to maintain a conspiracy of silence. But just so long as she didn't know *now*. So long as she hadn't guessed right at the beginning — hadn't been humouring him all this time. That was the thought which haunted him.

'In you go.'

He became aware that Hugo was holding open the door of the canteen.

'OK?'

He said yes, because it seemed pathetic to say no; he was glad, all the same, of Hugo's hand beneath his elbow. The last occasion on which he had made a foray into the canteen at this hour of the day had been when he still retained just sufficient residual vision to make such an enterprise at least feasible, even if somewhat precarious. He was forced to realise now that without Hugo at his side he would be lost, disoriented almost totally by the continuous low babble of voices, of clattering dishes and rattling cutlery, and the confusion of traffic to and fro. Hugo obviously sensed an uncertainty in his demeanour.

'This way.' Firmly, he shepherded him through the mêlée. 'Do you want to come and sit down while I get you something?'

He was torn between the ignoble desire to surrender — to give up the battle before it had even begun; allow himself to be led, like a child, by the hand; to be sat down and waited upon — and the instinctive rebelling of his own pride, not yet quite ready to lie down and die even now. He pulled a face.

'Start as you intend to go on.'

'What's that supposed to mean?'

'It means that I would like very much to go and sit down, but I don't think I ought . . . just make sure you hang on to me and don't let me go bumping into the furniture.'

'You won't bump into any furniture,' said Hugo. 'Not with me around.'

It was what he had said last night, when they had yanked him off to the pub to get all filled up with booze.

'You won't bump into anything . . . not with me around. Just put that —' he had taken Paul's hand, placing it on his arm — 'there, and you'll find you can't go wrong.'

'You want to bet?' Paul had laughed; self-deprecating; joking because he was embarrassed. He had thought Rose might quite likely put an arm about his shoulders: he had not expected Hugo to be the one to take him in charge.

'Trust me, kiddo.' Hugo had patted his hand, with an air almost paternal. 'It's what you should have done a long time ago. . . .'

Perhaps it was. Certainly, in many ways, life had

become a great deal less fraught since his confession. The worst part had been in the telling, but even that had been nowhere near as difficult as he had anticipated. They had done their best to make it easy for him.

'Why in God's name didn't you come to us before, you great berk? Apart from anything else, only think of all the breakages that could have been avoided!'

'My pot,' said Rose.

'Sod your pot! What about my shaving mug? That was a present from Lossiemouth, that was. It said on it . . . *Present from Lossiemouth*.'

'I remember it.' Gratefully, Paul had picked up on the theme. 'A hideous thing in pink tartan with a gold rim. One of the very few objects I can genuinely say that I am pleased not to be able to see any more.'

'That was no reason for going and smashing it! I shall never forgive you for that. All for want of a little humility.'

'You should talk of humility!' Rose, as usual, had leapt to Paul's defence. 'I'd like to see *you* ever turn round and admit you need help.'

'Me? I wouldn't hesitate! I'd turn round and *demand*, I'm not proud — and neither should you be, you great daft loon! Go and grab your jacket, we'll take you down to the Saracen's.'

He had thought it would be Rose who made herself responsible for him: he had not expected it to be Hugo. The placing of his hand on Hugo's arm had made him initially feel quite gauche and awkward. He had been at a loss to understand why this should be, for he and Hugo, after all, had known each other for more years than he cared to remember. They had seen the best of each other: they had seen the worst. Whence, then, this sudden discomfiture? This shrinking back like some shy virgin from any form of physical contact? He had worked out, in the end, that it was not the physical contact which caused him unease so much as the shift in their relationship which it undoubtedly marked.

Once they had been equals: now they were no more so. From this point on, it must always be Hugo who extended the hand, Paul who took it — and as with Hugo, so with the rest of the world. He could either enter graciously upon his state of dependence, or he could reject it with contumely and go blundering on alone. He had made a conscious decision and opted for the former. It might not show much fighting spirit, but it seemed, in the long run, more dignified.

'Hey, dozy!' Hugo was digging him in the ribs with his elbow. That was not dignified. He snapped to attention.

'What?'

'What do you want to eat?'

'Oh . . . whatever's going.' He reached out for a tray. He had been reaching out for trays, quite successfully, for the past few weeks. He had never before failed to make contact. That was because he had come up to the canteen by himself and had taken the trouble to count his steps: ten from the door to the angle of the counter, turn sharp left, five to the starting point, where the plastic trays were kept in their little cubby hole. Today, because he had come with Hugo, he hadn't bothered counting the steps; as a result, where the trays should have been, he encountered only nothingness.

'Here —' Hugo took his hand, guiding it in the right direction. He did his best not to mind; not to think of the people who were watching. There was no disgrace attached, they all knew by now that he couldn't see. It was something he was going to have to get used to. *Enter graciously upon your state of dependence.* . . .

'So what are you having?' said Hugo. 'Steak and kidney, chicken curry —'

'Whatever's easiest.' Whatever he was least liable to make a mess of. 'Roll and butter and a yoghourt.'

'Don't be a cretin! We had all this out last night.'

They had insisted, last night, on standing him a meal. He hadn't wanted a meal — not, at any rate, in public.

He had practically given up eating in public. It embarrassed him too much, chasing bits of food round the edge of his plate, never quite sure what he was putting into his mouth or what he'd slopped over on to the table. Hugo had told him not to be so ludicrous — 'as if anyone cares'. Rose had said: 'As if anyone *notices* . . . I never have.' That was because he'd not only practically given up eating in public, but practically given up eating in front of anyone at all. The last time he'd sat down to a meal with Rose and Hugo had been the morning Rose had cooked kedgeree, and he had dropped half of it down his sweater. He'd only known about it because Caroline had mopped him up, as if he were a two-year-old. He'd sworn then, never again.

Rose said: 'Oh, Paul *really*.'

'Talk about being over-sensitive —'

'In front of *us*.'

'What are you going to do? Starve yourself?'

'You can't stop *eating*.'

They had forced him in the end to have a plateful of steak and chips. It had embarrassed him acutely. Not only had the chips been razor sharp, so that they kept bouncing off his plate as he tried to spear them, but Rose had had to remove the fat from his meat for him because without using fingers he couldn't tell where one stopped and the other started.

'Have a curry,' said Hugo. He banged something down on Paul's tray. 'You like curry.'

I don't like curry. I loathe curry. I can't eat it without making a mess. Why for Christ's sake can't I be allowed to eat what I want?

'Pudding?'

'You choose.' He would anyway, so what difference did it make? 'Don't tell me, it'll be a nice surprise.'

His tone was obviously more sarcastic than he had intended. Hugo said: 'I'm sorry, I didn't mean to patronise. Tell me what you want. If you don't fancy curry, I'll put it back.'

'Oh, curry will do.' He spoke grudgingly, aware that he was being piglike. All this fuss over a bit of food. What the hell did it matter? So he slopped it over the table and made a mess, so they could mop it up after he'd gone. He should worry.

Someone from behind was jostling him. He edged forward and bumped into Hugo.

'For crying out loud!'

This was ridiculous. He should never have come. In future he would wait till the rush was over and eat by himself, in private. He wasn't fit to be let out amongst other people.

From his rear a voice he recognised as belonging to Virginia said: 'Paul?' It sounded doubtful; as if perhaps he might not be. As if losing his sight had stripped him automatically of his identity. 'How are you?'

'Fine,' he said. Blind as a bat, but otherwise quite normal. Nothing to write home about. 'How are you?'

'I'm all right.'

She paused, delicately. He cringed: let him at least be spared Virginia's outpourings. . . .

'I was so sorry,' she said, 'when Madame told me. I couldn't believe it. I said, *Paul*? I mean, I just would never have *known* . . . I feel so absolutely dreadful! Going on about you not reading that stupid note . . . I can't understand why you didn't *tell* me?'

'Oh —' He shrugged. 'I guess at the time it just didn't seem worth it.'

'But I would *never* — I mean, *obviously* —'

Obviously? Obviously what? Obviously never have got mad at him? Well, one wouldn't, would one? Not with a blind man. It wouldn't be right. It wouldn't be kind. From now on he must be treated considerately, gently, with kid gloves and soft words, as if he were an imbecile.

'It must be too utterly ghastly for you.'

Utterly. And the most utterly ghastly part of all is when people go on about it. I know you don't mean to go

243

on about it, I know that you are only trying to demonstrate sympathy, but I should be most awfully grateful if you would just keep quiet.

If you would just *shut up.*

Hugo, for God's sake! Get me out of here before I go mad. . . .

As if catching his sense of urgency, Hugo put a hand beneath his elbow, moving him on.

'Tea or coffee?'

'Coffee.' At least he was allowed to make up his own mind on that one. He wondered if he would also be allowed to decide for himself whether or not he had milk and sugar.

'Two white coffees,' said Hugo.

'I'd like mine black.' He was only being cussed. He couldn't stand coffee without milk; he always had white. Why for heaven's sake did he have to be so churlish?

He wasn't being churlish: he was merely asserting what little was left of his independence. If he couldn't even choose the colour of his coffee, then he might as well give up.

Patiently, Hugo said: 'Sugar?'

Since when had he taken sugar? From behind, Virginia's voice rang gaily in his ear: 'You watch those calories! If ever you feel like going jogging, by the way, just let me know ... I go every morning, round the park. I'd be happy to take you.'

On a tow rope, no doubt. He could think of nothing more degrading. In any case, jogging was a futile occupation at the best of times.

'Well?' said Hugo.

'Well what?'

'Do you want sugar in your coffee or don't you?'

'Of course I don't!'

There was no need to snap Hugo's head off; he was doing his best. It was not everyone would want to spend his lunch hour carting some great useless

244

millstone around with him. The least the millstone could do was try to show a bit of gratitude.

He reached out for Hugo's hand.

'Mea culpa.'

'Don't give me any of that papist crap . . . shove your tray along. It's a clear run to the check-out.'

Making payment fortunately presented him with no problems: he had long since acquired the habit of sorting both paper money and small change into different denominations and distributing them in various pockets about his person before setting out in the mornings. It was another of those laborious tasks which he cursed at the time but which ultimately saved much embarrassment. Carrying his tray across a crowded canteen was likely to be the most hazardous part of the operation. As a rule, because the place was empty, he simply slid into the nearest chair. He thought, once again: I should never have come. And then he got mad and thought, for Christ's sake! Pull yourself together and don't be so flaming wet!

'OK, McDuff.' Clasping his tray with one hand, he placed the other on Hugo's arm. 'Lead on.'

A brave gesture, but quite unnecessary:

'There's a table right here,' said Hugo.

He supposed that given time he would grow a second skin. Hopefully, by then, his own gaffes would no longer bother him.

They shared the table with Meat Loaf and Virginia. Meat Loaf he didn't mind: he could have done without Virginia. He had nothing against her, but he didn't exactly relish the idea of her sitting there, directly opposite, watching as he slurped curry over the side of his plate and felt about with his fingers for odd bits which eluded him. Virginia had always been so fastidious. (Rather like Diana. He wondered what *she* would say, were she to see him now. Nothing very complimentary, if past memories were anything to go by. Heaven knows, she had found him boring enough even when he'd had all his faculties.)

'I must dash.' He heard the scrape of a chair, as Virginia stood up. 'I've a million and one letters to type and Madame's on the war path.'

'I, too.' Meat Loaf, more ponderously, rose to his feet. His shoes creaked as he moved round the table: a hand descended on Paul's shoulder. 'Am glad you vent to Papa Jo, Vas right thing to do; yes?'

Lightly, he said: 'So what are you angling for? A gold star?'

'No star; iss only vhat anybody iss advisink.'

Anybody, thought Paul, who happened to have noticed. So far, discounting Ludmila, and by extension Papa Jo, Meat Loaf was the only one who showed any signs of having done so. He wondered again about Caroline. He wished he could be certain. Yesterday evening, before he had broken the news to Rose and Hugo, she had telephoned him from Paris. He had informed her, quite casually, as if it were a matter of absolutely no moment, that he had handed over the conducting to Hugo. She had said 'Oh?' And then: 'Why's that?' He had so nearly told her. The words had actually formed themselves on his lips — 'To be perfectly honest, I can no longer see well enough to do it' — and then Rose had come in from the shop, clip-clopping in her Scholl sandals, and abruptly he had changed his mind, mumbling instead some feeble rubbish about 'leaving things to the experts'. He didn't know whether she had believed him or not: he had passed her over, at that point, to Rose.

'Feel like another coffee?'

'I'll get them.' He could walk a couple of yards to the counter and purchase two cups of coffee unaided; he wasn't totally useless. He felt the need, suddenly, to demonstrate the fact.

As he returned in minor triumph to the table, Hugo said: 'Not just a pretty face, huh?'

'You'd better believe it ... bit of practice, I'll be performing juggling acts.' At least with Hugo one could laugh about it. It was hardly what one would call a laughing matter, but anything was better than sympathetic gush.

'Talking of juggling,' said Hugo, 'you'd better start getting your act together . . . we'll be wanting you to do a bit on our behalf in the near future. Same like what I done for you — except that yours was a posh do, in a church and all.'

'Don't remind me.' The church had been Diana's choice, as had the notice in The Times and the photographs in all the top society mags. *Diana, eldest daughter of Colonel and Mrs H.C. Tohourdin* (pronounced Tawden) *of Dorking, Surrey, to Paul, only son of the late Mr and Mrs Patrick Salinger* (pronounced Salinjer) *of Tenterden, Kent*. Looking back, he realised the whole thing had been a farce from the very start. Hugo and Rose were at least going into it without blinkers. 'So when exactly.' he said, 'is the big day?'

'Week after the Festival.'

'Won't Rose be rather —' He made shapes in the air.

'She will, rather. Will it bother you?'

'Embarrass me frightfully.'

'So how about it? Can I rely upon you to come and sustain me in my hour of greatest joy?'

'You'll be taking a risk.'

'I'm prepared.'

'You mean it won't bother you if I go and hog all the limelight by doing something stupid?'

'Like what?' said Hugo.

Like almost anything.

'Falling flat on my face? Tripping over the altar rail?'

'It's a registry office,' said Hugo. 'You can't do much damage in a registry office. In any case —' He paused. 'We're rather hoping that Caroline will be here.'

'I see.' Carefully he felt round for his coffee. He hadn't wanted to talk about Caroline with Papa Jo, he didn't want to talk about her with Hugo. Last night, in a state of maudlin intoxication (they had made him drink double brandies, as well as eating steak and chips) he had wept all over Rose, talking about Caroline. It was the first time he had wept in more years than he cared to remember. Fortunately he had left it until they were back in the Lodge, and fortunately Hugo, at the time, had been out in the kitchen making coffee. (He had his suspicions that Hugo may have come back in the middle of it and been sharply sent away again, but he couldn't be sure. There were so many things, now, that he couldn't be sure of.) Rose had been sweet, and kind, and understanding, just as one would expect her to be. She had stroked his hair and pressed his face to her bosom and made soothing noises into his ear. She had done everything that could be done, and he had woken next morning feeling the biggest fool in Christendom. Weeping hadn't helped restore his lost sight: it wasn't going to help restore Caroline. Caroline was in Paris with Larry, and soon she was going to be in San Diego with Larry, and that would be that. Finis. Over and done with. The end. He didn't want to talk about it.

'If Caroline were here,' said Hugo, 'you wouldn't get the opportunity to hog any limelight ... I should give her strict instructions to keep an eye on you.'

'Really?' Paul finished his coffee and stood up. 'I've got a class at one-thirty.' He turned, in what he fervently hoped was the direction of the exit. 'Are you going to help me fight my way out of this rabble, or do I have to fend for myself?'

Under the shower, Larry sang lustily: Daniela's theme, from the new ballet that he was writing. It was a good part, Daniela; strong, lyrical, full of passion. A part any dancer would give her eye teeth to have written for her.

Caroline stretched, luxuriously, beneath the covers. The sheets were made of silk, the bed, a four-poster, was draped in rose-coloured hangings. The whole apartment was quite ridiculously lush. Overhead, which was a waste, since it couldn't be seen through the rose-coloured draperies, the ceiling was a riot of little pink cherubs, all naked and rolling about: in the bathroom the fitments were of gold, with shell-shaped porcelain in flushed crimson. It was all quite hideous, but he had chosen it for her, because he thought it was what she would like; and so, of course, she did. It was the first time in their relationship that he had ever consulted her inclinations (what he conceived to be her inclinations) rather than his own. She could not but be touched — the more so, as the place was so unspeakably revolting. Somehow, if he had gauged it correctly, found somewhere discreet and unpretentious, in impeccable good taste, such as Paul would unerringly have chosen, it would have seemed too slick; too planned. The hotel Marie-Victoire, in its unashamed vulgarity, struck exactly the right note.

Larry called to her from the bathroom: 'Where d'you want to go this evening?'

'Oh . . . anywhere you like. I'm not fussy. Maybe we should do a night club?'

Since he had made an effort for her, she would make an effort for him. Strolling hand in hand along the banks of the Seine might be her idea of a good time, but she knew it was not his. Paul would have enjoyed it, but then Paul had never been one for the high life. Crowds had always been a torment to him. She supposed, now, that they would be even more so. She really ought to call him again. She turned on her side, reaching out for Larry's watch — the latest in digital gadgetry, with an alarm which he kept setting every half-hour to remind himself to do things: call home, take his blood pressure, swallow a pill. It rang now, as she picked it up. From the bathroom came a yelp: 'Jesus! Eight o'clock already?'

Time for another pill. He had carted a whole load over with him. Bettina, it seemed, had discovered homeopathic medicines, which could be taken for everything from pre-menstrual tension to allergic rhinitis. Bettina was taking them for her migraine and her asthma, both brought on by periods of stress, such as divorce proceedings. Larry was taking them for high blood pressure, hay fever, nasal congestion and gastric ulcer, none of which he suffered from but any of which might attack at a moment's notice, owing to a predisposition in the family. She shook her head, indulgent. Larry in her absence had gotten to be quite an old woman. He had reminded her last night that he would be forty next birthday.

'That's a great age, I'll have you know. I'm entering upon the era of the coronary. From now on, I have to be humoured. I have to lead a life without strain. I need to be looked after and cosseted . . . what do you say to flying down to Nice for a few days?'

If that was what he wanted: she was in a mood to please. She had made only one stipulation, that she should be back at Bampton in time for the first performance of *Jane*. He had not been too happy about that; she had known he wouldn't be. He had taken it for granted they would be flying back to the States together from Paris, had already booked them on to a flight — to coincide, whether by accident or design, with Day One of the Festival. Grumpily, after a bit of wrangling, he had agreed to put it back by twenty-four hours.

'But not a minute longer . . . I want you back here the following day, all packed and ready to go. Agreed?'

'I guess so.' There really wouldn't be much point in staying on more than the one day; not if she'd made up her mind to go.

'Not good enough! Say "yes, I agree".'

'Yes . . . all right! I agree! Anything to stop you getting nasal congestion.'

As so often with Larry, she hadn't so much made up her mind as had it made up for her. It was a habit she had come to Europe with the specific intention of breaking; had thought, until that moment, that she had succeeded in doing so. It was no excuse to say that he had used unfair tactics, although undeniably he had. They had been in bed at the time, sensuously entwined in the slinky silk sheets, enclosed in their tent of rose-pink draperies, with the naked cherubs, out of sight if not out of mind, erotically cavorting overhead. Nonetheless, she could have said no.

She turned, and replaced the watch. She really ought to call Paul and tell him her plans. She had spoken with him briefly last night, but the conversation had been stilted; awkward on both sides. It had left her with a feeling of dissatisfaction — of business unfinished.

He had told her, quite casually, just tossing it out at the tail end of the call, that he had handed over the conducting to Hugo.

'Oh?' she had said. She had known that it must happen. They had all of them known that it must happen. Still, it had startled her to hear him actually say it. 'Why's that?'

For just a second she had thought he was going to tell her — and if he had, what then? Out to supper, back to bed, make love in the silken sheets, sweet dreams of bliss everlasting 'neath the canopy of copulating cherubs? The question had not arisen: at the last minute, his courage had failed.

'Oh . . . I reckoned it would probably be best. Seeing as he's the expert.'

He obviously didn't want her to know; he preferred that she should remain in ignorance. It behove her, therefore, to go on pretending to that ignorance. Easiest for her, easiest for him. Make love in the silken sheets. Go to Nice. Dance Daniela. Forget about Paul, he had had his chance.

Still and all, she ought to call him.

The telephone, sitting on a small, marble-topped

table with wrought-iron base, was a delicate *objet d'art*, painted white and decorated with twining rose buds. It seemed almost sacrilegious to use it as anything so workaday as a telephone; the presence of Larry, also, was an inhibiting factor. He didn't like her calling Paul. They had almost had — not a row, but a degree of unpleasantness about it.

'Can't you be away even five minutes without you have to call the guy? What's the matter with him, for Chrissakes? He need a wet nurse, or something?'

She wouldn't call him again, once they were in Nice, but she couldn't go off with a clear conscience leaving things as they had been left yesterday. Determinedly, she drew the flowered telephone towards her, into the pink draperies. What with the shower turned full on, and splutters of Daniela's theme still issuing forth, Larry probably wouldn't be able to hear in any case.

It was Rose who answered. Paul, she said, was not there: he was up at the school with Hugo, attending a rehearsal.

'So how is he?'

Not too bad, said Rose; all things considered. Everybody now knew the truth, and everybody was doing their best to be helpful and make life easier for him. (Except Caroline, who was going to Nice with Larry.) Meat Loaf, especially, had turned up trumps.

'Even the Lady Virginia, can you believe, has offered to take him jogging?'

Jogging already. *Big deal*.

All right, Ramirez! So what are you offering to do? In a nutshell: nothing. You just slouch off down to Nice and leave him to get on with it. Who cares if he walks into a few closed doors or trips up the odd kerb or two? There's enough people around to pick up the pieces. He doesn't need you.

'He's told all the kids,' said Rose. 'He said that was the part he dreaded most, but apparently they've been really good about it. They've formed a sort of protection league — keep popping up out of the woodwork and asking if he needs anything. Hugo says it's quite touching . . . they'd even blow his nose for him if he let them.'

With so many willing hands, what need had he of her?

'Sounds like he's coping OK.'

'On the whole: most of the time. At least he doesn't have to pretend any more. We didn't let on, by the way — we just said we'd been a bit worried about him. We said we'd felt there was something wrong, but we hadn't quite been able to work out what.'

'Does that go for me too?' said Caroline.

There was a perceptible pause before Rose replied.

'We thought perhaps we should leave that to you. We didn't know what you'd want.'

'It's not what I want, so much as what Paul wants . . . whatever is going to make him happiest.'

'I can't tell you that,' said Rose. 'Paul's the only one that can tell you that.'

She raised an eyebrow. Did she detect a hint of antagonism?

'All I can tell you,' said Rose, 'is what he *says* would make him happiest.'

'What's that?'

'That's for you to go straight back home from Paris without ever realising.'

'You mean, not come to the Festival?'

'Well, obviously, if you came to the Festival he's scared someone would be bound to let the cat out of the bag.'

'So what are you trying to tell me? That I ought to stay away?'

'I'm just telling you what Paul says would make him happiest.'

She frowned.

'You don't believe him?'

'Do you?' said Rose.

253

Do you, don't you, do you, don't you ... what was this? An inquisition? She had come over to Europe to sort out her own problems, not get embroiled in Paul's. How was she expected to read the inner workings of his mind? If he said he didn't want her to know, then she had to accept it at face value: he didn't want her to know.

'Did he say if there was anything could be done about it?'

'We asked him. It seems there isn't.'

'You mean, they can't operate, or —'

Or what? Feed him homeopathic medicine?

'He says not,' said Rose.

She refused to believe it. These things didn't happen. People didn't get blinded in automobile accidents. They got scarred, or they got brain damaged, or even paralysed for life; they didn't get blinded. There had to be something that could be done.

'Has he really gone into this?' she said. 'I mean, consulted people? Specialists — eye people —'

'I know he's consulted one,' said Rose.

'One? He ought to be consulting half a dozen!'

'That's what Hugo said.'

'Then Hugo's right. For crying out loud! What does he think these people are? God, or something? *Infallible*?'

'If you came back over,' said Rose, 'you could tell him. He might listen to you.'

Why? Why should he listen to her, rather than Hugo? What did Rose want of her? Really?

She knew what Rose wanted of her. It was what Papa Jo wanted of her. What Hugo, in all probability, wanted of her.

What Paul wanted of her?

No; not Paul. He wanted her to go back to the States. He wanted her to go on feigning ignorance. Ultimately, no doubt, he would write and tell her, and she would write back, expressing surprise and dismay. She would tell him, in exchange, that she was going to marry Larry. He would understand, even if the others didn't. Paul knew too well what had gone before.

'Do you want him to give you a ring,' said Rose, 'when he gets back?'

'No, that's all right. Tell him —' she was on the point of saying, tell him I'll send a card from Nice. 'Tell him I'm going down to Nice for a day or so and I'll be in touch ... oh, and tell him, won't you, that I send my love?'

14

Rose and Hugo had gone off for the day. They had pressed him to go with them, but he had declined, ostensibly on the grounds that he had work to do. It was true that he did have work to do, but over and above that was the desire, at all costs, not to be a burden. Rose and Hugo were already bending over backwards to help him. He was there, like an incubus, when they woke in the mornings, when they went to bed at night. Always, it seemed, there was some minor task he needed to have done for him — a letter read out, a telephone number looked up, a missing object run to earth. They took him down to the village, they drove him into Cheltenham. Rose insisted, in spite of his protests, on cooking his meals, and yesterday had also attempted to do his washing and clean his room.

'Just until you get things sorted out. You can't learn everything all at once, and anyway your room is disgusting. It looks as if it hasn't been touched for weeks.'

That was probably because it hadn't been. He had felt guilty about it, and said that he would do it himself. He would spend the whole of Sunday cleaning his room *and* doing his washing. He didn't see why Rose should be expected to do it for him. In the days of Diana they had had a pearl beyond price called Mrs Pomeroy, who had kept the place spick and span as never was. Unfortunately, during Paul's spell in hospital Mrs Pomeroy had suddenly taken it into her head to up and off to Weston-super-Mare, there to reside with her widowed sister who ran a boarding house. By the time he had returned home, with vision already somewhat hazy, though not as yet sufficient to seriously impede, the Lodge had reverted to its normal, pre-Diana state of shambles. Somehow or other, it had been that way ever since.

'I mean, we *could* look for someone else,' said Rose, 'if you wanted.'

She said it at fairly regular intervals, roughly about once a month when the place became unbearable, but Hugo washed his hands of such matters, and Paul left it to Rose, which was a mistake, since things left to Rose rarely tended to get done. He knew it perfectly well, so had no one but himself to blame. If now he had to waste precious minutes of his time fighting losing battles with domestic chores the like of which, during the reign of Diana, he had never been troubled with, the fault was entirely his own.

Laboriously, with all the skill and expertise of an untrained two-year old, he felt his way across the bedroom floor with the vacuum cleaner. From somewhere downstairs, Rose's grandfather clock struck the hour: he had been feeling his way across the bedroom floor for the past fifteen minutes. It wasn't even a large floor; not as floors went. He straightened up, easing his aching back. He couldn't remember which areas he'd done and which he hadn't. Cautiously, he bent down to feel the patch of carpet immediately to his right. Not quite cautiously enough: he had forgotten that in his peregrinations to and fro he had hauled bits of the furniture about. Something sharp, as he bent, caught him a nasty jab just above his right eye. He swore; loudly and uncouthly. If he didn't start learning to put out a hand before making these ill-judged forays into uncharted space he was going to do himself a serious injury. His forehead, even as it was, was already covered in a network of blemishes from past unthinking episodes.

He examined himself gingerly with the tips of his fingers, feeling for signs of broken skin. Fortunately, there didn't seem to be any. If Rose and Hugo were to come back and find him with yet another wound to add to his collection, there would be all hell to pay. They nagged at him like a couple of old women.

'What in God's name have you been up to *this* time?'

'*Honestly*, Paul . . . you must take more *care*.'

He switched the vacuum cleaner back on. Immediately, above the ear-splitting racket of it, there came the sound of the telephone. For a moment he was tempted to let the thing scream, but then he thought, it could be Caroline. She had telephoned the other day, when he was up at the Hall, and told Rose she was going down to Nice. She had said that she would be in touch. He wouldn't want to miss her a second time.

He switched off the vacuum cleaner, felt his way with due caution through the maze of furniture, and hurtled down the stairs.

'Hallo?'

It wasn't Caroline, it was Diana. He recognised her voice at once: the light, crisp, slightly barking tones of upper-class Surrey. Strange that he should have been thinking of her — but yet perhaps not so strange after all. He quite often did think of her, even now. You couldn't be married to a person for five whole years and expunge them from memory all in a matter of months.

'Where are you?' he asked.

She was in Cheltenham — 'just passing through'.

'I had to be in the district, so I was wondering whether I might stop by and see you . . . or would that give you problems?'

'No problems,' he said. Certainly not emotional ones. He could see Diana again without any pang at heart, and with a bit of luck, for the short time that she was likely to be here, could hide the fact of his incapacity from her. (He felt, instinctively, that he must hide it, for quite other reasons than those which made him so anxious to keep it from Caroline: if there was anyone whose sympathy would be intolerable to him, it was Diana.) 'The only slight difficulty that does arise is that I can't come and pick you up ... I don't run a car any more.'

'That's all right, I've got my own.'

He noticed she showed no surprise at his lack of transport. With her knowledge of local conditions, he would have expected her at least to query it.

'I'll come straight over. Be with you in about half an hour.'

He pulled a face: half an hour didn't really give him as long as he would have liked. Even if he hadn't been stinking like a pole cat after his exertions with the vacuum cleaner, he would still have shied away from the thought of Diana discovering him unshaven, in old T-shirt and washed-out jeans.

He had just the time, before she arrived, to set the bedroom to rights (why did he bother to do that, he wondered afterwards?) to take a quick shower and make himself presentable: to ferret about in the kitchen until he came across a packet of salted something or others — cashews, by the taste — dump them into a dish, carry them through to the sitting-room and feel his way round their somewhat meagre selection of bottles until he could be reasonably certain of locating anything she might happen to want. (Unless she was on one of her difficult-to-please kicks, and demanded some way-out cocktail he'd never even heard of. If she was in one of those moods, she could go hang. He wasn't running the risk of taking her down to the Saracen's: he knew his limitations well enough by now.)

The door bell rang. Not without certain inner trepidations, he went to answer it.

'Diana?'

'Paul —'

Slight hesitation on both sides; scarcely surprising. The last time they'd met — if meeting it could be called — had been in the divorce court. It had all been very restrained, very polite, no mud-slinging or recriminations, but hardly conducive, a bare four months later, to normal social intercourse.

'Come in,' he said.

She walked past him into the hall. He caught the familiar fragrance of her scent; some expensive little number by Dior, no doubt. Diana had always had excellent taste. He wondered whether to take a chance and offer to relieve her of her coat, then decided against it. It was the end of April, the weather was warm, she might not be wearing one. Better not risk it.

'How are you?' she said.

'As you see me. And you?'

'As you see me?'

There was a definite query in her voice. He froze. (What was he doing that was wrong? Looking in the wrong direction? Looking straight past her?) Lightly, with a finger, she touched the tip of his nose.

'You're not wearing your glasses.'

'Oh! No. I —' He what? 'I went back to contact lenses.'

Why did he bother to lie? What on earth was the point? Like everyone else, she was bound to discover sooner or later. Even if he didn't go and blow it in the next few minutes by performing one of his favourite parlour tricks, she would hear it through the musical grapevine, or read about it in one of the papers. (From now on, he knew, he was doomed to be not just 'Paul Salinger, the composer' but 'Paul Salinger, the blind composer'. He wondered if Beethoven had had to suffer similar indignity: Ludwig van Beethoven, the deaf composer. . . .)

'So what are you doing in this neck of the woods?' he said.

'Just visiting. I thought while I was up here I might as well look in and see how things were going . . . how *are* they going?'

'Fine.' He didn't bother telling her about *Jane*. It was a project which had been in hand even before their break-up, but he doubted she would remember; or even if she did, would not be interested. 'How about you?' He led her through to the sitting-room. On the whole, he felt pretty safe indoors. If he just stopped to think before he did things, he couldn't go too far wrong. 'Are you living at home, or —'

'Town. I've still got the flat.'

Of course; he had forgotten the flat. A snazzy little pied à terre in a luxury block near Marble Arch. He had only been there a couple of times. That had been during the final run-up, when their relationship had already reached a point of no return. She had taken the place originally as a protest against being expected to bury herself in the depths of the country, leading the life, as she had bitterly complained, of a Carmelite nun. It hadn't exactly been like that of a Carmelite nun: the physical side of the relationship at least had lived up to expectations. That was one area in which they had not failed each other. Still, he could appreciate now, far better than before, the frustrations she must have experienced, shut up at Bampton without an audience. Diana had not been born to blush unseen. She needed a circle of admirers before she could properly flourish and be her true self.

'What will you have to drink?' He moved, competently, to the cabinet where he had ranged the bottles. 'Sherry? Whisky? Gin?'

'A sherry would do nicely.'

That was a surprise for a start. He had never in all their years together known Diana accept what was offered her. It had sometimes seemed to him that as a matter of principle she had to be contrary.

'Dry? Medium?'

'Whichever. I don't mind.'

Curiouser and curiouser. He poured a couple of La Inas and took them carefully across to the small table which he had set squarely in the middle of the room, along with the dish of salted cashews.

'Take a seat.'

He heard the creak of wicker, and knew that she was on the opposite side of the table, sitting in the aged rocker donated by Rose's great-aunt from Bognor Regis. (The same as had blessed them with the striking clock, now become such a godsend.) He himself made use of the sofa, which happened to be in a direct line. There was a pause.

'Well!' he said. 'You're looking good.' It seemed a safe bet. She would never have stopped by if she hadn't been; and anyway, she always did. 'What are you up to these days?'

'Not very much. Same old boring routine.' Boring old parties. Boring old Monte. Boring old Cowes and Ascot and Glyndebourne. 'How about you?'

'Not very much,' he said. 'Same old boring music.'

'Your Festival thing is on soon, isn't it?'

'That's right.' The Festival thing, where first they had run foul of each other.

'I take it you've written something?'

'For my sins.'

'I suppose, really —' he heard the rocker creak, as she leaned forward for her drink — 'one ought to come along.'

'Not on my account, I beg.'

'But, darling, you're growing quite famous! I hadn't realised. I was at a party the other day and I happened to mention your name to someone, just casually, the way one does, and he said — he actually *said* — I mean, it sounded like a line out of some third-rate play — he actually said, not *the* Paul Salinger?'

'So you said, no, the bum I was married to.'

'I didn't say anything of the sort! I asked him if he knew your string quartet, and he said yes, he'd heard it just recently at a recital of contemporary music at the Queen Elizabeth. We had quite a long chat about it.'

He wondered how she had managed that. Amused, he said: 'But you don't know anything about my string quartet.'

'Darling, of course I do!' She sounded reproachful; almost hurt. How could he possibly have forgotten? 'It's my favourite of all your music! It's what you were playing when we very first met.'

'Of course!' he said. 'How foolish of me! I remember now . . . you thought the slow movement was sublime.'

'And still do! It puts me in mind of the slow movement from the Schubert Quintet.'

He was even more amused. Schubert Quintet, forsooth! Diana couldn't tell the Schubert Quintet from a concerto for sackbut and wind band. She had obviously been storing useful snippets of information from her friend at the party. He wondered whence the sudden interest. What, really, had she come for? To see how well he was managing without her?

'How are Mummy and Daddy?' he said. Not that he really cared; they had never gone a bundle on him. His background may have been right (just about) but his attitude certainly was not. If Diana had to go and get herself tied up with a musician, then at least, for God's sake, let it be one who was prepared to play the social games and observe the social niceties. 'I imagine they must have been pretty relieved when we finally decided to pack it in.'

'That's not a very nice thing to say.'

'Why not? I wouldn't blame them. I can hardly have been a very satisfactory son-in-law, from their point of view.'

'They didn't understand you,' said Diana. 'Any more than you understood them.'

He grimaced.

'Any more than we understood each other?'

'Oh, now, don't start on that!' He could almost see her pouting, in the way that she used to — the way that had so captivated him during those first few months of heady rapture. 'I came here hoping we could manage to be civilised.'

'Weren't we always? We never threw things. We didn't hurl insults — apart from you telling me how boring I was. And how introverted. And what an isolationist. Fancy another sherry?'

He was taking a chance, but he had dug out their only two proper sherry glasses — originally part of a set of six, which had come from Bognor Regis, along with the striking clock and a threadbare Persian rug which would have been worth 'untold thousands' had it any of its basic pattern left. Rose was always telling them: 'That rug would be worth untold thousands if it had any of its basic pattern left.' The sherry glasses wouldn't have been worth untold thousands, even if they had still been six instead of two, but they were nonetheless exceedingly genteel. They only held a couple of mouthfuls. He defied even Diana, at her most ladylike, to make a couple of mouthfuls last longer than five minutes.

'Give us your glass.' He held out a hand: obediently she put the glass into it. Really, he thought, everything was so simple if you just went to the elementary trouble of thinking it out beforehand. Pleased with himself, he poured a couple more sherries and bore them back again, to the table. He even felt confident enough to continue the conversation as he did so.

'We never actually, so far as I remember, came to blows. So if we were civilised then, I really don't see why we shouldn't be civilised now.'

'Quite,' said Diana.

He was startled: her voice was not coming from where it ought to have come. She must have gone and moved, while his attention was elsewhere. She must be sitting on the sofa. Why was she doing that? And how had she got there? He hadn't noticed the rocker creak. He had thought, by now, that he was alert to every sound.

'Come and sit down.' She took his hand, pulling him on to the sofa beside her. 'Last time I saw you, you still had a scar. From the accident. Has it gone yet?' She swept his hair back, off his forehead. Had he realised what she intended, he would have stopped her. Too late: she had already seen. 'Darling, what on *earth* —'

Impatiently, he jerked his head away.

'Some silly little devil left a music stand lying around. Don't worry about it. Tell me about Mummy and Daddy.'

'Never mind Mummy and Daddy! They're boring. I'd rather talk about you.'

Why? What did she want to talk about him for? She knew all about him. She'd lived with him for close on five years.

'There really isn't anything to talk about,' he said. 'I'm here at Bampton, just as I always was, writing my boring old music, being introverted —'

'Paul! Hush!' He felt her lips upon his. Warm; faintly scented. 'Be civilised! Where are Rose and the dreaded McDonald?'

'They're — out,' he said.

'Down at the Saracen's?'

'No. Out for the day. They've gone —' He couldn't remember where they had gone. They had told him at least six times. 'I wish you'd change your mind and come with us,' Rose had kept saying. Maybe he should have gone with them. Maybe it would have been better. Certainly it would have been safer. Sitting here, alone with Diana —

'Just fancy,' she said. 'The McDonald managing to do something tactful for once . . . I bet if he'd known I was coming he'd have clung like a limpet.'

It was, he supposed, inevitable that they should end up in bed together. Diana had quite obviously come here for that purpose — if not as a main objective, certainly with thoughts of it in mind — and in all honesty he could not have said that he himself was averse to the idea. Since the night at Marden, when he had so shamefully made Caroline cry, he had led a life of unsullied purity; partly by way of self-punishment, partly, be it admitted, because the opportunities had not offered. Virginia, no doubt, would have been willing had he cared to cajole her. Several times this past week she had intimated that for her part she would have no objections to letting bygones be bygones. If he felt like resuming the relationship where they had left off.... Once or twice he had been tempted, but always, at the last minute, thoughts of Caroline had intervened.

If they did not intervene now, he could only excuse himself — limply — on the grounds that prolonged abstinence had weakened his resolve. Or, more accurately, that he was not sufficiently strong-minded to stand out against Diana's powers of persuasion. In truth, he scarcely needed any persuading. She had lived with him too long: she knew too well how to rouse.

Afterwards, complacent — but yet with just a faint hint of challenge? — she said: 'We were always good in bed together, weren't we?'

'Our only common meeting place ... the one area where I could perform to your satisfaction.'

'And still can.' She leaned over to plant a kiss on his brow. He felt her breasts brush soft against his arm. 'Allow me to congratulate you ... you haven't lost your touch.'

'Did you expect me to have done so?'

'Not really. But after everything you've been through —'

He frowned.

'What have I been through?'

'Well ... the divorce, for a start.'

'We've both been through that.'

'Yes, but then you had that ghastly accident to cope with ... poor lamb!' A finger wandered gently over his forehead, tracing the outline of his various cuts and scratches. 'You have had a rough time of it, haven't you?'

He shifted, uncomfortably. He could feel her breath, warm on his cheek, and knew that she was looking down at him; studying him. It gave him a distinct feeling of unease. He did not care, these days, to be subjected to too close scrutiny. Rose had assured him that 'no one could tell . . . not just by looking,' but he didn't altogether trust Rose. She was too kind-hearted. She would say anything to anyone if she thought it was going to make them feel better. He still remembered the way Papa Jo had reacted when he removed his glasses. There was obviously something; something that people sensed —

'It's all right,' whispered Diana. 'You don't have to turn away.' She leaned closer: he felt her lips brushing his eyelashes. 'I do know.'

He was silent a moment.

'How?'

He couldn't think of any way in which she could have found out. She had come to see him in hospital a couple of times, when he had still been bandaged up like a mummy, but so far as he knew she had not spoken to any of the medical staff, and even if she had they could not have told her anything definite; not at that stage. At that stage there had still been grounds for optimism.

'Someone mentioned it to me — I can't remember who it was now. Probably the person I was talking to about your string quartet. He must have got it from somewhere . . . you know how these things fly about.'

He was all too well aware, but still it was difficult to imagine how this particular piece of news could have hit the streets so soon. It was only a fortnight since it had become common knowledge at Bampton. Unless, perhaps, one of the soloists — not Peter; he would be too discreet. But Martina — she was a talker. He wouldn't put it past her to have spilt the beans. Not that he could blame her, if she had: he had enjoined no one to secrecy. He had hoped it wouldn't be spread around before the Festival, but unless you actually put someone like Martina on oath it was probably asking the impossible, expecting her to maintain silence. There was, after all, no reason why she should.

'Tell me —' lightly, Diana traced a finger over his eyelids — 'did you know all that time ago? When I came to the hospital?'

'I knew there was a possibility.'

'And yet you never mentioned it to me?'

He shrugged.

'I didn't see why you should have to be bothered. We'd already agreed on a divorce. I didn't want to run any risk of you suddenly feeling duty bound to stick by me ... poor old Paul, how's he going to manage? Any of that sort of crap.'

Not that there would have been much likelihood. Diana was not the sort to offer herself up in the rôle of martyr, and even had she attempted it, in a rare fit of altruism, he would not have let her.

'I suppose, the way things were —' she sounded for a moment almost regretful — 'it wouldn't have been wise.'

'I'm quite sure it wouldn't.'

'Do you still feel bitter?'

'Not in the slightest. Do you?'

'Not at all. That's part of the reason I came back — that, and to find out how you were.'

'Poor old Paul? How is he managing?'

'Well, obviously,' she said, 'it came as something of a shock. When I heard what had happened —'

'I'm sorry, I ought to have told you. I didn't think.'

'It's just that it made it a bit awkward ... knowing what to say.'

'Yes; I suppose it would.'

'It would have been easier if you'd — well!' She gave a little laugh; self-conscious. 'If you'd *looked* as if —'

'As if I were blind,' he said.

'Yes. I mean — oh, you know what I mean! If it had been obvious.'

If he'd been carrying some mark of identification. Maybe he ought to take to wearing a label round his neck: BLIND. STRING QUARTET AND TEN SYMPHONIES TO SUPPORT....

'Anyway,' said Diana, 'you can't wonder at my being worried about you.'

'You don't have to be, I assure you. I'm doing fine.'

'You don't look as if you are.' She swept his hair back again, off his forehead. 'You look as if you spend your life crashing into things.'

'One is bound to be a bit clumsy,' he murmured, 'just at first.'

'The McDonald should take more care of you.'

'He does his best. He can't be with me every minute of the day. Besides, I like to crash into things occasionally . . . keeps me on my toes.'

'Paul!' She rubbed her cheek, reproachfully, against his. 'You need looking after.'

'I'll get myself a guide dog,' he said.

'Silly . . . that's not what I meant.'

'But guide dogs are wonderful! People have crossed Dartmoor with guide dogs. You can even go on tube trains with them.'

'And that is the height of your ambition? To go on tube trains?'

'At this moment in time,' he said, 'it strikes me as the very summit of achievement.'

'Don't be so pathetic!' She ruffled his hair back into place. 'Why don't I come back again and look after you?'

The suggestion took him by surprise: it was something he had definitely not been prepared for.

'What's the matter?' said Diana. 'Don't you think I'd look after you properly?'

He was moved to protest: 'I don't need looking after!'

'Darling, that's a very brave thing to say, but totally

self-deluding ... look at you! Covered in cuts and bruises! I can tell you one thing: *I* wouldn't let that happen to you.'

No, he thought, with a cynicism born of long habit where his dealings with Diana were concerned: it spoils my beauty. He could hardly be displayed with any sense of pride, pockmarked as he was by layers of scar tissue. But then, even without the scar tissue, the days had gone when he could be displayed with any pride. Diana was not the sort to cart a cripple round with her. What on earth did she want to come back to him for?

'It's a nice idea,' he said, 'but you know it would never work. you wouldn't be any happier living here now than you were before. The situation wouldn't be any different — just worse.'

'When you say, living *here* ... you don't mean you're going to try and continue teaching?'

'What else would you suggest?'

'I would have thought it would be more to the point to concentrate on writing your music ... after all, you are *the* Paul Salinger.'

'Diana, we had all this out before! You know as well as I do that it's not practical. I may be *the* Paul Salinger, but I am far from being *the* J. Paul Getty.'

'But, darling, you don't have to be!'

They had had all that out before, as well. It was one of Diana's oldest arguments: what was the point of marrying a Woman of Means if you didn't intent to take advantage of it? *She* was perfectly willing to support him. Daddy, of course, would huff and puff, but then it had nothing to do with Daddy. The means were Diana's and she would use them as she chose. Unfortunately, for once — though for different reasons — Paul had seen eye to eye with Daddy. He had refused point blank to be supported by Diana. It was not that he had any objection in principle: only in practice. He had seen himself doomed to a life of lap-dogdom — the pet composer, trotted out at parties with a bow in his hair for the edification of guests. And in any case, over and above all else, there was the fact that he actually enjoyed his work as a teacher. Diana had never understood that. She had always insisted on taking it as an example of stubborn masculine pride.

'Surely *now*,' she said, 'it wouldn't bother you?'

'If it bothered me before,' he said, 'don't you think it would bother me even *more* now?'

'Oh, but that's just foolishness!'

'Is it?'

'Well, of course it is!'

What she meant was that now he had a legitimate excuse: nobody, now, could blame him for giving in and living off her. Not even Daddy. In his condition, what else was he supposed to do? Go and tune pianos? Answer telephones?

'Paul, darling, do be sensible! How can you possibly go on teaching? Look at all that paperwork you used to do — all those *hours* you used to spend going through the kids' exercises. How will you be able to? *Now?*'

'I don't know yet. I'll find a way.'

'But why? Why bother? When you could give it all up tomorrow and devote yourself full-time to writing your own stuff? Otherwise, when will you ever get the chance? It just doesn't make sense! And what happens when Rose and Hugo aren't here? Let's face it, Hugo's not going to bury himself at Bampton for ever, he's got ambition. So what's going to happen when they move away? You won't be able to manage by yourself.'

They were all of them, he had to admit it, points which had already crossed his mind. He would not pretend that it didn't occasionally frighten the hell out of him, lying awake at the dead of night, contemplating a future of dependency on others. He knew (who didn't?) that some blind men managed to perform wonderful feats of daring such as slalom racing or water skiing; there were probably some mad bastards who had even dragged themselves up the south face of the Eiger or jumped through hoops of fire. It didn't alter the fact that ultimately they were still dependent on the goodwill of their fellows. *No man is an island, brother* — but some of us, he thought, aren't even peninsulas.

'Paul?' Diana had snuggled down again into the bed. She had her head nestling where it had always used to nestle (when they hadn't been engaged in internecine fighting) in the crook of his chin. Her hand, persuasively, stroked his thigh. 'Why don't you give it up? It really isn't important any more — you don't *need* to go on teaching. You've done your bit. What's important now is that you should concentrate on your own work ... tell Papa Jo you're leaving, and I'll start looking for a larger apartment — or a house. Would you prefer a house? Somewhere quiet and secluded ... Hampstead, Holland Park —'

He laughed at the idea of Hampstead or Holland Park being quiet and secluded. They probably were, to Diana; but he and she had always entertained different notions as to what constituted seclusion. It seemed they still did. There was no reason, of course, for either of them to have changed — save that his situation, now, might be deemed to have made him less obdurate. Less inclined to stand out against her wishes.

'How about it?' she said. 'Don't you think it might be worth a go?'

There were attractions to the idea; he would not deny it. If nothing else, it would relieve him of all practical worries, and that they still found each other physically more than acceptable had just been amply demonstrated. Still, with regret, he shook his head.

'Diney, I'm sorry,' he said. 'I don't mean to fling it back in your face, but — I have to say no.'

'Why? You don't think it would work?'

On the contrary, he thought it probably stood a great deal better chance now than it had before. Circumstances altered cases, and his had certainly undergone a most radical change: it had affected his outlook in more ways than the obvious. For all that, he could not go back to her.

'Is it — someone else?' she asked.

He jeered: 'You really think that's likely? With me in this state?'

'Why not? You're just as attractive now as you were before. Some people might say, even more so. . . .'

'Then some people would be idiots.' He swung his legs over the side of the bed. 'Let's go and grab some lunch.'

Since there was nothing, any more, to be concealed, he took her down the road to the Saracen's — or, to be strictly accurate, allowed her to take him. She was not as adept at it as Hugo. Hugo was able to do it casually, almost inconsequentially: Diana, being Diana, could not do anything inconsequentially but had to make a big production of it, possessing herself of his arm and purposefully steering him, with loud running commentary, for his benefit (and the benefit of half the neighbourhood) on the various obstacles they were by-passing. He found it somewhat of a trial: even a white stick would be preferable to this.

Over lunch (which he was at least permitted to choose for himself: to do her justice, she made no attempt at bullying him into eating what he had no wish to eat) they talked quite easily and amiably of nothing of much import. Diana was obviously in a mood to create goodwill. The failure of her mission had not noticeably upset her — indeed, he had the impression that it had been more of a spur-of-the-moment idea, born of post-coital euphoria, than a seriously thought-out plan of campaign — nor did she evince any great desire to probe the question of 'someone else'. Only towards the end of the meal, in tones just a little too bright for comfort, she said: 'I never asked about Caroline, did I? How is she after all this time? Still dancing?'

He concentrated on trying to break up a portion of

gooseberry tart without sending a shower of pastry over the side of the dish. It was a task which needed concentration. Most tasks did, these days.

'She's in Nice at the moment.'

'Really? What's she doing there?'

'Working,' he said.

Even as he said it, he wondered just who he thought he was kidding — himself, or Diana? Caroline hadn't gone to Nice to work, she'd gone there to enjoy herself and be with Larry. And why shouldn't she? It was her life: she had every right to enjoy it.

'Is she still with her choreographer?' said Diana.

What did she mean by 'with'?

'Yes,' he said. He speared with his fork at the gooseberry tart. 'She's still with him.'

'They've been together quite a while now, haven't they? I remember they were together that time we went to see her dance.' There was a pause. 'Darling, I hope you won't mind my mentioning it,' said Diana, 'but you are making rather a mess of that tart . . . would it insult you if I were to just lean over —' he felt her doing so — 'and cut it into *slightly* more manageable pieces?'

Afterwards, as they walked back up to the Lodge, she said: 'Well! That was all very civilised, wasn't it?'

'Apart from me throwing bits of pudding around the place.'

'Oh, don't be so silly . . . as if it matters.'

True; as if it mattered. There were, when all was said and done, more important things to worry about.

Yet still it mattered.

They turned in through the Lodge gates, their feet scrunching over gravel.

'I'm glad that I came,' said Diana.

Nobly, he said: 'I'm glad you did, too.'

'Do you really mean it?'

'Of course I really mean it.' He did, on the whole.

'You don't think I was just being nosy? Poor old Paul, I wonder how he's coping?'

A fleeting smile crossed his lips.

'If you were, I daresay it's only natural.'

'But I wasn't,' she said. 'Not entirely.'

A silence fell.

'Oh, well!' She loosened her grip on his arm. 'I'd better be getting a move on. I wouldn't want the McDonald coming back and catching me here.' Briefly, he felt her lips brush his. 'Look after yourself.'

'And you.'

'Oh! I always do. You ask the McDonald, he'll tell you . . . self-preservation is one of my most prominent characteristics. Do you want me to see you to the house?'

'I believe I can manage,' he said, gravely.

'The gate is right behind you.'

'Yes.'

'Well, if you're quite sure —' He heard the car door open and slam shut; then the window was wound down. 'I'll be off. Keep in touch.'

'I will.'

The engine started up. He suddenly remembered something: 'Diana . . . who was it who told you about me?' He didn't believe her story of 'someone at a party' and 'not remembering who'. Even allowing for a certain measure of frenzy in her social life, and his own relative unimportance in the scheme of things, such a claim to amnesia seemed a trifle too contrived to ring true.

'As a matter of fact,' she said, 'it was Ludmila.'

'Ludmila?'

That was the very last name he had anticipated. Martina he had been prepared for; but *Ludmila*? He had not even been aware that she and Diana had maintained any contact, though it was true Ludmila had never shared the rest of the school's antipathy towards her.

'She rang me,' said Diana, 'about a couple of weeks ago. She said she thought I ought to know.'

'But why?' He was flabbergasted. What in the name of God did it have to do with Ludmila?

'Well, it's not unreasonable,' said Diana. 'I do have *some* interest in your welfare. And anyway, she was only thinking of you.'

Was she? He wondered about that.

He went on wondering for the rest of the day.

15

Caroline waited a full week before calling Paul, and then when she did he wasn't there. It was Hugo, this time, who came to the telephone: Paul was up at the Hall, rehearsing. It was only what she should have expected. In these last few days before the Festival he would probably live up there, putting finishing touches, having last-minute consultations. She was only surprised that Hugo was not up there with him.

'In fact,' he said, 'I was just on my way. You caught me quite literally as I was going through the door.'

'In that case, I won't keep you. I only called to check how he feels about having me come over for the first night.'

She paused, waiting for Hugo to make some comment, offer some opinion; but all he said, businesslike, matter of fact, was: 'I'll get him to give you a bell when he's through rehearsing. Probably be about an hour. You going to be around?'

'Yes,' she said. 'I'll be around.'

'Does he have the number?'

She gave it to him.

'OK, I'll make sure he gets it. We've got a good scheme going now ... cassette machine by the telephone. Any messages, we simply put them on tape for him. Likewise, anyone gives him an address, or something he wants to make a note of ... it works pretty well. Anyway, how about you? Having a good time? Not gambling away all your fortune, I hope?'

'Not the way I play.' It was Larry who was the gambler, not her. One spin of the roulette wheel and he was anyone's. 'How are things your end?'

'So-so. The ex called round the other day.'

'Ex?'

'The Divine Diana.'

'Oh. Really?' She strove for the right note of unbiased interest. Interest that Diana should have called; but no personal concern of hers. 'What did she want?'

'I gather she had this bright idea they should get together again . . . suddenly fancies herself in the rôle of ministering angel. Leading him round on a pair of silken reins . . . fortunately he had the good sense to say no.'

And if he hadn't?

If he hadn't, it would still have been no concern of hers.

'So how is he managing, generally?'

'Up and down. He gets a bit depressed, which I guess isn't to be wondered at. He's being stupid over food at the moment — got this thing about making a mess when he eats. Totally irrational.'

It wasn't irrational, she thought; it was perfectly understandable. She had tried, the other night, just for a few moments, eating shellfish with her eyes shut. It had proved next to impossible. Larry had looked at her irritably and said 'For God's sake! You're splatting that stuff everywhere. What in hell do you think you're playing at?' She could hardly say to him, pretending to be Paul. . . .

'Maybe when you're back,' said Hugo, 'you can talk some sense into him. Point out that no one gives a damn. I'll tell him you called. Expect to hear from him in about an hour. About nine o'clock. OK?'

She waited an hour, but he didn't call. She guessed that the rehearsal had probably run over. She would have waited longer, but Larry was growing impatient, wanting to go out and eat before heading for the tables.

He had been pretty reasonable thus far. She had anticipated a scene — 'Why in hell should we hang around waiting for that bozo?' — but for once he had demonstrated quite unusual restraint. She had no wish to antagonise him. She agreed, in the end, to leave a message with the desk clerk.

'If a Mr Salinger should call me from England, would you tell him I had to go out? Ask him when it would be convenient for me to call him back?'

They dined, most evenings, in a sea-food restaurant they had discovered conveniently close to Larry's favourite casino. They had been there barely five minutes, had just settled down at the bar with drinks, when Larry, melodramatic, clapped a hand to his forehead.

'Holy shit!'

'What's the matter?' she said, alarmed.

'I forgot my pills.'

'Forgot your *pills*? Oh, come on, now! You can surely survive just one evening without?'

'You don't understand.' Larry had no sense of humour where his homeopathic medicines were concerned. 'You can't juggle around with these things. I have them all timetabled. If you're not prepared to keep to a strict schedule, you might as well not bother.'

She didn't know why he did bother. Bettina's influence, she sometimes suspected, was rather stronger than it ought to have been. Certainly, on this particular subject, it carried more weight than hers. No amount of teasing could shame him out of self-induced hypochondria: he was convinced, without his pills, that death from cerebral haemorrhage was just around the corner. (If not cerebral haemorrhage, then gastric ulcer — 'and that's no joke, I can tell you.')

'You stay on here, I'll grab a cab. Back in ten minutes.'

In the event, it took him nearer twenty.

'What kept you?' she said.

'I couldn't find the damn things. Would you believe it? I couldn't *find* them?'

'You ought to tie them in a bag around your neck.'

'Believe me, I'm thinking of it. . . .'

It was gone three in the morning when they arrived back at the hotel. She asked the night clerk if there were any messages for her, but there was none: Paul, it seemed, had not called. She guessed the rehearsal had probably gone on until the small hours. There was no cause for concern. The chances were, he would call her first thing.

He did not call; instead he sent a cable. It came up with the fresh orange juice and hot rolls at eleven o'clock.

CARLY STOP WOULD HONESTLY PREFER YOU NOT COME OVER FOR JANE STOP WILL EXPLAIN ALL LATER STOP LONG LETTER TO AWAIT YOUR ARRIVAL SAN DIEGO STOP ALL MY VERY BEST LOVE PAUL.

She sat, staring at it, wondering why she felt pole-axed.

'What is it?' Larry held out a hand, across the breakfast table. Numbly, she passed it to him. A breeze, warm yet with a faint malevolence, wafted fresh flower scent across the balcony. 'Well, that's one problem solved.' With an air of satisfaction, Larry folded the cable. 'Maybe now we can fly back home together as planned.'

'Maybe.' She picked up her orange juice. 'Don't rush me. I need time to think.'

'What's to think about? The guy doesn't want you there. He couldn't say it more plainly if he tried.'

Except that he might not be saying, thought Caroline, what he seems to be saying.

'He obviously reckons it's going to be a wash-out. You won't be doing him any favours. Let's face it, we all have off days . . . remember that ballet I did? *Street*

Games? I sure as hell would have given a lot to have some people not see that. I certainly wouldn't have thanked anyone flying in specially when I'd gone to the trouble of asking them not to.'

'No.' She spoke doubtingly, unconvinced by the argument. 'I suppose not.'

'Look,' said Larry, 'the way I see it, if he's asked you not to, then he's asked you not to. That's all you need concern yourself with. So he has problems? So it's up to him to sort them out. Just don't you go getting any guilt complex over it.'

'Why should I get a guilt complex?'

'Well —' He hunched a shoulder. 'Knowing you . . . always such a soft touch.'

'I don't see what point you're trying to make.'

'Look, the guy had his chance with you and he blew it. Am I right? Right.'

She frowned.

'Who told you that?'

'Told me what?'

'About Paul —' Having had his chance and having blown it. She had never mentioned anything of their past history to Larry. 'Where did you get it from?'

'I guess I've known all along. It didn't take much figuring. Why else do you suppose I've never pressed Bettina for a divorce? Because I knew darn well you'd only taken up with me as a means of getting even with him.'

There was just enough truth in the claim to make her stop and think. It sounded plausible enough — and yet the argument, basically, was false. She had not taken up with Larry as a means of getting even with Paul, but in an effort to forget Paul. For the last five years, Larry had had her exactly where he wanted her: in his bed and dancing in his ballets. Where he had not wanted her was at his side, walking down the aisle. Probably still didn't, if the truth were known.

'OK,' she said. 'So while we're on the subject . . . how *about* that divorce?'

'Shit to the divorce! I told you . . . the divorce is going through. All the more reason I don't want you suddenly getting soft in the head just because the guy's had a bit of a rough time and can't get his act together.'

Slowly, she set down her glass.

'How did you —'

'Huhalova told me. She called me, just a couple of weeks back. She said you were on the verge of sacrificing your career, and if I didn't want to lose one of my best dancers I'd better get over here pretty damn sharpish and do something about it. So I did. Not because I didn't want to lose one of my best dancers, but because I didn't want to lose *you*. OK? That satisfy you? You happy now?'

She supposed she ought to have experienced a warm and comforting glow of fulfilment radiating outwards through her body, such as radiated outwards through the bodies of all right-minded females when their menfolk declared a passion for possessiveness. Instead, all she experienced was a tidal wave of cold anger. God *damn* Ludmila. What right had she to go meddling in other people's lives? At least when Papa Jo tried it on he did so quite openly and obviously. He never went sticking knives in behind one's back. No wonder Ludmila had been so gushingly eager for her to abandon the kids and go jauntering off to Paris. Considering that it was she who had engineered the whole thing —

'So what's up now?' said Larry. Plainly, as far as he was concerned, the matter had been neatly finished and parcelled up. 'Now what's bugging you?'

'Oh, nothing,' she said. Her voice was heavy with sarcasm. 'Nothing at all . . . I just really enjoy having people manipulate me.'

'Manipulate? Who's manipulating? Because I don't want to lose you, that's manipulating?'

'Don't go on,' she said. 'I thought it was a spontaneous gesture.'

'Well, it was, wasn't it? She called me — I reacted. What could be more spontaneous than that?'

'What, indeed?' said Caroline.

She did not stay on with him at the casino that night. As a rule she sat around, watching as he played, trying to pretend she was having a good time. Tonight, she finally admitted that she was not.

'I'm going back to the hotel,' she said.

'What for? You feeling bad?'

'No . . . just a bit giddy, watching roulette wheels go round'

'You want we should play something else?'

'Not particularly.'

'So what're you gonna do?'

'Go to bed,' she said, 'and read.'

She went to bed, but she didn't read. She didn't sleep, either. She was still awake when Larry returned, a couple of hours later.

'I came back early,' he said. 'It wasn't any fun without you.'

Despite coming back early he was still sunk in slumber when she awoke the next morning. She propped herself on an elbow, watching as he slept. His jaw was slack, his mouth gaping slightly open, small buzzing noises issuing from it as he breathed. His hair, which had been thick silver-blond when first she had known him, was now noticeably growing thinner, its colour less bright. On the bedside table beside him were his digital watch and his collection of homeopathic medicines for the prevention of high blood pressure and gastric ulcer. She couldn't remember what other ailments it was he was seeking to ward off. Nasal congestion? Fallen arches? Haemorrhoids? She shook her head, and in a moment of affection bent and dropped a kiss on the tip of his nose. For all his undoubted self-preoccupation, she could still find it in her to feel fond of him.

Downstairs in reception, twenty minutes later, she

was handed another cable. Her immediate thought was that it must be from Paul, countermanding his orders of yesterday, but it was not. It was from Rose. She stared, with blank incomprehension, at the message it contained:

I SUPPOSE I HAVE TO SAY CONGRATULATIONS STOP ALL BEST WISHES STOP LOVE ROSIE.

What in the name of God, she thought, was going on now? There was only one way to find out: she put through a call to Bampton. Seconds later, she was speaking to Rose.

'I just got your cable. It was really nice of you to send it, but —'

'I thought I ought,' said Rose. 'Seeing as it's the done thing.'

She gave it a beat, then: 'What is?' she said.

'Sending congratulations.' Rose sounded surprised. 'Don't you do it the States?'

Oh, sure, thought Caroline. All the time. For absolutely no reason.

'Look, Rosie,' she said, 'I don't want to seem obtuse, but what exactly are you congratulating me on?'

'Getting engaged,' said Rose.

'I'm getting engaged?'

'Well —' A note of sudden doubt entered Rose's voice. 'Aren't you?'

'If I am, nobody told me. Could I ask who told *you*?'

'Paul did ... he said you were going to marry your choreographer and that you wouldn't be coming to the Festival because you were going straight back home to the States.'

'Paul said *that*?'

'Yes,' said Rose. She sounded puzzled — as well she might. She was not the only one to be puzzled.

'When did he say it?'

'The other night — the night he called you.'

'Hang on a minute! Let's just get things sorted out

here ... which night is this?'

'The night before last. When you spoke to Hugo. You left a message saying Paul should call you back —'

'Which he never did.'

'But Caroline, he did! I was there when he did it.'

'You were actually there when he got through?'

'Yes! I heard him ask for you.'

'He may have asked for me: he certainly never got me.'

'Well, he got *someone*,' said Rose. 'I heard him talking.'

'Did you by any chance hear what he was talking *about*?'

'No; I didn't listen. I went upstairs. Then when I saw him afterwards he said that you were getting married.'

'And he told you that *I*'d told him?'

'Yes. Well — I *assumed* it was you who'd told him. Seeing it was you he was ringing.'

But not me, thought Caroline, that he was speaking to.

'Rosie,' she said, 'do you happen to remember what time it was when he called?'

'About twenty past nine. He got back just as the news was finishing. He said he had to call you straight away because Hugo had said he'd be in touch by nine, only the rehearsal had run over and he hadn't been able to. He said he didn't want you having to hang about and wait.'

She hadn't hung about and waited, had she? She had allowed herself to be talked into going off and having dinner. That must have been at about five minutes past. At about fifteen minutes past, Larry had made the momentous discovery of his forgotten pills and had gone back to the hotel to pick them up. And at twenty minutes past, Paul had telephoned her —

'Something very odd is going on here,' said Rose. 'Why should he pretend that he'd spoken to you if he hadn't? I mean, that was definitely the impression he gave. And he *definitely* said you were going to get married. Why should he go and make up a thing like that?'

'I don't think he did make it up.' Caroline spoke slowly. 'I think someone did tell him — it's just that that someone didn't happen to be me.'

'Ah. Light begins to filter through the mists ... I thought it was a bit of a mean trick, to go breaking that particular piece of news at this particular point in time. I *told* Hugo it wasn't like you. I mean, it didn't surprise me that you were going to marry your choreographer — I mean, if you *were* going to marry your choreographer — but to break it to him *now* —'

'Did he take it very badly?' Caroline asked.

'Not on the face of it. On the face of it he's being terribly British and stiff upper lip ... you know Paul. Valiantly pretending that it's all for the best and he really didn't want you to come along tonight anyway, so —'

'So if he really didn't,' said Caroline, 'he'd better brace himself for a big disappointment.'

There was a pause.

'You don't mean you're *coming*?' said Rose.

Yes: that was precisely what she meant. In that moment, she had made up her mind.

'You really think I'd miss out? On a first night? Not a chance! I'll be there. Listen, I'll call you as soon as I get in to London. Let you know I'm on my way. But don't say anything to Paul; not just yet. OK?'

'*Okay*,' said Rose.

Back upstairs she found Larry awake and swallowing pills.

'Where have you been? he said.

'Downstairs.'

'Doing what?'

'That,' said Caroline, 'is what I should like to ask you.'

He peered at her, owlish, with sleep-filled eyes.

'What are you on about? I haven't been downstairs!'

'The other night.'

'Which other night?'

'The night you came back here for your medicines.'

There was a silence.

'Larry,' she said. 'Why did you do it?'

'Do what, for Chrissakes?'

'Tell Paul we were going to get married.'

'Shit!' He banged down a glass of water on the bedside table. 'Why shouldn't I tell him? Considering you've spent the last three years hassling me about it ... what's your beef?'

'I don't like being manipulated, that's what's my beef! And two can play at slamming things around.' She screwed up Rose's cable and hurled it at him. He recoiled, indignant, as it hit him in the face. 'I am sick to death of intrigue and secret telephone calls ... I'm beginning to feel like a glove puppet! Every goddamn person I come into contact with thinking they have a right to shove their hand in and start dictating which way I move. Well, I have had just about enough of it. From here on in, I do the dictating: it's my glove, and it's my hand in that glove. Get out of my way!'

'What are you doing?' said Larry.

'That's my nightdress you're sitting on!' She yanked it out from under him. He watched, blinking, eyes still foggy, as she marched across to the closet.

'What do you want with your nightdress?'

'I'm packing. That's what I want with my nightdress.'

'What are you packing for? We don't leave till tomorrow.'

'Correction: you don't leave till tomorrow. I happen to be leaving right now. I have a flight to catch, remember? It departs in approximately one hour.'

'Caroline, for fuck's sake!' He was out of bed now, trying to wrestle with her as she opened the closet door. 'Be reasonable! The guy already spelt it out ... he doesn't want you over there.'

'And why doesn't he want me over there?' She turned on him, furiously. 'Why don't you have the guts to tell me? Tell me what you actually said to him . . . go ahead! I dare you!'

'So, all right! I'll tell you! It's no big deal. I put it to him straight . . . you were going to marry me, this was like our honeymoon, I didn't feel too happy at the idea of losing you for twenty-four hours . . . OK, so I make no bones about it! I was being selfish. I told him I was being selfish. I admitted it. I said if it was up to you you'd go flying back there because that's you. That's the way you are. And he agreed that that's the way you are. We both agreed . . . you're too soft for your own good. It was all perfectly amiable. The guy understood. No hard feelings.'

Caroline took a breath.

'Just tell me one thing,' she said. 'You didn't by any chance happen to suggest that I might be suffering from a guilt complex?'

'N-no. No, I don't believe I mentioned the word guilt. Guilt did not come into it. Not as far as I recall. No. I think I can say quite definitely not. I just put it down to your kind heart and the fact that — well — you felt in some measure it was your duty. Which, let's face it, you do. The guy's lost his eyesight, and that is tough. That is really tough. I would pity anyone that was in his position. And I can quite appreciate that you being you feel you owe it to him to make this one last gesture. In your place I would probably feel the same way. Undoubtedly I would feel the same way. It's a very good and laudable way to feel. However —'

'Larry,' she said, 'did you let on to Paul that you knew he couldn't see any more?'

'Hell, no! What do you take me for? I didn't want to make the guy feel bad. *She thinks she has to come over and listen to your lousy opera on account of you being blind and her feeling sorry for you?* Shit! That would be really sick.'

'It would,' said Caroline. 'And furthermore it wouldn't even be true. I'm not going back because I feel sorry for him, I'm going back because I want to be with him — and because I don't intend to let myself be manipulated any more. Not by you, not by anyone. Now, will you please let go my arm so I can start in packing my bag?'

'Caroline,' he said, 'you can't do this to me.'

'Larry,' she said, 'I am.'

'But for Chrissakes! I need you!'

'Then we have an irresolvable problem, because I need Paul.'

'Are you crazy? When the guy already did the dirty on you? You have to go running back and make a doormat of yourself?'

'A doormat is what I have been for the past five years. What I aim to be now is one half of a partnership.'

'What you're going to be now is an unpaid guide dog!'

'You can't have it both ways,' she said. 'I can't be a doormat *and* a guide dog. Would you be kind enough to pass me that hanger?'

He did so.

'This is ridiculous! Throwing everything up just to go and play Florence Nightingale to a guy that's already kicked you in the teeth ... what's with you? Are you some kind of a masochist or something? You get a buzz out of making a martyr of yourself?'

'Larry, will you just get one thing into your head? I am not making a martyr of myself. I am going back to Bampton because I want to go back.'

'And what about the ballet?'

'You mean ballet in general? Or your ballet in particular?'

'My ballet in particular! I've written that damn thing for you.'

'No one's indispensable,' she said. 'You'll find someone else ... Michelle, for example? I'm sure she'd jump at the chance.'

'Fuck Michelle!'

'I thought you already had?'

It was a cheap jibe, but it struck home. His face grew mottled: she noticed that he made no attempt to deny it. It only confirmed what she had long suspected, that Michelle had by no means been the first — and would almost certainly not be the last.

'And how about the divorce?' He spoke sullenly. 'What am I supposed to do about that? Tell Bettina I've changed my mind?'

'I'd go ahead, if I were you. You're bound to meet someone else.'

'I don't want to meet someone else! Hell's teeth! I was only doing it on your account.'

'Larry, I'm sorry,' she said. 'Truly I am.'

'A helluva lot of good that does!'

'Try to understand . . . it just came too late.'

It should have happened a year ago. Since then, there had been too much — Michelle; the abortion; Paul —

'Anyway,' said Larry, 'I don't know what you're packing your bags for. . . . you won't be getting on that flight.'

She paused; a pair of sandals suspended in mid-air.

'Just what do you mean by that?'

'I cancelled,' he said.

'You *what*?'

'Yesterday. After you got the cable . . . I called the travel firm, and I cancelled.'

'Jesus Christ, Larry!' She slammed down the sandals. 'There are times when you can be the absolute pits. . . .'

'Let me take one last look at you.' Paul submitted, meekly, as Rose held him at arm's length. 'Yes, that's fine.' She tweaked at his cuffs, brushed something off his collar. 'You look good.'

He couldn't have cared less, at that moment, how he looked. Had he had his way, he would have remained backstage, in old sweater and jeans, listening to the performance over the loudspeaker relay. He had no wish to sit out front, dressed up like a penguin, exposed to the gaze of all and sundry. As usual, he had not had his way.

'Of course you must sit out front! Don't be so silly. You're the composer, you can't go skulking round the back like some troglodytic gnome.'

He felt like a troglodytic gnome. Give him a large damp stone to hide under and he would be in his element. The thought of being stared at by a milling horde of people was not one that appealed. He said as much to Rose, hoping for sympathy, but instead found himself crammed forcibly into evening dress, subjected the while to a tirade of abuse.

'I never heard anyone make so much fuss! It's pathetic! Anyone would think you were being asked to face a lynch mob, the way you're carrying on.'

'It feels like a lynch mob, when you can't see what's happening.'

Even that appeal fell on deaf ears. Rose had suddenly become a woman of stone. She was adamant: he must get himself dressed up, he must go and sit out front, he must get up on stage afterwards —

'I'm not getting up on any stage!'

'You'll do what you're told,' said Rose. 'And anyway, what about the reception? You can't go to *that* in old sweater and jeans. Don't be so affected! Just put this jacket on and shut up.'

He didn't want to put the jacket on. He didn't want to go to the reception. It might have been different if Caroline had been with him; but not by himself.

'You won't *be* by yourself! I shall be there, and so will Hugo. We're not going to abandon you. In any case, for all you know Caroline might yet turn up.'

She would not turn up. He had sent her a cable telling her not to do so, and he knew that she would respect his wishes. She might not understand them, but she would respect them. Her very silence confirmed it. It was no use going on thinking about Caroline. She was going to be married, and that was all there was to it. He must strive to put her from his mind. Last night, in an attempt to do just that, he had written her a four-page letter, typing it laboriously with two fingers on Rose's portable typewriter. He had said things in that letter which might more profitably have been said a long time ago. Had he ever before told her that he loved her? Casting back through the shadows of his memory, back over the years, he could not remember a single occasion on which he had done so. Always, he had taken it for granted that she knew. It occurred to him — belatedly — that he had taken rather a lot for granted where Caroline was concerned.

Hugo had decreed they should drive up to the Hall. He said that it was for Rose's benefit, though Paul suspected it was more for his. One of the adverse consequences of revealing himself to the world was a growing tendency, on his part, to become dependent. Previously, dependence had been a luxury in which he could not afford to indulge: sheer necessity had created its own bravado. With the need for pretence removed, his courage had dwindled to proportions somewhat less than heroic. Whereas once he would have struck out boldly, unaccompanied and almost without giving the matter a second thought, on the half-mile journey from the Lodge to the Hall, he now relied upon Hugo's arm for assistance; and if Hugo's arm were not available, then, to his abject shame, he would descend to the level of soliciting. He had said to Christopher the other day: 'Want to see me back home?' He had said it lightly, half joking, trying to convince himself that he was only humouring the child. In fact, the hard truth was that as vainglory had departed, so timidity had set in. It was something he was going to have to conquer — something he *would* conquer — but just for the moment he had enough on his plate. If Hugo sought to spare him the indignity, on this first night, of being seen to arrive escorted, like a zombie, then he would accept it for what it was: a tactful gesture.

The opening day of the Festival was also an open day for the School. Guests had been arriving since shortly after lunch. Some, at about this time, would be wandering down into the village to seek sustenance at the Saracen's. Others would be picnicking in the grounds, or having purchased special 'supper tickets' would be eating supper in the Conservatory, on tables laid out amongst the potted palms. A few — the select few — would be dining privately with Ludmila and Papa Jo.

'Whatever you do,' said Rose, as they left the car, '*don't panic.*' She slipped her hand into his. 'There'll always be one of us here. Just sit back and listen to the music and try to enjoy it.'

'Enjoy it?' said Hugo. 'You have to be joking! He'll spend the entire evening sitting there simmering, thinking what a far better job *he* would have made of it.'

'Mm-hm.' Paul shook his head. He had been through that scene; he was done with regrets. 'I leave it in your hands . . . entirely and utterly.'

He went backstage and stayed there, with the cast, until Rose appeared at his side and said the house lights were starting to dim and it was time they were taking their seats.

'Incidentally, I've been told to tell you that someone called Layton Berry is out front.'

Layton Berry? His lips twisted. The irony of it! How Caroline would gloat, if she were here. . . .

'Hugo seems to think he's important,' said Rose. 'Is he?'

'He is, rather,' agreed Paul. 'Yes.'

'You don't sound exactly overjoyed'

How could he be overjoyed? When Caroline was not present to savour her triumph? It was she who had lured him — she who had gone to dinner with Rod

293

Kaufman and beavered away on Paul's behalf. Now he was to be denied even the simple pleasure of saying thank you.

'According to Hugo —' Rose ushered him through the pass door: he felt the warm air of expectancy coming at him in waves from the auditorium — 'Layton Berry is practically a cause for celebration in himself.' She lowered her voice. 'He's sitting in front, by the way, with the cognoscenti.'

Papa Jo had wanted him and Rose to sit in the front, but he had begged to be let off. This would be the first public ordeal to which he had subjected himself since the descent of what he was quaintly pleased to call the Great Darkness: he was, quite frankly, apprehensive. If he had to sit out front, then at least let him sit somewhere relatively obscure and unexposed. Papa Jo had objected, vehemently.

'What when you have to take your bow? You cannot come creeping all the way!'

Since he had not the least intention of taking any bow, no matter what Rose or Papa Jo might have to say on the subject, he had brushed the objection to one side and argued himself into a seat as far back as it was possible to go. Rose had promised to sit with him. She had said that at six months pregnant she felt the need for obscurity every bit as much as he did, and that in any case she wanted to see what her costumes looked like from a distance. He didn't believe a word of it, but was too craven to sit by himself.

'Here we are.' She brought him to a halt, placing an arm about his waist and turning him slightly. 'Take the second one along. I'll be back in just a couple of shakes.'

'Why?' Panic gripped him. 'Where are you going?'

'Don't ask questions . . . just do as you're told!'

Before he could remonstrate, she had disappeared. He groped his way to the second seat along and sat in it, feeling abandoned and betrayed. He felt as he had felt as a small child, when his parents, off on some tour or other, had put him on the train and told him to 'sit there and be a good boy until you get in at the other end'. At the other end, in those days, there had been the Aunties, faithfully waiting to take him back to Marden for milky tea and home-made cake. These days, there wasn't anyone. Even Rose, now, had deserted him. A voice nearby said: 'I see the girl who's singing Jane is still a pupil at the school.' He didn't know whether the remark was addressed to him or to someone else. He didn't know whether to say 'Yes, that's right, she is', or whether to ignore it. The sweat broke out on his brow. He knew a moment of idiocy, and wanted to jump to his feet and be gone. The only thing that stopped him was the fear of making a fool of himself on the way. . . .

The cab turned in at the Lodge gates. Caroline glanced at her watch — the umpteenth time she had done so in the past hour. One minute to eight o'clock. Eight o'clock precisely as they rolled to a halt outside the Hall. She paid off the driver, grabbed her bags and hurried for the entrance. Rose was there waiting for her, ivory pale and very obviously pregnant in a dress of virginal white.

'Am I in time?'

'Just, if we hurry.'

She dumped her bags in the vestibule and hastened in Rose's wake. The earliest flight on which she had been able to find a seat had got her into Heathrow at three-twenty. From there it had been a mad rush through customs, tube to Paddington, fifteen-minute wait for the next Cheltenham train; finally a frenzied drive in a minicab through winding country lanes to Bampton. It was from Paddington she had telephoned Rose, and again from Cheltenham, to say that she was on her way.

'Does he know?'

Rose shook her head.

'I said I was just popping out for a second. He thinks I've abandoned him. He's in a frightful state of jitters, poor love. Partly first-night nerves. Partly —' she pushed open the door of the auditorium — 'other things. Understandable, really. It must be a bit nerve-racking. There.' She pointed. 'On the central gangway. I'll leave you to it.'

The overture was just starting up as Caroline slid into her seat. Paul said: 'Rose?'

'It's not Rose.' She felt, in the darkness, for his hand. 'It's me.'

There was a moment's stunned pause, then: '*Carly*? What are you doing here? I thought I sent you a cable?'

'You did send me a cable.'

'So what are you doing?'

'What do you think I'm doing? I've come to hear the opus.'

'But Larry said —'

'Forget what Larry said.' They were conversing in whispers, their heads almost touching. 'Larry's a fantasist.'

'But what are you —'

'Sh!'

'What are you going to —'

'*Quiet.* You're upsetting people. Just stop talking and listen to the music ... I want to hear it even if you don't.'

The applause at the end of the act was prolonged and enthusiastic. She was not surprised. *Jane* seemed to her to be one of the strongest things he had ever done. She tried to tell him so, but he only looked tense and shook his head.

'Better reserve judgement ... there's more to come yet. You might not care for the second half. Let's make a move before the mob starts up.'

'You want to go backstage?'

'Somewhere quiet. I have to talk to you.'

'Later,' she said. 'We'll talk later.'

'Not later, Carly ... now! There are things I have to say —'

'There is nothing you have to say.' She drew his arm through hers. 'I've come back, and I intend to stay back, and there is nothing you can possibly have to tell me that's going to make me change my mind.'

'But —'

'Paul,' she said, 'will you just stop arguing?'

On their way backstage they bumped into Ludmila, looking regal in black velvet with a headdress strongly reminiscent of Odile's from *Swan Lake*.

'Why, Caroline,' she said. 'How nice that you could get here . . . I quite thought you'd have gone back to the States by now.'

'I know,' said Caroline. 'I'm sorry. Larry did his best, believe me. He made a most gallant rescue attempt. Unfortunately I guess I'm just too stupid to be worth rescuing . . . I came back here, instead.'

Ludmila's gaze rested for a moment on Paul.

'The cards,' she said, 'were unfairly stacked.' She reached out and took Paul's arm. 'Come, young man! There's someone I want to introduce you to. Caroline, why don't you go and talk to Papa Jo? Tell him your news . . . it'll make him very happy.'

If the first act of *Jane* contained some of the most powerful music that Paul had ever written, the second, thought Caroline, must surely contain some of the most moving. She wondered, as she listened to the final soaring duet between the returned Jane and her blinded Rochester, whether Paul had had premonitions as he wrote it. Had he guessed, already, what fate had in store for him and drawn parallels? Was that the inspiration for these soul-searing melodies of his? She could appreciate now, as she had not fully been able to before, the desperate urgency of his desire to conduct. Could he only have held out for just a few weeks longer. . . .

The applause swelled to new heights: her fingers tightened, in a gesture of encouragement, over his arm.

'You'll have to go up there.'

'No!' No way. They could push him so far, but no farther. Wild horses were not dragging him on to that stage.

'Paul, you must . . . come on, now!' She urged him to his feet. 'Don't be a coward.'

She didn't know what she was asking of him. No one had told her. He had thought Papa Jo might, but obviously he had not. He himself had tried to, but she hadn't let him. If she knew the truth, she wouldn't be bullying him like this. She would understand how impossible it was. She would know that he couldn't do it. He couldn't get up there, in front of all these people.

'Carly —'

He stumbled, and flung out a hand.

'It's all right,' she said. 'I'm here.'

She took him to within a few feet of the stage.

'You want to do the last bit on your own?' He didn't; she could feel it. Could feel the waves of panic coming at her. *Carly, don't leave me* . . . deliberately, she hardened her heart. He would not thank her, tomorrow, for having given in to his pleas. This was one moment above all others when he needed to walk alone. 'Off you go, now.' She gave him a little push.

'Carly' he whispered, 'I can't!'

'Yes, you can.' Gently, she took his hand, placing it on the rail at the side of the ramp. 'Just keep a hold of that . . . Hugo's up there. He'll get you.'

He knew, then, as with teeth clenched he climbed the ramp, that she had been right: there was nothing he had to tell her. Nothing save the one thing. The thing that should have been said years ago.

He wondered why he had ever found it so difficult. . . .

Epilogue

'Perhaps now,' said Papa Jo, 'you will grant that he knows what he does, this boy.' He tapped a finger to his nose, as he manoeuvred his wheelchair to the side of the bed. 'Did I not say to you, she had not yet decided? And have I not been proved right? There are not so many flies on the old man after all, eh? He knows what he is about. When he puts his meddlesome old finger in the pie, then just some time he pull out a plum. This time, I think —' Papa Jo nodded, well content — 'he pull out the biggest plum of all . . . maybe now you will thank him, and say to him, well done.'

'Papa Jo,' said Ludmila, 'I have only one thing to say to you.'

Papa Jo beamed.

'And what is this?'

'You,' said Ludmila, 'are an old fool,'

Papa Jo's beam faded, to be replaced by a look of hurt indignation.

'You say this to me? Now? When it is I, with my meddling —'

'You with your meddling? It wasn't you with your meddling, you darned old fool, it was me with mine! Which I guess,' said Ludmila, wryly, 'makes me even more of a darned old fool than you . . . you darned old fool!'

A WOMAN OF TWO CONTINENTS
by Pixie Burger

From the elegance of the London Season, to the plains and mountains of Argentina . . . from a luxurious villa on the Riviera, to an Estancia in South America . . .

She was an Anglo-Argentine – clinging fiercely to the old life-style – to a world of Edwardian garden parties and formal elegance, a woman in a land dominated by men . . .

First Edie, then her impetuous daughter Yvonne, and finally her granddaughter, fought for their identity in the cruel, beautiful, mysterious world of Argentina, searching for happiness and an answer to their passionate need for love . . .

0 552 12142 8 £2.50

THE SUMMER OF THE BARSHINSKEYS
by Diane Pearson

'Engrossing saga . . . characters who compell . . . vividly alive'
Barbara Taylor Bradford

'Although the story of the Barshinskeys, which became our story too, stretched over many summers and winters, that golden time of 1902 was when our strange involved relationship began, when our youthful longing for the exotic took a solid and restless hold upon us . . .'

It is at this enchanted moment that *The Summer of the Barshinskeys* begins. A beautifully told, compelling story that moves from a small Kentish village to London, and from war-torn St Petersburg to a Quaker relief unit in the Volga provinces. It is the unforgettable story of two families, one English, the other Russian, who form a lifetime pattern of friendship, passion, hatred and love.

'A lovely, rich plum of a novel. Read it and enjoy'
Jacqueline Briskin

'The Russian section is reminiscent of Pasternak's *Doctor Zhivago*, horrifying yet hauntingly beautiful'
New York Tribune

'Something about the beginning of this book caught at me and I read it, then had to read it through more or less in one fell gulp. It comes across with the genuiness of a *Lark Rise to Candleford* . . . a compelling story and a splendid read'
Mary Stewart

0 552 12641 1 £2.95

THE DAFFODILS OF NEWENT
by Susan Sallis

They were called the Daffodil Girls, spirited and bright, enduring, loving and dancing their way through the gay and desparate twenties.

APRIL	who married the tortured and sexually suspect David Daker, convinced she could blot out his memories of the trenches.
MAY	pregnant by her handsome music hall star husband who didn't want to settle down.
MARCH	loved and betrayed by the man who had fathered her child, and who still wanted her.

The Daffodils of Newent – three wonderful girls whose story began in A SCATTERING OF DAISIES.

0 552 12579 2 £1.75

A SCATTERING OF DAISIES
by Susan Sallis

Will Rising had dragged himself from humble beginnings to his own small tailoring business in Gloucester – and on the way he'd fallen violently in love with Florence, refined, delicate, and wanting something better for her children.

March was the eldest girl, the least loved, the plain, unattractive one who, as the family grew, became more and more the household drudge. But March, a strange, intelligent, unhappy child, had inherited some of her mother's dreams. March Rising was determined to break out of the round of poverty and hard work, to find wealth, and love, and happiness.

0 552 12375 7 £1.95

OTHER FINE NOVELS AVAILABLE FROM CORGI BOOKS

While every effort is made to keep prices low, it is sometimes necessary to increase prices at short notice. Corgi Books reserve the right to show new retail prices on covers which may differ from those previously advertised in the text or elsewhere.

The prices shown below were correct at the time of going to press.

☐	12281 5	JADE	Pat Barr £2.95
☐	12142 8	A WOMAN OF TWO CONTINENTS	Pixie Burger £2.50
☐	12637 3	PROUD MARY	Iris Gower £2.50
☐	12387 0	COPPER KINGDOM	Iris Gower £1.95
☐	12565 2	LAST YEAR'S NIGHTINGALE	Claire Lorrimer £2.95
☐	12182 7	THE WILDERLING	Claire Lorrimer £2.50
☐	11959 8	THE CHATELAINE	Claire Lorrimer £2.50
☐	12503 2	THREE GIRLS	Frances Paige £1.95
☐	12641 1	THE SUMMER OF THE BARSHINSKEYS	Diane Pearson £2.95
☐	10375 6	CSARDAS	Diane Pearson £2.95
☐	09140 5	SARAH WHITMAN	Diane Pearson £1.95
☐	10271 7	THE MARIGOLD FIELD	Daine Pearson £1.95
☐	10249 0	BRIDE OF TANCRED	Diane Pearson £1.75
☐	12607 1	DOCTOR ROSE	Elvi Rhodes £1.95
☐	12367 6	OPAL	Elvi Rhodes £1.75
☐	12579 2	THE DAFFODILS OF NEWENT	Susan Sallis £1.75
☐	12375 7	A SCATTERING OF DAISIES	Susan Sallis £1.95

ORDER FORM

All these books are available at your book shop or newsagent, or can be ordered direct from the publisher. Just tick the titles you want and fill in the form below.

CORGI BOOKS, Cash Sales Department, P.O. Box 11, Falmouth, Cornwall.

Please send cheque or postal order, no currency.

Please allow cost of book(s) plus the following for postage and packing:

U.K. Customers—Allow 55p for the first book, 22p for the second book and 14p for each additional book ordered, to a maximum charge of £1.75.

B.F.P.O. and Eire—Allow 55p for the first book, 22p for the second book plus 14p per copy for the next seven books, thereafter 8p per book.

Overseas Customers—Allow £1.00 for the first book and 25p per copy for each additional book.

NAME (Block Letters) ....

ADDRESS ....

....